PRAISE FOR *OHIO* BY STEPHEN MARKLEY

"Markley [does] some extraordinary things with the structure of the book. . . . Casual details suddenly take on new surprising significance. There's real pleasure in this hopscotching narrative: with each new point of view, a clearer sense of the hidden story emerges as the reader slowly pieces together some shocking revelations. . . . The most moving parts of the book are those that step back and let the events and the actions speak for themselves, as when one character (the shy bookish one from high school) recalls his first tours in Afghanistan. The beautifully precise details are all the more vivid for their lack of accompanying commentary. The real core of this earnestly ambitious debut lies not in its sweeping statements but in its smaller moments, in its respectful and bighearted renderings of damaged and thwarted lives. It's the human scale that most descriptively reveals the truth about the world we're living in."
—Dan Chaon, *The New York Times Book Review*

"[*Ohio* is] a descendent of the Dickensian 'social novel' by way of Jonathan Franzen: epic fiction that lays bare contemporary culture clashes, showing us who we are and how we got here. . . . Markley's prose [is] as lively as a bonfire, crackling with incisive details. . . . Markley's gift is keeping one eye on these intimate specifics and the other on the expansive landscape of modern American life."
—*O, the Oprah Magazine*

"*Ohio* isn't just a remarkable debut novel, it's a wild, angry and devastating masterpiece of a book. Markley's debut is a sprawling, beautiful novel that explores the aftermath of the Great Recession and the wars in Iraq and Afghanistan, and a powerful look at the tenuous bonds that hold people together at their best and at their worst. [*Ohio*] is intricately constructed, with gorgeous, fiery writing that pulls the reader in and never lets go."
—NPR

"Genuinely absorbing . . . *Ohio* burns with alienation, nihilism, frustration and finally love for a place that gave birth to all of them."
—*The Washington Post*

"A book of genuine substance and style . . . Markley's skill is apparent . . . Both a lament and a love letter, *Ohio* is a reminder of the wealth of stories hidden in small towns, and of how much 'history and pathos could accumulate in errant pockets on any given night.'"
—*The Wall Street Journal*

"Markley's ambitious foray into fiction reunites four high school class-mates on a fateful summer night in their Ohio hometown, in what reads like a darker-themed epilog to *Friday Night Lights*. . . . Markley's prose sparkles with insight and supports an intricate narrative architecture that recalls Nathan Hill's *The Nix* and Patrick Somerville's *This Bright River*. . . . Highly recommended for all literary collections."

—*Library Journal* (starred review)

"Reporters have fanned out in search of answers to Middle America's decline and Trumpist desperation, but Markley is one of the first novelists to fully reflect the social forces at work without sacrificing an iota of character work or narrative tension. Drawing on the reunion-novel tradition, he brings together four alumni of the same (fictional) Ohio high school on one momentous evening a decade after graduation, each with their own pattern of escape and return—and their own mission of repentance or retribution."

—*Vulture* (Nymag.com)

"[*Ohio* is] a thoughtful examination of the neglected corners of a trauma-tized country—and one that will pierce your loyal, loving heart."

—*Entertainment Weekly*

"[A] standout debut . . . Markley's novel is alternately disturbing and gorgeous, providing a broad view of the anxieties of a post-9/11 Middle America and the complexities of the humans who navigate them."

—*Publishers Weekly*

"[*Ohio* is] so rich in complex storytelling and literary excellence that it's difficult to believe it's a fiction debut."

—*Publishers Weekly*

"Timely and of vital importance, *Ohio* delves into the spectrum of issues consuming contemporary America's Rust Belt, exploring topics like joblessness, addiction, terrorism, sexuality, religion and sex, to name a few. Markley's disturbing masterpiece reads like the offspring of Harlan Coben, Jonathan Franzen and Hanya Yanagihara: an illuminating snapshot of our current era masquerading as a twisted character-driven thriller, filled with mordant wit and soul-shaking pathos . . . an edifying and unforgettable read that leaves [readers] breathless."

—*Bookpage*

"The characters walk and talk like real, messed-up people; the author cares about them, and so does the reader. The prologue–four sections–coda structure works because Markley took the time to connect everything in a masterful set of flashbacks and flash-forwards that parcel out enough information to make the conclusion both shocking and inevitable.

Ohio is a big novel about what happened after 9/11, the initial euphoria and the long depression that grips us still."

—*Seattle Times*

"Effectively four tart, well-turned novellas bundled in a symphonic prologue and epilogue. . . . Markley writes each of these character studies with powerhouse command and painterly detail about socioeconomic distinctions. . . . Markley's novel is in line with a dark strain of Midwestern fiction that runs from Edgar Lee Masters to Gillian Flynn. Its bleakness and style are appealing."

—*Minneapolis Star Tribune*

"[A] knockout debut . . . fully engrossing from the start, save moments when you're taken aback by how good the writing really is, how flawless the storytelling. . . . *Ohio* is a ceaselessly beautiful and gut-wrenching debut."

—*Chicago Review of Books*

"Ambitious and suspenseful."

—*Columbus Dispatch*

"The kind of book that people rarely attempt to write anymore. . . . A Big American Novel that seeks to tell us where we live now."

—*The Millions*

"In his bold debut novel, *Ohio*, Stephen Markley visits the fictional northeastern Ohio town of New Canaan to paint in vivid colors the shattered dreams and stunted lives of young adults removed by roughly a decade from their high school graduation. It's an intensely realistic and keenly observed portrait that puts a human face on subjects often obscured by statistics and expert opinion. . . . A dark and deeply felt examination of a generation confronting problems that can't be solved quickly or with ease . . . It has earned a place in any conversation about the important role fiction can play in reflecting life back to us when we look squarely in the mirror."

—*Shelf Awareness*

"Markley is a knockout storyteller, infusing each section with realistic detail, from the drudgery of Walmart work to war to the fleeting ecstasies of drugs to violence, especially self-harm."

—*Kirkus Reviews*

"Important and ambitious."

—*Salon*

"Beautifully descriptive . . . an insightful, tragic story."

—*Booklist*

OHIO

A NOVEL

STEPHEN MARKLEY

Simon & Schuster Paperbacks

New York   London   Toronto   Sydney   New Delhi

Simon & Schuster Paperbacks
An Imprint of Simon & Schuster, Inc.
1230 Avenue of the Americas
New York, NY 10020

First Simon & Schuster trade paperback edition June 2019

SIMON & SCHUSTER PAPERBACKS and colophon are
registered trademarks of Simon & Schuster, Inc.

For information about special discounts for bulk purchases,
please contact Simon & Schuster Special Sales at
1-866-506-1949 or business@simonandschuster.com.

The Simon & Schuster Speakers Bureau can bring authors to your live event. For
more information or to book an event, contact the Simon & Schuster Speakers
Bureau at 1-866-248-3049 or visit our website at www.simonspeakers.com.

Interior design by Carly Loman

Manufactured in the United States of America

1   3   5   7   9   10   8   6   4   2

Library of Congress Cataloging-in-Publication Data is available.

ISBN 978-1-5011-7447-6
ISBN 978-1-5011-7448-3 (pbk)
ISBN 978-1-5011-7449-0 (ebook)

For Andy Finke.
Because I still owe you for that old mattress
and the time you picked me up at the bus stop in Cincinnati.
We all miss you, man.

PRELUDE

RICK BRINKLAN AND
THE LAST LONESOME NIGHT

THE COFFIN HAD NO BODY IN IT. INSTEAD, THE STAR LEGACY 18-Gauge Platinum Rose casket, on loan from the local Walmart, had only a large American flag draped across its length. It rode down High Street on a flatbed trailer, tugged along by a Dodge RAM 2500 the color of an overripe cherry. A blast of early winter cold had invaded October, and a hard, erratic current of air tore across New Canaan with the unpredictability of a child's tantrum. One second the breeze was calm, tolerable, and the next a frigid banshee shriek would rip across High Street, chilling the assembled, scattering leaves and loose litter, drowning out petty chatter, and carrying voices off to the sky. Before the truck and its cargo left the fire station, the staging ground for all of New Canaan's parades from Thanksgiving to the Fourth of July, no one had bothered to secure the flag, and as the show casket reached downtown, a gust of wind finally took it. The Stars and Stripes flapped, undulated, parachuted through this mad breeze, as several sorrowful gasps issued from the crowd. Nothing could be done. Each time it began to drift back to earth, another gust would catch it, toss it, bear it aloft. The flag made its way to the square, where it finally snagged on the gnarled branches of an oak tree and shuddered there.

The procession for Corporal Richard Jared Brinklan had originally been scheduled for Memorial Day. KIA in Iraq in the final days of April, the timing made sense, but then an investigation into the circumstances surrounding his death delayed the body's return.

Once that wrapped up, the display of hometown pride was planned for the same July day as the funeral. Unfortunately, a monstrous summer thunderstorm overran that afternoon. A flash flood of the Cattawa River and a tornado warning kept all of New Canaan indoors. At that point Rick's family did not much care whether there was a parade or not, but the mayor, sensing the electoral hazard of failing to honor the third son New Canaan had lost to the current conflicts, insisted on scheduling a parade for October. People tended to roll their eyes at this small-town politicking and then go out and vote based on it anyway.

The town was sleeved in red, white, and blue. Small flags spaced every fifteen feet in the grass-lined High Street for over a mile leading to the square. Flags in windows, as car decals, clutched in children's pink hands and adults' scummy gloved ones, even drawn with red, white, and blue frosting onto an enormous sheet cake being sold by the slice outside Vicky's All-Night Diner. The road's trees, rich with autumn reds and yellows, clashed brilliantly against the gunmetal sky. Meanwhile, the wind tried its goddamnedest to emancipate the leaves of these quaint elms, alders, and oaks. Two New Canaan Police Department cruisers led the way, lights silently flickering, an errant *woot* from the sirens every few hundred yards, followed by the sheriff's cars, the SUVs, and every other vehicle the police department could spare for the son of one of its own: Chief Investigator Marty Brinklan's youngest boy. Volunteers on motorcycles followed, some driven by vets, but really anyone in town who owned wheels was there. American flags and POW-MIA banners flapped from the backs of the bikes. Following this long hodgepodge of vehicles crawling slowly down the city's main thoroughfare came the flatbed with its flagless coffin. Some stepped out of their homes that bordered the east side of town only to scramble inside after the casket passed. Some huddled in Ohio State jackets and New Canaan Jaguar sweatshirts. Some pulled bright blue

GORE-TEX hoods around their heads, tugged toboggan caps low, and many, misjudging the weather, let their ears turn bright red and painful to the touch. One questionable soul wore nothing but disintegrating jeans and a No Fear shirt with the sleeves cut off, exposing arms inked solid with tattoos. Some held toddlers or gently rocked bundled babies in strollers. Older children stood with their parents, twiddly and bored, shifting weight anxiously from one leg to the other. Unsupervised kids chased each other through the legs of the adults, oblivious to the sorrow around them. The teenagers, of course, treated the whole affair like a social function (as Rick himself might have once). The girls flirted with the boys, while those boys waited to be chosen. They talked too rapidly, they laughed too loudly, they carved their initials into trees with pocketknives. There was a man wearing a Desert Storm Veteran ball cap talking to the lone TV reporter who'd made the long trip from Columbus. There was a girl holding a piece of cardboard that said simply *#25*. Another held a poster board that read: *We LOVE U Rick!!!*

They worked at Owens Corning as engineers and data specialists, at the Jeld-Wen plant as general labor manufacturing doors and windows, in the antique and clothing shop on the square, using a doming block and hammer to mold Buffalo nickels into ornamental buttons for purses and shirts. They worked at Kroger and on road crews and at First-Knox National Bank and the local DMV, which ran with such brisk efficiency that wait times rarely exceeded five minutes. They worked at the county hospital, the town's largest employer, as nurse practitioners, doctors, janitors, technicians, physical therapists, and physician's assistants—as private practices found it harder to get by, the hospital bought them up until the entire county relied on this single entity for its medical care. Many worked in the vast network of old age homes, retirement communities, hospices, and of course a few worked in mortuary services and were not thrilled by Walmart's intrusion into the casket business. The residents of New Canaan owned the county's lone liquor store, veterinary practices, a sporting goods store that made seventy percent of its sales on guns and ammunition. They were psychologists and podiatrists. They drove trucks for potato chip suppliers. They worked as health inspectors. They built porches, installed hot tubs, fixed sewer systems, and landscaped. Some had tried to flip houses. One of them, age twenty-three, had taken a loan from a bank, then another from his father, and was now looking up bankruptcy law online. Some worked for New Canaan's only newspaper, hands going carpal tunnel today trying to collect quotes about Rick. One of them coached the high school football team and his praise for Rick was an indomitable waterfall (*One of the finest young men I've ever coached selfless dedicated best teammate I've ever seen cared about every guy from the quarterback to the last guy off the bench*), an Appalachian-accented wind. Those who'd lost children thought of the ways they'd been taken: leukemia and hunting accidents, suicides and car wrecks, liver tumors and drowning, cars that overheated in the summer sun with rescue just a few feet away, standing in line at the dry cleaners. Some had terrible dreams and woke frequently to sweat and confusion. Others shot up, showered, and went to work.

Their children went to one of the six elementary schools, the middle school, and New Canaan High. Many of the adults had known one another since that first awkward day when they were dropped off at preschool, and in tears, clung to their mother's skirt or jeans or overalls. Some grew up and became teachers at these very same schools. One remembered Rick as a funny little loudmouth always rubbing zitty cheeks. Another recalled the card Rick had given her on the last day of seventh-grade pre-algebra. On the front: *Teachers Deserve A+s Too!* Inside, a coupon for a free Little Caesars cheesy bread. Another thought of a paper Rick had written for Honors History, which this teacher still, on the day of the parade, was convinced the star football player had plagiarized.

There were former cheerleaders and volleyball players and stars of the girls' basketball team. One still held the record for points and assists, for three years using her ample rear end to back defenders down all the way to the basket. Some were loaded from a breakfast of Stoli and orange juice, a few kept watch for estranged children they saw only at public gatherings, and one twisted a cheek-shredding ring on his finger: it depicted the archangel Michael, commander of the Army of God, blowing his horn and leading a battalion of angels into battle, all crammed into the hard gray metal of this one enormous ring. Some dreamed of making a home in California or vanishing down southern highways or pointing a finger at a map and lighting out for wherever the digit landed, while others lived on the beneficence of an SSDI check. Many were at the cellar floor of the country's economic ladder.

A few, who'd grown up playing among the wreckage of salvage cars on a family property known as Fallen Farms, cooked methamphetamines and sold pills at a markup. They shot at bottles and old engine blocks and the kick of the weapons would dispel ancient anxieties for seconds at a time. Some made money hocking stolen merch on craigslist, laptops practically attached to their hips. Others posted to Internet message boards about the coming invasion of babies from lesser civilizations and white people's last chance to turn the tide.

Many came home to find an orange Sherriff's Notice on their door. These were the days of foreclosures and evictions from one end of the county to the other. Some of the homes the banks took had the usual roaches and water stains but many had skylights and plasma TVs. They left value behind: gas grills, furniture, jewelry, vinyl albums, Beanie Babies, plaques with framed prayers, frozen steaks, the entire Bible on a set of CDs, bikes, and one eccentric left thirty-odd ducks penned in beside a small backyard pond. Some people just vanished, whole families blinked out of existence like the Rapture. Some moved in with parents, siblings, or friends, some into motel rooms and cars. Others had to be chased out of the city park or the Walmart lot. Marty Brinklan would tell you why serving an eviction was his most hated responsibility: how hurt and angry and truly terrified a man or woman who lost a home could be. One old man, widowed, well past his working years, had fallen into Marty's arms in tears, no dignity left, begging him not to do this because he had nowhere to go. Marty would see that guy everywhere now, trucking around his worldly possessions in a shopping bag that said BIG SALE on the side.

A few in attendance saw something gravely wrong with the whole scene, while others twirled those small flags in cold, chapped hands and felt paroxysms of pride and ownership and faith. A ceremony for a fallen soldier was an opportunity to decorate and reinvent the town as its residents wished it to be. Cradled in the state's northeast quadrant, equidistant from the cities of Cleveland and Columbus, one could envision her home as an imaginative space, a specific notion of a white-picket-fenced (and let's face it, white-skinned) Ohio. Far from the redlined black neighborhoods in Akron or Toledo or Cincinnati or Dayton, distant from the backwoods vein of Appalachia running along the borderlands of Kentucky and West Virginia, most of the parade's attendees clung to a notion of what their town was, what values it embodied, what hopes it carved out, though by 2007 its once-largest employers, a steel tube plant and two plate glass manufacturers, were over twenty years gone and most of the county's small farms had been gobbled up by Smithfield, Syngenta, Tyson, and Archer Daniels Midland. Many of those residents who had not been born in this country but who'd made their way from Kuala Lumpur or Jordan or Delhi or Honduras waved those flags the hardest when the casket went by.

Nothing spoke to this imagined homeland quite like the 2001 football team. Led by Rick's fearsome running game, a reliable quarterback, and the merciless hits of one particular linebacker who everyone thought would make it to the NFL, it was New Canaan's first team ever ranked in the state. In a community of roughly fifteen thousand, the high school always held on to its D-1 designation by a thread, but as Coach often pointed out to boosters, no one moved there. The athletes all came from the same pool of peewee football kiddos, and if a couple weak years went by where the teens were more into skateboarding, you were screwed.

Most of the famed team was there that day, except the reliable quarterback, who'd died of a heroin overdose half a year earlier. He simply cooked up too much, shot it into his knee pit on the stoop of his stepfather's trailer, and that was the ball game. One minute he was admiring icicle-mimicking strings of Christmas lights, the next, he slumped into a puddle, face smacking its mirror image. As the casket passed them by, many remembered how Rick and the quarterback used to wrestle in the locker room before games to get hyped. Pure horseplay, but they would slam each other violently into lockers. Slick with anxious sweat, wearing nothing but a jockstrap, his ass like two flower bulbs spilling out of white elastic, Rick would grapple with the QB until their skin was pink from meat slapping meat, the cheers and hoots of their teammates egging them on. Then they'd all strap their pads tight, punch lockers, smack helmets, and storm across the parking lot to the field. They'd fought as brothers to earn the enormous plaque that still graced the glass display case at the entrance of the high school, yet few of them had the skill or the grades to make it to the next level. Eighteen years old and no more Friday nights under stadium lights, pep rallies, bonfires, or freshman girlfriends. No more dances, forum shows, homecomings, or raucous trips to Vicky's Diner, slinging fries at each other across the booths. Now they worked at Cattawa Construction, at Jiffy Lube, as line cooks at Taco Bell, as real estate brokers. They spent paychecks quickly, smacked pool balls or blew raspberries on their babies' bellies. They recounted long-ago football games, which seemed to produce hard evidence that they'd once been something. Many suffered from lovely high-gloss dreams where they were back on the field. A few lived with constant sub-audible guilt about what they'd gotten up to with the girl they called Nasty Tina.

Rick's short life had intersected with a great many people in this place, partly due to his father's status in the police department and the salon his mother owned, but his family went back generations in New Canaan. His mother could trace her ancestry all the way back to the first settlers who'd come to farm land grants after the Revolutionary War. One great-grandfather had emigrated from Bavaria, and he and his people brought with them glass-cutting skills that would eventually become Chattanooga Glass. Another great-grandfather made a living as a canal worker in Coshocton County, moving timber through the locks. Rick had farmers and bankers in his lineage, factory workers at Cooper-Bessemer, which eventually became Rolls-Royce. The parade-goers knew Rick from when he and his friends were just little ones, hellions around town, always running off to play with grape jelly still smeared on their faces. They'd watched him grow up. They'd watched him crash through defensive lines. They'd watched him play a sexy Amish farmer in the senior skit. Five young women could call Rick their first kiss. One had been paired with him for Seven Minutes in Heaven, and in the closet he'd drooled all over her chin and grabbed a handful of everything there was to grab. Another got so keyed up after kissing him beneath the bleachers at an eighth-grade basketball game that it was all she thought about for the next month.

Many were hungover from toasting Rick in the Lincoln Lounge the night before. Over cheap beer and well drinks, they shared classic stories, brave recollections, and dark musings. The rumors, the gossip, the urban legends ran wild. New Canaan had a curse, their peers decided. Their generation, the classes of the first five years of the infant millennium, they were all stepping through life with a piano suspended above them and bull's-eyes on the crowns of their skulls. This was different from (but probably a companion to) the garbled small-town myth known as "The Murder That Never Was." Whoever came up with that particular phrase wasn't much with grammar, but it stuck nevertheless, debated and ruminated in bars, salons, and diners, sometimes whispered, sometimes not—particularly that night when the speculation was belted out across the dim pall of the Lincoln. The Murder That Never Was held that there was someone who went missing or not, who died accidentally or not, who was gruesomely murdered or not, who faked his own death or not, who made off with a heist or not, who burned rubber out of town laughing like a demon or not. Now in the light of day, in the queasy suffocation and sluggish eternity of a hangover, how silly that all sounded.

The driver pulled his truck to a stop, bringing the flatbed in front of a stage that had been borrowed from the high school and erected beneath the square's hundred-year oaks. On that stage, Rick's parents and his brother, Lee, stood among a scrum of friends, family, the mayor, the sheriff. "Amazing Grace" played over a jury-rigged PA, and as the final chords reverberated, the pastor of the First Christian Church, where Rick and Lee had so frequently fidgeted, farted, and fought with each other every Sunday (two of the most disruptive kids to ever grace the pews, according to most), delivered the opening prayer. "Jesus, take your son Rick into your arms, and give his family and friends the strength to endure this loss," he said. Boilerplate stuff.

Following that, four people were to speak that day.

One of them, Rick's high school girlfriend, would never make it to the mic. Kaylyn Lynn was so stupefyingly high nothing seemed to matter at all. The wind whipped unwashed hair about her pretty face and bit through Rick's football jersey (#25), which he'd given to her after the team banquet his senior season. She hated that Rick's parents had asked her to speak. There was no fairy tale here. They broke up the summer after senior year. She basically cut out Rick's heart and ate it in front of him. Pawned the engagement ring he tried to give her. Fucked his friends. Told him how much she loved him only to make sure he'd never really leave her. The pastor's prayer wound to a close, and she watched a crow pick apart a piece of the flag cake selling outside of Vicky's. There was red and blue frosting all over the bird's beak as it dug into this treat smeared across the asphalt. Ill with guilt, when her time came, Kaylyn simply kept her eyes lowered and gave Rick's parents a panicked shake of her head. Hid her high with bereavement. She rattled and sucked on her inhaler, her eyes as vivid as Cassiopeia.

Marty Brinklan stepped to the microphone, stroking his bleach-white mustache, his face weary, good marble covered by bad clay. He looked to his wife sitting in a metal folding chair, squeezing a handkerchief the color of a wet plum and staring catatonically at the ground.

"Husband, Christian, patriot, public servant," said Marty. His eyes flitted up from the piece of paper he gripped, peeked at his friends and neighbors. "But most importantly, once you're a father . . . that's what you learn about being a father: it becomes the first thing you are, and everything else had better make way for it. Once you're a father," he repeated.

Marty wanted to be done with the public part of this. He was good at quarantining his grief, saving it for appropriate moments when he could have it to himself, take it out to tenderly care for like an antique pistol. He wasn't sleeping or eating well or taking care of himself. Hell, he'd even taken a couple of drinks. The first day of his workweek he'd gotten a call about a nineteen-year-old girl, dead of an overdose, found facedown in an overflowing toilet. A gruesome

scene. Then he'd served an eviction for one of Rick's former team-
mates from the football team, a wide receiver who wept and cussed
him out until Marty found himself putting a hand on the butt of
his gun. The former wide receiver looked at him just before he tore
out of the driveway and sneered, "Rick would be so proud, Marty.
Too bad he couldn't see this." That jolly job had been just yesterday.

Jill Brinklan felt like she was on one of the cruelest reality TV
shows ever dreamed up. She acknowledged Marty and his speech
with a tight smile and nod, but she couldn't meet his eye. She hadn't
been able to look at him since they got the news. She also found she
couldn't stand very well, hence her sitting in the metal folding chair.
Lately, when on her feet, she sometimes lost her equilibrium. Squeezing her handkerchief, she stood, thanked everyone for coming, for
being so kind, and sat right back down. She wondered if she'd ever
forgive her husband for his pride. This was what pride got you.
Anyone who'd read the Bible knew that. That morning, Marty had
asked her which shirt he should wear, and she'd hissed at him like
a cat and fled their bedroom. She went to the kitchen, obsessively
running her hands over the stove because she was thinking of apple
turnovers. Before Lee's or Rick's football games, she'd always made
apple turnovers in the morning. When they first began the tradition,
she let Lee handle the skillet, stirring the apple slices in butter, while
Rick flattened the dough with a pizza roller. How funny little boys
looked cooking, the way they got hyperventilatingly excited at each
step. And later when they were ogre-like teenagers, total galoots,
how amusing it was to watch them spread the apples daintily in
the squares of dough and pinch them shut. The obscene exchanges
she had to regulate—how did they even dream up such vulgarities?
(*Rick, wash your hands, we know your thumb was knuckle-deep
in your ass last night; I'll dip my scrotum in your eye, Lee.*) That
morning, stroking the stove, all of this came over her in one of those
crippling waves that arrived as unpredictably as each freak gust of

wind. She went out to the backyard, staggering past her garden to the fire pit, which still had singed Bud Light cans resting in the ashes from when Rick was last home. She lost her balance and sat down in the grass. Wanting to dig down through layer after layer of dirt until she found her son, until he was safe, until she could no longer smell this long-gone scent of burning.

Of the four planned speakers, however, the one who truly broke the hearts of the assembled was Ben Harrington. Ben, a college dropout struggling to make it as a musician, hated coming home. To him, downtown New Canaan had this look, like a magazine after it's tossed on a fire, the way the pages blacken and curl as they begin to burn but just before the flames take over. How vibrant and important and tough and exciting this place had seemed through the scrim of boyhood, back when he, Rick, and Bill Ashcraft rode their bikes all over kingdom come. They knew every spigot where you could fill up a water balloon and the best spot in the Cattawa River to go swimming and the best hill for sledding and the best wall to use for pushing on a guy's chest until he passed out and had weird, twitchy, oxygen-deprivation dreams.

On that stage, Ben told a simple story from their boyhood. Once, on the banks of the Cattawa, wading around, feeling the mud between their toes, Rick had caught a frog. He held the squirming trophy in both amazed hands while Ben, blond locks whiplashing over his eyes, stumbled away.

"It's just a friggin frog," said Rick.

"Don't get near me with that!"

"Just touch it."

"No."

"Just touch it."

"No."

"It's not poison. That thing about it giving you warts idn't true either."

"Get away, Rick."

Then Rick heaved the frog at Ben, who'd shrieked and fled, while the terrified frog ribbited the fuck away from these psychotic kids. Bill Ashcraft laughed deliriously. Ben cried, called them assholes, then sat down on the bank while they played in the water. After about five minutes, Rick came up to him, hands on his hips.

"Go away."

"C'mon, Harrington. Would it help if I ate a bug?"

"Huh? No. Wha—"

Before he could say anything else, Rick snatched up a grasshopper that had been hanging out on a leaf and popped it in his mouth. He gave it one hard crunch, swallowed, and then immediately choked, doubled over, and puked in the dirt. Ben had never laughed so hard in his young life. They were both in tears, Ben from cracking up and Rick from trying to hock up the grasshopper's exoskeleton. After a while they ran back into the river as if nothing had happened and splashed around and spat water at the sun.

Laughter and a fresh round of sobs passed through the crowd. A father holding his teenage daughter's shoulders suddenly gripped her, as if she might be borne away by this hard wind.

Of course, Ben didn't share the story of the last time he saw Rick, in the spring of '06. Home from his first tour, Rick had added even more layers of muscle to his beastly frame. He looked like he wore a full-body Kevlar vest. He got skunk-drunk, and Ben tried to broach the subject of Bill Ashcraft. Rick and Bill, friends from the crib, hadn't spoken to each other in nearly three years. But Rick had only grisly stories of bravery, of the fun he was having in the Iraqi desert. "One time, thought I saw this rat carrying around a piece of beef jerky. So I thought, where's your stash little buddy? Turns out it was a finger! Little cutey-tooty rat carrying around a finger!"

"Jesus, Brinklan."

"Aw, don't be a puss. It's just war."

Rick wouldn't talk about Bill, and he wouldn't talk about Kaylyn, but he did want to go out to Jericho Lake and smoke a joint.

"Don't the Marines piss-test you?"

He barked a laugh. "Bullfrog, you little twat." This was the thing about Rick: how his coarseness, his incivility, could never mask—and was in fact tied to—his great love for you.

And they did drive out to Jericho, too drunk, cruising up over the horizon of their snow-globe town. Ben wanted to write a song about Rick, this kind of guy you'd find teeming across the country's swollen midsection: toggling Budweiser, Camels, and dip, leaning into the bar like he was peering over the edge of a chasm, capable of near philosophy when discussing college football or shotgun gauges, neck on a swivel for any pretty lady but always loyal to his true love, most of his drinking done within a mile or two of where he was born, calloused hands, one finger bent at an odd angle from a break that never healed right, a wildly foul mouth that could employ the word *fuck* as noun, verb, adjective, or gerund in a way you were sure had never existed before that moment ("Having us a fuckly good time," he'd said, as they sat in the grass, staring out at the glistening midnight sheen of Jericho). Yet his friend was in no way standard. He was freewheeling, mule-stubborn, and cunning as a coyote trickster. He had whole oceans inside of him, the wilds of the country, fierce ghosts, and a couple hundred million stars.

"There's nothing left, man. Nothing to go back to," Rick cryptically declared that night. He freed his runty dick from his jeans and pissed so close to Ben that he had to scoot madly across the grass to avoid the splash. "Just you and me, buddy. Just you and me and this last lonesome night in each other's arms."

What was he talking about? Hard to say. Rick didn't much understand himself, but something about what, in just three short years, had happened to him. To them. The places he'd seen, the things he'd done. On his last day home before his redeployment, he got obliterated in his backyard at the fire pit, chucking cobalt-blue cans of Bud Light into the flames even though his mom always scolded him for this. He took a walk down the road, to the field where, like an idiot, he'd once tried to give his girlfriend an engagement ring. Dusk settled in, and it was that odd midwestern temperature where the remnants of winter kept stealing day after day of spring. Scabs of melting snow lingered in the brush of the field. Beyond it stretched the forest and the scotched, brush-wire look of the leafless trees. Aqueous daylight came slanting over the horizon. Like a filter, it rendered the color of things differently, so that the field's distant cows looked maroon and yellow in this kaleidoscopic sunset. He stood, smacking a melted puddle with his foot, waiting on the crows. You had to have faith, he figured. Faith that whatever pain you had in your life, God made up for it later.

Crows had taken to roosting in the woods near the industrial park about a mile away. Foraging in the dumpsters and the hackberry bushes, multiple flocks teamed up to become a larger and larger horde. His dad called them the "mega-murder" because of what happened at dusk. Rick watched his image wobble in the puddle, and when it went still, he would smack it, and his features would get that horizontal interference all over again. He was drunk and got to thinking. Thinking about this cage he lived in, this prison where it felt like he'd spend the entirety of his life, cradle to grave, measuring the distance between his most modest hopes and all the cheap regret he actually ended up living. You passed your time in the cage, he figured, by clinging pointlessly and desperately to an endless series of unfinished sorrows.

Then the crows lit out, thousands of them, pouring across the sky's last light. They seemed to swell with a violet hue, creatures somewhere between rats and angels, cawing, descending into the forest in an eerie blanket, covering every naked winter branch . . .

When all was said and done with the parade, the crowd converged around the stage and those on it fell into their embraces and prayers. The wind sneaked up their sleeves, gouged at their eyes, and seemed to hustle them toward departure. Jill Brinklan dropped her plum handkerchief and never picked it up. Marty Brinklan turned to hug Lee, so he wouldn't have to look at his wife. Kaylyn hopped off the stage quickly. Ben Harrington smeared tears across his cheek with the back of a cold hand. Vehicles from the procession began to peel off. A city maintenance truck arrived to fish the flag out of the branches of the oak tree. The casket was returned to Walmart. It was October 13, 2007.

In terms of our story, the parade was perhaps most notable not for the people who showed up but for those who were missing that day. Bill Ashcraft and Nasty Tina. Former volleyball star and First Christian Church attendee Stacey Moore. And a kid named Danny Eaton still doing his time in Iraq, a few years away from losing one of his pretty hazel eyes. Each of them missing for reasons of their own, all of them someday to return. It's hard to say where any of this ends or how it ever began, because what you eventually learn is that there is no such thing as *linear*. There is only this wild, fucked-up flamethrower of a collective dream in which we were all born and traveled and died.

So we begin roughly six years after the parade thrown in honor of Corporal Rick Brinklan, on a fried fever of a summer night in 2013. We begin with history's dogs howling, suffering in every last nerve and muscle. We begin with four vehicles and their occupants converging on this one Ohio town from the north, south, east, and west. Specifically, we begin on a dark country road with a small pickup truck, the frame shuddering, the gas tank empty, hurtling through the night from origins yet unknown.

BILL ASHCRAFT AND
THE GREAT AMERICAN THING

WHAT WE HAVE HERE IS A TRUCK CRUISING ALONG ON A HOT July night with a small unmarked package strapped to the underside of the wheel well. This after a fourteen-hour drive from New Orleans to Ohio with the driver cranked out of his moon on LSD. This after Bill Ashcraft had pulled into his hometown and encountered two relics of his country's imperial, war-savaged heart. After he found bemedaled hero Dan Eaton strolling aimless and hollow-eyed on the twilight roadside. After visiting Rick Brinklan's cool, glass-smooth grave, his first time since Brinklan's fractured body came home. After the bar fight suddenly extinguished by Eaton's inventive use of a glass eye. Then throw in a few other schoolyard ghosts he'd yucked it up with at that bar: Jonah Hansen, the scion of a housing dynasty, and former Rust Belt football icon Todd Beaufort, and what a web of truly vexing remembrance these aging boys had constellated within him. Tuck all that away, though. Dan Eaton will explain all that eventually. For now just understand that *stuff went down*, but for Bill, the mystic, intertwining energy of the night was not exactly decelerating. From the moment he popped the tab onto his tongue and pulled into the swamp-ass heat of the bayou highways, he understood he'd be navigating some bends in the river on this one, but even by his standards the path felt ox-bowed, unpredictable far beyond what one expects when returning to your frayed and haunted hometown to make a shady delivery to a figure from your deep, dank, dark damning past, which is to say, *Dear Territory: I'm a stranger here myself.*

Then, after dropping Eaton off at the Eastern Star Retirement Home to chase his own two-toned demons, the goddamned truck ran out of gas.

Hard to blame anyone but Bill Ashcraft on this count. He hadn't anticipated so many distractions, and his truck's gas gauge had the accuracy of a creationist biology textbook. Mostly he'd been thinking fondly of his bottle of Jameson, which had run dry in the spooky twilight amid the gravestones.

The old Chevy S10 clicked, tinkled, rattled, and wheezed to a halt, sounding like she pissed herself before her engine gave out completely. Bill guided her to the shoulder, coming to rest with a scrape of tall dry grass on the undercarriage.

"You dry bitch," he told the truck. "You old, foul, no good—" He screamed bone-dry laughter. "Naw, I'm just kidding." He wrapped the steering wheel in an embrace. "I still love you, girl. Ryde or die forever, boo."

The headlights cut an off-kilter block of light over the yellowed crabgrass on this limp, tree-lined stretch of State Route 229, maybe a mile outside of New Canaan.

"Remember that time we drove out of Kansas with the entire fleet of staties chasing us like bank robbers? That was fun."

He released the wheel and sighed. Neither Bill nor his truck had ever been to Kansas.

He was pretty fucking drunk, which for him was saying something. He was also still pretty wired from the acid. These tabs lasted For. Fuck. Ing. Ev. Er. You really had to be prepared to step into another dimension, accept the deregulations of that particular nuthouse, accept that you were never coming back, and imagine life under these new brain-bled, torch-fever-fed circumstances.

It was okay. This crazy rat of a day would just have to steam a little longer in its shithouse.

The thing of it—Bill mused—was this: You ran into people from high school whenever you came back to The Cane. That was double bogey for the course. But to spot Eaton on his way to visit Rick and then later sit across from Beaufort, who, having used up all nine of his football lives, now looked like a sad, soggy, bloated-corpse version of the titan he'd been in high school, on this night of all nights—well, that was pretty goddamned cosmic-hand mysterious. Though they'd been teenage enemies of a sort, he also felt the fraternity: once handsome, marbled, small-town athletes who couldn't understand why they hadn't conquered the world.

Whatthefuckever. Tonight the universe was a-humming. He could feel it through his urge to vomit. He didn't believe in God, fate, or coincidence, but that left precious little to actually explain anything, and sometimes the right asteroid just strikes the right planet so the lizards lose a turn, and the motherfucking monkeys take over.

"Planet of the Apes!" Bill shouted into the cab. "It's our planet. What a twist."

He was at least a couple miles from the nearest gas station, and he'd thrown his cell phone out the window in Arkansas after briefly becoming convinced the NSA was tracking him. He plucked the kitchen timer from his pocket: 02:37:47. He would have to hoof it. He went rooting around in the glove compartment and found the roll of clear packing tape. Flicking off the headlights, exiting the cab, he walked over to the back left wheel. Crawling beneath, he found the small package secured to that nook with a complicated mess of duct tape and twine. He spent a couple minutes freeing all this handiwork, peeling at gobs of tape that lacquered his fingers, plucking drunkenly at knots, marveling at how the black configurations of an internal combustion system could look like a phantasmagoric dream-empire likely ruled by a barbaric autocrat (the dried mud, he decided, was the upside-down wasteland where most rebels were defeated and crucified), before the load fell away.

He crawled back out, dusted himself off. The package was a rectangle, the length of a standard No. 10 envelope. A few centimeters thick. A nice long brick secured so tightly beneath efficient rolls of plastic and tape that it gave away absolutely nothing about the texture, color, odor, or variations of the contents. Bill unbuttoned his flannel, laid it over the truck, and stuck the brick lengthwise along his spine, right in the small of his back, a strip of packing tape attached. He then wound the tape around his back and belly, fixing the brick to his person. When it felt secure, he tore the tape, which split with that smooth-butter silence that leaves one agog at the variegated achievements of industrial civilization. He tossed the roll into the truck bed. He peered at his stomach.

"Only too late did he realize that when he arrives he'll have to rip this fucking tape off," he said to his gut. His stomach hairs, mashed to the skin with suffocating, cloying adhesive, were now terrified little buggers.

Before he could follow the thought, he turned and barfed into the grass, which he knew would sober him up quick and be a true bummer in the near- to mid-term.

Returning briefly to the cab, he plucked a photograph from the visor and slipped it in his back pocket. This picture had taken a mercurial path. Many times he'd thought of leaving it wherever the wind happened to have blown him. How many dorm room corkboards or hostel bathroom mirrors or apartment refrigerators had he tacked, magnetized, or otherwise affixed it to, always with the thought that here would be its final resting place in this kingdom. That he'd leave it there like he'd left behind every other artifact. Somehow it was always the thing he remembered, the one crisp piece of buried nostalgic schist that he'd unearth before moving on. He sometimes wondered if this sticky photograph had its own agenda.

Then he set off toward the lights of the town that was still, for lack of any other concrete options, his home. After walking maybe half a mile down the road, he realized that while remembering the picture, he'd left the keys in the ignition and a thousand dollars in the glove compartment.

He didn't bother going back.

Bill had chosen this particular weekend to make the return trip because he knew his parents would be out of town, so that when he stumbled up to his childhood home, a dark, pristine castle in the country with a neat lawn and a basketball hoop in the driveway where he, Rick Brinklan, and Ben Harrington had balled until the daylight gave out, he could be sure to wreck around the house half-wasted without his parents asking a thousand questions about what their twenty-eight-year-old semi-estranged son was doing with himself these days.

Estranged was a hell of a word, and not exactly accurate. His parents were more like *exasperated* with him: his postgraduate wandering, his lost jobs, his remarkable ability to filch money even after they'd increased security around their ATM pins, PayPal accounts, and jewelry boxes. There was also the possibility that his parents were divorced and just hadn't bothered to tell him. His mother, a journalism student who gave up a New York City career to follow her dentist husband to his hometown of Corn & Rust, Ohio, where they would supposedly raise a son away from—well, from what? Violence, fear, minorities, pollution? A joke like that surely had an expiration date, right? Love was a marketing strategy, but every ad campaign lost its zest in the end. Every romantic bond eventually turned into the Yo Quiero Taco Bell dog.

More to the point, they were at his cousin's wedding in Cincinnati.

Beyond his mission and all its implications, he was also eager to escape the gun-blast heat of New Orleans for a few days. That place already felt as claustrophobic as New Canaan. It was really all he'd discovered from his travels: No matter where you went or how novel it seemed when you first pulled into town, it always turned into the same bars, same food, same women, same politics, same liquor, same drugs, same troubles.

He'd been writing media releases for a wetlands conservation group, an organization that had sprung up following the 2010 BP nightmareathon. Dedicated to helping residents and the environment of the Louisiana coast, rumored to have some Oscar winner's money behind it, pushing back against the oil and petrochemical interests that ran the state like the British ran colonial India. It didn't exactly take a policy wonk to understand that the state and local governments were obsessed with slurping up every last drop of oil from the wells off the coast, and the wetlands—as far as the vast majority of the state legislature was concerned—could go take a flying fuck on the spaceship *Challenger*. No two ways about it: the city was fucking doomed. It wasn't clear if he'd been fired for his desperation, his drinking, or an impolitic remark to his boss (the prissy, lecherous, Vermontonian *Treme* superfan), "Try fucking your wife for a change," but fired he had been.

So if he ever went back to New Orleans, it would be to clean out his apartment. After securing this new gig, he made a diplomatic mission to the French Quarter where he found a saxophone player willing to sell him a tab of acid. He then smuggled himself past his self-loathing and straight out of town. From there, he drove north.

The first part of the job went off without a hitch. He met the guy in the empty, forsaken lot of a shuttered warehouse, the chain-link fortification rusted and collapsing, scoured NO TRESPASSING sign in the dirt, weeds taking back the concrete through any crack rain and sunlight dared penetrate. Just another abandoned industrial Leeziana outpost, nothing on the approach but grief, churches, cancer clusters, and gut-loving bayou cooking. The man also drove a truck but not a cheap, used beater like Bill's. This Cajun good ole boy drove a shiny new F-350, bloodred and fierce. He had a salt goatee and a camo trucker's hat with a cross dead center. He'd come from somewhere that put mud on his boots, and he spoke in that Creole dialect that a kid from Ohio could never fully decipher. He instructed Bill to smash the burner cell underfoot. The two of them got under Bill's truck together, and Bill handed the guy tape and twine while he fixed the package to the truck's guts. Then he gave Bill an envelope stuffed with twenties.

"Drive the limit. Don't go talk to no one. And you get pulled over, don't got drink nor drugs in your cab."

"I got cruise control and white skin, my man. Pigs can't even see me."

The Cajun didn't look amused, and Bill didn't have time to explain that the comment was ironically racist, a satirizing of the power structure—or that he fully intended to do psychedelics on the trip. (Lotsa stuff left out of that convo.)

Thing was, Bill had a hard time driving long distances without being some kind of altered, and pulling from New Orleans to Northeast Ohio in a day to deliver mystery contraband would require strong mojo. He only had the one mishap when he tossed his phone, a bad idea because he'd been told to show up for this exchange at an acutely specific time. He remedied his mistake by stopping at a pharmacy where—unable to locate a section with wristwatches and feeling the searing eyes of the staff—he purchased a small kitchen timer and, after stumbling into a display of self-tanning lotion, the bottles clattering and careening down the sleek aisle like bowling pins, set it to **15:00:00**, which was a fine guesstimate of the schedule he'd been given. Solving that hiccup seemed to activate the LSD's magic. For ten to twelve hours, he smoked cigs across the bleached-out American landscape, up through the deltas of Mississippi and stars falling on Alabama, he watched the sky shift in burning purple and orange wars. Armies cascaded across the plains and planes died in beautiful violent violet clashes. Dust thick enough to taste billowing off the fields serving up their corn and soy. Black birds clutched black telephone wires and watched him with black eyes. The flags ran up the polls of the clouds and an amber smoke drifted in and out of time, crept up into other levels of existence and sailed back, changed. The CD player useless, the clock broken, and the radio his only companion, he kept for company the vast panoply of American broadcast eccentricity: pop radio, country doggerel, and Evangelical dreamers hoping against hope that Jesus would make it back sooner rather than later. Through Tennessee and Nashville and the bluegrass hills of Kentucky, through July, a month of electric heat hallucination and erotic moons, the fields were on fire on all sides, and the flames rose thousands of feet in the air until they scorched the underbellies of passenger jets. Only the highway was a cool river of water through which he could be assured safe passage. The rest of it burned like blood on fire. Cruising along Eisenhower's interstate baby with the setting sun on his left spilling some mystic aurora across the addled sky, he thought he could feel his brain bleeding.

But these visions began to tame as he neared home, and when he crossed the Ohio River near Marietta, that familiar thirst was there, riding him, demanding satisfaction, that whole beautiful flow of mid-American freshwater looking like a goddamn bathtub full of booze. He pulled into a liquor store, bought the cheap shit, and drove across the gloaming blue of the Ohio, taking his first pull at the moment the fading color of the twilight sky perfectly matched the water.

He'd been on a bestial three-week bender since getting fired, but that was more like a culmination of a four-year bender since getting fired from Obama's Columbus office, which itself may have been an extension of a prolonged drinking spurt that dated back to New Canaan High School. Hard to say, really. Bill had spent this last three-week leg drinking and smoking and snorting and popping in such an unreflective stupor that, in a way, the acid had almost woken him up, brought him reeling out of a safe place into the vampire-incinerating light of day, and now this whole moment of existence was a protracted, muscular mindfuck of remembrance and poetry and wonder. Really, the way a good trip should be. He hadn't eaten in a day. Every time he took acid, he'd forget to eat for thirty-six hours and wake up famished, wanting to drain the blood from a rabbit.

He trotted along the dark country road, a shambolic gait through whispering trees wrung wild. Big stars overhead. Sweatshop Nikes crunching over the gravel edge of the road. Too sober following his purge. The long walk into town took him over a bridge with low concrete barriers. Below, the swiftly flowing Cattawa River whispered. His childhood river. The grass on the banks was a dirty, dry summer yellow. The night felt formless here, and it wasn't just the alcohol's cool washcloth on his mind or the lingering effects of the LSD—this was something elemental he was hearing. The river spoke and its singular trail churning through the earth, shaping its contours, told profound stories of time and apology and geology. This was the sound or absence of sound he sometimes felt when he drove from New Orleans to the wildlife refuge to hike the trails through the bayous and watch the world waste away. Trying to catch a glimpse of the part that had maintained, that had survived, at least for now, the pestilential lust of humankind's brief party.

The tape wound around his torso stretched and bit with each step.

He had time to kill—02:18:24—and the liquor store, coincidentally, lay right in his path. He fingered the shard of torn napkin:

Jonah had jotted the phone number on it while they smoked outside the bar. Beyond the urge to drink and get the vomit taste out of his mouth was the urge for something harder. And beyond the urge for something harder was the urge to remember—the worst addiction of all.

Boy, he thought, suddenly looking around, did Ohio look like shit.

The whole state for sure, but stumbling down SR 229 into the outskirts of the city limits, New Canaan looked like the microcosm poster child of middle-American angst. This little stretch of strip mall had lost all its signs, so you could see the ghostly outlines of the vanished businesses as well as all the smaller rust outlines where the screws once attached to the stucco. The rest of the road had all the familiar tumors. House with FOR SALE sign. House with FORECLOSURE sign. The rest for rent yet clearly unrented. Andy's Glass Shop, closed. Burger King, open. New Canaan Building Supply across the street, closed, FOR RENT sign. Subway, open. Gas station, open, sign burned out, weird old dude lingering by a pay phone watching him. (A pay phone! Still!) Gotti's Pizza, where Harrington's dad used to take them after YMCA soccer or basketball, shut down, gone, along with its excellent Hawaiian pie. Liberty Tax, open.

Ohio hadn't gone through the same real estate boom as the Sun Belt, but the vultures had circled the carcasses of dying industrial towns—Dayton, Toledo, Mansfield, Youngstown, Akron—peddling home equity loans and refinancing. All the garbage that blew up in people's faces the same way subprime mortgages had. A fleet of nouveau riche snake oil salesmen scoured the state, moving from minority hoods where widowed, churchgoing black ladies on fixed incomes made for easy marks to the white working-class enclaves and then the first-ring suburbs. The foreclosures began to crop up and then turn into fields of fast-moving weeds, reducing whole neighborhoods to abandoned husks or drug pens. Ameriquest, Countrywide, CitiFinancial—all those devious motherfuckers watching the state's job losses, plant closings, its struggles, its heartache, and figuring out a way to make a buck on people's desperation. Every city or town in the state had big gangrenous swaths that looked like New Canaan, the same cancer-patient-looking strip mall geography with brightly lit outposts hawking variations on usurious consumer credit. Those entrepreneurs saw the state breaking down like Bill's truck, and they moved in, looking to sell the last working parts for scrap.

"Hey-ho!" Bill toasted the night with an invisible bottle.

Passing into town he'd spotted several houses with their ROMNEY/RYAN yard signs still holding on nearly nine months after those two effete, moonbeam-colored Cylons bit it. He spotted other yard signs that appeared, as sure as the seasons, begging people to vote *Yes* on a doomed school levy.

He streaked for the pay phone, weird old dude trickling into the night with his shopping bag. Bill transferred the phone number from the scrap of napkin to the greasy buttons, each denuded silver rectangle likely a spa retreat for herpes and snot.

"*Drugs-d-drugs-drugs-drugs*," he sang to the tune of Sisqo's "Thong Song."

He got two rings and a voice on the other end.

"Jonah Hansen gave me this number. Can I get something?"

"Where? And what?" The guy's voice was light and buzzy, like when a fly drones by your ear.

"Weed preferably. But I'm open to other bad ideas . . ." His gaze fell on the Dunkin' Donuts, lights aglow. An employee pushed a mop. He was old and rail-thin, his face an archipelago of scabs, a few still looking open and wet, and Bill could almost smell decay through the glass. He noted a missing a tooth, a single incisor in the top row.

"I got plenty-a options, yo. Where you wanna meet?"

"I was on my way to the liquor store."

"Perfect. See you in ten."

A New Canaan PD cruiser slowed as it went by. Of course, he looked to see if it might be Marty Brinklan, but the cop was young, his head a cue ball, his face cruel and curious because this pay phone was likely used strictly for drug deals. Bill stayed on the phone as the dial tone began—just to make sure this oinker cruised on by.

The night knuckled down.

For perhaps the thousandth time in the last twenty-four hours, he wondered what he'd gotten himself into and wandered out of that wonder by singing an old Ben Harrington jam. The one that sounded kind of sailor-songy from the album where he was wearing that imbecilic pork pie hat on the cover.

"Everyone went off to war / Everyone got addicted to dope / Everyone woulda hanged hisself if it weren't for the price of rope." He reached a crosswalk, belting it out. A lone car idled at the intersection contemplating a green light. *"Everyone got an Ess-Tee-Deeee / Everyone set the banshee free / So now it's just ole you and me / With our sad, sick revelry!"*

At first he thought the driver had simply not yet noticed the green, but the car continued to sit, uninterested in its right of way. He guessed a drunk or a stoner lost in a daze. Surprise tingled his fingertips when he recognized the face.

It was his ex-girlfriend's goddamned mother. Bethany Kline sat in the lane heading south, so he could see right into the car. With her hands dug into the wheel at ten and two, she wept.

The plastic-green color of the traffic light made the moisture beneath her eyes shine. Bethany Kline looked even more swollen,

saggy, and ugly than he remembered. One spent so much time looking at the Botoxed and surgery-perfected visages of movie stars and
TV personalities that it was sometimes jarring to just see what an
average sixty-something woman, trampled by time and disappointment, actually looked like, let alone what she looked like crying.
She hadn't changed her haircut, still the unflattering midwestern
bowl of badly dyed brown. Bangs like a friar. Her eyes were in-
flamed red wounds. It almost made him angry. What the fuck did
she have to cry about?

He thought of her daughter at Jericho Lake wearing a black
bikini and Jackie O sunglasses, her skin with both the mocha and
the cream of her ancestry. Her taut, muscled build. Lisa Han had
cheekbones higher than the moon and a delicate lift to her eyes that
betrayed the half-exiled Caucasian in her. For the two keyest, binge-
drinkingest, fuckfestingest years of high school, Lisa surprised him,
drove him, maddened him. They met when she'd hunched forward
at her desk in geometry class, studying a returned test. She'd been
the only freshman in the class, bumped ahead a year by the Powers
That Will. Bill had been staring at her cleavage, the way her high
and tight tits pressed up out of this silver V-neck. She made a sound
like *"Blargh."* And he looked up.

"Problem?"

"Asian F," she said, showing him her ninety-one percent score.

It had been game on after that. The first time he'd gone over
to Lisa's house, he had to ask. There were just too many pictures
of this beautiful Asian girl with this family of Tupperware-looking
white people. Lisa explained how her father had fled after the fall
of Saigon, shepherded by distant relatives to Texas. He ended up
going to school at Ohio State where he met and impregnated a
young woman from his Bible study group. Like good Christians,
they married over a baby bump, but Papa was gone shortly after
Lisa was born, possibly to return to Vietnam to find out if his fam-

ily was still alive, more likely just another broke-dick father running away.

"Who knows," Lisa said, shrugging at the wall of family portraits. Bill was sorry he'd asked, as he could sense the embarrassment wafting off her. "Ole Bethany's told me the story about five different ways. She buzzes me off when I ask too much. It's why I refused to change my last name to Kline when she remarried. So she can't pretend I'm her nice white girl. Like she never had a premarital yellow cock in her."

He laughed at this haunted humor and looked back to the smiling pictures of Lisa perched before her stiff white-bread stepfather and chubby, dim-looking stepbrother. Then they went upstairs, and beneath her posters of Trent Reznor, Kurt Cobain, and a shirtless Nelly, simultaneously cast off their virginities.

All this was preamble to the protracted war between him, Lisa, and Bethany. From word one, Mrs. Kline did not like Bill. He enabled Lisa's rebellion, had her coming home late, had her getting caught with small bits of pot or condoms or bottles of liquor. Lisa informed him of Bethany's retrograde attempts to enact punishment, to "ground" her so to speak, but Lisa was too smart, too defiant, too fiery to treat like a child. He recalled picking her up, Bethany standing in the foyer with her hands on her hips, a cheek-chewing expression of fury rippling through her facial folds.

"Your mom totally despises me," he said as she climbed into the car. "We're never going to change her mind."

"Nah, Ashcraft, just get your tongue up her vagina. That's what turned me around on you." He threw the car into gear, laughing madly.

Weirdly, once Bethany learned that Bill's mother worked for the local newspaper, she took up writing letters to the editor as her principal hobby, gaining a more or less permanent position on the *New Canaan News* editorial page, where she expounded on such topics as the immorality of not allowing a moment for prayer in schools, the teaching of intelligent design, the dangerous possibility that teachers were not being screened for past sex offenses, and just generally that there was a holocaust going on in abortion clinics.

His dad would fume every time a letter appeared and wonder why the paper had to keep giving this woman space. Bill always figured his mom lived her entire life in a sub-audible state of misery over having left her native Queens to follow her husband to his dicktoon hometown. She'd interned at the *New York Post*, and Bill had the feeling that giving up her dream of someday writing at a major paper had been a bitter, softball-sized pill to swallow just so her husband could carry on the dentistry practice started by his own father. Bethany's letters became a constant source of tension in their marriage. He could tell his dad didn't like Lisa, didn't trust her even though she shared none of Bethany's odious views. On the Ferris wheel at the county fair that summer, Lisa was the one who climbed onto him and nearly sucked his lips off, grinding into his lap while the games dinged and the stadium lights spilled across the country band wailing away onstage. She was the one who'd gone down on him when they climbed up on the roof of the library, and she was the one who suggested they pee on each other, just to give it a shot. Yet she still called herself a Christian, still kept a pointless Bible quote etched into a wooden plaque in her room. William Sr. deeply distrusted this pretense of religiosity, and like Bethany, he seemed certain Bill would end up getting Lisa pregnant.

His mom, the quintessential purveyor of mom-reasonability, chided them both. At the paper, she was always ending up in the middle of these stupid small-town controversies, and she had the disease of seeing a false equivalence in everything, of lending credence to idiots and charlatans. She said of Bethany, "It's all she's ever known. People like her grow up in a small town and get the same kind of cruel ideas fed to them their entire lives, and they wrap it up in their worldviews because that's the context they understand. Her husband left her at a young age, and she had to raise a daughter alone for a long time. That's a hard thing."

Bill could never tell which of his parents he was in more of an argument with. How much of his nature could be attributed to spending his formative years arguing with his mother's on-the-one-hand-on-the-other-hand Obamaian pragmatic streak? It would strain their relationship enough that they stopped speaking for several years. Similar pointless, circular arguments ensued with his father, but that resulted from Bill's total disinterest in law school or med school or, God forbid, dental school. All that formal education just made people higher-paid fools or more articulate fools, but fools they remained.

Lisa was no fool. Never had been, never would be. They broke up the week before he left for college. Out at the Brew, parked in the shade of a tree where the moonlight couldn't reach, they sucked on each other, turned the interior of his Accord into a sauna, and that's how you broke up in high school. You fucked like a corporeal toast to the heartache of new beginnings.

"I can't wait to see where we'll end up," she said, playing with the hairs on his chest, letting free a few uncharacteristic tears. "If I had to bet, you'll be the only person in this town to do crazier shit than me."

"You think?"

"Of course. It's why I decided to let you love me for a minute."

A year later, when he heard what Lisa had done, he wrote to her to make sure she was okay. He'd heard rumors—gossip as currency, people all but bartering with it—about a pregnancy, about an abortion, about a blowout fight with Bethany.

In an e-mail, Lisa assured Bill that, no, she wasn't pregnant. She'd packed a bag, grabbed her passport, emptied her savings account, and bought a one-way ticket overseas. Told her mom not to bother looking for her. At first, Bill loved hearing all this. It impressed him, inspired him. Whenever he found himself lost or in danger abroad, he'd think of how Lisa had been doing scarier shit when she was just an eighteen-year-old kid. Six years after she left, when he found himself working in Southeast Asia, he went in search of her.

I'm in your neck of the woods, he wrote to her via Facebook.

Lisa Han 5/23 3:03 p.m.
No shit!? Where? Why?

Bill Assata Shakur Ashcraft 5/23 5:24 p.m.
Where to begin? Um, I've been in Cambodia buying up child prostitutes.

Lisa Han 5/24 9:07 a.m.
Can't say I'm surprised, but uh, yeah, please tell me that's a joke?

Bill Assata Shakur Ashcraft 5/24 11:11 a.m.
Ha no joke. But I mean like buying them out. So I was over here working for this NGO that frees girls from the sex trade, gets them back to their families, and sets them up with shit to do so they don't have to go back to prostituting (and so their families don't sell them back ☹). Get me? We like set them up with seed money and training to start their own markets, selling sandals or beads or fruit or whatnot.

Lisa Han 5/24 2:54 p.m.
Ah goddamnit I always knew you had some deep decency in you, BA. Don't tell me you've turned into an actual catch since high school? ☺

Bill Assata Shakur Ashcraft 5/24 3:44 p.m.
It's an adventure. You haven't lived until you've faced down a
Cambodian pimp.

He asked if she wanted to get together, but she never wrote back. He decided to go in search of her and rode a motorbike up the Ho Chi Minh Trail, stopping only to see some spider holes. The mission went to hell, though, after an unsettling near-death experience: dusk, an errant log, launching over the handlebars and past the ledge of the trail into pure jungle canopy, tumbling and falling for what seemed like such an enormous gulf of time, sensing a final impact that would surely end in a dry twig snap he'd hear first in the bones of his neck, trying to settle on a pleasant final memory to go out on and coming up only with Kunthea, an understandably shy nine-year-old girl with bony, collapsible limbs and a mouth of bent brown teeth.

(They'd successfully negotiated with her madam, an old woman who'd probably been the plaything of German businessmen when she was a child and understood this as the natural order. When Kunthea clung to the post outside the house, afraid to follow the four white people and Cambodian translator now hectoring her to come along home, Bill reached down and plucked a Jolly Rancher from behind her ear. While she busied herself with the wrapper, he loaded his fist and plucked out another: "This is insane. Your ear's a candy factory." She came with them after that, and before she went to bed that night, Bill found a toothbrush in her ear and taught her how to use it.)

A fine memory to die on. Until he came to land softly, improbably, in a bed of grass as comfortable as a down pillow. Eyes darting, lying in the noisy breath of the jungle, he checked to find himself completely intact. He spooked the birds when he screamed that he was fucking unbreakable.

A few days later, unable to track Lisa down, he caught a flight out of Hanoi with the last of his cash, and he never heard from her again. He wrote her several more times, but she never answered. He worried about all the typical things: if she'd found out about Kaylyn, if she'd always known about Kaylyn, if she'd long hated him, if she'd thrown her laptop into the South China Sea, etc. What it came down to, though, was this: like everyone else, she'd vanished from his life. He could only stare at the dark and wonder what had become of her.

Gripping the wheel with both hands, Bethany Kline took one last small roll of her head, as if saying to herself, *Sure, I guess I'll live with this miserable thought*, and punched the accelerator. The car went zooming off, carburetor rattling.

Then again maybe Bethany was another hallucination. An acid flashback materializing from the sweat-drenched electrical storm. Either way, he wished he could simply rip open the package and blindly snort away whatever was inside just to see where the cocktail took him.

"Wanna get a drink?" he said to a busted blue fire hydrant.

Closing in on thirty fast, he had an urge, undaunted by the temporal challenge, to find Lisa Han, wherever she was, and ask if she still saw passion and decency in him. If that young version of her could see him now, like this, a decade on, would she still recognize what she saw back then? How dearly he wanted to ask her if there was any chance she still believed in him.

In the liquor store, he scanned the shelves looking for the right potion, tickled by that lovely little thrill of unexpected booze. You could go high-end, he figured, groping a bottle of Johnnie Walker Black, or just keep on keeping on with the Jim Beam that had gotten him over the Ohio River. The decisions alcoholics had to make.

If sober people understood all the work that went into deciding how best to get loaded, they would get over themselves and sling a little fucking admiration his way. He selected Jack Daniel's in the end because they didn't have the right size Beam.

"I'll take a pack of Camels and a Bic too," he told the Indian cashier, who seemed to recognize him from all his efforts to buy booze in high school. Bill glanced at the analog clock hanging over the cashier's left shoulder, but the hands all pointed, dead and still, to the ground. He pulled out his timer. It was the size and shape of a large skipping stone or maybe some middling lizard's egg and felt good to hold. In the white plastic casing the stiff numbers read: **01:47:18**.

"You got ID, buddy?" he asked in his crisp accent. Bill used to try to stop guys on the basketball team from calling him "Apu," usually to no effect. He knew, likely, by the way of his mother, that this man had an engineering degree and had lost a child to leukemia. Now he was only an obstacle to a drink, and one with Cheetos dust in his mustache at that.

"I'm like thirty, bro," Bill rounded up, swiping his near-maxed credit card and snatching the bottle.

The cashier made no objection. Instead he said, almost tenderly, "Big storm coming later. Don't be wandering around all night drinking."

Bill left without acknowledging this, tearing the cellophane wrapping off the pack of smokes. He wasn't a smoker, but there was nothing like a cigarette when you were drunk (which basically made him a smoker). One thing he missed about the northern climes was having a cigarette during a brutal midwestern winter. Something about standing on frigid pavement, switching hands as each went numb, pulling in that silky cloud of nicotine. The warmth ran all the way to your toes. A buzz like a tuning fork going off in your core.

Clamping the little guy in his teeth, he unscrewed the cap from the whiskey and drank from his bottle of light.

Now he was really feeling no pain.

He wandered to the side of the lot where he could watch the entrance and took a seat on the curb to smoke his cigarette and wait for the world to happen. The tape around his midriff crinkled when he sat, and the package dug in, acted almost as a back brace so that he had to sit with preposterous posture. He recalled the night's loose-leaf events: a nose exploding to pulp under the fist of a drunk hick in the Lincoln Lounge. Interrupting a long conversation about The Murder That Never Was, the town's great isosceles-sided rumor, too crazy to be true, too ingrained to discount. He and Jonah outside, recalling when Harrington bricked two free throws with half a second left to almost cost them the conference championship. Harrington had been a better songwriter than basketball player. From there, he finally got to thinking about Kaylyn. The green-eyed island of heat.

He took the idle time to pull the picture from his pocket. At some point long ago he'd folded it into quarters, maybe to tuck it in his wallet when he was certain he would get mugged in a harsh neighborhood in Phnom Penh, and the paper had two tactile ridges bisecting the surface, cutting through the date (10.15.02). On the actual picture side these ridges were reversed into chalky white divots flaking away whatever chemicals formed the images, so that Bill's face, which had gotten caught in the fold, was scabbing away from his nose to his left eyelid. Like he was vanishing à la Marty McFly's family in *Back to the Future*.

He sucked on his cigarette and let his gaze travel from the center out. He had his arm around Lisa, his fingers just creeping over her neck. He wore a blazer a size too big and gray dress pants a size too small. He remembered how the waist had bit at him all night. The silver tie almost matched the pants. He had sideburns down past his ear, a teenager's demonstration of masculinity. Lisa wore a slim black dress with spaghetti straps and a deep V that exposed, in some of the mothers' opinions, an expanse of olive-brown cleavage too scandalous for a homecoming dance. Her hair popped off the back of her skull in an abrupt ponytail, and she was shaking her head so that the black strands were caught in inky motion. She'd chosen for her goofy face a model's squinch, her slim, smoky eyes boozed and dangerous.

On Bill's other side was Rick, face partially obscured by two fingers traveling John Travolta–style across his visage. He'd gone all out and rented a black tux, from which his football muscle practically bubbled. His butt protruded slightly toward Bill, and it looked like a couple of black balloons trying to escape. Beneath the coat, the vest struggled to stay buttoned. Behind the Travolta fingers, he wore his football scowl, his brow tight and formidable, already spilling sweat before the dance had even begun. His other hand clung to the stark green of Kaylyn's waist. Kaylyn had chosen to blow a kiss, and her lips, shellacked in purple lipstick, frozen in a pucker, passed the kiss to her open palm. Strands of her blond hair fell carefully to either side of her head, curled and bobbing timelessly in the stillness. Her lips reminded him of a single purple flower growing from a verdant forest floor. The way that color clashed with her dress certainly had to be intentional. Kaylyn knew how she would stand out in pictures, even in the background, and years later when people flipped through photo albums, they'd come to this homecoming section, and no matter if they'd known her or they were originally from Oregon and now married to a graduate of New Canaan High, their eyes would still be drawn to the girl in the green dress with the purple lipstick, and their gaze would track her in any photograph that followed.

Beside her, Stacey Moore had gone Bond Girl, both hands clasped together into a gun she held under her chin. In a long copper dress, the junior looked like a sexy penny fresh off the mint, the material catching all kinds of odd light from the cafeteria. Her blond was cleaner than Kaylyn's, but cinched back tight against her skull by unseen scalp mechanisms. Her long, slim limbs seemed to crowd her own boyfriend out of the picture. Though Bill had loved her, found her warm and lovely and amusing, Stacey had always appeared awkward to him. She slunk her shoulders—in this photo too—as if she wanted to erase some of her height, embarrassed by the longitude it took to accommodate her presence. One sharp elbow looked like it might dig into Ben Harrington's chest. He had been caught both trying to put his arm around Stacey and yet avoid catching that elbow in a rib. As a result, it looked like he was dancing badly to a rap song, his other arm dropping a finger to some unseen beat. (What might it have been in '02? "Hot in Herre"? "Bombs Over Baghdad"?) In his stasis the baby-faced Harrington seemed to be attempting embryonically to preview the musician garb he'd someday wear. Bill and Rick had tormented him for the black fedora, cocked forward on his head here, and the black jacket over a black crew neck with a single gold chain sparkling. Who had he even been imitating? More importantly, did he realize how brashly that sweet baby grin of his clashed with the ensemble? It looked like a Halloween costume. His sideburns were also too long, nearly down to his jaw.

There were other people on the fringes of this picture. You could spot the stunted Dan Eaton beside Hailey Kowalczyk, her voluptuous figure still years away from widening. She had a smooth plastic face with spots of rosacea on her cheeks and forehead. She appeared to have dragged Dan into the frame, behind her Rainrock Road crew of Lisa and Kaylyn, who at the point of this photo had undergone some bitchy high-school-girl falling-out. And poor Dan looked like he wanted to be transplanted off the planet. Into some Fortress of Umbilical Love where he could limply marvel at Hailey in solitude. When Bill had seen him earlier that night, Dan had been uninterested in this picture. He'd handled it like the thing might poison him.

The night this photo was taken, Bill and Rick stayed in the basement of Harrington's house, sneaking Kaylyn, Lisa, and Stacey in after midnight through a window. Rick and Kaylyn disappeared into Doug Harrington's tool-draped workspace and fucked on the edge of the table saw after Rick made sure it was unplugged. ("Had the worst vision outta a horror movie right when I got off," he drunkenly reported.) Harrington and Stacey took the bathroom, and after finishing, they sat in the basement rec area watching *The Princess Bride*, tossing M&M's into each other's mouths from across the couch. He and Lisa had gotten the night's activities out of the way at the Brew, and in the dark, he'd imagined her as Kaylyn the entire time. Her Vietnamese heritage bled out of her in the starlight and Kaylyn's German bled in, until in that dim halo he could see each girl as the other.

Funny, he thought, folding the picture back up, how you could look at anyone's high school homecoming picture from any middling town or suburb in America, and they all looked like stock photos, the image that came with the frame, identical teenagers doing identical teenage shit and hoping it wouldn't end because what lay beyond was too unknown.

He heard the door of the liquor store chime and popped his head up in time to see a short, unkempt figure stalk in. He sat finishing his cigarette.

After a moment the man reemerged and looked at Bill the way you'd check to see if a dog in the pound was actually the one your parents told you had run off. Unruly dreads bobbed around his face, playing Velcro with gnarly, gnatty stubble. Clothed in baggy jeans with white bleach stains and a dark zippered sweatshirt despite the warmth of the night. A big chain looped from his belt to a wallet in the back pocket. He'd added a bottle in a brown paper bag to his accoutrements.

"Whoa. Bill Ashcraft."

Bill held his whiskey aloft. "The one and only."

"Where in the pits did you come from?"

Bill studied the face: a coyote scowl, thick platypus lips, a disappointed menace in the eyes, but so very white bread underneath the posture—a specimen plucked from the suburbs and spray-tanned with disaffection. Familiarity flickered but winked out. "Sorry, it's been a fucking hippo of a day. We went to school together?"

"Dakota." He stuck out a small, delicate hand. His eyes were furious and careless and nihilistic. It was like locking gazes with a torturer.

Bill clamped the cigarette and shook the hand, though the name still meant nothing.

"Sure, man."

"Bill motherfucking Ashcraft. You back in town?"

The trigonometries of his patter were familiar. The Ohio drawl acting as interlocutor for an urbanized, hip-hop patois gleaned from interaction with young black men mostly via CD.

"Sure. Maybe. Who knows. Up here running an errand and Jonah handed me your number."

"No doubt I can hook you up."

Suddenly he remembered the kid. Exley. Dakota Exley. He'd been without dreads then, just a mushroom of bland brown hair. A petite little fucker a grade ahead, Dakota had skulked around with a skateboard and no friends. At least, he'd had the skateboard until Ryan Ostrowski, a football-playing Beaufort lacky, cornered Dakota in the parking lot for the LOLz. He'd torn Dakota's skateboard away, shoved him to the ground, and hit him so hard over the spine that it cracked the wood. Kids stood around watching the way they do.

"You backed me up. Sorta," Bill remembered, a glow of unexpected camaraderie blooming. "During that whole T-shirt debacle, you came up and said something to me that wasn't 'Go fuck yourself.'"

"What can I say? You had a point."

Bill slapped his new friend on the back and stood. "C'mon. Let's boogie."

They ambled away from the liquor store, searching out a place to make a deal. Clouds moved in overhead, blotting out the stars in large dark-white patches of spilled, glowing paint.

Let's call it a defining time of Bill's young life, but for very different reasons than it was definitional for most. This was fall of his junior year, right before basketball began, and all that was on his mind were those last days of freedom before the season swallowed all his time and energy. He and Lisa were having the kind of exhausting amounts of sex only teenagers can truly manage, and then, one Tuesday morning during earth science, Mr. Masoncup got a call. He hung up, turned on the television in the corner of the room just in time for the class to see the second plane crash into the World Trade Center. All they could do was watch in total, undiluted awe as the first tower fell. Hailey Kowalczyk sat beside him in that class, and when the South Tower began pancaking down in a cascade of gory gray glory, she ate a breath of air, buckled back so fast her desk shrieked against the tile, and said two words that, for Bill, would come to define the event and all that came in the aftermath.

"Oh no."

Bill was immediately on the wrong side of the thing. In his social studies class, they talked about the coming invasion of Afghanistan. He'd stayed up nights reading the history. Some war-torn country literally known as the "graveyard of empires" and they were going to go bomb the rubble around and occupy? Good fucking luck. "Maybe we should be asking why people hate us so much," he said in that class as he felt Rick glaring at him, Lisa wishing he would be quiet. "Like is it crazy to think we had this coming?

Like, those people think God chose them, but here we all are just clearly thinking God chose us. It's in the pledge the state makes us say every morning." The class sat in silence, picking at their desks and fingernails.

In New Canaan High, 9/11 had this element of activation. At lunch, the boys crowded around the military recruiters who came through handing out pamphlets. Students were instructed to write and decorate messages to the troops on stiff pieces of cardboard, which would be "sent to the war zone." On his, Bill wrote: *Try not to kill too many civilians.* His social studies teacher informed him that this sentiment was removed from the pile before it was mailed.

His own activation had been a long time coming.

Adolescent identity is an odd thing, formed mostly for hypermasculine young men by their chosen extracurricular activity. Since seventh grade when he and Rick were breaking out as up-and-coming stars of their respective sports, they'd each had a taste of that oozing, slippery product called popularity that had something to do with health and something to do with wealth but simply couldn't be predicted. Prior to this moment, the two of them made sense. Maybe his parents were college educated and Rick's parents worked as a police officer and ran a salon, respectively, but who cared about that? About their parents' levels of education or incomes or worldviews or politics? He, Rick, and Harrington had stories dating back to the second grade. In seventh and eighth grade, they took to quizzing each other on basketball and football plays and joked about Rick's eerie ability to recall running routes after only a glance ("You're like Redneck Rainman, Brink"). They made weird bets at parties to set lawn chairs on fire or jump into scummy ponds for Little Caesars breadsticks coupons. They were whip-smart badasses, lambent troublemakers. They were *boys.*

Something began to change right around the time the shit-eating Texas governor snookered the 2000 election from the doughy and ineffectual vice president. They'd always busted each other's balls about everything, but this felt different. It bothered Bill. For that period of months when they were counting chads and maneuvering to the Supreme Court, the two of them argued about it the way you'd argue about a bad foul call in the NBA playoffs or an Ohio State touchdown that got called back for offensive pass interference. When Bush got crowned, Rick needled him at every opportunity, including slapping a W STANDS 4 WINNER bumper sticker on Bill's locker, which he had to scrape off with a razor blade.

Then two planes hit the World Trade Center towers, one hit the Pentagon, and a final one dug a crater in a Pennsylvania field, and almost that same day, he felt a divergence occur between them. Bill observed the flag-waving, the brainless nationalism, the invocation of military might as panacea for sorrow, and it felt to him like a bad movie, a gloss of convenient worship for shared bloodletting. Rick got into it. Really into it. He put a bumper sticker on his car: LET'S ROLL. He took down every football poster and hung a massive American flag in his bedroom, the kind that belongs on a pole outside a civic building. He seemed genuinely disappointed when the operation in Afghanistan came to a quick conclusion (or appeared to). When he turned eighteen the summer before senior year, he would get his first tattoo: a claw mark on his shoulder where invisible talons revealed the Stars and Stripes beneath the skin. Meanwhile, Bill felt like he had to ingest everything he could to counter this jingoism suddenly ejaculating from his best friend's mouth. His favorite album became *Let's Get Free* by Dead Prez, while he checked off all the required reading of a young radical struggling to make sense of history and the social order: *The Autobiography of Malcolm X, Manufacturing Consent, A People's History of the United States*. The bug gestated, and when he began to see the way the world *is*—not the way the corporate media presented it, not the way his parents and teachers told it, not the way he wished it was so he wouldn't have to feel guilt—once he saw the way the world *is* in its most gritty, tactile, overwhelming sadness and injustice—well, he could never unsee it.

Maybe at that age he was aping left-wing provocateurs, not yet ready to author his own opinion, but Rick was just a Fox News fire hose spraying invective at anyone he saw as insufficiently war-hungry.

So a few months after the attacks of September 11, as the administration began murmuring about a second war, Bill came to school in a black T-shirt with a mug shot of Bush and the words WANTED: INTERNATIONAL TERRORIST.

He'd been in the building less than ten minutes, enduring the stares and glares, when Rick found him by his locker. He'd never seen his friend so angry.

"Are you fucking kidding me?" He pushed close. Put his face breath-to-breath with Bill's. Rick had this particular scent, a pre-sweat musk that hovered around him even after he showered. It smelled almost of bean burritos.

"All right, don't get all fucked up over it, Rick. It's a goddamn T-shirt." He pretended to look for something in his locker, which was a disaster of folders, textbooks, errant clothing he kept forgetting to take home. He found his varsity jacket and searched the pockets, found his car keys, which seemed like a reasonable excuse to not face Rick and a fury that, he had to admit, surprised him.

"Would you wear that shit around someone who died fighting for your right to wear it?" Rick asked, the muscles of his face taut and demanding a real answer. Even his acne appeared redder.

Bill gave him a quizzical look. It was times like this he yearned for Kaylyn the most. The resentment felt like wolves breathing on the back of his neck.

"You mean like would I wear it around them in the afterlife? Not sure I understand."

Harrington had been milling near his locker with Stacey and left her to walk their way. They had a crowd now. Clusters of their book-clutching peers stopped to watch this juicy scene unfold. Rick plucked at the shirt, pinching Bill's skin in the process. "This is some sick shit, even for your unbelievable dumb ass."

Despite Rick's Creatine muscle, spreading over his young frame like an exoskeleton, Bill felt the impulse to take a swing and see where it led. He was still four inches taller. Rick had to gaze up at him.

"How's this . . ." He thumped a palm hard off Rick's chest, hoping it would back him up. "Any fucking different from putting that idiot bumper sticker on your car? Just exercising my free speech rights. Isn't that what you want to go off and kill a bunch of Third World farmers for?"

Rick's face in motion always reminded him of an angry little boy. It was a face of small features—tiny ears, tiny nose, beady brown eyes. When he smiled, his eyes almost disappeared in the manner of a little kid caught in gut-busting hysterics. Maybe this was because Bill had known him since they were toddlers, but it's what he always saw when the guy laughed. Now this sense of Rick disappeared, and after this moment Bill never saw him that way again.

Harrington finally spoke up. "Dudes. This is dumb. Let's chill the fuck out? Everyone's already agreed you owe us all a dollar every time you bring up politics. So Ashcraft that's five dollars for wearing the shirt, and Brink that's five dollars for getting pissed about it."

Rick pretended not to hear. He jabbed a finger into Bill's chest. So hard it stung. "I see that shirt after today, man, we're gonna have words."

He stormed away, swollen arms held adrift from his body, as if allowing them to hang normally by his sides might give the terrorists succor. Bill turned back to his locker, tossed his car keys back into the pocket of his varsity jacket.

Harrington stared at him like a dumb puppy.

"What?" said Bill.

"Nothing." He began walking back to Stacey, who stood at the end of the hall, hips cocked, chewing on her lip with her pixie-cute face wrenched in worry. Over his shoulder, Harrington said, "Have it your way, Ashcraft. Just have it your way all the time."

But the day didn't end there. After third period, he was walking through the upstairs hallway, talking to Eric "Whitey" Frye, a sophomore and one of the only black kids in lily-white NCHS. They were pushing through the crowd, talking hoops, feeling the first pre-lunch pangs, Bill explaining how Coach Napier was going to have him play a two guard even though he had height—

And then a hammer landed on his chest, sent him sprawling to his ass before he even realized it was his books and folders flying. They slapped back down to hard hallway carpet as Frye made himself slim against the lockers. Bill looked up to see a shoulder and above it, a delighted smile, both belonging to Todd Beaufort, the football team's co-captain.

"My bad," said Beaufort, and Bill had a flyby thought of how this was such a move from some bad teen comedy. The cliché offended him as much as the physical act. "Maybe don't make treason against your own country? Just a thought."

Bill hauled himself to his feet, face hot from the whispers and snickers. Beaufort's girlfriend, Tina Ross, stood a few feet back snickering with delight. For some reason—as Bill stepped toe-to-toe with Beaufort—this is what pissed him off the most. This stupid, pretty girl giggling at her steroidal fuckbag boyfriend, playing the good little Christian virgin while the high school's football star used her like a blow-up doll. Beaufort was born to be a bully, oversized and stupid. What excuse did she have?

"If you wanna go . . ." Beaufort mused. He and Bill were about the same height, but the kid probably had thirty pounds of muscle on him. For the first time in high school, he felt the isolation of the easy pickings. He wondered too if Beaufort was acting as Rick's proxy.

He felt a hand on his shoulder.

"Get moving," Mr. Clifton said to Beaufort. "And, Bill, come with me."

Beaufort smirked as Bill was led away, and he saw Tina give him this look like she'd never been more delighted to see someone knocked down a peg. He'd bought her a milk shake at Vicky's once, and they'd even made out in one of those long-ago grades (Seventh? Eighth? Who remembered?). He hated her more than Beaufort.

"This isn't you in trouble with me," Clifton assured him on the way to Principal MacMillan's office. "This is about your safety."

"Seems like it's about censorship."

Mr. Clifton took a hand from his pants pocket and smoothed his mustache. "I admire your passion, Bill. I always do admire people with passion. But you need to learn the difference between passion and provocation."

In Principal MacMillan's office the bureaucratic lump took one look at him and said, "Turn it inside out for today. Then I don't want to see it again, or it'll be a suspension."

That afternoon after classes let out, Bill went to the screen printer in town and had a shirt printed with the quote:

Returning violence for violence multiplies violence, adding deeper darkness to a night already devoid of stars

This too landed him in the principal's office. Mr. Bonheim, the football coach and also a history teacher, spotted him in the hallway.

"We been put on notice about this," he said, examining the words, trying to ferret out what radical meaning they might possibly contain.

Bill spat it out before he thought it through: "It's Martin Luther fucking King."

He entered MacMillan's office with the rage of the righteous. He was ready to shout. To threaten. To take a stand. He pictured a Supreme Court case. He pictured the *New York Times* editorializing on the courageous determination of this humble kid from Middle America. He pictured an Oscar-winning biopic.

"You have a choice," MacMillan told him, hands tented. Bill glared at the way his baldness was happening—a streak of fallow follicles crawling up his scalp from where he parted the limp brown. "Coach Napier tells me you're a hell of a ballplayer. Either you can keep up this nonsense or you can play basketball this year. You cannot do both."

Like that, his fury drained. His skin went clammy, the way it will when dread chokes away false courage.

"That's what he said?" He hated the way his question came out: frightened, childish. Suddenly, his surroundings returned to him. The drab, uncluttered office space of a public school warden. Clichéd inspirational posters making success sound as if it had nothing to do with socioeconomics.

MacMillan nodded. "It's not his decision anyway. Now, Bill, if you want to get the ACLU involved, be my guest. Meanwhile, you won't play basketball."

Bill threw away both shirts that day. Only one person ever acknowledged him for what he'd done. A squirrely outcast named Dakota Exley approached him in the hallway after school, likely when he was sure Bill would be alone. This skinny, scraggly upperclassman with a face like a rhesus monkey, Bill had to look around to make sure it was him the guy was speaking to. "Heard what happened with your shirt. Just wanted to say fuck those dickless cogs," he said while blinking too much. "Someone should knife 'em all and put 'em in the dirt."

Though he didn't really condone the closing sentiment, Bill was so relieved to have anyone side with him that he thanked this hallway apparition, whom he'd never given a second thought to, and who soon stalked off. It was the last thing they'd say to each other until more than a decade later on a summer night the temperature of warm blood. The strictures of high school cliquery were simply too much for another interaction—let alone a friendship—to propagate.

Whatever burgeoning political rage he'd felt, he was also still a child. Precocious, maybe, but a kid who loved the joy of the dribble, the Zen of a ball ripping through a net, and when he saw that this could be taken from him he had that little-kid feeling of wanting to cry down to the bottom of himself. It was a lesson he'd learn over and over again—in college, in activism, with his finicky, conformist parents. Like MacMillan and the clique of teachers and coaches who all went to the same church and barbecued at one another's houses, much of the country's small-bore civil servants were itching to do some repressing of their own. Millions of Dick Cheney wannabes swelling the ranks, enjoying their little authoritarian fiefdoms. His disagreements with Rick ebbed and flowed but like storms on a warming planet, grew in ferocity. Maybe his popularity was grandfathered in because he won basketball games with his J, but even when he slipped into a cloak of conformity, his isolation followed him like a hot sweet smoke. What an important lesson for every young person to learn: If you defy the collective psychosis of nationalism, of imperial war, you will pay for it. And the people in your community, your home, who you thought knew and loved you, will be the ones to collect the debt.

Bill watched an owl—possibly imaginary—streak magnificently across the diving darkness. "You hated me?" he asked.

"I wasn't exactly sitting at the center of the lunchroom."

He walked slightly behind Dakota, each of them swigging whiskey. Bill's shirt was baggy enough, but he worried about the bulge on his spine. He stretched his back, the tape stressing skin. He had to get this shit off. But the idea of smoking some green or snorting a rail had wormed too deep.

"You're down with Jonah Hansen now," Bill noted. "He was like the social chair back when."

Dakota had a look of permanent resentment carved into his features, which made him impossible to read. He kept picturing the kid with that clean part right down the middle. The spasming dreadlocks must have been the work of years. "Doesn't mean we're tight."

"Had a few beers with him tonight. Eaton and Beaufort too."

"Yeah, I see 'em around."

"Ever talk to Beaufort?"

"Nope."

Bill scratched his balls. "And I thought I was the sad-sack, washed-up ex-jock."

Because he'd had that beer with Beaufort, now he couldn't get Tina Ross off his mind, and all the weird shit that had gone down because of her. All these years later, he still saw her snickering at him, that image somehow the totem of all that had gone on with his stupid T-shirt wars. When had their brief fling happened? He remembered the milk shake and making out on the couch in his basement (pretending to watch a movie, his mom pretending to do laundry to keep an eye on them). He remembered how she'd petted his dick without taking it to the next step. When her mom picked her up, Bill curled into a fetal coil in his bed, feeling that ache in the testicles that made you want to simultaneously come, shit, vomit, and die. She'd ghosted him after that. Why had he been so furious at her? Wasn't her fault. She hardly had a thought in her head that hadn't come from her youth pastor. Yet when he heard the rumors, he'd felt glee. His turn to laugh at her.

"Thought I'd still loathe him. Beaufort, I mean." His memories kept jerking him around in bumper car collisions. His mind had the consistency of quantum foam. "I actually felt sorry for him."

They passed an ExxonMobil station, bright sign beaming its massive con. The searing fluorescent white cast a fog over his speeding, bleeding brain. Then he admitted the obvious:

"I suppose in high school I would've hated me too."

"It's relative. You and Harrington, y'all two were cooler than most."

His friend's name echoed in the stillness, the very sound a weary refugee dragging an ache to his dry throat. "Ever listen to his music?"

"Huh?"

"Harrington. His albums."

Listlessly kicking a plastic Slurpee cup, sending it skittering across the road, memory gave birth to memory in botched C-section bloodletting. Dakota rolled up a sleeve, and he saw a tattoo on his forearm in florid script: *Money Power Respect.*

"Maybe I checked 'em out a while back. Didn't care for it. Kid had a dim view on things."

"A dim view? Can you even blame him—"

"No offense, man, but you buying anything?"

They came to the intersection of South Main Street and Newark Road, where a cardboard box of a building, which had over the years shuffled through being a sub sandwich joint, an athletic apparel store, and a real estate office, currently idled in vacancy. Brown paper taped to the interior of the windows obscured whatever copper-wire-salvage scene lay within. They stopped at the crosswalk. Dakota was right; he really needed to be on his way. Get this deal done and the night on-withed. Then he remembered his truck.

"Fuck," he muttered.

"Yo?"

The thousand dollars he'd left in the glove compartment seemed more important now. "Forgot my cash. Don't suppose you'd take plastic?"

Dakota threw up his hands. "You call me all the way out here and ain't even got cash?"

Bill *pffff*ed. "One of those nights, man."

The glowing mid-stride crosswalk guy beckoned. Then he felt the dealer's stiff hand tap his shoulder, guiding him to cross the street.

"Hey. We gotta move."

"Kinda need to be on my way."

"No. I mean we really gotta move."

Bill followed his gaze to the distant traffic light where a police cruiser waited, the hood looking like a hungry lion. Dakota picked up the pace, and even though they weren't doing anything—just a couple old acquaintances out for a late-night stroll—he knew Dakota had illicit this or that on him, and Bill, well, he had no idea what he might have in tow.

"Don't want those fuckers even seeing us. Let's get to the football field. Then we can talk deals."

The prospect that Dakota might spot him a joint—hell, that sounded like honey in the famine. They hustled toward New Canaan High. Bill hummed another Harrington song, one of home and sky and heat and road, as they made their way toward his chosen place of worship.

He was never sure who he missed the most, but Ben Harrington was the friend he frequently found himself talking to in his head. Harrington who'd had a tenderness, a disinclination toward a hard heart. Hell, Harrington's real name was actually William, and he'd gone by Will until kindergarten when the two of them became friends. Just like that, he began going by his middle name, Ben, to settle the confusion—the kid changed his name for their friendship. As a boy he probably spent more time at the Harringtons' than at his own house, flirting with his sisters, nosing around Doug Harrington's incredible garage with every dangerous power drill, saw, and sander one could imagine. He had a special fascination with Harrington's father because he'd been a star guard at New Canaan back in the seventies. He was also a hard, often unpleasant man. When he heard the song "Trouble in Hand," which included lyrics like *Born in the same town you'll die in dumber*, he wondered what Doug thought.

"Way back, I planned to write the album so he'd stop speaking to me," Harrington said. "Turns out I didn't need to work so hard."

By then Harrington was living in L.A. Bill found this appropriate, as the kid had always looked the part. Floppy blond locks, a year-round tan, and big white teeth straightened with seventh-grade braces to resemble wall plaster. He was Americana prepackaged, belonging on the glossy spread of an Abercrombie ad. His love songs all sounded like they were written for Stacey even though, like Bill and Lisa, they broke up in 2003. There was a sappy, precocious energy that reminded Bill of the way Harrington had doted on her.

Maybe he should've looked closer at his friend back in high school: the anxiety, the uncertainty that probably fueled a lot of artist types. He'd smoked more pot than the rest of them, but so what? When they visited each other in college, Harrington would always want to score prescriptions. Once he showed up with a bottle of Vicodin. Another time they snorted Oxy, and Bill discovered the one drug he hated because for whatever reason it made it so he couldn't piss no matter how full his bladder was. Over the years, he watched his friend's music career accelerate, watched him play in bars and small clubs, saw fans begin to attach themselves. His sound was retro-Dylanish, pretty but insipid, not really Bill's thing, but he at least appreciated all the references, the inside jokes. They'd met up in Chicago while Harrington was on his second self-financed van tour. Before the show, Bill had himself a peek into his friend's backpack, which looked like a fucking pharmacy. Vic, Val, Oxy, Hydro, Norco—Harrington had a serious set of pals. But Bill operated by the principle that you don't intervene in people's coping mechanisms—however they faced down the storm. So he stole two Vals, and went about feeling like sexy melted marshmallow the rest of the night.

Since meeting in kindergarten, they'd had only one serious fight. When Rick was killed. Harrington could not believe, could not stand, could not countenance that Bill wasn't going home for the funeral.

"Whatever happened between you two, it's going to last after the kid's dead?" They spoke by phone, and Bill walked out of his college apartment. The semester was over, and he stood in the street watching a sorority girl try to pack piles of dirty laundry into her SUV.

"We didn't all drop out, Harrington. I graduate next week."

Harrington's end of the line was silent.

"It's not about Rick," Bill continued, trying to explain the inexplicable. "It's about what the spectacle represents. As long as the Rick Brinklans of the world are held up as heroes, and we're celebrating their pointless deaths with patriotic parades, all this shit rolls on."

Harrington still said nothing.

"Dude," he demanded.

"I don't know what you want me to say, Bill. You don't hear how selfish you sound? You're hiding behind some bullshit political reasoning because you're still mad at him over—over who the fuck even remembers."

Bill's skin crawled with righteousness. "You don't get it, and why would you? You always wanted to stand in the middle and play peacemaker. Not because you can't think for yourself but because you're afraid."

"Man," Harrington started, then stopped. "Stacey's not going. Lisa never wrote me back. I'm just— What the fuck is with you guys? He was our friend."

"Christ, Harrington, we were children. We didn't have a choice who our friends were. Oh, this kid lives down the road from me? I can ride my bike to his house? Sure, let's be best pals. That's over. And yes, what I'm telling you is that he no longer means anything to me. Not enough to go be a part of some jingoistic spectacle. It's a narrative, man. It's a narrative they want everyone to swallow— that what he did was honorable. It wasn't."

That phone call ended badly, but unlike with Rick, they patched things up.

Four years later, after Cambodia and the Ho Chi Minh Trail, Bill was back in Columbus looking for a job, ranks of temp agencies failing to call him back for ten-dollar-an-hour call center work, when he saw the story on CNN. He booked his bus tickets, routing through Pittsburgh, that same night.

He spoke to Harrington on his way to New York, telling him that depending on what happened in Zuccotti Park, maybe he'd come stay with him in L.A. afterward.

"And take a corporate airline?" said Harrington in his gentle tenor. The voice that made twenty-year-old coeds mad with desire. "You already selling out, bro?"

"Harrington, the day you figure out your albums are radical documents of protest . . ."

"You know those evil sons of bitches only take money, right? Have you heard of money? Currency? Here, I'll give you a primer . . ."

His Occupy experience was a novel in and of itself, complete

with villains and minor antagonists and a low-rent threesome he
had in a tent one night with a Palestinian dude and a woman who
smelled of onions. The park thronged with Guy Fawkes masks,
kempt reporters with stiff hair products, percussive music that
thrummed in the fillings, gawkers, NYPD standing at the perimeter,
rigid and bored, the active murmur of hundreds of simultaneous
conversations convening to a river's roar. It was thrilling, it was
maddening, it was fascinating. He made friends he thought he'd
stay in touch with the rest of his life. They would smoke cigarettes
at night and watch the glowing cinders of the park. Mere blocks
away, the new One World Trade Center tower glowed the color of
molten steel. As the movement grew and other occupations erupted
across the country, then the world, he and his new friends had the
sensation of a wildfire catching the right wind.

Yet he wasn't around in the end when the weather turned
cold and the park filled with drug addicts, the mentally ill, the
homeless—all the people society had cast off, drawn like moths
to the flame of Zuccotti. He wasn't around when in November
the police put on their riot gear and cleared the park; armed
with NYPD vans, corrections buses, plastic zip-tie handcuffs, and
pepper spray, they carried the bodies of nonresistant occupiers
while helicopters thundered above and searchlights beamed up
the apostasy. Flatbed trucks stacked with metal barricades moved
in while a backhoe clattered down Broadway like an Imperial
Walker, loading the books, boxes of food, sleeping bags, tents,
duffels, clothes, suitcases, and mattresses into soggy dump trucks
that delivered it all to nowhere, just more cast off effluvium of the
American experience.

He wasn't there because five weeks into his time at Liberty
Square, he saw he had a voice mail. Only his parents still left voice
mails. He had to walk down multiple blocks to get enough quiet
from the drum circle, and then he called his mom.

It was difficult to hear her and even more difficult to process. "Ben," she choked. "There was an apartment fire. I can't believe this—I'm so sorry, baby." His skin went cold, and he thought irrationally that this was his fault. That he'd somehow brought this on.

The details were even more harrowing. Harrington had overdosed in bed with a lit cigarette in his hand. Heroin, according to the autopsy. He also killed a couple who lived above him, newlyweds from Mendocino, who'd just moved in the month before. They died of smoke inhalation. Bill slipped into that kind of stunned that settles in after impossible news, those random acts of freewheeling madness that change everything in one blood-draining beat.

He hung up on his mom and sank against the side of a building outside a deli. He stank. He hadn't showered in a week. Occupiers chanted from down the street. We. Are. The Ninety-Nine Percent. Bill found himself thinking of grade school. They'd had this thing called the Angel Award that went to the most well-behaved student, which Harrington won every single year, much to his dismay. They gave him such shit about it. Called him "Angel in the Outfield." Then when they got to sixth grade, their lunch table gathered a pool of money for the man brave enough to poop in the girls' bathroom. Harrington stood up, shrugged, and said, "No more Angel Award, so I've got nothing to live for." He took a detention for it and everything.

Bill lowered his head into his lap as despair erupted in his chest. Then he wept for a long time. The way you will.

He thought about staying in Zuccotti. Who knew where all this was going? How could he leave now? Harrington wouldn't know the difference, and maybe this was it—the event that would change things. But of course it wasn't. In the end he caught a bus back to Ohio for the funeral and watched the NYPD clear Zuccotti on the TV in his parents' basement.

Following the funeral, Bill got in touch with his Occupy friends.

One was in prison for assaulting a police officer. The cop had grabbed her breast during the clearing, and she'd cracked him with her elbow. To put a five-foot-nothing woman away for such "assault" was to codify the illegality of dissent. Another friend, Arthur, told Bill he was going to Mexico for this collective farming thing, and Bill promised to meet him there. Bill's became a life of Greyhounds, sunglasses, and overpasses; of weeded lots and dry-docked cars on cinder blocks; of joints rolled and smoked just out of reach of the street lamps. A week later he was in the cracking, sunbaked plains of Sonora, getting advice from a kind woman with a snaggletooth and gnarled arthritic hands on how best to avoid confrontation with the cartel enforcers who not so secretly ran the town. Arthur never showed.

"The song's not racist," Bill told Dakota. "It's about the desperation of the narrator. He's looking to lash out, to blame anybody available."

"I fought that nigger again," Dakota quoted, reading the lyrics from his phone. "I fought that nigger again / I said, 'Boy, don't you know, you stole my granddaddy's soul / Now I got my enemies as kin.' "

"Right, he's talking to a specific person. *That* nigger, who's now somehow a part of his family. Who he thinks stole from his grandpappy, probably with the Voting Rights Act or some shit."

Dakota's face remained skeptical as he read more of the song.

"I killed a man again / I killed a man again / I stuck a knife in his ribs outside a bar in West Texas / I got his ATM pin.

"I beat my son again / I beat my son again / I said, 'Kid, don't you know, this hard world grows you cold' / I broke his arm again.

"I raped his mother again / I raped his mother again / I met her on a FOB over in Afghanistan / I killed her heart with my sin."

"Exactly," said Bill. "They're expressions of the dispossessed. It's about a dude who can't even understand why he acts out in these ways. People dismiss him as a monster because that makes it easy on *them*. But he's been bred and brought up, almost like a dog, to be vicious, to be cruel. The song's about his remorse. Very Johnny Cash."

Dakota arched his eyebrows. "If you say so."

From what his parents told him, Harrington's music had been fairly polarizing back home. Certainly no sign was going up at the city limits: HOMETOWN OF WILLIAM BENJAMIN HARRINGTON. He'd had a following, he'd played the festival circuit, but he'd never really broken out. He'd certainly never made money. A gruesome OD may have since helped record sales and mythos, but rock stars don't get remunerated for the good career move of dying at exactly twenty-seven years old.

"At the bar tonight we were talking about this New Canaan rumor—you heard of this? The Murder That Never Was?"

Dakota checked over his shoulder, the road empty. "Sure, everyone's heard of that."

"Right. So someone decides to make it up for a laugh. But it sticks, it spreads. It's like any urban legend, like the guy with the hook for a hand who murders kids on lovers' lane. That's so teenagers will stop having sex at the Brew. It serves a social utility."

"You lost me, man. Lost me good."

"You know," Bill said, waggling both hands in the air as he tried to capture his point. "It's trying to provide meaning and narrative where there is none. The murder rumor is like a conspiracy theory in that way. People don't want to believe dark, terrible violence can just spring out of—or onto—bored normal folk. Look at the kids we grew up with. How many ODs do you know?"

Dakota snorted a laugh. "That are dead or that just OD'd and started shooting up a week later?"

"Curtis Moretti, Ben Harrington."

"If you're only counting from the popular cliques. My class alone had eleven. If you're talking jail, you got Tony Wozniak? Ron Kruger? And are we counting the Flood brothers? They're like on frequent flyer miles. Still not sure what you're steering at."

"It's the Harrington song, man. It's all part of the same phenomenon in the end. You either fight for your dignity and some fucking justice or you lose it—no other way. And once you start to really lose it, the rot sets in."

He knew a bag of weed was hidden somewhere in the substratum of Dakota's jeans. The guy had a scent like a cyclohexane refinery.

"We're here on business," Dakota warned. "Don't fill my ear with your liberal bullshit."

Bill stopped, his feet skidding in the gravel berm, and regarded him. "Thought you were down with my T-shirt protest back in the day?"

"Didn't mean I was no Democrat. Ain't like I voted for Barack O-fucking-bama."

In the wind, the leaves looked like an addict's agitated fingers, stroking night and sky. They turned onto New Canaan Avenue, which ran by a few industrial lots, the bowling alley, the park, and over the Cattawa. For some reason the town had never felt it necessary to put a sidewalk on this road, so they walked on the berm, uncapping their booze and swigging, vigilant for the NCPD patrol car.

"Yeah, well, neither did I. The second time, I mean. I was in Mexico anyway."

"Doing what?"

Bill went on to describe his many aborted journeys: the reservation, Cambodia, Occupy, the cartel town. It sounded a hell of a lot more exciting than it actually felt to live, sitting unbathed in interminable airports waiting on delayed planes; broken phrases in disparate languages; chopped English and hand-gesture communication; keeping your whole life strapped inside a forty-pound Osprey pack. Of course that was after he lost his job on the 2008 campaign.

"See," said Dakota. "Democrat."

He laughed, thinking of when he got fired for an "outrageous, indecent, indiscriminate" tweet (*Ready to string up these Wall Street fucks & their families from light poles on Park Ave #JacobinTime*). He hadn't bothered cleaning out his desk, accidentally leaving behind a glass cube with a piece of the net from when Harrington tipped in his own missed free throw for the conference championship. Self-fucked, out of the whole incident Bill regretted this the most.

They passed under a street lamp, one of those sodium-vapor deals that cast the worst kind of orange-soda color and made half the streets in America look washed-out and sick. Only under its glare did Bill now realize that roughly a third of the lights on New Canaan Avenue were dark, which created large pockets of sallow shadows.

"What you learn's like: the American system . . ." He flicked his cigarette into the road. "It's not like this conspiracy of Illuminati. It's just this adaptive, fucking assimilating, smooth motherfucker. It gives you cars and credit and religion and television and all this other comfort that we go and call 'freedom.' Problem is, there's no raging against the machine because the machine just consumes whatever objection anyone makes about it."

"Hey, can I bum a smoke?"

"Sure." Bill fished in his jeans for the pack of Camels. He popped the top with one hand, offered the pack to Dakota, and then drew another for himself with his teeth.

"But it's— Here, I got a lighter." He snapped a flame for Dakota and then lit his own. "It's way more subtle than that. Like anyone trying to say her piece," Bill explained. "You'll just get commodified, assimilated, appropriated. You'll get a tenure-track teaching job or a record contract or your own TV show, or God forbid, a publishing deal. Now you're owned by the status quo. By GE or Comcast or Pearson PLC or worst of all, some neoliberal Ivy League university."

Dakota ashed with expert flicks and ticks of his fingers, like an old-timer sitting on the porch matter-of-factly recounting the moment his wife left him. They passed the varsity baseball diamond and neared the secluded safety of the football field where—eons ago it seemed—he'd graduated on one balls-dripping-hot summer day.

"Democrat? Liberal? Duckfuck. At this point I'd rather be called a Nazi. Liberals are the Harvard grads interested in diversifying the plutocracy. And if you're *really* causing trouble, if you're *really* being heard, and it needs you to shut up? It'll find a way."

Dakota appeared bored by this, but at least he was someone to talk to. Bill had never actually met a person to whom he did not enjoy ranting.

"Ever seen that John Carpenter movie? *The Thing*?" Dakota asked, smoldering Camel sticky-tacked to his lower lip.

"Yeah, Kurt Russell?"

"Right. Great flick. Yo, let's cross here."

They waited for a lone pickup truck to pass, its lights sweeping over their faces, one of the two dim, nearly padiddled out.

"The monster in *The Thing* is like this alien parasite that takes the form of the people it eats. It can become whatever it's parasiting off of, if you get me."

"Let's assume I do."

"So. You're talking like the *Great. American. Thing*, man."

"The Great American Thing?" he asked, amused because he could hear Dakota placing the capital letters. He sucked on his cigarette. There was a pothole in the road and sticking out of this pothole was a stuffed animal, a lobster. He swore to Christ it was waving its claw at him. He started laughing really, really hard, choking on smoke and light. "Shit," he said when he finally recovered. "The Great American Thing. That's pretty goddamn hilarious."

They arrived at the stadium: two sets of bleachers presiding over a football field now rough and patchy from drought and the cleats of summer two-a-days. A cancer patient refusing to shave her skull and letting the hair fall out in irregular tracts. Stadium lights stood sentry over the bleachers, and on the north and south ends of the field the orange goalposts took the watch. On the backside of the western set of bleachers, an enormous mural looked out at the road: a ferocious black jaguar bursting through a wall of orange, fangs bared, grapefruit eyes gleaming with savage Darwinian murder. The whole town was awash in black and orange, but this mural was the epicenter of the tsunami.

"Climb the fence?" Bill asked.

"Sure."

Bill tucked his bottle of whiskey into the back pocket of his jeans. They each took to the chain links, digging the toes of their tennis shoes into diamond-shaped holds and scaling the eight feet only meant to keep out the laziest of intruders. They swung their legs over the top and dropped to the other side.

They made their way around the crossbeam jungle of the bleachers' interior, pieces of litter from long-ago football games still decorating the dirt. Dakota returned to the earlier conversation.

"I dunno, man, it all rings kinda hollow to me."

"What does?"

"You're a prep, dude. College boy and a rich bitch back in the day."

"What? My mom works at the paper. My dad's a dentist. Do you have any idea what the word 'rich' actually means?"

"Not just that—good grades, good at sports. Hot girlfriend. Popular."

"Not for a long time I wasn't. Popular, I mean."

Take for instance, the last home basketball game of his junior year in 2002, a must-win against Mansfield. Butterflies in the days leading up to it, he'd arrived in the stadium lot where the underclassmen parked wearing his good shirt and tie (as the players always did on game day). The start of the season seemed to be pumping water under the bridge in regards to the situation with his T-shirts the previous fall. He'd played a great season. People were forgetting. Then a car pulled alongside him, the back and passenger windows down, and two classmates he didn't manage to get a look at opened fire on him with paintball guns. Multiple hits to the torso, back, and butt, one to the head that coated his hair in neon and made his skull ring, and one that drew blood when it cracked open the skin of his elbow. He'd stood stoically, feeling the snickers and whispers of the dozens watching. Turning back to his car, he winked at some anonymous sophomore and knew she would remember him forever. He drove home to shower and change. The pellets left enormous, painful welts, but he didn't shed a single tear. He went back to school clean and furious and scored twenty points that night to prove to those who'd shot him, watched him, or gossiped about him, that he could not be fazed.

They climbed the rows of aluminum-can-colored bleachers. Dakota's dreads waggled and his wallet chain splashed against denim. Bill took the opportunity to check his timer (**01:18:23**) and idly ponder how he'd slip away from this kid in the next half hour. Over the wrecked wind and quiet homes lay his destination and, he hoped, answers: to the contents of this package, to his guilt, to this last lost decade and its discontents.

"How 'bout here?" Dakota asked, pointing to the third row down from the top.

"Looks good."

They sidled into their seats. Bill propped his legs up on the row in front of him and leaned back. His whiskey was about halfway gone and he made himself wait a bit before the next swig.

Dakota ashed his cig with two smug taps. "Think what you want. That's why I live the way I do. No one owns me, no one tells me what to do. It's more than most can say."

"Oh, fuck me," Bill started and stopped, hated that he could never let things go, and plunged ahead anyhow. In his idle moments, he prepared soapbox ramblings for arguments that would never happen. Like Rick would climb out of the grave to finally have a conversation of reckoning about the Iraq War. "You believe all the rap albums you grew up listening to, I get it."

"Fuck you, man. I made my own way. I got mine on my own. No one helped me or gave me a fucking thing. Nobody took me shopping for the right kind of jeans when I was a kid." He jerked his skull at Bill's lap. "And believe me, I paid for that shit. For years in school I paid for that."

Bill smirked. Amazing the way social dislocation manifested itself, the raw wrath roosting in the small towns, suburbs, and exurbs of Middle America. It could be the worst if your family had money and could afford to wall itself off behind home security systems and inside megachurches. If you weren't rich or religious you could bang your head to thrash metal and ICP and wait to have your alienation harvested. If your job options amounted to "Paper or plastic?" you could deal dope and call yourself free. Some people thought they were born without the capacity to obey, and yet their only act of defiance was to believe they could never be conned by the powerful. Retain only the savory flavor of their own certainty. What had Dostoyevsky imagined at the end of *Crime and Punishment*? Raskolnikov dreamt of a virus that spreads the world over, causing each and every person to believe he or she is the sole possessor of Truth.

Dakota sniffed. "If all this shit is so evil, Ashcraft, what are you doing out here getting loaded? Go blow up some banks! Shit, I'll point you in the direction of Fallen Farms right now and the Flood brothers will hook a white boy up. Otherwise, keep away from me, my porn, my money, my drugs, my life. Every man for himself and every man free."

"You'll see how all this ends," he said.

Dakota made his scorn no secret. "How do you figure?"

"Eh," he grunted, and batted a hand. "They won. They fucking won. It's the divine right of kings updated for the secular age. Convincing people like you diddling on the fringes of their empire to subscribe to their philosophy. And for the rest of us to be so jaded we throw up our hands and allow all this exploitation to roll on until we all hurtle into total ecological and economic collapse. The usual."

Dakota shrugged a shoulder. "So we go live in space like in *WALL-E*. Problem solved." Then he angled one slim butt cheek higher and farted.

This let the tension out of the conversation, allowed Bill to laugh. "Dakota Exley, anarcho-capitalist. And I thought my life was weird."

They sat in silence for a while staring out over the dusty field. The smell of a waterfall in Angkor Wat returned to him. He felt the strangeness of being alive and a part of time, the specificity of death and the holy beat it put in your pulse.

"You remember Rick Brinklan?" Bill asked. "Senior year we had a game against Marysville. Big conference rival—"

"Couldn't have given less of a shit."

"Well, Marysville was a bunch of mean wiggers. Rick used to tell me stories of being at the bottom of the pile and guys would be trying to punch him in the kidneys, squash his nuts, spit in his helmet. Anything for an advantage. There were fights on the field for three years in a row, fights in the stands, fights outside the stadium. It got to be where the cops would send extra bodies just to make sure a riot didn't break out. But senior year, with Beaufort graduated and Rick captain, he tells me, 'I'm gonna switch it up. I'm just gonna be real nice to everyone on the field. Even if we're in the pile, and someone sticks a thumb in my ass, I'm just gonna be like, "You jokers! Good one, guys!" Total reverse psychology them. Freak 'em out.' And he totally did it. He was going around during the game patting Marysville guys on the back, telling them, 'Nice tackle, bro! Love your *sticktoitiveness*!' Rick's girlfriend, Kaylyn, and me, all our friends—we were crying laughing in the stands. But I guess it worked. Psyched Marysville out of their gourds. We ended up winning by four touchdowns and Rick ran for like one fifty or something."

That night, while the football team was still showering, he'd slipped out of the dance to meet Kaylyn. *So this is something we're doing?* she'd said, but not shamefully. Playfully. Grotesquely. Joyfully as a fucking rainbow. Later, when he and Lisa drove out to the Brew, he'd worried that his dick still smelled like the condom.

"That guy," he told Dakota, giggling. "He was pretty fucking funny sometimes."

He was about to bring up another story concerning Rick when blue and red lights erupted in sweeping whorls to their left, and a spotlight as bright as being awake on the operating room table came blasting over their faces, wrenching them from the safety of darkness's sticky womb.

Before Kaylyn reached out to him after the Marysville game, he thought it was over. It was always up to her if they would meet, when and where, and she hadn't texted him with their funny little code word—*grandmas?*—in nearly four months. It began to infuriate him, madden him, make him lose sleep. Every time he saw her with Rick, he found himself dangerously close to becoming the guy who snatches an arm and demands an explanation. But then she sent him the code, and he slipped away. They pulled their cars side by side in the part of the parking lot where the lights didn't meet.

Because it was already wrong, because they were already ashamed, Bill did things to her. Lisa was wild, but Kaylyn—she wanted punishment or humiliation or degradation or maybe something Bill couldn't even think to give her. He almost couldn't find the low level within himself that she actually wanted. Pull her hair, dig into her ass with a finger, choke her, come on her face— afterward she'd seem bored with it, disappointed in him. By winter of senior year, when they'd been doing this under everyone's noses for nearly a year, he feared that all he could give her was the thrill of what would happen if their friends found out.

"We could get a hotel room sometime," he suggested. She brought her knees to her chest in the backseat and slid her under-wear up her sleek calves, then hoisted up her butt to pull them all the way on.

"We could," she agreed. She went searching through her jeans pockets, brought out her inhaler and a pack of gum. "What are you doing now?"

"I guess going to the dance." Bill tugged the condom off, buzzed the window down just low enough to toss it. A frigid gust of winter wind sipped inside and chilled his naked skin. She got her jeans on but then settled back against the door and watched him, her flesh pocked with goose bumps.

"Rick texted you?" he asked.

She chawed her gum thoughtfully. "Only about twenty times. I told him I had to run home after the game to do some stuff for Barrett." Her mouth curled the way it did whenever she mentioned her autistic younger brother.

"Want to meet this weekend?"

She shrugged with her eyes and jaw. "Maybe." She kept her curious gaze on him. Before he'd known her, when all the local elementary schools fed into the only middle school, he'd watched her across the lunchroom, marveled at this stunning girl. She had this long, taut body, small hips, small breasts, small round ass, and it was all narcotic to a teenage boy in the grip of hormones, but it was really her face that caught his breath. Gorgeous Germanic features with a dusting of farm daughter freckles on a slim, sharp nose. Green eyes that she must have known were hypnotic because she so frequently wore pale green sweaters and scarves and shirts that set them off. Her small teeth bent slightly into her mouth and were just crooked enough to be charming. She kept her hair long and knew how to play with it; to leave it messily tossed over one shoulder or draping down across her breasts as she did now. He loved burying his hands in the thickness; it felt like you could pirate-swing from the mast of a ship with it. Of course, she had the tattoo she'd gotten with Rick, and that night, pumping into her from behind, he'd stared at it and wondered what could have possessed her to foul a piece of her lovely body this way.

"Do you ever think you hate anyone?" she asked. She propped a foot on his lap, and he kneaded her toes, small as corn kernels.

"George W. Bush," he said.

"I'm serious."

"So am I."

"Bill."

He thought about it. "I don't know. I don't hate Rick if that's what you're asking. That's not why I like being with you."

"Sometimes"—she chewed and laid her bright green eyes on the fog of the windshield and the gloom of the park beyond—"I get this idea in my head. Like all my frustration gets focused on just one person, and everything that goes wrong—whether, you know, I'm like messing up in a class or I have a lousy game, it all goes into that one person. Usually a girl. And I just can't even be around them—I can't look at her without this feeling like I want to just claw her face off."

He always had trouble reading her but especially now.

"You feel that right now, you're saying?"

Her chewing quickened. She tilted her head and swept her hair to the side. A big tent of blond stayed aloft for a moment before easing back down to her skull. "Maybe. A couple years ago, this girl . . ." She let out a single laugh that sounded like *Eh-ha*. "I just got so much pleasure out of hating her."

"Who?"

"Doesn't matter. She was just. I don't know. Like looking at her upset me, but she was just around all the time. I had to see her all the time."

"And you still hate her?"

The fog they'd steamed onto the windows had turned the scene outside opaque. This, he realized, was what he loved about her. She was inscrutable, unpredictable. She wore a small gold crucifix around her neck, and now she picked it up to feel the edges. "You know, I did whatever people do. I messed with her a little. Got it on tape. Then got over it."

He admitted, "I'm a little lost here."

Her eyes found him again. She leaned across the backseat, naked from the waist up, her nipples still erect because the heater couldn't quite warm the car. Pausing a few inches from his face, she breathed on his lips twice, then kissed him, and he was hard all over again.

This all began the previous year after her father died very suddenly. About a week after the funeral she'd called Bill out of the blue to ask if he could give her a ride to her grandmother's house to pick up her forgotten medications. Dover was about an hour's drive east, and Rick was on a college visit that weekend. On the drive, they talked about her dad. He'd only known Mr. Lynn by reputation:

a surly, depressed alcoholic who could never hold a job and who occasionally got into gossip-inducing physical altercations with Kaylyn's mother. Dead of his second heart attack at fifty-three. The funeral was Bill's first open casket. There lay the stiff, embalmed, made-up version of what was once a man. His beard looked like it belonged on a mannequin, the hair a toupee. Kay's mother, a frayed woman with tics in her face like multiple metronomes, blinking as though constantly trying to clear her eyes of debris, spent most of her time handling Barrett. Thirteen and hopeless, Kaylyn's brother was an incomprehensible jack-in-the-box of illogical outbursts. He brayed, he whined, he screamed, and it all seemed to have no tether to anything that was happening around him. Bill could see how quickly he wore the family out.

Somewhere on the barren state highway, he asked Kaylyn if she was okay.

She didn't answer for a moment, kept staring at the gray rotten-tooth fields on her side of the road. "I guess I'm fine. People keep asking me that, but what do you say?"

"Uh: 'I'm awful, my dad's dead, so get fucked and eat a dozen dicks'?" Bill suggested.

Joy swelled when the smile cracked her face and spread.

Mr. Lynn had long resisted moving his mother out of her home in Dover, but now he was gone. Barrett needed a lot of help, the family needed money, and Grandma Lynn would have to pitch in by going to decay in the Eastern Star Retirement Home in New Canaan. Replete with those fabricy, doilyed, glass figuriney touches of an elderly woman, the small home made Bill unbearably sad. Kay didn't know what her grandma needed exactly, so she scooped the entire medicine cabinet into a brown paper bag. Then a thunderstorm rolled in. Lightning split the sky and a downpour turned the street outside to a molten river. They found peach schnapps and gin in a cabinet. They talked about death, about how Bill didn't believe in God and never would. "I've been waiting," she admitted. "It's like I've been waiting forever to feel it, but I still don't." And he kissed her. She tried to push him away, but he wouldn't let her. "Don't," she said, but only once. The storm lasted the rest of the day and night. It was still raging when he pulled her hair and snapped her head back. Then she lay with her legs clutching his torso, and they listened to the rain together. The wipers were barely capable of peeling the deluge from the windshield on the drive back.

You don't know the lengths you'll go to, Bill figured. The people you'd risk hurting. He'd been infatuated with her for years, and of course Lisa had been his consolation prize. Of course, he'd long resented Rick for pinning Kaylyn to his hip. They had a certain Ohio symmetry Bill could never mimic. They were sweethearts who were born in this town and believed in it, believed they were fated to raise a family here and cheer for all the Jaguar teams as long as civilization stayed standing. Bill was a transplant, a New Yorker who accidentally grew up in this struggling shitburgh, who just happened to fall for its native daughter. As he and Kaylyn began meeting more often, driving halfway to Akron just to figure out a place to get on with it, he began to understand what an enigma she was to him, a fantasy he filled up even as he swore she was too clever, too self-aware for a sincerity-generating cliché like Rick. He wasn't sure what her inner monologue was like, what she thought about, what she cared about. He suspected she carried more pain than anyone he'd ever known. He felt like she pursued their clandestine affair because when they were together, he could relieve that damage, maybe not take it out of her but at least tamp it down for a time.

That winter of senior year, in the park, after a frigid football game against their conference rival, she stretched one long leg to the passenger seat and, using nothing but her big toe, picked up her bra and shirt. Bill said, "I want to see you again. Soon."

She curled her leg in and collected her clothing. "You don't know a thing about what you want." Her eyes evaded his. "None of us do."

She found a place within him for all of time. Through the years, the sound of the rain against her grandmother's house echoed in his head, became a minor chord. A song in the skin.

They ran.

The lights kept strobing—blue-red-blue-red-blue-red—washing over the football field in this hallucinatory diurnal carnival, and sure, Bill felt panic, he felt the terror of the tape jerking his torso flesh, knowing there was no way to get his shirt off, let alone rip the package from his person (and for real, how *evil* were the contents?). Yet also, overwhelming the panic, he had this glee, like: *Finally, we're having some fucking fun!*

On the other side of the field, he and Dakota snatched the chain link. The metal bit into each finger in that bone-pressure way as he scrambled up over the top. Then they were both at a dead sprint through the ghostly parking lot where he'd once died in a blaze of paintball rounds. As they approached the long, low structure of the high school, the brick and mortar ganglion of their youth, the ultimate haunted house, Bill saw the pipe that made the roof accessible.

"Roof," he huffed without further explanation. And then mostly to himself, "Unless they moved the dumpster." He and Harrington used to climb to the school's roof in the summer and smoke joints until they didn't know their own names. He quickly assessed that the Powers That Will still kept the dumpster in its position next to the pipe.

"Looks like they never wizened up," said Dakota.

"Authority never does."

They quickly pushed the dumpster over so that it was directly under the pipe. The lights of the police cruiser were still distant because it had to drive the long side of the "L" around the football field, but this Barney Fife wasn't fucking around. The patrol car turned down the drive that led to the school, and he was hauling, maybe fifty or sixty in a twenty mph zone. They only had to climb onto the dumpster and make a small jump to grab hold.

He reached the roof, pulled himself over the top. His whiskey remained miraculously tucked into the back pocket of his jeans and now, as he fell to his butt, he rewarded himself with a long, fiery pull. He was having a hard time staying drunk with all this activity. Dakota followed, wallet chain clattering Jacob Marley–style, and they huddled in hiding where he and Harrington had first smoked weed amid the vents and gutters of the gritty black surface, approximately above the southern end of the basketball court where he'd honed his legend.

Back to the wall, Bill positioned himself so the package didn't dig into his back. They waited and watched the strobing lights chase the sky as the cruiser slowed. The spotlight studied the brick, the bushes, the rows of trees that separated the school from a residential neighborhood. Of course, it occurred to him it could very well be Marty Brinklan giving chase, but he was in no mood to find out. Then the spotlight's glare angled over their heads. Dakota heaved breath beside him. Bill marveled that he was actually in pretty good shape, his lungs buoyant hot-air balloons.

When the spotlight went searching elsewhere and the lights dwindled to the other side of the school, Bill peeked his head up and looked out over the town. Flecked with radiance, it cupped light in its palm.

"We wait here a minute. He might circle back or call another patrol over." Dakota shuddered his dreadlocks out of his eyes. He too had not let go of his whiskey. "You gotta be careful with these

NCPD psychos. Man, they will fuck you up for nothing. 'Member that Ostrowski kid? He's a cop now. Anybody who likes fucking up people when they're young, you can bet they'll end up military or police. You wanna talk 'bout The Murder That Never Was? I'll tell you, I'd look at them first."

"What's that mean?" Genuinely curious.

"Means I might be down the food chain, but there's skeletons all over this town." He popped his head up to check on the patrol car, a paranoid-snake motion. "I mean literal fucking skeletons. You know here and the three surrounding counties have double the missing-persons reports?"

"Double of what?" Bill asked, but Dakota wasn't interested in explaining his arithmetic or citing sources.

"Jericho Lake—there ain't no bottom to it is all I'm saying." Bill didn't bother pointing out the inaccuracies in this statement. Every New Canaan kid had heard the story of Jericho, most likely in Mrs. Bingham's seventh-grade history class. When the lake was built in the fifties, the engineers had needed to buy up and flood an entire town. Supposedly, gangsters from Youngstown had financed the project so they had somewhere to dump bodies, but Bingham was always telling gory tall tales to keep kids awake in class. Dakota kept peering over the roof, but there was no sign of the police. Not even the glow of distant headlights. "We should all be more paranoid."

"Have you even heard me tonight?" Bill gulped, wiped a sleeve over his mouth, thought about sucking out the excess sleeve-booze, rejected it. "I already got all the paranoia I can handle."

Dakota turned his head to show that he did not care. Bill lapped the last vestiges of his whiskey and kept right on staring out over the lights of the city. Fireflies hung in the night, a vascular chandelier. He thought of all the places he'd been.

Dakota surprised him by raising his bottle in a toast. "Here then, Ashcraft. To The Great American Thing. Long may it run."

Bill saw purple in the corners of his vision and figured it for sorrow manifesting on the ultraviolet fringes. "Long may it run," he agreed.

He gulped down the last of the bottle, tasting mostly of the accumulated saliva at the bottom. He pulled the kitchen timer from his pocket. **00:48:37.**

He looked up to see Dakota remove a pipe and plastic bag from the zippered pocket of his sweatshirt.

"Since we got time to kill, this high'll be free of charge."

Bill stared at the small rocks in the Ziploc, dread swelling.

"Doesn't look like any weed I've ever seen."

"Glass," said Dakota. "Prior experience?"

"None. And I'm not sure I care to."

"See, I didn't actually bring any weed, son."

Now Bill felt the crossroads. Crystal felt kind of over-the-top, even for him. Yet he smelled the ash descending from the sky, mixing with the rain and wind. Markers to measure the coming storm.

"One hit," he warned and promised.

Dakota had already lit the pipe, a blue glass job the color of Walter White's product. He held the smoke in his lungs while passing to Bill. Without giving too much more thought to the entire sad episode, Bill put the pipe to his lips and lit. As the wet axe blade scraped the back of his throat, he immediately hacked on the smoke. He and Dakota dueled coughs. His head spun two ways at once. Through his tears he could see the stars that appear above a cartoon character's head blending with the lights of downtown. When his coughing began to abate, he said, "I really need to go. I gotta be somewhere."

"So go," said Dakota, whose head had fallen back against the wall, jaw slack. "No matter what you think, it's still a free country."

Bill tried to relax. The key to any new drug was to understand that there was some small chance you might freak and try to claw your own eyes out. If you knew these mental appeals would come you could resist them.

"Whoa," said Bill—because there It was. It came flooding over him in one titanic wave that may have resembled chemically induced sensations he'd felt before but only the way a silent film resembles a modern-day summer action movie. Like take a child from 1922 and sit him down for *Transformers: Dark of the Moon* in 3-D. There was a semblance of familiarity but not really. It was pure bliss that sublimated every anxiety and sorrow that had built in him for the past fifteen years. All those faces that produced such deep shame and guilt and nostalgia and love, now a mist torched by the dawn. He felt only unattached, unwarranted, pure-as-the-driven-snow happiness. His skin warmed and tingled, every pore orgasming at once. He watched the loves of his life writ brilliantly across the mystic sky river, carrying summer stars, satellites, and dust from the beginning of creation.

As we all know, the way memory works is that the sweep of your life gets explicated by a handful of specific moments, and these totems then stand as narrative. You must invent the ligature that binds the rest. After LSD mixed with methamphetamine, with an interregnum of several quarts of booze, one really begins to interrogate those incidents that blaze neon, and this cocktail was creating particularly interesting transpositions of time. It was like taking a virtual reality walking tour of his own past, like he could hold his little egg timer, rub it like a lucky time machine, and zip back to the morning he woke up in a diaper in Rick's backyard to the heart-shitting sound of a shotgun blast.

Obviously he fell right out of the lawn chair where he'd passed out. His central intelligence came back in denuded bits of soggy puzzle pieces:

Where am I? Who am I? What the fuck was that sound? I'm Bill. Brinklan's backyard. Why? We got fucked up last night. Where? His parents are in Arkansas 'cause his older brother's wife had a baby. Bottle of Smirnoff, bottle of Jameson, case of Miller Lite. But where? Kaylyn and Lisa got it for us. How? In the backyard lawn chair. Good-looking girls can always get booze. What the fuck was that sound?!

Rick stood by the backyard porch, cackling, his dad's shotgun jutting from his hip to the sky. "Aw, did I wake you?" he asked.

"You're a hick psycho," Bill wheezed. He looked down at himself. "Oh for fuck's sake."

"You passed out first," said Rick. "It was mostly Harrington's idea."

Hard to take it all in. Charred logs and shards of beer cans the fire had left behind. He was naked from the waist up and covered in Sharpie ink. He had about a zillion mosquito bites. And of course he was wearing an adult diaper.

He started laughing very hard. "Why the fuck am I wearing a diaper?"

"Hey, we didn't like undress you and put that on," Harrington called from inside the house. "The Sharpie-ing was my idea, but *that* was your idea!"

Bill looked to Rick for confirmation. Rick was wearing nothing but gym shorts and an apron that said *You Don't Need to Kiss Me but You Could Get Me a Beer.*

"You said you wanted to try a diaper—who was I to stop you?"

"But . . ." Bill looked down at the ridiculous pair of plastic underwear moistly clinging to his skin. "Where did I even get this?" He couldn't stop laughing.

"They were left over from when my grandpa lived with us," said Rick. "Don't laugh! It was a sad situation."

His head was splitting but this made him laugh even harder.

"Did I actually piss in it?" he asked.

"Like we checked? C'mon in, I'm making breakfast."

Rick set the shotgun against the garage door and went back to the skillet where, from the smell of it, he was making eggs, bacon, and pancakes. Harrington sat at the kitchen table reading the *New Canaan News*, and Bill could see his mother's byline beneath the top headline. Most of the night trickled back to him. Their girlfriends had stopped by briefly, but this first night of post-graduation summer vacation had been designated as a guy's night. They built the campfire in Rick's backyard, shot at a bowling pin until they filled it with enough birdshot to kill it good, and then sat around getting loaded until the first person passed out.

"Great night," said Harrington, sipping coffee. "Exactly what I was looking for."

On Bill's stomach, his friends had drawn two arrows pointing to his crotch. One said, LADIES, I CAN'T MAKE IT GROW while the other read, INSERT INTO ASS END OF DONKEY.

"Oh you guys are hilarious," said Bill. "Some real grade-A wits."

"We had a lot of trouble deciding what to write," Rick agreed. He stretched his arms over his head, exposing the pale sockets of his armpits and the mad-scientist hairs that had first sprouted in sixth grade, when the two of them had stolen a shopping cart from Kroger, pushed it all the way back to the high school, and then, in order to impress some girls, rode it off a small cliff—really more like an abutment—into the Cattawa River. "So we compromised, but I agree it might not be our best work." He tossed Bill a digital camera sitting on the counter. "But at least we got it documented."

He only needed to flip through the first few to get the idea.

"Okay, but you gotta delete this one," he said, showing them the image where Rick and Harrington both had their testicles hovering obscenely close to his face.

Rick shot him a terrified eyebrow. "You kidding? I'm deleting all of 'em. My dad would fucking send me to boot camp if he knew we were drinking in his house. Speaking of—y'all are coming over tonight and helping me clean this place top to bottom."

Bill toggled through a few more photos. He cracked up again. "All right, this one's pretty funny." Harrington and Rick both wore suits and ties. They had draped his naked, dead-limbed arms over their shoulders. Both of them grinned like they were posing for a wedding picture while Bill's head lolled back with his tongue hanging out of his mouth.

"That one was a lot of work," agreed Harrington, flipping a page of the newspaper.

He now noticed the word *Bullfrog* scrawled across Harrington's back like a tattoo.

"Yeah, I passed out second," he admitted.

"Here." Rick handed him a plate. "Hearty breakfast for a hearty boy."

The scent was simultaneously nauseating and intoxicating. He tried to force down scrambled eggs while taking in the view through the Brinklans' kitchen window. Because they were like seventh-generation New Canaan, the Brinklans had worked their lineage into one of the county's finer bucolic perches, a high grassy hill that descended into forest, beyond which their town carpeted both sides of the Cattawa River, looking nineteenth-century quaint, like the tuba solos were always on the verge of bursting forth during a Fourth of July parade. He'd loved waking up to this view since his childhood when Jill Brinklan would make them cinnamon rolls and Marty would sip coffee through his walrus mustache and mostly say nothing.

Rick broke his revelry by thwapping a small item below the fold of the newspaper. It was an AP story: *Rumsfeld Confident Major Operations in Iraq Finished.*

"See? Don't you owe me an ice cream cone or something?"

He tried not to take the bait. "We will see, pal."

Rick hoovered down a strip of bacon in a bite, hairy legs spread. "One thing you at least gotta admit is that with technology now they can really strike targets with precision. This was one of the most humane wars ever waged."

Bill belched eggs, whiskey, and Bud Light. Tried to meet him halfway.

"Okay, right, sure, this wasn't Vietnam or whatever, but you know they're talking like seven or eight thousand civilians killed in the initial attack? That's not counting like tens of thousands of Iraqi Army deaths—are we really talking about this?"

"Yeah, summer's for hangovers and jerking off," agreed Harrington.

Rick grinned to show this was all friendly. No more bitter arguments over T-shirts and bumper stickers. His small, squinty eyes only made his smile maddeningly big and bright. He had a single Himalayan-sized zit on his temple, of which Bill could see the crags, blood vessels, escarpments, and other skin-tectonic features. With his head now shaved into a stiff flattop, the sides of his skull milky and gruesome, he looked his part. Like he'd stepped out of central casting for Hillbilly Ohioan. Part of Rick's appeal had always been that he knew this and played into the stereotype in a self-effacing, often hilarious way. It wasn't until the last couple of years that the caricature had blended with his real thinking, which kept leading them to confrontation over just about anything: war, politics, Todd Beaufort's sexual deviancy. "That's war, man. You sit around in your safe little town your whole life, and of course it seems totally ridiculous that you'd have to fight for that safety. Then three thousand people get killed in the attacks—"

"Rawr! And for like the billionth time, dude, Iraq had nothing to do with 9/11. I don't know how many different ways to say it at this point. Like should I tattoo it on your arm *Memento* style?"

"If you hadn't passed out first, you could've written it on me in Sharpie."

"Guys," said Harrington, setting the paper down. "Dad says cut it out. No one—I mean no one—not me, not the girls, not anyone—wants to hear you idiots debate this another second."

Across the room, Harrington's funky ringtone bleated out of his cell. He went to answer.

"Maybe Iraqy-raq had nothing to do with it, and maybe they did." Rick turned back to Bill, still smiling. "But this is bigger than any one country, man. It's civilizational. It's two different ways of seeing the world, and sometimes you've got to show strength. Hit back with all you got, so they know what you're about."

The hot pit of fury this put in Bill's head. It was a black hole with a gravitational force that pulled every last atom into its dense, infinite sphere. He refused to take the bait, Lisa's voice in his head. She thought he and Rick were engaged in macho, horn-locking, dick-comparing bullshit. She said he had to chill out when Rick goaded him. Not turn every petty issue into the Lincoln-Douglas debates. She was the one person he considered possibly smarter than him, so he'd lately been trying to listen to her. As Harrington wandered to the back porch to take the call, Bill let go of the conversation in his own particular way.

"Tell you what," he said to Rick, "I'll admit bombing Iraq to submission was easier than I predicted if every time you bring up 9/11, you have to suck my cock."

Rick arched an eyebrow. "Now does that mean to completion each time? Or like one up and down gulp per September Eleventh observation?"

"Hey," said Harrington, poking his head back in, holding the phone to his bare chest. "The girls want to go to the beach today."

"Jericho?" asked Rick.

"Booze?" asked Bill.

"Stacey says Lisa and Kaylyn can hit the liquor store on their way."

"Plus, we still got a thirty rack of Coors," said Rick through an *Oh shit, this could hurt* face.

"Christ," said Bill. "My liver."

"Is that a yes?" asked Harrington.

"Well, it ain't a fucking no. You can sleep when you're dead, Ashcraft."

They spent that hot summer day of 2003 at Jericho Lake. The chain of calls early Saturday morning tumbled through the ranks, and half the high school showed up. They pooled pilfered booze. Hailey Kowalczyk brought armfuls of wood, and she and Dan Eaton built a fire pit on the beach for later that night. Stacey teased both Dan and Rick that the sun was invented in a time before boys with such reflective skin. Jonah Hansen turned up twirling the keys to his dad's boat, docked a half-mile's walk down the shore. Ron Kruger and Eric "Whitey" Frye arrived with patched-up black inner tubes and five bottles of Zima. Tina Ross came, and in her swimsuit you could see all the weight she'd lost, her bones looking as fragile as those of a featherless bird. Tony Wozniak and Mike Yoon brought a football, cornhole boards, and beanbags. They backed Yoon's Explorer to the edge of the parking lot and blasted 93.7 FM, pop music from Columbus.

Bill watched Rick and Kaylyn standing in waist-high water. Rick's Stars and Stripes claw marks glared at him. Kaylyn skimmed her fingers across the surface, and when she turned he saw the tramp stamp on her lower back. He'd always hated tattoos, but Kaylyn's made him especially disgusted—a blue butterfly with symmetrical curlicues spreading across the once-perfect crest of her ass. She wore a lime-green bathing suit and held a hand over her brow to block the sun, squinting. Rick's lower lip puffed out from dip, he took her by the hips, his eyes hidden behind Oakleys. Bill thought

Kaylyn's gaze flitted to him, but she might have just been turning away from the sun.

Later that afternoon a cop cruised by, and they all madly hid their alcohol. Jonah took a group down to his boat, and Stacey's top came off in the water, so they all got a glimpse. Lisa hooted and clapped and shouted, "Leave it *off*, Moore!"

Bill lay beside his girlfriend in the sun, giddily, meltingly drunk. Normally in those days, he felt up to his nostrils in guilt, desire, and self-disgust—disgust with oneself being a thing as cherished and protected as any bit of ego or pleasure. But not that day at Jericho. It was the last time he could really remember when they were all just young, arguments lacking permanence, sins missing any real vital evil. He had lovers, yes, but he loved them. He was hurting his friends, sure, but they were still childhood brothers. With all that had passed between him and Rick, the friendship felt constantly volatile in his hands, like unstable explosive. Yet even with Kaylyn standing there in the water, looking as gorgeous and iridescent as a dragonfly, he felt a surge of love and regret unlike anything he'd experienced before. Because they were just kids, and that day they drank and they danced and they laughed at the sky-blue heavens, and it really felt like anything could be fixed and anything could be forgiven.

He had no idea how long he sat there. His gaze drifted from the stars to the city lights to the fireflies winging their Morse code. He listened to the crickets on their motorcycles, revving engines. He marveled at the beauty of It, how he could see everything about the universe down to the molecular level or up to the cosmic—the broken streetlights, the scratchy gravel of the roof beneath his fingertips, the empty spray paint can clutched by a cornice, the nuclear fuel of distant stars.

At some point, he remembered Dakota sitting beside him, fingers dug deep into his dreads, staring into space, eyes glassy. It looked like he'd buried his hands in a pit of earthworms now writhing over his fingers.

"Jesus Christ," said Bill, getting to his feet. He jumped in place for a moment, reaching higher and higher with each release of his toes. He glanced down, and the roof looked impossibly far away. He could suspend in the air for superheroic seconds. "Wow," he said. "Wow, wow, wow."

Dakota still hadn't moved, but now Bill found himself with an appetite for the night.

"Fuck that cop." He continued jumping. "Is the liquor store still open? Let's go back to the liquor store."

Dakota slowly rose to his feet, surveying every possible direction. "Yeah, man."

"Mothafuck the police!"

He skipped over to the edge of the roof, haphazardly swung his legs over the side, grabbed the pipe with both hands and swung down onto the dumpster. Barely pausing, he leapt to the asphalt, knees bending to absorb the shock.

"I get It," he said as Dakota followed him less gracefully. "I totally get It. Even though I'm intellectually aware It's just the methamphetamine releasing an excess of dopamine to my central nervous system, you can't quantify a feeling like this in terms of dopamine and nervous systems, you know? Jesus-fucked-up-Christ, It's like taking a shot of Jedi."

"Good shit, right," said Dakota, still distant, eyes like glazed donuts.

They walked back across the parking lot with Bill bouncing every few steps. When The Thing appeared overhead, some happy, bopping music issuing from speakers in its guts, he wasn't even mildly surprised.

"Wowzers."

The Thing was a never-ending python-amoeba of circus lights and seductive tunes, of venerated faces pushing up through the slime of its skin and a vacuum hose appropriating the dead and setting them up on marble pedestals jutting from its back. Slithering through the sky, The Thing bulged a muscle and barbed appendages caught souls on their sticky tips like insects. Robotic arms lowered with mechanized whizzing, tipped with hypodermic needles injecting stronger and stronger barbiturates into the masses, while oozing jelly limbs slithered into every other corner of the American night, places so dark and lonely, even the echoes fled.

He looked in all directions. "I think I'm going to go do some cartwheels on the football field. How's that sound? Is that weird?"

"Nah, man," said Dakota. "You do you."

Bill took off sprinting for the fence, arms pumping, lungs as powerful as blimps. He ran beneath the watchful gaze of this Leviathan, this opaque creature that knew only control and hunger, that no person not under the helpful influence of three different types of narcotics could even see because to look at it was to miss it. Turn your eyes in its direction and it evanesced back to vapor. It watched Bill curiously, thirty-seven million microscope eyes crawling the surface of the naked country.

He snatched the chain link, scrambled to the top, and vaulted over. He hit the ground, rolled, collecting grass stains on his elbows, and sprung back up in a dead sprint toward the field. He crossed the black polyurethane surface and then his sneakers were crunching over the dry grass. He tipped his body, lowered his hands, and flung his legs back in a flailing cartwheel. He was a particle accelerator crashing protons and neutrons together. He could see the electrons slipping between realities, taste the quantum ghosts. This ended with him sprawled on his ass. The sky spun, and The Thing vanished back to stars and carbon. How rad. He did snow angels in the dust. He laughed and laughed.

"History's all the same story, man—the consolidation of capital and political control."

They were walking back along New Canaan Avenue, beneath the broken streetlights and past the dark park, the threat of the cops obliterated in a fog of dopamine. For a moment, a cigarette butt glowed orange in the distance, a bright coal in the space beneath the picnic shelter. Inhaled back to life. It held for a moment, glimmering as the exhaled smoke curled, warping the air. Then it went dark as if it had never existed. Bill was talking very fast and neither he nor Dakota noticed.

"But it ain't just the military, man . . ." He went on to haphazardly describe: corporate media, real estate covenants, the medical-industrial complex, reality television, student loans, pharmaceutical companies, military contractors, industrial agriculture and factory farming, coal, oil, and gas interests, consumerized sex, the carceral state, neoliberal trade agreements, advertising, auto title loans, social media, narcotizing political messaging, and corporate data collection. "Any way to make a buck from people's misery, man, they're there."

Always something of a borderline Timon, for Bill, perhaps smoking crystal methamphetamine wasn't the best prescription after a long, sleepless, drug-addled, alcohol-soaked day because even as his mouth and tongue and lips masticated this feverish disquisition on U.S. foreign, social, and economic policy, a dark purple cloud began to creep into him, somewhere between the visible spectrum and his kaleidoscopic intellectual preoccupations.

Dakota had yet to say anything since they'd left the football field. He walked beside Bill with his hands stuffed in the pockets of his ratty jeans, the denim swishing noisily as he ambled along, his eyes with a bulging-orb quality. Like he was staring at a scene happening in another dimension.

The cloud descended and Bill's voice was divorced from what transpired in his head. The purple cloud had a notion. It swept down on top of him like smoke billowing from fallen towers. The possibility that all his work and all his travels and all his passion was just farce. His way to engineer the world to make sense. His way of coping at four a.m. on a West Texas highway. His heart thundered, and he dreamt the Truth, but each discovery was as slippery as a fish in the hand, and every time he tried to catch one, it would simply wriggle its tail and be free. His chest felt tight. He was having trouble catching his breath.

He turned his head and vomited a laundry-detergent capful of his guts but barely missed a syllable.

"The reckoning is coming too, man." He wiped bile from his lips. "I'll tell you something. I see the future sometimes. I don't mean I can see it all, but I have dreams where I see it. Dreams of buildings falling down and people spilling out of the cities. Already ninety percent of large fucking fish in the oceans have been exterminated. Yeah, you heard about that? Tropical forests will be gone in our lifetime. Phosphorous will peak, and there goes your fucking fertilizer. The West Antarctic Ice Sheet is toast. There goes your coastal cities the world over. Refugee flows like no one's ever imagined. Get ready for your helping of all the chaos and murder and sodomy you can handle. And the shit that the Powers will do to hold on? It'll make the tyrants of the twentieth century look like Disney characters."

"Shit," said Dakota, bending over. "A quarter." He pinched it up.

There were worse things in the purple cloud, though. Terrible shit he probably kept so deep that to let it out might overwhelm. Like inside of him was a passion and a darkness, and he could never tell the difference between the two. He only knew they were intertwined, tangled together like a snake with a head at each end.

They cut through the alley behind a storage facility, and everything was crushed plastic soda bottles, beer cans, broken glass, and loser lotto tickets. Alley detritus speaking of the empires swaying back and forth in the breeze, precarious. Bill had always believed he and Rick would figure it out. When he came back home. And this thought led him to all the petty evils to which he'd borne witness. The dismembered hands he'd seen in Sonora, nailed to the doors of a church. The children he'd visited with in Hanoi, orphaned and limbless thanks to American ordinance still lying around the countryside. The wetlands of the Gulf eroding to oblivion. And it was all part of the same human sickness that filled him with such ancient exhaustion, that made him want to puke up his soul.

He didn't know how long he'd been lost in his own head. He looked around, trying to remember where he was. His hands were sticky with whiskey.

Stair step. When you came down minutely from a high, Harrington had called it a "stair step." He felt how his breath connected to the thud of his heart inside its rib prison. Ventricles and muscles made for such a delicate slaveholder. One broken piece, and you sacrificed your entire consciousness? Seemed like a shoddy system.

"You're a real weird motherfucker, Ashcraft." Dakota rummaged around in his pocket. "I mean, you need to, like, chill out and take yoga classes or some shit."

He exhaled a memory of the New Mexico desert, hot and red as Mars, where he went to work after getting fired from the campaign in '08. He'd been seeing another teacher out there. Their stipends hadn't allowed them much fun, but in lieu of dinner and a movie they used to fuck a lot in the shower of their dorms. She'd had wonderful bundles of black hair. On their way back from a visit to Durango they'd come across a spectacular drunk-driving wreck burning like a pyre in the night. This flaming car throwing light over the sweeping grasslands and distant mesas—how awful and awesome. He and this girl watched it for a long time. Now he couldn't remember her name.

"Dude, you home?" Dakota snapped his fingers in front of Bill's face. They stood in spilled garbage bags, fast-food wrappers, a pile of wire coat hangers, and five empty forties lined neatly in a row. "C'mon, man, let's pop a squat over the river."

They crossed the street to the bridge, home to the train tracks where no trains ran anymore. Dakota took a seat with his legs dangling over the side. Bill joined him. The Cattawa flowed on in near silence.

"So I gotta ask," said Dakota. "Whatcha got strapped to your back?"

The meth was doing something to Bill's brain, joining up with the expiring veins of LSD and getting up to devious shit. He could feel the worming quality of a greasy electrician's fingers rewiring circuitry.

"Long story."

"Saw it when you were doing cartwheels." Dakota reached behind him in a practiced motion anyone would recognize from the movies. He set the gun in his lap. The way the grip of unexpected fear feels on the skin: like on a warm day when a cloud suddenly blocks out the sun. "Maybe I need to get that story."

Bill had seen the future before, but he'd never seen his own death. That it could be something as stupid as this made him want to sob.

"'Cause it's drugs?" he asked, the words dumb and taffy in his mouth.

"We kinda got a situation worked out in the county where we don't like new business."

All moisture fled from his throat. He said, "Anarcho-capitalism."

"Don't know nothing about that. What I know is we can't control the sale of anhydrous ammonia, but we can control some things."

The water of the Cattawa looked good. Maybe better to slip off the bridge. Feel gravity carry his every molecule into the water. Bill dared a hard look at the gun. It had severe angles and weight, like a shrunken anvil. He hallucinated the crimson flash of a discharging bullet, the heat of the hammer on hot steel. Dakota had worms writhing on his scalp again. His pores opened up into enormous caverns gushing with toxic black juice.

"Look, man, it's my livelihood." Dakota's voice had yet to waver from its stoned calm. Now he took the pistol and pressed the barrel to the top of Bill's skull. The bullet would burrow straight down through his throat. "You gotta understand, all the shit going on round here—it makes people paranoid and violent. Just tell me if you're moving product."

The gun pressed a dream into him, a dream of the last time he and Rick spoke. The night bulged. The darkness swelled and collapsed like the beat of a heart.

"Honestly," said Bill, as carefully as if trying to speak around a capsule of cyanide held in his cheek. "I don't know what it is. It's a favor for a friend."

"Lemme tell you something, Ashcraft." Dakota took the gun away from his skull. His trigger finger looked so utterly calm and reasonable. "This ain't the same place we grew up. People are expecting a certain level of discipline. You think this is fun and fucking games? I can assure you it ain't. I wasn't fucking around about Jericho Lake—that's what some of these dudes wanna start doing. I want you to answer honest: This a onetime thing?"

Bill felt out words with his tongue. "For sure, man. Seriously."

Dakota finally set the gun on his lap and sighed, as if bored with the whole affair. "Got the feeling you're the kinda dude people are always giving passes. This one's mine."

Sounds returned: the river below gargling like a throat. In the distance, a soft wind stirred the drought-fried corn cowering in its husks. His relief felt gastric, intestinal, as if the old children's myth had come true and he'd swallowed a seed that grew tendrils through the juicy soil of his belly.

"My senior year, woulda been your junior . . ." Dakota replaced the gun in the back of his jeans, and Bill felt the anguish of relief. He still didn't dare twitch, let alone stand and try to leave. "I thought I might kill some people at school."

Bill waited and when he didn't say more, asked, "How do you mean?"

"Those kids who did Columbine, Klebold and Harris? I, like, read about 'em. Studied 'em. Dreamed about 'em. I just thought, how cool would it be to be remembered like that? You know, no one would remember anybody from New Canaan, Ohio, *ever again* except me. It would be a Me day. So I brought a gun to school. My mom's. And I was planning on walking into the cafeteria and just start mowing fuckers down. I didn't know if I could break Klebold and Harris's record, but I thought I could come close."

Bill's throat clicked, depending on which lunch period Dakota was talking about. He thought of how cruelty created chain reactions, how one act could set off events, could eat through floors like acid, so to think of all the systemic cruelty in the world was to think of acid burning from one floor of a skyscraper down to the basement.

"But you didn't do it," he said.

A shake of his head. The worms made juicy noises. He shimmered between the person he was now and the kid he'd been then. "Can't really remember why not."

Bill felt dizzy, vomity, his heart slammering like a drunk kicking at the foot pedal of a drum kit.

Dakota nodded slowly, blinkless eyes fixed on the river. "I mean maybe I pussed out or maybe I just figured too many people would get away. I'd end up killing pointless kids. Not the ones who mattered." Dakota swung his legs back and forth, childlike. "Gotta say I'm glad I didn't. Might've been you, and then we could never have had this weird night. You got a good heart, Ashcraft."

At this uninformed description of himself, Bill felt a crashing surge of guilt and remorse. Because that's what he'd always hoped, and even though he knew it to not be the case, he nevertheless ached to hear someone say it.

They were both quiet for a long time, the tricks playing light on them.

Finally, Dakota stood. "Okay, man. I gotta head out. Got a bedtime story to get to."

He didn't know what else to say other than, "Thanks for not murdering me."

Dakota cocked his head, and the worms on his head whip-lashed. "You try to fly from evil, but evil will always come to you."

And then something pretty strange happened.

Dakota began walking backward from the bridge to the road, and as he did, his body began to swell the way the night had, and then it was morphing. Unlike his vision of The Thing, this wasn't happening in his eyes but their own physical reality. The skin along Dakota's arms and sides grew into course, leathery flaps. His clothes shredded and fell away. His face contorted, and soon it was no face, just a grotesque collection of folds and bones. His fingers stretched into gnarled autopods, and the ulna of his forearm deformed into the angled zeugopod of a bat. The creature, this deformed angel, flapped harder and achieved liftoff as gray hairs sprouted from every pore. The digits webbed, and the gnarled face grew stranger still as huge worms came writhing from the orifices and fell to earth in wet clumps. The angel sailed higher and higher as the muscles in its back thickened and added power, percussive thumps of its wingspan crippling the wind. They grew to the width of a city street. The feet metamorphosed into talons and the knees buckled inward. It climbed into the dead sky, singing, screaming a song, until the air slipped open. A vortex of blue light spilled across the pavement, the streets, the downtown buildings, swirling violet violence and a piercing hiss as the oxygen was sucked into another dimension. It flew backward into the hot cerulean spiral, gazing mad black eyes, and when it passed over the edge of existence, the puncture in the universe wheezed painfully and then zipped up like a wound stitching itself shut.

Bill watched in awe as the worms left behind sizzled on the ground, vanishing to steam.

He spat into the water, feeling a real nice stair step bringing him back to the moment, excising some of that paranoia. The water gurgled over its carve of sediment, a murmur of voices rolling like time, telling rumors of the past. The wind, hot and fecund, deposited its consoling coat. Above this, a bizarre bleating sound. It took him a moment of looking around to realize the electronic squawk was coming from his pocket. His kitchen timer read **00:00:00**. He couldn't figure out how to silence it, so he chucked it into the river where the water immediately swallowed the tinny noise. It was time to make this delivery. And then ride off into the sunset like a good cowboy.

He followed High Street north, past downtown and into the rows of colonial homes. The cars had all but vanished at this late hour. The night grew quiet, introspective of its nightly self. The colonials gave way to two-family homes and dilapidated aluminum siding. Here was more flaked paint and sagging porches. Less care went into the lawns and more flotsam was left to accumulate spiritual inertia. Tricycle, garden hose, kiddie pool, another ROMNEY/RYAN yard sign halfway trampled, clinging upright by one wire spike, trampoline with rusted springs, white plastic lawn chair, swing set with runty plastic slide, an undulating brick street with drips and drabs of concrete patching the potholes, American and Buckeye porch flags vying for attention. One particularly parochial home had the state flag with its red-and-white bull's-eye floating in a field of stars. The Confederacy was decently represented as well.

He heard a car idling ahead and then in a huff it continued down the road, tires drubbing the brick. His body tensed as the headlights spilled over him—surely this was the NCPD patrol car, finally caught up now that his legs had no sprint left. But it was a minivan. A dingy burgundy Chrysler with a pink stripe like a thin belt. The window was down, an emaciated arm hanging nearly to the outer handle. As the vehicle passed, the driver turned to watch him. Though Bill had known this person only by reputation, Dakota had name-checked him earlier. Frankie Flood had spent most of his teenage years in juvie for stabbing his stepfather. His face was cut-and-pasted from adolescence, affixed to a shriveled shoulder and completely inked arm. Bill turned his gaze to the ground before their eyes could meet.

He hurried on. His hands were still sticky with whiskey.

His sneakers scraped across a dry wild-flowered lawn as he cut over to Sandusky Street, checking the house numbers. 705 Sandusky bloomed before him and with it enough heartache and regret to fuel a vessel straight through the flood at the end of the world. A low and cramped two-family with white vinyl siding and a roof blacker than the night around it. He didn't hesitate, though he'd suspected he might. The tape rubbed and creaked against his skin. Behind cheap venetian blinds, a low-wattage lamp left on for him. And there was his heart picking up. There was the sweat breaking out in his pits and on his back. There was the sinking in his gut, like a bowel movement going off in the wrong direction. There was his fist rising to knock on this cheap hollow door the color of cool stone. There was the door cracking for him, the dusky light washing into the night.

And there, of course, was Kaylyn Lynn, ten years on, a beautiful memory downloaded to flesh, with a bubble of a stomach jutting toward him like a beach ball about to pop.

Citing cause and effect here might be difficult. It would have been more satisfying if his transgressions had found daylight. If Lisa had just learned about Kaylyn. She would have said whatever needed to be said. But she never found out, and instead of resolution, there was fracture.

Everyone thought his disagreement with Rick was political, but it wasn't. Nor was it the kind of machismo jealousy Lisa always suspected. There were deeper subterranean features that allowed Bill to feel no particular regret about sleeping with Kaylyn—why, in fact, he'd almost engineered it. His resentment began with this thing—this bizarre, fucked-up, only-in-Ohio story about a girl who'd once laughed at him.

Junior year, uneasy rumors circulated about Tina Ross. Rumors are immaculately fucked things in small towns. Embers often make the jump across roads and spark fires in other forests. Bill and Rick were spending the night at the home of poor Dakota's teen tormentor: Ryan Ostrowski—Strow, as he was known. Bill had planned to go to Harrington's, but the kid was again at war with his father, so he called Rick looking for something to do. This was after the T-shirt debacle, when it seemed like they were finally getting back on decent terms. Many drinks into the night—a group of maybe ten jocks from different grades hammering back cheap gin with lemonade—Ostrowski took out a digital camera.

"Check this out," said Strow, and they gathered around the

squat, powerful senior, a living, breathing concrete abutment on the offensive line. Though Bill saw the others laughing, covering their mouths in disbelief, when the camera landed in his hands, he wasn't ready. To his wild surprise, it was the girl he'd tried to court in middle school with a Vicky's milk shake. He couldn't remember what he thought at the time, he was so wasted, nor did he recall Rick's reaction.

He did remember Strow saying, "We got a video of her first time too."

Bill woke on a sticky sofa in the basement, Rick nudging him, first light spilling through a ground-level window. Driving home with Rick, a hangover throbbing between his eyes with each beat of his pulse, he had to be reminded of what he'd seen.

"We should say something to someone." Rick's eyes traveled from the road to Bill. It was as much uncertainty as he'd ever heard in his friend's voice.

"What?" This made his head thud harder. "To who? Why?"

Rick rubbed a hand over the stubble of his skull. He had a way of furrowing his brow where he could go from looking mean and handsome to genuinely distressed, the expression of a young boy about to burst into tears.

"Because they're still doing shit like that to her regularly."

"Didn't look like she was objecting, if I recall."

"That's not the point."

Rick's self-righteousness pricked his headache. "You're going to tell who? MacMillan? Coach Bonheim?"

He was thinking ruefully of his T-shirt ordeal. MacMillan, Bonheim, even Coach Napier, whom he loved like an uncle, no way would they make trouble for Beaufort, the star linebacker who was going to sign at a D-1 program. Rick didn't get that the people in charge could be as cloistered and gutless and frightened as teenagers.

"It's not that I want to snitch," said Rick. "But you think she deserves that?"

He could feel the blood in every single vein in his skull. "Brink," he snapped. "Those guys are your fucking friends. That was your call to hang out at Strow's place last night. I don't see how this is our problem."

Rick let it alone after that and dropped Bill off. He managed to chat amicably with his dad for five minutes before he retreated to his room with a glass of water and a flask of spit-stirred whiskey to get a little hair of the dog in him. As he lay in the dark beneath his poster of Malcolm X, he mused that his objections to making this a federal case weren't exactly on the up and up. Truth was, he had gotten a thrill from the pictures. He'd thought of Tina laughing at him in the hallway after Beaufort put him on the floor, and here was proof the snotty, Jesus-loving brat was more deep-down pathetic than he would *ever* manage to be. He recalled drinking a milk shake with her, the way a head of large brown curls spilled over each shoulder onto her varsity jacket. An air of fragility surrounded her, not only of her porcelain features or compact frame, but her very presence in the world, small and thin with dusty skin and large owl eyes. She played her part as the ingenue, the chaste. These Jesus kids all got away with this facade, dripping with self-righteousness while they pulled all the same shit the rest of the sinners did (and occasionally much worse). A few of the images of Tina did create a certain feeling, like spiders scuttling on the inside of his stomach, but he enjoyed them nevertheless: not for any sexual reason but for the gratification of discovering hypocrisy in exactly the place he expected. If he did harbor any guilt, Stacey's older brother helped relieve him of it. He was friendly with Matt Moore, who'd been impossible to miss in the pictures, so he simply asked.

"Aw, that mother-frickin Ostrowski." Matt rolled his eyes. "He should not be showing those off."

"But it's . . ." Bill searched for the word. In one snapshot, Stacey's brother had worn a Jags football shirt and nothing from the waist down. "She's okay with it all?"

Matt arched two red-blond eyebrows. He could never decide if he thought Stacey was weird-looking because she looked so much like her older brother or if Matt was weird-looking because he looked so much like his little sister. "That girl," he said, nodding each word, "is the craziest little freak ever. Ever, Ashcraft."

Fall progressed to winter. Football season ended and basketball season took over. Beaufort signed to play for the Buckeyes. Bill and Rick had another conversation.

"Curt Moretti was drunk the other night," said Rick. They stood outside the Brinklans' house by the field overlooking town. "He got to talking."

Bill glared at the ground, not wanting to have this conversation again. He'd eaten dinner at his friend's house, Jill Brinklan's glazed salmon that he always scouted out days in advance so he could come over. It had long been Marty's joke that Bill was their third kid on salmon night.

"We gotta tell someone." But Rick sounded anything but certain.

"Tell them what, dude? What is it you're planning to say?"

"Alls I know," said Rick, "is I keep thinking about Kay, you know? She and Beaufort went out in middle school. Like it's not out of the question that a few years back maybe things go different and she ends up with Beaufort instead of me. And he tries that on her. It makes me want to kill him just thinking about it."

He still felt nips and pinches and fleabites of jealousy at the way Rick had to reassert, out loud, again and again, that Kaylyn was "his girl." Like he'd conquered mountains, slain dragons, dedicatedly collected enough proofs of purchase from cereal boxes to win her. *My girl* was Rick's incantation of possession, and though Bill first told himself his loathing of it was somehow feminist, he knew his reason to be baser: he coveted Kaylyn and always had.

"This isn't grade school where you can just tattle to the adults and all your problems go away. Fuck, man, most of the people in charge at that school are the fucking problem."

The sound of dishes banging around in the sink reached them from the kitchen window, and they both silently agreed to move farther down the road, past the Brinklan mailbox with an American flag etched into the metal. They stood in light jackets, watching a dense fog twist and distort the distant lights of the town.

"I know why you're not bugging Harrington with this shit," Bill grumbled, then told him what Matt Moore had said. A helpful reminder to Rick that whatever had gone on—was going on—could affect a lot of people.

"Beaufort and Ostrowski," said Rick. "They call Tina their 'fuck pig.' "

Those words made a gristly, nauseating sound together. Bill would not forget them for as long as he lived.

"I'm planning on having kids someday, which probably means a daughter or two. How do I live with myself knowing this about guys I play with? That I high-five every day?"

Reluctantly, Bill found this an alarmingly mature notion. He felt his friend's honor then, his electric core of decency. Made ever more stark by a world he was coming to see as increasingly honorless. And yet it wouldn't be until years later that he'd be able to admit this to himself. At the time, it just made him more furious that Rick was trying to rope him into playing chivalrous knight.

"Brink, I've heard grown fucking adults say 'Beaufort carries the town's hopes.' Medium-case scenario is they ignore this. Best-case scenario is also the worst, which is that the whole school finds out, sees those pictures—or Jesus, there's a video? Yeah, so Tina will be humiliated, and people probably blame her for fucking up the life of the star linebacker. Just because you think what Tina and all them are doing is gross doesn't give you the right to insert yourself like this."

It had rained that day, and the air still smelled like damp stone. Rick breathed it in now, pulling through flared nostrils. "You're not hearing me on this," he said, and then tucked his hands and stalked back to his house before Bill could reply.

Bill pointed to Kaylyn's stomach. "That mine?"

Her face, wide and worried and as expectant as her pregnant gut, collapsed into a laugh. A beautiful expression. She could still light him up like a firefight.

"Get in, Bill."

He staggered inside, and she eased the door closed, eyes lingering on the night.

"You're late," she said, turning the deadbolt. She peeked through a blind and studied the street before turning back to him.

"Sorry, lost my phone. Had to go buy an egg timer. Then there were some hiccups, some weird happenings, but . . ." He lifted his shirt to show her the brick strapped to his back. "I don't really see the point of a recap. Long story short, my truck broke down and I had to hoof it here. Might've smoked some meth on the way."

A momentary stare, then an accommodating laugh from the corner of her mouth. Sure, he'd left some stuff out, but he figured narrators were always conveniently forgetting essential shit. In the last decade everyone had learned to be a truth masseuse.

"We might have to cut that tape off you," she said. To hear the nimble honey of her voice again. What a holy song. Seeing her in full glare of the lone, cheap lamp, though—the decade had battered her. Her eyes still floated in a splash of freckles like two sapphires tossed onto a white-sand beach, but the skin around them was creased with a thousand worries. Her teeth were nicotine-dimmed, yellowing on their way to brown. Her limbs looked skinnier, knees and elbows knobbier, perhaps accented by the grotesque bulge that almost looked fake. An actress strapping on a prosthetic for a role. She still wore her hair long, but instead of the strawberry blonde she'd favored in high school, it was now that tacky platinum blonde, the color of a Post-it note. She'd chosen to greet him in black sweatpants and a simple green V-neck.

Yet an ache still surfaced that hadn't stalked him in years. Here is longing even when you bury it alive in the dirt of your heart.

"It's going to hurt," Bill said matter-of-factly, scanning the room. "I'll probably need a drink for numb-the-pain purposes. Know what I'm getting at?"

"I have wine and vodka, that's it." She had a pimple on her chin and a scrim of sleep burned away by the nervous edge of waking abruptly.

Bill exhaled, long and dramatically. "Yep, that sounds like it can locomote me to the right place."

Kaylyn smiled again. A real wormhole to the soul. "I'm not sure if it's reassuring or totally terrifying that you have not changed like one iota."

He heard from Harrington that Rick had proposed to Kaylyn and she turned him down. This was after he and Rick had stopped speaking but before Bill left for college. How simultaneously furious and overjoyed this had made him, imagining Rick on one knee with some flimsy blood diamond that nevertheless must have cost the kid his savings.

Rick left for basic training two weeks later, and Bill never spoke to him again, so he never got his version of the story, but Kaylyn admitted it had happened. He tried to persuade her to let him drive to Toledo where she enrolled that fall.

"What for?" she asked with hostility he couldn't understand.

"To see you." He gulped down the silence that followed. "Kay?"

"Don't you feel guilty? About Rick? And Lisa?"

"Not really," he admitted.

"You kept fucking her. The whole time we were— Are you still?"

"Lisa?" He was confused. "We broke up. I told you. What? Are you jealous?"

"I don't understand why you don't just be with her. You guys have your little book club; you'll both be superstars in college. Why not just be with her?"

"Maybe I'm not getting something, Kay, but—Jesus Christ— I've made it so clear how I feel about you."

"You're both smart. You'll have money," she said. "You should just be together. Just be with that pretty Chinese bitch and leave me alone."

Bill almost choked—on rage, grief, and disbelief, on not understanding what the hell was going on with her. "Who gives a fuck about Lisa?" he blurted, though he did. He just wanted this cruelty out of Kaylyn. He wanted back the confident girl he'd fallen for so long ago in the sixth grade. The fearless one.

Then she stopped answering Bill's texts and calls. The last thing she ever said to him before opening the door of her rental on Sandusky Street in 2013 came via text in October of 2003. *I know you won't like this but I don't think we should talk for a while. Sorry.*

Now he saw himself a decade on, directionless, staggering through life, learning to tell fast lies and leaving a burning landscape behind him everywhere he went. He never thought Lisa would flee to the other side of the world, never to return, or that Rick would catch a bullet in Baghdad or Harrington would die glazed and asleep in a flame-soaked room. He'd never expected any of them to get old or sick or sad or dead. He never thought any of them would be afraid. But Kaylyn was the first person he really lost, and the one who left him wide awake and staring pointlessly at the dark.

He stood in her living room with his shirt off as she used a pair of scissors to cut into the clear packing tape, studying the small, sad unit. A two-seat couch faced a small TV. Piled beneath it, a helter-skelter collection of DVDs, the kind of ancient, soon-forgotten rom-coms with Jennifer Aniston or Paul Rudd you got for three bucks in the bargain bins of gas stations. The coffee table was a mess of *Us Weekly*s, a plate of half-finished, lipstick-red spaghetti going cold, and her inhaler, right next to an ashtray with two fresh cigarette stubs, the stench heavy in the air. He saw back to the sliver of bedroom, the unmade bed, a closed laptop on a pillow, and a disaster of clothes scattered on the floor. His gaze lingered on the pair of enormous, muddied work boots kicked into a corner.

"*Ow-uh!*" said Bill as the tape screeched from his skin. The black hairs on his chest appeared to him as scuttling insects.

"I don't understand why you taped it to you."

"Felt right. Real *Midnight Express* shit."

He cried out again as she ripped more of the tape free. She held the package in hand and looked visibly relieved. "Want me to do it like a Band-Aid or peel it off an inch at a time?" He didn't remember her having this much Ohio drawl in her voice. Like it had deepened.

Bill batted her hand aside and ripped the rest of the tape free in two skin-burning, flab-stretching, hair-shredding tugs. This took with it a good deal of the hair on his torso and left behind tormented red skin. The room shimmered all around him, hallucinations and weariness coming like a fog.

"So what is it, Kay?" Bill asked, patting his tender flesh the color of massacred civilians.

She held the gray brick like she was contemplating Yorick's skull. "I don't know."

When she'd sent him the Facebook message a month ago to ask if he was really in New Orleans and if he'd like to make some quick money, Bill had felt stir all those forgotten parcels of himself. Whatever line she was throwing him, asking him back into her life after all this time, he couldn't resist it. But she'd been all business. She named the price for taking a package from Louisiana to Ohio. Having just lost his job anyway, it seemed like a win-win. Progressively, things skewed stranger. She told him to buy a burner phone, and they spoke twice to arrange the details for where and when he would meet the man who'd give him whatever it was to take north. Even as the sketchiness of the operation increased, Bill found himself more compelled. He ate up adventures. And this one would allow him to lay eyes on her again. He couldn't remember being as nervous about anything—and keep in mind, once, in Mexico, someone had disemboweled a dog and left it on the steps of his rental trailer.

"You're paying me two grand to carry it, and you don't know what it is?"

"I guess." She considered the brick. "It's complicated."

Bill pulled his shirt on, popping the buttons back in place. "Why me?"

"You were in the area, and I knew I could trust you."

"How'd you know that?"

She motioned for him to follow her to the kitchen. "I'll get you that drink."

Her ass swished in front of him through the sweats, juicier with the pregnancy. Her shirt rode up just enough that he could see the butterfly tattoo, the ink now faded. He imagined scraping it away a layer at a time with a razor blade.

Over the last decade he'd followed her movements only through refractions and reflections from other sources. What frustrated him the most was that he knew he could have helped her. After she dropped out of Toledo after just one semester, she returned to the same provincial piece-of-dawdling-shit town that she'd sworn on all those nights in the backseat of his car she would never go back to. He didn't even want to think of all the one-act men she'd kept busy with. It killed him to imagine what the father of this child must be like, how he must think, dream, behave, and love.

"Drugs?" he asked, nodding to the brick now resting on the kitchen counter.

"It's not important." She poured vodka over ice cubes in a coffee mug.

"Except who pays that much money to haul one little brick of coke or heroin or Oxy?" wondered Bill. "No way is that worth two grand on the street."

Kaylyn's eyes didn't move from the package. "Doesn't matter what it is. Just that we're getting paid for it."

She was lying. He went to the kitchen, and she handed him the drink.

"I'm thinking counterfeit thousand-dollar bills," he said. "Or smuggled Chinese microchips." She smiled without teeth. He raised his mug. "Or Marsellus Wallace's soul." The vodka smelled pleasantly isopropyl and tasted of relief. Out here on the edges of the fracturing economy, people muled mysterious packages back and forth across the scorched American landscape. Getting all the dirty deeds done.

"Not your problem anymore," she said. She opened the silverware drawer and reached beneath the divider. She handed him an envelope. "You can count it."

Bill accepted it and wondered at the odds that the other half would still be in his truck. "Not necessary." He stuffed the envelope in his back pocket. "You didn't really answer my question. Why not go down and get it yourself?"

"I don't have a car. Plus, this doesn't make travel all that easy." She rubbed her belly affectionately. Bill watched her. This story was such garbage. He wondered how much that even mattered to him. He wondered how blinded he was by seeing her after all this time. He drank.

"So who's the father, Kay?"

He felt the sensation that people called the heart moving into the throat, but that didn't exactly describe it. It was more the throat closing off in anticipation of dread.

"It's such a long story, Bill. Let's just say he's still deciding if he's sticking around, and I'm pretty far from sure I even want him to."

Her face morphed into those of his dead friends: Rick and Ben. For a moment she looked like Lisa, until her freckles and eyes returned. He blinked and tried to keep his voice even. "What does that mean?"

Her eyes darted to every part of the narrow kitchen: the saucepan soaking in the sink, an owl clock on the wall shifting its eyes back and forth with each tick of a second. She palmed her swollen belly. "Sometimes I'll sneak a glass of wine. The doctor said it's okay every once in a while, you know? Why don't we go out back and you just let it lie. Okay?"

And because it meant she'd spend a drink's worth of time with him, he accepted.

Out on her back stairs, beneath the frozen ligature of the stars, she sat a couple steps up from Bill facing the yard while he reclined against the faded spindles of the railing. He told her about visiting Rick's grave earlier in the night. "A mostly purposeless endeavor," he finished, with a shrug and a chug.

Kaylyn bit her thumbnail, peeled it off, and flicked it to the cement. "I haven't been out there in a while. I'll see his parents around sometimes, but . . ."

Marty and Jill, prototypical kind, plainspoken midwesterners.

He thought of Marty with his white walrus mustache giving him shit about staking out salmon night. The backyard looked out over a cement walkway leading to a dingy single-car garage. This path was flanked on either side by strips of pale grass. The fence obscured almost any view of the neighboring homes, so they only had the dome of the sky above. There were stars in this dome, and they were mighty and beautiful.

"Do you miss him?" said Bill, though he did not want to hear the response.

She was quiet for a long time. "Not sure I know how to answer that. It's messed up but when I heard, I was . . . relieved, I guess. He'd never come home, and I'd never have to face him again. I got to see my dad drop dead at dinner, but having to spend all that time with Marty and Jill at the funeral, then the parade, was one of the worst things. I don't know. Just how hard parents can cry."

"Do you think Rick knew about us?"

She sipped the wine she'd poured from a box. Delicately licked the purple stain off her upper lip. "I don't know. I know he would've forgiven me."

He scrambled the ice cubes at the bottom of his mug, then cradled it gently in both hands, the way you would a baby chick. Bill thought of how he'd felt when she stopped returning his calls, that cold, comingled rage and grief. He and Rick had that in common till the end.

"He had our lives here planned out down to when he'd get the head coaching job. Then you and I got, you know, close. And you always wanted to go out and live life. You won't remember this, but one time, maybe junior year, we were all at Vicky's after a dance and you were going on about how you wouldn't stop before you'd seen both the northern lights and the Antarctic ice. That's exactly how you put it: the northern lights and the Antarctic ice."

"Haven't seen either."

"Yeah, but it mattered to you. It sounded very brave and romantic to a girl who'd never been on an airplane." She bit into a nail. "You had this hunger that Rick never did."

He felt that pang in his throat again and the cool bore of the wind. He knew seduction was just another con.

Bill took the photograph from his back pocket. He unfolded it, handed it to Kaylyn.

"Senior year. Homecoming."

She took it like it was made of ethylene glycol, held it in that way people hold old analog photos, with their fingers on the sides, afraid to get their smudgy prints on the surface.

She studied it a moment before handing it back, voice anodyne. "We look like babies." He folded the picture, his eye catching Lisa's sultry squint, Kaylyn's purple pornographic kiss, Rick's playful menace, Harrington's goofy-ass fedoraed smirk, his own vanishing face flaking into oblivion.

He pulled the pack of cigarettes from his pocket and chucked one between his lips. Lit it, sucked in yet more poison. Kaylyn did not object.

"I was at the bar tonight and ran into a bunch of people from high school. And you know, I found Dan Eaton while I was driving around. He was just walking along the side of the road, looking like a ghost crawled up his ass and into his eyes. Wouldn't surprise me if he's homeless in five years living under a bridge. That's what happens to kids like him. Sometimes I can't believe how much we've lost. And even that's only a fucking omen for what we might have left to lose."

He glanced over at her. Her eyes had lightning in them, flashing like the violent skies of Venus. He wanted to tell her the story of what Rick had done about Todd Beaufort, but why? And why, since he saw the fat, faded kid in the bar earlier that night, could he not stop thinking about him? He realized he was having another hallucination, but this wasn't a vision. This was honest-to-Christ time travel. They were all time travelers. Shit, every time you glanced at the sky you were getting a glimpse of the ancient past, stars burned out or traveled millions of miles from where their light once shone, and the stronger the eye you constructed—say the TMT on Mauna Kea in Hawaii, with a thirty-meter mirror telescope—the further back in time you could look. Some people were just more attuned to it than others.

"Kay," he said softly as all time and space raced backward around his eyes. "Tell me what's in that package."

In early 2002, a few months after the night at Ostrowski's, Rick called him on a Saturday night. He said he needed Bill's help, but he didn't explain. He only said he'd pick him up shortly.

Rick pulled into his driveway, his old Explorer coated in a hazy film of white salt. The winter night had rolled in quickly, the town bathed in darkness by six p.m. He asked Bill to grab his papers and a bit of weed.

"All I have are scraps."

"Just get it."

So Bill went up to his room and dug into the shoebox for his latest eighth, now mostly dust pinched into the corner. In the Explorer, Rick asked him to roll a joint.

"Dude, where we going? Aren't we meeting at Harrington's later?"

"After this."

They bounced along 229, passing a trailer park, Bluebaugh Auto Body Repair, a metal-fabrication shop, and then Rick turned off Dudgeon Ditch, a real backcountry road that alternated between pavement and gravel. Meager moonlight cut through the branches as Rick's SUV crackled across gravel and leaves, snapping twigs and just missing a couple of horny raccoons darting through the elms.

Rick pulled into a long driveway marked only by a battered black mailbox, twisting back through the woods, arriving at a one-story double-wide in disrepair. The siding was dull with dirt, awash in the hideous orange glow of a porch light, and the windows had storm shutters thick enough for a hurricane. When he spotted the black truck parked by the side of the house, the frame lifted high above the wheels so that it looked dinosauric, he understood.

"What the fuck are we doing here?" Bill asked.

"Just gonna talk," he replied, yanking the key out, engine dying.

"You fucking kidnapped me? What are you trying to prove, Brinklan?"

"Shut up." The anger in his voice actually caused Bill to do just that. "For just once in your life, shut the fuck up." They sat in the car a moment, engine ticking. "We're not here to fight him. You don't have to say shit. Just stand there and offer him weed."

Before Bill could say anything more, Rick bounded out of the truck. Cursing his friend's meddling nature, his bullshit chivalric simplicity, he followed. Behind the small house there was a fenced-in yard that must have ran for an acre to the rim of the woods, and he could hear an army of dogs barking, mewling, yipping, screaming like angry little girls, and as the two of them passed by, the mutts all crowded by the fence or pulled at their leashes and gave plenty of warning as visitors neared.

Todd Beaufort pulled the door wide before they reached it. He wore black shorts that swamped his shins and a sleeveless T-shirt with the New Canaan jaguar crushing a football in its jaws. He looked confused, first by Rick and then very much by Bill.

"Yo what's up, Fifty-six," said Rick, extending his hand. They slapped palms and traded a few manipulations. Bill remained below on the porch steps, like a child on his first day of kindergarten hiding behind his dad's ankles.

"Nothing. What are you two getting into?" Beaufort cast his eyes on Bill.

"Your mom home? We got some bud. Need a place to smoke up. We were driving around, and I remembered you lived out here."

It was a thin excuse, but Beaufort seemed to find it reasonable. Bill attempted to scowl and it felt false, a mask rather than an attitude.

"What up, Ashcraft." Beaufort extended his fist, which Bill dapped. Their first exchange since Beaufort leveled him in the hallway that fall.

"Hey," he replied, thinking of their childhood. News of the alpha athlete of each class always filtered down, and he got his first glimpse of Beaufort during sixth-grade Little League, screaming at his mother in the parking lot. Bill watched this hefty woman the shape of a slope-shouldered lemon smack her kid in the face hard enough to spin him around, his heel skittering in gravel.

"My mom's at work," Beaufort said, and surely Rick had known this. He led them into his home, which smelled of wet dog and something sickly, like the vomit of infants. The kitchen, living, and dining areas bled into one another in a mess of furniture too big for the space. A couch and two chairs crowded around a forty-two-inch TV, nearly banging into the dining room table and its mismatched chairs. Stacks of video games, copies of the *New Canaan News* (mostly the Sports section), catalogues, and bills overflowed a coffee table. *SpongeBob* chirped on the television. A pustule of plugs was suspended along one wall, extension cords running in every direction from its vertex, one fixed behind the only decoration, which was a tacky ten-cent painting of Jesus, hands in supplication, eyes fixed Fatherward because he suddenly understood he wouldn't be carrying on the family name.

"I got a lighter," said Beaufort, and then they went about talking football for a while. This recruit Clarrett for the Buckeyes—man, he was going to be fearsome. Not to mention Beaufort's teammate soon.

Bill sat on a blue couch and felt parts of the fabric that had turned stiff from long-ago spills never cleaned. He could see the little black pocks from dropped cigarettes. Rick took a seat in a chair opposite Bill so that the two of them flanked their quarry; he waited until the joint had made the rounds and Beaufort had his first drag.

"I wanted to ask you something," said Rick. Beaufort had one leg up on the coffee table, resting his heel from a position of maximum lounge. The fabric of his shorts slid down, exposing a thigh of fine blond hairs. "I been hearing rumors about what you guys are up to with Tina. Gotta say it sorta has me disturbed."

Beaufort said nothing. He frowned, then leaned forward to pick up a mug already full of cigarette butts to ash the joint.

"Don't see how that's none of your business," he said finally and reclined back.

"No." Rick clasped his hands. His knees rose and fell like he was keeping time. "If you're hurting her, it sure is. If you're taking pictures, filming, doing shitty things to her . . ." He rubbed the stubble on his chin, his hand looking powerful.

"It ain't anything she don't want," said Beaufort, genuinely confused. "She's got no objections."

"Not sure I believe that."

They stared at each other. Bill wondered what he'd let himself get pulled into. It was only now, stoned eyes wandering the room because this scene was so uncomfortable, that he spotted amid the clutter of the coffee table a wicked knife resting on, of all things, a *Guns & Ammo*. The knife looked like something a Klingon would carry, curved and jagged with a mean black grip. He was sure Beaufort had picked it up when he heard the dogs barking.

Now the linebacker murmured a laugh. "That why you came out here? To play moral police with me and my girl? Sure this ain't about *your* girl?"

Bill would always wonder what Beaufort meant by that, was never even sure if he heard the kid correctly, but Rick rolled over it too quickly.

"Nah," he said. "It's about what you're doing to someone you got power on. And it's over, man. You're done. I'm telling you you're going to break it off with her. You're not going near her again."

Beaufort leaned forward, amused. The dog tags he always wore dangled, two stiff, lazing flags. Bill saw how the ugliness would grow in his face when he aged: his wide nose, heavy brow, and thick, buttery lips. They looked firm and boyish right now but in a few years they'd go Mongoloid. By contrast, Rick looked brutishly heroic.

"You should ask me who gave me all the help popping that cherry, Boy Scout," said Beaufort, a depravity in the hard contours of his jaw. "Doesn't matter though. Season's over. We ain't team-mates anymore." He jerked a thumb toward Bill. "Take your faggot boyfriend and get out. Or me, Curt, and Strow can make Kaylyn our fuck pig instead."

Bill stared at the grotesque beige of the carpet and saw chip crumbs. He knew he had to look up, and when he did Rick's face was a haunted mask, maybe fear there, maybe panic, but certainly grim determination.

"It's like I go to all these camps," said Rick following a long pause. "And I see these black kids from the cities, and they've just got something in them that I don't. It's like they know this is it, this is what they've got to get themselves out of where they're from, and if it doesn't work out, they're fucked. So when the moment comes, they don't flinch. You can be big, you can be athletic, but when you're running the ball, it's all about that moment when you're about to get crushed, and you can't hesitate. You can't think about your family or your friends or your home or your girl because then you'll flinch and the guy coming at you will pop your fucking head off. I feel like I got so many reasons to flinch. So sometimes I do."

His tricep twitched, and it sent a pulse through his whole arm.

"Now you got a reason to flinch, Todd. You break it off. Leave Tina alone. The other guys, they don't go near her either. You delete all the pictures, all that shit you took of her. You do it by the end of this week. And if you don't, I got a copy of that video. The first one you made. And if you think you'll be able to hold on to your scholarship after I hand that over to my dad, the school board, her parents, everyone, then you're even stupider than you look. You'll never get outta here, you'll never have a shot at the pros, you'll never do fucking anything. You'll grow old and fat and broke in this house with your mom, and that'll be that. This ain't a negotiation, man. This is me telling you how it is."

Bill watched the cloud of doubt descend over Todd Beaufort, and it frightened him. He'd never seen the dark clarity of having another person's fear in the palm of your hand. Rick stood. Bill's eyes passed over the knife. He imagined Beaufort buying the dagger, trying to dream up what opportunity might allow him to stuff it between somebody's ribs. He wondered if he should make a move for it.

"Brink." Beaufort hadn't moved from the couch. He sat draped onto it. Relaxed. "I ain't spending another minute in New Canaan, man. You fuck this up for me, I won't have a reason to do nothing but kill you."

Rick stopped just long enough to shrug. "Alls I'm saying is do what I tell you, and we got no problem." Then he popped open the door and Bill followed him out, glancing back at Beaufort one last time. What he saw there rearranged some things. As his cold blood mingled with the frigid winter air, he saw how much uncertainty this kid lived with. When Beaufort plowed into Bill in the hallway, it was because he was utterly without control over his own capacity to respond to his circumstances, getting played over and over again while believing fervently he had a grip on his own fate. He figured Beaufort would probably do what Rick asked. Then he would go to Columbus and get his head pounded to jelly for the NCAA, and when his body gave out, he'd wind up as a cog in some other machine. He'd live feeling only brief respites from confusion, and even these would pass quickly, like the gaps of sunlight in a massive anvil thundercloud.

On the drive back into town, out of the entombing darkness of the country, on their way to Harrington's to be with their friends and lovers, he said to Rick, "The tape? You don't have any tape."

"Yeah, but he doesn't know that. And those guys made enough copies, he thinks I might."

"What's even on it?"

Rick shook his head. "Doesn't matter."

"What, so Todd Beaufort is suddenly going to see the light and behave himself? Treat his girlfriends and everyone else with empathy and respect? Fuck, Brinklan, you've got a worldview like an eight-year-old watching a bad action movie. Steven Seagal doesn't really save young girls with karate."

Rick chewed his tongue. "Someone had to give that guy some consequences."

"Yeah, so he can get to college and do it to another five, seven, ten women. You probably just doomed some other poor moron to getting used by him. At least Tina Ross is dumb enough that she probably doesn't even know the difference."

"Man, what *is it* with you?" He snatched a hot, furious look at Bill.

"Keep your eyes on the road. This is like the deer holocaust strip."

"You know . . ." He gritted his teeth, hissed through them. "Jesus, Ashcraft. You think you have all these friends and admirers, man, but that's not what they are. You think you're this charming, slick dude. People think you're *arrogant*, man. They think you're full of yourself. They all talk behind your back about how fucking phony and unpleasant and unhappy you are. They feel sorry for you, Bill. I guess that's what makes it that much more disappointing. Because I *am* your friend. I stick up for you when people talk shit, man. This will always make me wonder about that. The fact that I asked you to try to do something halfway decent for a person you know and grew up with, and you kicked and screamed the whole friggin way. It's cowardly."

That was what really started their unwinding. That little speech on their drive back from Beaufort's. Bill put it away, but he brought it back out. When he took Kaylyn to her grandma's that March, for instance. Every time he needed to resurrect the unbridled, unhinged hatred he had for his friend, he just called up that moment and he had it in his grip again. He knew how you could grow resentment for a person over time, water it, care for it so that every word exchanged in every interaction—every glance even—could be loaded with this enmity.

He barely even remembered their final exchange the summer of '03. It had been late July, maybe a month after he woke up at Rick's with the diaper on. A huge group of guys from their senior class had been drinking at Mike Yoon's house, and he and Rick had ended up jawing about the war, as usual. He had been so loaded he didn't recall the lead-up, just that somehow it escalated. They'd been in the backyard, the woods looking as dark as a black hole fallen to Earth. For whatever reason, Rick had called him a coward, and this reminded him in a savage way of the year before, when he'd used the same word driving back from Beaufort's. Then Bill was screaming—and sure, it might have been incoherent at the time, but if you dressed it up without the alcohol it would be something that hurt, something like: *You're the one who talks all his patriotic blood-and-honor bullshit and then goes to OSU to become a fucking math teacher. Go coach your high school football team someday, Brink. What a warrior! Yeah, Saddam and al-Qaeda are shaking in their boots at you. Talk about a fucking coward.*

Rick had gone at him then, which was probably good because Bill had already hitched in the breath to move to Total War, to spill everything, to stand in front of all their friends and recount how Kaylyn had crawled onto his face in her grandma's bed and how her skinny thighs quaked when she came. Lucky for Bill, their buddies pulled them apart before he revealed all. Later, when he heard from Harrington that Rick had dropped out of OSU to join the Marines, Bill had to wonder if that night of wasted heat had something or everything to do with it. That night was the last time he ever spoke to Rick Brinklan.

Four years later, Bill's dad called him as the final semester of his senior year of college was winding down. He'd been in a bar on a weeknight watching the Cavs finish off the Wizards in a first-round playoff game. He told the story about playing fourteen-year-old LeBron one-on-one at a basketball camp because there was a beautiful blonde who'd joined them, some friend of a friend, and she had pearl earrings, a preppy popped collar, and an attractive curve to the bridge of her nose. She kept looking at him, and he at her. He went outside to take his dad's call, and while Bill was easing in to his take on the game so far, his dad goes:

"Hey, I've got something that you need to hear. I just got off the phone with Marty." And of course Bill knew what was coming. "Rick was killed in combat yesterday. They're planning a parade, and—you know, if you want to come home." His dad went silent, his voice caught, like a sweater snagged by a nail, on the moment of telling his only son that his best friend from childhood, a kid who'd eaten Fruit Roll-Ups in their kitchen and played basketball in the driveway and sneaked liquor from above the stove, was gone.

He got his dad off the phone as quickly as possible, but not because he needed to weep. Because there it was. Rick had gone off to fight a pointless, bullshit imperial war waged for the profit of a small elite, and he'd taken one for the team, hadn't he? He got exactly what he wanted—to die a supposed hero. Bill went back inside the bar, watched the Cavs triumph, and fucked that pretty, preppy girl twice that night and once in the morning.

Kaylyn twisted her wineglass and watched the liquid chase gravity at the bottom.

"It's not important, Bill," she finally said. "You helped me when I needed it. That's all that matters."

He'd finished his cigarette and stubbed it out on the step, but he still held it between his fingers, twirling the blackened end. A Camel talisman. "What I'm saying . . ." He dropped the cigarette butt and put his hand on hers. "If you need help, I want to help. If you need money, if that brick is what you're doing to make ends meet, I can—"

"Bill." Her voice trembled, and very abruptly tears shimmered in green irises. "I cannot—I mean it—I cannot tell you. All I can . . . I've messed up. Got involved with—just—some bad people. I did some incredibly stupid things, and . . . Now I'm just trying to save myself, stay out of prison, stay clean, and give Barrett and my mom and this baby any chance. And I can't tell you what this involves because I don't want you involved. You just have to trust me."

Her throat clicked. A calving cloud passed overhead. He gripped the bones in her hand.

"I've done those stupid things too," he finally said. "And that's even when I've been trying to do good. Nothing feels like it does any fucking good. Because people only act—they only change—with a gun to their head. I've been depressed, I've been miserable, I've hated myself. But through all of that, Kay, you know what I keep coming back to? You. You've never been out of my mind."

She took her hand back and held her eyes with the tips of her fingers. "You don't understand what I've done."

Then, with Bill working around her obfuscations—excavating much, but deducing little—Kaylyn told her story. Not so much an explanation as a fogged, opaque confession.

In the long list of regrets, mistakes, and nightmares, the thing that haunted her when she couldn't sleep wasn't even the worst thing she'd done. She'd given them all an order and moved those rankings around depending on what shame she wanted to fill herself with on a given day. She tried to decide when she'd learned to be so cruel. At a middle school dance, she'd ridiculed Hailey Kowalczyk for wearing a basketball jersey: "You look like a boy with smaller tits," she'd quipped to the raucous laughter of those within earshot. Later, before her mom picked her up, she saw Kowalczyk wiping at tears. But that was the thing about having younger friends. Now that Hailey and Lisa were in middle school with her, they got clingy, called every night, tried to trade on their friendship with the girl a grade above them. The flipside was that they never doubted her, never questioned her knowingness.

That's how two years later, during a game of Seven Minutes in Heaven, she got Kowalczyk to give Curt Moretti a blow job. She told the participants she would join them in the bathroom to make sure things went well, and after the hoots and cheers, Curt sat on the closed toilet while Kaylyn perched on the rim of the tub and directed her younger friend: On your knees. Put the bath mat under them so they don't get sore, etc. Kaylyn watched with her chin propped on her hand and felt both lascivious and powerful. Hailey kept her eyes open, a dumb bovine quality to her expression.

"You want to join in?" Curt asked her as Kowalczyk mumbled the kid's cock.

"You wish, Moretti."

But she did put her hand on the back of Hailey's head to test her limits. Kowalczyk had no idea what she was doing, and in fact, when Curtis blew his load, she just swallowed and kept right on going. He came again a few minutes later. She'd never had a thrill like that before. She wasn't sure why she'd picked on Kowalczyk, this cute, funny little tomboy chick, who played point guard for the basketball team. Everyone fawned over her for how she took on the household responsibilities when her mom got diagnosed with bone cancer. Lisa called her "Triple Threat," and the name spread. Hailey could do it all, they claimed. Therefore, Kaylyn wanted to make her try it all, and in doing so, she discovered Life in all its manipulative, wet, pornographic glory.

"I can't believe you did that," she said to Hailey later that night.

Hailey averted her eyes. "Had to happen sometime."

When Lisa heard, she was horrified. Not at Kaylyn, but at Kowalczyk. Kaylyn couldn't have cared less that Lisa and Hailey stopped speaking. By then, she was with Rick, the brawny stud football player of her class. He did her math homework and got just the right amount of jealous.

As an adult she'd wonder where this streak in her came from, if she'd just been born bored and intrigued by the lengths people would go to in order to please her. When her father crashed to the floor while eating dinner, she knew before her mom dialed 911 that he was about to leave her. Growing up, if he was on his double-digit wine cooler of the night he'd tell her she was the moon and the stars and the sky, the only thing that kept him going. Kaylyn took this to mean he hated her mother and Barrett as much as she did. When he died and left her with them—a crumpled shell of middle-aged passivity and her only sibling, not an ally or a friend or a person she could lean on, just a vicious, mean-spirited lunatic no one could control—she was furious and something else. Envious of him maybe?

By then she was already on to the Third and Fourth most terrible things she'd done, having grasped the incalculable pleasure that could be wrung from manipulating people to her desires. The addiction was like a wet washcloth, no matter how many times you twisted it, water would always wring out, even if in diminishing returns.

She should have been more on the lookout for the other addictions. When Ben Harrington started having certain meds around, she stole or cajoled them. Once a month he'd come by her locker and offer her an aspirin bottle with three or four Percs rattling around in it. Once, after school with the hallways empty and eerie, she dipped two fingers into the pocket of his jeans and pulled him close, not because he was giving her pills but because he would complete a satisfying triple crown.

"No, c'mon," he said, turning bright pink in the high parts of his fine cheeks and pulling his hips away from her. "That's not even funny."

How did the line go in his song? *Pretty, sad girl / offering a glance for pills / pretty, sad girl / throwing her battered heart into the hills*. She hated him for that.

The Fifth and Sixth worst things she'd ever done toggled between a few contenders, but lately not marrying Rick was pushing up in the order. Not that an eighteen-year-old girl should be on the hook for an idiot boy's sense of romanticism. When she turned him down, she wanted to add, "Are you insane? Don't you realize that you were an accessory like a purse or a nice pair of earrings?" Later, she took a flashlight, found the ring he'd hurled into the woods by his house, and pawned it for nearly a thousand dollars.

The problem was, by the time she got to Toledo, she'd moved on to Oxy, which was a hell of a nice feeling, but expensive and all-consuming. She had to find a couple of guys who were willing to share their stashes, and this project took up so much of her time, she never even completed a course. She dated Mitch, this *American History X*–looking guy who had a direct line to all kinds of party drugs. Together, they went to basement raves on the outskirts of the city with metal raging through speakers, the whole joint rigged to be a fire hazard. He was an amazing lay. They'd snort a line of crystal and fuck for hours, then snort an Oxy so the comedown wasn't too harsh. It was the most carnal and delicious period of her life, the evolutional training for food and sex and other pleasures suddenly rendered cheap and inert by a sniff.

When she ran out of money, she lost her apartment and her enrollment in the same week. She went to live with Mitch, which she quickly understood to be a mistake. He'd leave her alone with his friends for days at a time, and she would lock herself in the bedroom because they all had the glazed quality of rapists who were just too tired to make the effort. Once, when a particularly evil-looking guy was spending time there and she was in a paranoid mood, she even stuck her butt out the window to pee so she wouldn't have to leave the room.

She knew she had to stop with the crank. One night she left a few shards of it on a butter knife and passed out. In the morning she saw the coating of rust it left on the metal and began having horrific visions of the insides of her lungs and sinuses. She'd heard of people developing sores, their teeth falling out. In the end, her vanity probably saved her from herself.

She stole as much Oxy as she dared and went home, crushing

and snorting the pills in her childhood bedroom to help with the tweak. For days, her body shook like she had Parkinson's.

New Canaan was flush with glass, though, and she needed the occasional bump to get through her waitressing shifts. It allowed her to work seventy hours a week sometimes so she wouldn't have to be home with her mother and brother. She could pull off the long hours and then settle down to sleep with an array of prescription meds. That helped lead to what was obviously the Most Terrible Thing she'd ever done, the summer of 2004, when she set in motion a thing she could never take back and never make right (and when Bill pressed and pressed her on it, she finally said, "No. Stop. I'm not talking about that—let it be," and he did).

Not long after that, Hailey laid it out: "I'll help you if you promise to get help."

Kowalczyk was a smart cookie and now her last friend. She drove her to NA meetings for the rest of the summer until she left for school at Bowling Green. The problem was, at NA they basically wanted you to confess all your sins, and there was no way Kaylyn could do that. No way. Her solution was to go to one of those doctors at a pill mill and complain about an aching back. She stopped going to NA but she was no longer messing around with meth, so she counted it as an improvement.

In high school she remembered days when she couldn't leave the house, when the thought of stepping outside filled her with so much panic that her chest cramped up and she couldn't breathe. Sometimes she'd put a disc on in the boom box in the bathroom and take hour-long showers. Her mother accused her of preening, and wasting all the hot water while doing so. The truth was, she used this time to cry. To weep and weep until her stomach ached. It wasn't until she found the relief of an opiate dose that she realized she'd needed this for as long as she could remember.

In the years that followed, the pill mill worked just fine.

Dr. Redding would pull out his pad, scribble, and she'd be on her way. Sure, there was the interminable line where she would get harassed by the scuzziest refuse of Northeast Ohio, where fights would frequently break out in the parking lot, where broken old men would offer her pizza for a kiss, but at the end of that rainbow was a scrip to get her through the month. If she needed more, all she had to do was complain about the pain getting worse and Dr. Redding would oblige. She liked his no-nonsense business model. As long as she had cash.

When she stopped going to work and lost her job, he wasn't as accommodating.

"Please," she said. "I can't find work without it. You get it? Like in order to get a job to make money, I need it or I'll crash and I'll never show up and I'll just get fired all over again." She heard how frantic she sounded but was helpless to stop.

"We could make an arrangement," he offered. That same all-business attitude. She wouldn't have expected it from him. He had the thinning peach-fuzz hair and frumpy midwestern features of an asexual toad. It wasn't a pleasant solution but she could sleepwalk through it. Bend over the exam table and after fifteen minutes or less she'd have the scrip. Of course, she never did find a job. Not when she had this simple a trade.

Events passed her by, and she was indifferent to all of them. Curt Moretti died of a heroin overdose and all she thought was, *That's why I'm sticking to the safe stuff*. Her mother kicked her out for stealing, and all she said was, "I'll find other arrangements." And she did (though she kept going back to fleece what she could until her mom changed the locks). Rick was killed, and she went to the funeral and parade, but she was high for both, her mind as blank as a Buddhist monk's. There were a lot of people there whom she hadn't seen in a while, and they all kept coming up to her—Rick's sweetheart—and she had to fake like she was stunned. Marty and

Jill insisted she stand with them at the parade, still looked at her like she and Rick had been in love. Like she'd spoken to him since high school. Like she cared.

What she did care about was when the pill mill shut down and Dr. Redding lost his license and came under indictment. There were two months of full-on panic when she was rationing her stash, scraping together money to buy from some of the dealers in town. Later, she'd learn the term "junky luck," which perfectly described what happened to her. Dr. Redding gets shut down and Hailey walks back into her life with a proposition.

"I'm getting married," she told her.

"Congratulations." They had this exchange in La Paloma, New Canaan's most mediocre Mexican. "To who." Not that it mattered. The last thing she wanted to do was catch up with a childhood chum. She'd crushed one of her last pills that morning.

"Eric. Frye."

"That black kid? Wasn't he a little weirdo?"

"We reconnected. He's actually a great guy."

"What happened to Eaton?"

"We broke up. A while ago now." She looked sick that Kaylyn had forgotten this fascinating piece of trivia about her dating life. Like a goddamn breakup with Danny Eaton was any kind of monument in time.

"Okay. Cool. Congrats, Kowalczyk." She sipped a Corona and thought of choking this girl on Curt Moretti's dick. The memory brought her a lot of satisfaction.

"I'm pregnant," Hailey said. "And also, we're just in a tough spot right now. Both Eric and I have so much student debt, and he's substitute teaching, and that's like—you know, he might as well be working for free."

"Yeah, it's hard times. They're calling it the Great Recession, if you don't catch the news."

"Well. So." She fidgeted with a fork. "What I wanted to ask you is. I work at the retirement home."

"I know. My grandma died in there, remember?"

The waiter arrived with their meals. Hailey left hers untouched.

"What I want to know is—I have access to a lot of stuff. Like a lot of different prescriptions. I know a couple of the nurses already do it."

Junky luck.

For three years, this worked about as brilliantly as one could hope. Hailey made some money while Kaylyn got her fix and a modest income. She could stay in her fog undisturbed, passing the days watching television, drinking nights away in the bars, walking the railroad tracks out over the Cattawa so that she felt like she was traveling to distant lands, like she didn't miss anyone or regret anything. Like all the awful things she was responsible for were the faraway memories of another woman.

Then in 2011, not long after Ben overdosed, Kowalczyk pulled the plug on their operation. A girl had been caught stealing prescription pills at Eastern Star, and she was going to jail. "Eric and I are doing well. He's working, we don't need this anymore."

"You don't understand," said Kaylyn. "These people I'm working with, you can't just walk away from it."

"I don't have a choice, Kay. I've got a daughter—I'm not going to jail for fencing prescriptions for a few extra bucks. I'm sorry." Kowalczyk had gotten so fat. Kaylyn hated the bloated look of her face, like she'd just had her wisdom teeth out.

What Kaylyn failed to mention was that she actually owed the Flood brothers a bit of money. She'd been holding on to more of their supply but taking the payments with promises to supply the rest of the pills later. Instead of paying these local dealers back, Kaylyn instead kept buying more from them on the false pretense that her supply would return. So she was good for it. Owing a bit of money became owing a lot of money. She went smurfing in drugstores to try to pay it down, but there was only so much pseudoephedrine you could get away with purchasing at the few locations she could walk to. Then these guys cut her off. That's when she started catching rides down to Columbus where heroin cost as much as a six-pack. She snorted it, smoked it, promised herself she'd never inject it, and within a few months was shooting it between her toes.

Amos Flood, who she'd known since Elmwood Elementary, came to her, and very apologetically put it to her like this: "We need you to do us a favor. It'll be later this year, maybe summer. You do this, all your debt's forgiven. You don't, well—you gotta think about if anyone would even miss you."

She was to make a trip to New Orleans to pick up a package. On top of that, she hitchhiked to Planned Parenthood in Mansfield to have something checked and found out she was pregnant.

Coming down from the fix she'd allowed herself in an Arby's bathroom—slumped against the grimy tile, all terrors forgotten, all nightmares vanquished—she realized she had nowhere to go. She couldn't go back to where she'd been staying. The father of her child had kicked her out because she was dragging him back into this life. Her own mother wouldn't let her through the front door even if she were bleeding to death on the lawn.

She found herself ringing the doorbell at Hailey Frye's. When she answered, Kaylyn could see into the warm light of the dining room, where Eric (bearded, so much older than she remembered him, but still with a boy's cheeks and the same wide, freckled nose) and a dark-haired, light-skinned little girl peered at her with curiosity. The kid demanded to know who it was.

"It's Aunt Kay," Hailey told her. "Hold on." She stepped outside and closed the door, regarded her with crossed arms: *I'll listen to you, but I won't let you near my family.*

"I'm in so much trouble, Hailey." Kaylyn started crying. She told her story with snot pouring out of her nose. She spilled everything except for what Amos Flood was asking of her.

Hailey went back inside to get her car keys. She came out with a piece of fried chicken and made Kaylyn eat it while they sat in her car. When Kaylyn finished the chicken, Hailey wrapped the bones in a napkin and held them on her lap.

"It seems like you think you have no choices, Kay, but you really only have one. You get clean."

Kaylyn held her mouth in her hand. She'd never wanted to kill herself before, but she thought about it then. She definitely had enough junk left to OD. She could hike out to the Brew or Jericho Lake and put it straight into the pit of her elbow.

"I'll drive you right now," said Hailey. "I know a treatment place in Columbus. I'll help pay for it and you can stay there as long as you need. That's your only option. Then we can talk about what you want to do about the baby. Who knows, maybe that little gal will save you. Maybe she'll give you a reason to make up for everything."

Kaylyn wept harder. When Hailey guessed at the sex, she saw, vividly, what a daughter of hers might look like.

"There's no way I'll make it," she said. "There's absolutely, one hundred percent no way."

Hailey pulled her into her arms, rested her chin on Kaylyn's head. Her friend's body was warm and soft, a mother's body. "Of course you will."

"Why are you doing this?" Kaylyn demanded, wanting to strangle her. "I've never done anything for you. I've never been anything but a fucking monster to anyone."

"Oh, I don't know about that," said Hailey. "You had the only Teddy Ruxpin on Rainrock Road, and you let me play with him all the time."

She didn't find this funny.

"I can't take back what I did. Not now. I've lost myself."

Hailey pulled back, looked at her with a severity, but also a kind of demented humor, a *Look at where we find ourselves in this grand cosmic joke* sort of face. She took Kaylyn's gaunt cheeks in warm, moist hands. "It's never too late to start over. You and I know that."

"Why?" Kaylyn pleaded. "Why do you keep helping me?"

"Jesus Christ, Kay." She pushed a handful of greasy blond off her forehead. The ruddy bulbs of her cheeks gleamed brightly, filling with embarrassment. "Because I've loved you too long. We do anything for the people we love. That's what I've learned from you."

She woke the next morning in the large house of the Volunteers of America of Greater Ohio sicker than she'd ever been in her life. Vomiting and diarrhea like her insides were unspooling out of her. Her bones and muscles ached so maddeningly that she wanted to scratch her skin open and rip the whole infrastructure out. She itched everywhere. Her vagina felt like an open sore and she wanted to burn it shut. She thrashed in the sheets. She thought she could feel the baby eating her from the inside and dreamt of cutting it out of her stomach. She wanted to stab the nurse when she came by with water, and she puked it all over the floor instead of the toilet just to be spiteful.

And yet.

The morning after that, in the midst of a host of pains so unfathomable she thought they might drive her to permanent madness, she got out of bed and went to the window. The sun was rising. Alum Creek to the east, and the green expanse of the Franklin Park Conservatory to the south. There was a song playing in her head. From Ben Harrington's second album. *This pretty, sad girl, lost for so long even the devil had gone and forgotten her name.* She watched the clouds pass over the sun and spears of light pierce through their gossamer veil. The song played and played in her head until she went to the toilet to be sick again.

Bill could hear only the ticking clock in the kitchen and the sound of his own breath.

"You don't have to be alone with this," he said, putting his arm around her. "Whatever it is. I can help you." As he pulled her into his embrace, he wasn't sure if the pulse was his or hers or the baby's.

"You don't understand," she said again. "I've done awful things to people I cared about, people who were my friends, who I was supposed to love. I look back sometimes, and I can't believe the person I was. Who I am."

Kaylyn shimmered before his eyes, and there was something always out of his reach, something more to her than the mourning Ohio beauty, more than an unexpected sexual audacity discovered in her grandma's house in Dover, more than the girl he'd tried to drink away in a dozen countries on a thousand nights. He'd go to the underworld, he'd stand on the bitter rock, he'd eat the sticky bodies of the vilest subterranean insects, and still he wouldn't have her. Hades abducted Persephone and made her queen, but the motherfucker was the enemy of all life, all gods, all men. How to pull apart a story like hers? He felt in her things he'd never seen, processes of cunning none of them had ever understood, and the way she looked at him, her eyes now black pits with dark tongues lapping in the depths, he wondered if he should fear her. That was her power. That he'd never really know. And even when the waters rose at the end of civilization, he still wouldn't.

"You need to go now," she said.

Panic feasted as she led him back through her house. At her front door, he clutched the meat of her bicep. He pulled her into him once more, gripped the bones in her back and felt all of this like he was being buried alive.

She kept her hand on the doorknob. He scrolled through their ancient conversations, searching for an explanation and got nowhere except the memory of her clutching a towel to her skinny, small-breasted body when she emerged from the summer water of Jericho Lake. He couldn't bring himself to believe all this longing he'd carried was just a well-stretched scam by a cruel, ignorant pill junkie.

"I'm sorry." He let go of her, sucked in a needed breath.

She smirked, wiped tears from her eyes. "What an un-Ashcraftian way to depart."

"Maybe a good-bye kiss? Or a good-bye blow job?"

She laughed and wiped a few tears away as she popped the door open, the lamplight spilling over the concrete steps.

"That's more like it." She kissed him somewhere on the fringe between mouth and cheek.

She closed the door behind him, and Bill hurried into the night. The whole world felt like a sleight of hand. Their lives: all part of some larger parlor trick, an expert misdirection, and here they were, reeling, grasping. He needed the comfort of the liquor store again and aimed in that direction.

He'd gone only five blocks before he understood how exhausted he was, how strung out and ready to collapse onto the crummy red brick. As he neared the square, he heard a low rumble in the distance. The rumble grew until the sound familiarized: helicopter blades thudding dully at the air as they kept their cargo aloft. The red lights of the chopper cruised up from the south. He stopped in the middle of the street and watched it. It was too low, nearly skimming the tops of New Canaan's tallest three-story brick edifices, tilting back and forth with uncertain piloting. The nose dipped, as if for a moment it would dive kamikaze straight into the guts of this rank neighborhood, and then it achieved more lift, adding clearance. This close, the blades positively thundered. It passed overhead, weaving chaotically, and Bill got a look at its black belly, tinted blood red by anti-collision lights looking like wet, blinking eyes. Pointed due north, it sped toward its destination, as if drunk and desperate, as if fleeing. Like the angel, the chopper vanished into the same inter-dimensional chute of ashes and blue light.

He heard sirens in the distance, and not just one vehicle. It sounded like a response to a three-alarm fire, and he remembered they would still be looking for him. If they found him, they would lift up his shirt and see the flesh outline of the package and know what he'd done—whatever that was. He did the only thing he could think of, what all children eventually revert to. He cut over to the Dunkin' Donuts and dialed collect the only adult he could trust. He said, "Hi. It's Bill. I could use some help."

Then he sat down on the curb and let darkness close around him.

When he came to, strong hands were hauling him up, guiding him into the backseat of a car. "If you're gonna be sick it's gotta be back here."

He fell into the cushions of the backseat. A car that still had that old man, Barcalounger scent: fake leather and stale, sneaked cigarettes. Through the slits of his eyelids, he watched Marty Brinklan walk around the front and get in the driver's seat. He looked almost the same, a big unkempt cap of stiff white hair that never receded and the mustache, now more handlebar than walrus. Bill was too far gone to note if he looked any older, any paunchier, any grimmer, but these all seemed reasonable. He still had a busted boxer's nose, as crooked and malformed as a knot in a tree. He'd broken it four times, most recently when he and Rick were kids and an angry woman beamed him with a flowerpot to the face during a domestic disturbance call. Rick's mom had to wear earplugs for the snoring.

Bill tried to apologize to Marty, but he wasn't sure of the words he was saying.

"I get it. It was either me or a night sleeping it off in county." Marty's baritone had a sandpaper rasp. Bill tried saying something else but an unseen palm held the lids of his eyes. He felt the centrifugal pull of each turn, the rumble of the road. It vibrated inside his teeth.

"Said your parents are gone?" Marty asked him.

Bill wasn't sure how he responded.

"I'll take you to the house. You can pass out there. I gotta go back out, though. We got a call. Nasty business out on Stillwater Road." He sniffed allergies into the back of his throat. From childhood, Bill knew what would come next. Marty cracked the window and sent a loogie shooting off the tip of his tongue. Through the window he could only see dark veins of purple swimming by, and in that purple a mask with bottomless eyeholes that watched him as they drove.

He must have asked what happened. He was sure the nasty business was his fault.

"Can't say, Bill. Don't know all the details." Then Marty, who was the quintessential man of few words, said something that chilled him even through his haze. "From the sound of it, though, it'll be the next thing in this town that keeps me up at night."

When he came to again, he was in the Brinklans' house, his arm slung over Marty's thick shoulders. Marty carried him to—where else—Rick's old room.

"Where's Jill?" he thought he said.

"She doesn't live here anymore," said Marty.

Rick's room had been stripped bare. Posters and trophies and the flag and torn out pinups from *Sports Illustrated* swimsuit issues were all gone. The walls spackled and painted blue. The guest bed overflowing with pointless throw pillows. He collapsed into them.

"I've gotta get out to Stillwater. If you gotta throw up there's a trash can by the bed. We'll get you some breakfast in the morning."

Bill tried to open his mouth and say it: What he'd admitted to Dan Eaton earlier that night. What he'd wanted to say ever since he'd understood his own hapless, coward's heart.

Instead, Marty's mouth moved just below his wounded eyes.

"You and Rick both had this idea. That if you can't save all of mankind, you've completely failed. I know he forgives you, Bill. Even if you'll never believe it, he forgives you."

But maybe Marty Brinklan did not say that. As soon as the silence returned, it only felt like another hallucination, and on the last few words Marty's mouth opened into a portal where he could see ancient battlegrounds and sharpened bayonets. Marty left Bill there to listen to the sound of the car turning over and backing down the driveway. He closed his eyes and met his visions.

He dreamt of how his and every other story would end in shame. He pictured Earth after the profiteers had finished carving up every last shard. The planet would go dark, and every animal would devour itself or fall, pale and listless, into a black acid sea. The oceans would boil away, and eventually this rock of humble miracles would go silent. Spend the rest of time adrift in its slot of space, the land gray and ashen like a crater, and nothing would notice or remember what had gone on here. It was as inevitable as the next drink he would take. He thought of all that he'd lost and tried to summon his friends—their faces, their voices, their holy souls entombed in his despair. He could wish that the dead only waited patiently off stage, their makeup still on, longing for salvation when they'd take their bows. He could let his memories be the noose from which he'd swing at dusk.

Or.

Or he could climb out of this abyss. As he slipped into sleep, he told himself there was no going back to the slowly drowning swamps of the Mississippi Delta. There was a thousand dollars still in his glove compartment, a thousand more in his back pocket, and another quest, another vision, lying in wait. Even after all this, there was always a reason to stand again. To summon the courage to live and to be alive. To rage against the faceless entropy, the savage logic of accumulation that would return them all to exile, that aimed to strip them bare of everything, every place, and every person they'd ever loved. To find hope in defiance, in the subterranean fire, and to always and forever endure the Truth and struggle to extinction.

He stumbled on in his dreams, mourning the rivers and fields of his homeland. He saw it burning in blue fire, and he prayed for the strength to defend it, to fight for it, to bring it back alive.

Stacey Moore and a Theory of Ecology, Literature, and Love Across Deep Time

ON THE DRIVE BACK HOME TO DELIVER AN OVERDUE LETTER and meet the woman she'd feared and hated her entire adult life, Stacey Moore stopped to scoop her hand into the ground and tear away a handful of dirt. Five miles outside town, well before the sign that welcomes you into the city limits—weathered, aging, yet still admonishing that here lies America's heart—she had to pull to the side of the road, her bladder begging for release.

Her nerves rising alongside that internal pee ache as she neared New Canaan, she realized she wasn't going to make it. No matter how old you get, a swollen bladder always takes you back to childhood, especially if you grew up with older brothers and everyone rolled their eyes when you were the one who instigated bathroom stops on road trips. She always held it just so her dad wouldn't give her that skeptical glance in the rearview mirror, but her brothers, Patrick and Matt, were like fucking genetically advanced camels the way they could store water.

Trooping into the woods with dusk rapidly drawing down and only the faintest blue-gray light lingering, the world a fading Chinese lantern, she got situated with her back against the tree—the key to peeing outside, her mom once explained. The very process still elicited memories of campfires, her mother's s'mores, and the fecund scent of summer nights in Mohican State Park. As a little girl, maybe six or seven years old, Stacey squatted beside her and watched. "Afterward you gotta kinda wiggle your butt around," she said, demonstrating with a little "Twist and Shout" dance. Attempting to imitate, young Stacey promptly fell on her butt into her own pee, and her mom laughed like she was having a seizure.

Now Stacey was an expert, having peed in locales as diverse as the Brazilian Amazon and Croatian alleys, none of which had anything on this deeply satisfying gush of kidney-processed coffee and Diet Pepsi, as delightful and relieving as snapping one's neck in that chiropractic way that releases half a dozen kinks at once. Alone in this bedraggled piece of the county except for the thunderous buzz of the crickets and the careful winking of the fireflies, she allowed herself an audible, pleasured moan, then a little laugh at the borderline-sexual severity of that moan.

Finishing, she wiggled her butt around, per Mom's instructions, and pulled her underwear back on. Around the deep-blue flower print, the white of her dress glowed, and she remembered Lisa pulling it off the rack in a Columbus thrift store many years ago. "I think your ass will look like a million bucks in this dress, Miracle. For fifteen bucks, math-wise, that's substantial savings." That she'd worn it tonight was a coincidence.

The night roared with those Ohio crickets, their hopes, jokes, disagreements, and bullshitting all wrapped up in a crackling symphony. And now that she was home (or at least the place she could never stop thinking of as home), all the errant memories began to spring forward, unbidden, clamoring for attention. Whac-A-Mole ghosts. Which is why she stopped before she reached her Jeep, pulled haphazardly to the berm of the road. She reached down and scooped up a handful of dirt. Mr. Masoncup had lectured his earth science class not to call it that, like it was a slur. *Soil*, he'd implored, and she'd replied with something like *Looks like dirt, Mase*. That typical manner of hers. The character she'd played in high school: witty, coy, knowing anyone would forgive her teasing because she'd been demarcated as beautiful by the patriarchy (that's a joke, but not really). Teasing people, she learned, endears them to you while also keeping them off-balance. It was a social lesson she mastered early.

Lisa Han was in that same earth science class junior year. They'd both written papers on dirt. Lisa sat two rows ahead and one over due to a randomized seating chart (a real bugfuck lottery for Mr. Masoncup to pull on the first day), and Stacey would catch her looking sometimes. She'd have to avert her eyes because chances were she'd been staring at Lisa.

That was the year everything changed. The year she changed. She used to think it was mostly about Lisa, but maybe she'd never given enough credit to that earth science class. She squeezed the fistful. Cool and wet, born from the explosions of stars and coalesced into life, it took the shape of her palm. When you're a child you think nothing of touching dirt, but as an adult, how often do you pick it up and feel it this way? Feel it the way you'd feel a lover, give it the reverence you'd give to a body. She held a solar system of mycelia gnashing away at plant matter, returning it to the cycle, renewing. "What's more important?" Masoncup asked them. "Humans or dirt?" And the answer was that it wasn't even close—even as Ohio's monoculture farms massacred the soil, a veritable mycelia genocide, and then pumped in nitrogen fertilizers to keep it alive, zombielike.

Maybe it was dirt that had started her down the road to losing her faith.

But what a silly way to put it. She released her handful like a magician revealing a dove. The soil looked like an extension of the dark tattoo on her forearm, like the ink was sliding off the skin.

Because by shedding the hyper-restrictive construct of religious thinking—what some people call "losing your faith"—Stacey had gained the Universe.

* * *

Before leaving Ann Arbor that afternoon, she'd gotten coffee with Janet, and her primary advisor said something disturbingly insightful.

"You view writing like those scenes of Bruce Wayne putting on the Batsuit." Her eyes bulged in her peculiar, excitable way. Janet's hands and eyes were always in motion, crumpling a used sugar packet, tapping the wooden stirrer against the side of her mug, peering over the rim of her matronly glasses at passersby, Stacey, and back to people watch. "Like those scenes with Christian Bale or Michael Keaton putting on each piece of the suit in this onerous process."

"Don't forget Clooney and Val Kilmer."

"Body armor, click on; gloves, click on; cowl, click on." She made the motion for each piece. "You need to learn to just sit down and write without putting this pressure on yourself."

Janet had become an English professor mostly to indulge the huge pop culture nerd hiding beneath her work on Faulkner. Stacey had yet to witness her in a conversation she couldn't somehow turn to *The Walking Dead*.

"It's just getting past that feeling," said Stacey, "of everyone being totally fucking brilliant and then the paralysis when I realize I'm not."

Janet rolled her eyes, a motion that took her entire head in a loop.

"Chill out, Stacey," she ordered. "You're a first-year student, for Christ's sake. Take a week off when you go see your parents. Write something nonacademic. Just write something for yourself." It felt like Janet had pulled it out of her head: because she'd spent an awful long time writing something for herself the night before. It was now sealed in an envelope on the passenger seat of her car. "Give transnational modernism and ecocriticism a rest."

When she'd been casting about for a grad program, she'd chosen Michigan because it was by far the best school she got into, and now it freaked her out to think that had she chosen differently, she might never have met their horror- and sci-fi-obsessed Faulknerian, who had become not only a mentor but a woman with whom she was engaged in an absolutely shit-stomping case of hero worship.

"Saw that Maddy dropped you off."

Stacey responded with a furious heat in her cheeks.

"Hey," Janet reassured her. "Literature and sex are the primary methods we use for demarcating intervals of our lives. You're reading this person and fucking this person during any given period and they tend to change over with weirdly similar timing."

Stacey had no defense for sleeping with her ex, who was about to go chase adjunct positions in the wide blue world. Maddy had somehow dragged her back into her fold. When they first started hooking up, Stacey found her butch midwestern frankness appealing, not to mention those squat legs of a power lifter. Maddy had an awesome androgynous punk coif, and courted her by cutting Stacey's hair into a sort of Mia Farrow pixie cut she was still in love with. When she began describing her embryonic notion of an idea for her dissertation—ecology and world literature—Maddy kind of scoffed at her first-year naiveté and asked if she'd ever read Goethe, who supposedly invented the genre. "The world at large, no matter how vast it may be, is only an expanded homeland," she quoted. Later, Stacey decided she had to date outside the handful of women in her program, preferably a half-straight girl who never quoted anything.

"Forget Maddy," she told Janet. "I've got enough making me crazy right now. This trip home . . . It's just like this total sense of doom. Like having to think ecologically all the time, it creates this impulse to barricade yourself in a house, town, region, country, planet—hell, that's doom." Stacey laughed nervously at her babbling. "Wait, maybe we should go back to who I'm fucking."

Janet smiled, her mouth two rows of gravestone teeth. Her

professor could quell from her mind all eloquence, leave Stacey stammering, staggering around mentally like Gregor Mendel in his library during an earthquake, books beaming her on the head.

"Anyway."

"Stacey, you're wound tighter than the girdle on a Baptist minister's wife." Janet's eyebrows danced. "This is your ex's mom?"

She'd already told Janet the story, editing out the more disturbing aspects. The parts she'd never told anybody.

"Listen, Stace, the past only has power over us if we allow it that power."

"That's easier said."

"And come on, girl, it's not the mom that's bugging you. It's *her*, doy!"

The night before when she hadn't been able to sleep, while entertaining visions of ancient narratives racing across the coalescing and dissolution of stars, drowning in Deep Time, she finally realized her preoccupation with ecology and literature had a trail of breadcrumbs leading back to Lisa Han's bedroom library. Stacey's love of reading began with Lisa, who pulled books from her foldable shelves and pushed them on her like a drug dealer, the pile of unread tomes growing so vast that Stacey only finished all of them years later while traveling in Europe. Stacey doled out to herself this strategic reserve of Lisa's favorite texts in careful drips, never reading two in a row. They were Stacey's reward to herself, her way of connecting back to this person without admitting that that's what she wanted. Almost all of them had Lisa's dog-ears and margin notes. Jaunty, clever quips, occasionally filthy, always charming: A huge smiley face at a perverted scene in *Lolita*. A sarcastic *"Thumbs-up, bro!"* at a bit of misogyny from Milan Kundera's *The Book of Laughter and Forgetting*. A *"Jesus I'm wet"* next to a scene in *Wuthering Heights*. It had been during these pusher days that Lisa had handed her James Lovelock's eco-classic

Gaia, warning of its density but also its mind-blowing capability. "After you read it, you'll be a totally new person," Lisa told her. "You won't look at flowers or lichen or dung beetles the same ever again."

Flipping *Gaia*'s pages in Lisa's bedroom, a photo had fallen out. It was of Bethany, Lisa's mother, swollen with pregnancy, holding her stomach and looking at the camera. "You in your mom's belly!" she'd exclaimed. "She's so pretty in this."

"Seventeen years and one kid ago," Lisa snorted.

Stacey flipped the photo over and squinted at the date. "Lis," she laughed. "This is from the day before you were born."

Lisa took the photo from Stacey, gazed at it a moment, searching for an unspecified clue to no particular mystery. Then she shrugged and stuck it back in the book. Or she must have, because Stacey would find that photograph nearly five years later in Croatia when she finally got around to reading *Gaia*.

She had never explained to Janet or Maddy or anyone that her preoccupations, what she wanted to write about, well, this girl from her hometown, Lisa Han, had always pointed the way.

"My advice?" said Janet, rapping her knuckles on the table in the coffee shop, clearly buzzing from her daily overload of caffeine. "E-mail her today. Now. The hot ex, I mean, not the mom. The longer you haven't spoken to her, the more anodyne and undramatic the e-mail. Just a cheery 'Hey, howzit going, whatcha up to?' Trust me, it'll suck the power right out of her."

"That," Stacey said, smiling, "seems an unlikely move on my part."

"We are all travelers, Stacey. The only difference is how much baggage we choose to burden ourselves with."

"Your aphorisms are always totally useless."

Janet blasted crazy air through her lips and flapped a hand like a bird caught in a tornado.

"Not only that, but I've got three ex-husbands who'd call bull-shit on that one. I'm nothing but baggage."

Though it lay several miles to the west, she felt the high school as she passed by. Without even laying eyes on that place, she could feel it like an ache. Some institutional slab of crap architecture with that sixties-era authoritarian aura to its brick Lego look. She marveled at the power the American high school experience holds on the imagination. She'd always noticed how people tended to view their high school days as foundational even if they didn't realize it. Get them talking about those years, and they suddenly had all these stories of dread and wonder you could wrap whole novels around.

She followed Zanesville Road to the center of town and was surprised to see what looked like a gleaming, brand-new Walmart bursting like a diamond from coal out of a remote area where before there was nothing but farmland. There had certainly already been a Walmart in New Canaan when she'd lived there, but this new one made the Walmart of her youth look like a sickly mom-and-pop. Even at this relatively late hour the parking lot, only appropriately measured in football fields, held hundreds of cars, and people strolled shopping carts in and out of multiple sliding glass door entrances. It took about three hours to get from Ann Arbor to New Canaan with maybe another hour to reach her parents' new home in Columbus, and along the way she'd have a choice of how many of these panoptic consumer centers? A dozen? A hundred?

The CD in the stereo, *Extraordinary Machine*, a college love, began skipping. The passenger seat was a stew of candy wrappers, empty soda bottles, her purse, and the crisp bleach-white envelope. She scraped through the mess until she found *Slow River* and switched out Fiona for her high school boyfriend's raspy tenor.

Halfway into the opening song, she pulled into one of the slanted spots in the town square. The mechanical scratch of shutting off the ignition, followed by the thudding silence as the stereo went dead, filled her stomach with the queasiness of a hangover. When Bethany first e-mailed her a few months earlier, she'd read with fury, triumph, pity, more fury. It was all pretty confused. She told Lisa's mother she had nothing to say to her, but the woman kept writing. All she wanted was to meet, she said. All she wanted was to talk, she claimed. Just a half hour of Stacey's time. And maybe it was curiosity that led Stacey to agree. She told Bethany she could stop in New Canaan on the way to see her parents.

Her boots—kick-ass, high, and black, with a zipper that nearly reached the knee pit, a ten-buck Salvation Army find—clopped over the street like a horse with two amputations. The square was surprisingly quiet, a few cars hesitating at the yield signs, distant stoplights winking through their programs. A small black purse on a spaghetti strap slung diagonally across her chest bucked rhythmically against her hip. An old man sat on a bench, one arm draped around a pink shopping bag that said BIG SALE, and she felt his eyes on her as she passed. Walking through the heart of town, she wasn't sure what to expect. She'd let New Canaan take up such gargantuan psychic space that sometimes she forgot it was just a place, and life carried on here as it did anywhere else.

Vicky's All-Night Diner had been the favored greasy spoon in high school, the place to be after dances. It was blue-neon signage, strange artifacts of Americana affixed to the walls, and your choice of two rows of booths or a bar with stools made of that red sparkly plastic material. The game where you pump in quarters and try to grab a stuffed animal with an impotent mechanical claw still stood in the corner. One night after a basketball game, Ben Harrington tried for half an hour to win her a prize. She recalled him spending nearly eight dollars in quarters going after a pink elephant while the group gathered around the plexiglass cried out each time the toy slipped through the claw's grasp. When a boy makes up his mind about you there is no challenge too trivial for him to peacock.

A man in a red trucker's hat and a green plaid shirt sat on a stool, a large expanse of fleshy white lower back and butt crack exposed to the harsh diner lights. An elderly couple occupied a booth near the door, eating in silence, silverware tinkling against a bowl of soup and a salad. A waitress pecked at the cash register. Another stalked back into the kitchen, her yellow sock-hop skirt bouncing behind a generous rear. A chintzy, prototypical hometown diner, decorated with the spare parts of someone's cleaned-out grandfather's house after he's passed. Skis affixed to a wall here, a picture of Marilyn Monroe there, a sign in block letters that read ORANGE 10 CENTS hanging above a World War I–era gas mask. Americana without purpose. Detritus for the critic to sift through and puzzle over the symbolism. There was a young man at the counter, no meal before him, fidgeting with a credit card. He saw Stacey and fixed his eyes the way men do.

She decided to kill time at the game Ben Harrington had tried and failed at so many times for her sake. Better that than waiting while this leering, rude motherfucker drilled eyes at her.

The first haunting piano notes of *Slow River*'s opening track played on repeat in her head. Between this and Vicky's claw, Ben's presence felt nearly material. His sweet grin, his compassionate laugh. In many ways Ben, the only guy she'd ever slept with, had also inadvertently built the road to Lisa.

Until they finally started hitting puberty, she'd been taller than nearly every boy in her class, her father's hearty Norwegian stock a total liability as an adolescent. She had a deep-seeded understanding of her awkwardness, how long her femur was inside the flesh, how razor sharp her elbows must have looked. It took her the first two years of high school to realize she'd become pretty. She'd carried her gangly, akimbo frame her entire life. Built like a collection of kindling, slim of hip and breast and ass, her figure filled out, and developing even the most passable bosom went a long way with teenage boys. That's how teenagedness works: everyone lives in a bubble of their own terrifying insecurities oblivious to the possibility that so does everyone else.

It was through volleyball that she fell in with Lisa and her friend of the assonantly awkward name Kaylyn Lynn, who was a grade older. Lisa and Kaylyn dated the crown jewels of the class of '03, Bill Ashcraft (dark-complected, arrogant, black eyebrows as sharp and dangerous as steak knives) and Rick Brinklan (a football star, he looked like Stacey's Jeep with fair farm-boy skin stretched around the frame), respectively. Their best friend, Ben Harrington, played on the basketball team with Bill, and they began hanging out by default and dating soon after. She well understood that by any measure Ben was truly gorgeous, a slender but chiseled teenager with a mop of gold hair, that lucky Caucasian skin that goes mocha in the summer, and a grill of teeth so white you had to make sure light didn't reflect off them and hit you in the eye. Until they started dating the summer before her sophomore year, Stacey had been convinced she wouldn't have sex before she got married. Sex ed in eighth grade was having couples visit from the high school to talk about what a gift it was to save themselves for marriage. Ninth-grade health class featured a woman who spoke of how deeply she regretted her abortion and the premarital sex that led to it. This assumption—one Stacey never questioned—proved ill preparation for when the smoldering Kurt Cobain equivalent of New Canaan High School suddenly took an interest in her, when he proved surprisingly sweet, and when he touched her in ways she'd not been touched before, around the ear and neck, in that way that tickled and chilled and warmed and made every last hair follicle stand at attention.

Lisa and Kaylyn sort of threw Stacey at him, like ground chuck at a lion, and when the matchmaking worked out, the two of them immediately took to treating her like they'd all been best friends for years. Almost overnight, she stopped hanging out with her best childhood friend, Tina Ross, while Lisa captured the bulk of her attention—probably more so than the guy she was actually dating. Lisa had this odd habit where she tied small strings around her left wrist. Remarkably, she could do it using only the fingers of her right hand, and as the strings gathered in a braided clump, Stacey found herself fixated. Then her eyes would flow up the length of her arm. They found her athlete's build—muscled shoulders and strong arms, very little curve to her hips, and a taut, round butt, difficult to not obsess over. They found the geometric tip of her nose, brown eyes like saucers of coffee, and thick, plum-colored lips. The tilt of her eyes gave her a perpetually mischievous quality. It was a face that knew how to razz people, fuck with them, knock them off-balance before they even realized they'd been standing. She could hold a person's gaze well beyond what most people found comfortable, like she believed the longer she held your eye, the more she'd have access to your mind and memories. Beyond that, she was a fire starter. Smart and sassy with a graphic, volcanic mouth, and the first person Stacey ever met who was just unapologetically herself.

At a sleepover with Kaylyn, Lisa gave them a description of her forthcoming autobiography.

"Obviously, much of it hasn't been written yet. It'll have great lovers and adventures and all that, but the entire first chapter is just going to be about how I discovered masturbating. How I basically didn't sleep from ages twelve to fifteen because I was staying up till three a.m. every night rubbing myself out."

"Twelve?" Stacey clucked. "I barely knew what my vagina did when I was twelve."

"I'm glad it happened that way." Lisa lay on her side with her head propped in her hand, deadpan expression, like a bored queen trying to decide whom to execute for the laughs. "A couple years ago, my mom told Alex how he'll grow hair on his palms if he touches himself. If she'd told me that I would have been checking my hands every day. My room was a pedophile's idea of a good website."

"What will you do when your kids read about your rub-out parties?" Kaylyn asked.

Lisa rolled her eyes. "Wouldn't expect a conformist New Canaanite for life to understand. I'm not having kids. I'm traveling the world and having Italian lovers and stuff. If I do have a kid, I'll raise her as a single mom, give her a weird name, and fuck her up real good by dragging her around the globe."

Stacey asked what the child's name would be, and Lisa looked at her like she was an idiot. "My kid? Darkheart McStabababy. Duh. Darkheart McStabababy Han. DH for short." Stacey clutched a pillow, laughing in that way that scrapes the inside of your breastbone.

That night Lisa also schooled her on condoms. When Stacey mentioned Ben wasn't using anything, and she wasn't making him, Lisa slapped her forehead and then pulled her cheeks down exposing the gross intake of her eye sockets. "Staaaaaaacey. No, no, no, no."

"He takes it out," she explained. It was the first time she'd felt truly naive around them.

"No, no, no. Common misconception. You can still get pregnant even if he just gets a splash in you. Even if it's just the pre-cum."

"The what?"

"Body's natural lube." Lisa sat up, clenching a fist. "See, this is Ben's beautiful, gigantic dick making you want to have unprotected sex. During this part, before he comes, there's some lubricant that comes seeping out, which is nature's way of greasing the pole." Kaylyn was cracking up, but blinding horror had descended upon Stacey, convinced she was already pregnant. They'd just had sex at the Brew the night before, her sixth time total, a count she would keep with obsessive specificity. "So because evolution is so clever, it's like, 'Hey, why not make this lube have some little hot Ben Harrington babies in it too? Then give those babies gigantic staffs, and let's keep the ball rolling.' Get what I'm saying?"

She did not. She still thought evolution was a conspiracy theory, but the next week Lisa gave her a ride home after volleyball practice and tossed a box of Trojans at her. "From now on, wrap it up, Miracle." And that's what Lisa called her from then on, "Miracle." Because Ben never got her pregnant.

Good girl that she was, Stacey truly could not recall why she let Ben deflower her. Somehow she justified and compartmentalized it, and then put on an abstinence play for her parents, youth group, and church while sneaking off to sleep with her boyfriend on the reg. Not that you really need an explanation. That's just being a teenager. Were He to exist, God would still have no power over the hormones, the longing, the urges that carpet-bomb you at that age. What could be said about her first time except that it hurt like hell, and she was mortified that she got blood on Ben's sheets and further embarrassed that she hadn't thought of that? They made the decision quickly, his parents and sisters still out for ice cream after his basketball game, thinking Ben and Stacey had gone to the dance. Stacey likened losing her virginity to getting her hand slammed in a car door: abrupt, shocking, painful beyond your ability to anticipate while causing no real lasting trauma (most of the time). Like they tell you, though, with practice it gets better, and before you know it, it's pretty much all you want to do. Then your young life becomes a fretful logistical equation of spatial and temporal factors to determine when you might next find the opportunity. It helped that Ben was more or less the perfect boyfriend for a sexually inexperienced nascent lesbian unaware or in denial of her own dyke-ish desires: easygoing and considerate in a way that many teenage boys cannot summon. Like so many men, he had an uneasy relationship with his father and therefore an uneasy relationship with himself. He was a fantastic musician, spectacular on the guitar, which he could complement with a soulful voice that now reminded her of Amos Lee or Josh Ritter. His father, Doug Harrington, was this old-school chauvinist who measured his own child's worth in feats of athletic performance and his ease or unease at wielding power saws or hunting rifles. Doug saw Stacey as the distraction that kept Ben from achieving on the court, but it was the other way around. For two years Stacey didn't do much besides hang out with his son.

It was hard for her to say what they spent so much time talking about, but she liked to remember it inaccurately, to recall the two of them pondering philosophy and literature while he plucked at guitar strings. Maybe he wasn't the love of her youth, but Ben Harrington had what her mom called a "great big heart." Even though she knew her relationship with him was part of her own inability to understand herself, and every sexual encounter had a claustrophobic quality—watching a frightening, beautiful alien planet from within a small glass box—she didn't regret a moment. They broke up when he went to college, but at that point her mind was already elsewhere. She saw him only once after he graduated but kept a close watch on his music career. He even put her in a song. *Pretty, sad girl / on her way to somewheres better / pretty, sad girl / she'll take you the next planet over if you let her.* A reference to what he said the first time they had sex stoned, which admittedly, really blows your hair back if you're not used to it. "I think I just woke up on a different planet," Ben said, and Stacey laughed and played with his beautiful sweaty blond hair.

She never saw what was coming.

In 2009, she got an e-mail forwarded to her from her dad, originally written by Doug Harrington. It said: *Respectfully, would you please ask your daughter to stop sending Ben money.* She wrote back to her father to say she had no idea what Doug was talking about. She hadn't spoken to Ben since they'd gotten lunch in 2005. That was the last she heard from him until the fall of 2011.

She'd just arrived in Ecuador and was taking some time to travel the country before she began teaching in Quito. It was in a hostel in the north, this small, out-of-the-way town called Cayambe, where she logged on to a computer with its greasy keyboard to check her e-mail. Her mom had written to tell her that Ben had set fire to his apartment in Los Angeles. Rather than reading the despondent obits on music-nerd sites—inflating Ben far beyond the reality of his lackluster career, Stacey found herself poring through pictures of the two people he'd killed: Christina and Eduardo Zayas, both twenty-nine, newly married. She bit into the side of her tongue as she scrolled past a picture of Christina rock climbing and one of Eduardo angrily jabbing his finger at another actor in the play *Wait Until Dark*.

She realized she had no quarters. While she waited on a waitress to come back to the cash register, she brought up the last e-mail Lisa ever wrote to her. Back in 2004, she'd said: *I'm sorry about everything. Be well.*

How hard her heart had beat, how she'd broken a sweat like a fever, how she'd wanted to scream and throw her laptop through her dorm window when she read that years ago. Even if she took Janet's advice, she couldn't reply to this. She opened a fresh e-mail. She didn't type Lisa's address. She mostly just wanted to stare at the white space.

The young man at the counter was still staring at her. He was short and wore an unruly beard like a stage prop, a greasy head of hair combed straight and humorless with a sheen that caught the fluorescents. He was dressed like a skateboarder or a grunge rock bassist, badly but unassumingly. While she tapped her dollar bill against the counter and worried over the blank screen, he simply stared and stared, and she resisted the urge to snap at him, *What's the problem here, bro?*

"Can I help you?" The waitress appeared, and she stuffed the phone back in her purse and slid her dollar across the counter.

"Just four quarters."

She was older, gray hair and a haggard, drooping face, skeins of weariness embedded in deep wrinkles. She click-clacked away at the register until it popped open. Scooping out the quarters, she nodded at Stacey's arm, "That's a nifty tattoo."

"Thank you."

"What's it mean?"

"It's from a poem."

The cursive script ran up the inside of her forearm from the spot where the Romans put the nails in Jesus's wrists to just short of the elbow pit. " 'All dreams of the soul end in a beautiful man's or woman's body,' " the waitress read. "Sexy."

"I thought so. It's Yeats."

"Can't say I know that one. You ever read John Hardee?"

"No, I haven't."

" 'While hollering and breathing so long so deep / Memory came on and dove down to my sleep / Dreaming this memory of space all around / Silence becomes breath becomes thought becomes sound.' " She winked. "Look him up."

"Shit." And she was filled with that sensation of interconnection, of Deep Time and all the myriad notions of wonder it promised. "I will."

The waitress hoisted a coffeepot and walked away.

*   *   *

Lisa had been her classmate since the sixth grade, but Stacey was sure they had not spoken more than ten words to each other until she joined the volleyball team in high school. Along with Kaylyn and Hailey Kowalczyk, Lisa was an Elmwood kid, and over at Grover Street Elementary Stacey and Tina had deep reservations about the trashy cliques from Rainrock Road. (And don't even get eleven-year-old Stacey started on what "jerkstores" they had at Rutherford Hayes Elementary; if you told young Stacey she'd grow up to date a cocky Hayes boy, she would've threatened to puke on your shoes.) That's how the social taxonomy of small-town high school works. You can *know of* a person for years without actually *knowing* her. Though they'd grown close through volleyball and their boyfriends, the second semester of their junior year both Lisa and Stacey took Mr. Masoncup's notoriously easy earth science class, where they learned all about dirt. Studying for one of Mase's exams was how Stacey discovered Lisa's obsession with popping zits.

"You have one on your back," she told Stacey gleefully. "I saw it at practice when you were changing."

"Perv."

"I'd really appreciate it if you let me take a crack at it."

She protested, and the conversation brewed into a healthy argument, their memorization of mycelium and other dirt components entirely forgotten.

"It's big, it's white, it's right on your shoulder blade. I need it. I want it."

"You're disgusting. And strange. You're too strange."

She twirled a finger at the sky. "Look, Miracle, you can act like a little muffin crumpet all you want, but I'm not helping you pass this test till I get at that sweet zit."

"Muffin crumpet?"

Even stones get run down by flowing water, though, and eventually Stacey caved. She sat with her shirt off, hunched forward to stretch her back skin per Lisa's instructions, and she could see her face in the dresser mirror, zipped tight with concentration.

"Han, you look like a psycho."

"Just hold still."

The knobs of her spine each looked like a knot in a rope, and she felt self-conscious about the size and number of moles that peppered her skin. Lisa bore down on it with two thumbs, and Stacey felt that little pop, even heard it, and cried out.

"Oh yeah," Lisa breathed, examining the pus on the tip of her thumb.

"You're so weird!" But she was laughing.

"Holy shit." Lisa stared at her back with a particle physicist's sense of wonder. "Look at that fucking thing bleed."

Stacey had always noticed women physically, but this didn't seem aberrant. She was self-conscious about her own awkward frame for long enough that her gazes felt like jealousy, not longing. By the time summer rolled around, after their respective breakups with Ben and Bill, Stacey was spending almost all of her time with Lisa. They might have shared a conversation about the dual solace they could provide now that their boyfriends had graduated, but if so Stacey couldn't recall it. They both had summer volleyball, trekking all over the state to play in scrimmages and tournaments. Lisa was the best setter on the team, could deliver a meaty ball into Stacey's palm right at the height of her jump. This was when Lisa began badgering her to read more. She and Dan Eaton were little bookworm neighbor friends from childhood. Then she and Ashcraft had traded tomes (though Stacey remained convinced he didn't actually read anything—he just liked upending his jock stereotype). Lisa hated having people in her orbit who were not readers. At that point Stacey had no idea she even liked literature. Other than the Bible, The Baby-Sitters Club novels, the Left Behind series, and the first couple of Harry Potters, she never picked up a book outside of class (this now seemed as incredible as the fact that she used to blow a boyfriend). Then Lisa got ahold of her that summer. Even though Stacey wrinkled her nose at the weight and length of Zadie Smith's *White Teeth*, she finished it in three nights, and Lisa rolled her eyes like *No shit*.

Lisa began eating dinner at Stacey's house. She knew this was partly because of Bethany; Lisa never made it a secret that they had been at odds ever since she started dating Bill, and Lisa wanted out of the house. Meanwhile, Stacey's parents loved having her. Partially they were relieved that she was spending so much time with a girlfriend instead of sneaking around with Ben, who'd graduated and who—as good of a guy as he was—just had the slick, honeyed look of a kid trying to fuck your chaste daughter.

Lisa could also set her charm wattage to "parent" better than anyone. She called Stacey's dad "Moore's Law"—not for any computational reason (her dad worked with mulch), but because Lisa told him, "We have to get Hollywood to green-light a sitcom about you, and it's gotta be called *Moore's Law*. It just has to, I'm sorry."

Stacey's father was the kind of buttoned-up Eisenhower-era holdover who loved nothing more than hard work and hustle, which for him were interchangeable terms. When he coached her sixth-grade YMCA basketball team, which consisted of her, Hailey Kowalczyk, and a bunch of girls who couldn't dribble, his most enthusiastic and frequent compliment was, "That's good hustle! Love that hustle." So when Lisa bopped out her sitcom music for *Moore's Law*, Stacey's mom would find it hysterical, and her dad, who had no sense of humor or irreverence at all, would always make the same joke: "Far as I can tell, it's just a show about Lisa Han eating my food."

Her mom, on the other hand, was a total goofball. She could scat off puns at a worrisome, embarrassing clip. During the avian flu scare of 2004: "Stace, have you been to the hawkspital yet? Owl always worry about you, even though I know you'll survive on a wing and a prey-er. No egrets, right? Boy, this dinner is parrotdise." Her dad laughed at most of these, which might have explained their entire marriage.

Her mom thought Lisa was a total firecracker. Once, memorably, the two of them got into an argument about senior pranks. The class of '03 held a milk-chugging contest in the cafeteria. Supposedly it was physically impossible to drink a gallon of milk in an hour, which, based on this experience, seemed accurate. All participants failed, vomiting dueling blue-white jets into nearby trash cans.

"It sounded like a plane landing on an aircraft carrier," Lisa told Stacey's mom, recounting the incident from the previous spring. It was one of the last times she found herself missing those friends: Bill, Rick, Kaylyn, and Ben. "Most unbelievable throw-up noise I've ever heard."

"Lisa, I'm so disappointed in you." Despite her mom's middle age, she still had eyes that somehow looked years younger. Bright and pale blue, they glittered when she smiled. As a child, Stacey envied her elegance, but as her mom aged and put on weight, Stacey felt herself wanting to stall time, to preserve her mother's joyous beauty in amber. "That's not even clever. You know what we did my senior year at Massillon? We found the frame for the make and model of the principal's car, and the boys assembled it on the roof of the high school. Not the whole car, mind you. Just the frame with the right paint color. Then my boyfriend at the time, he broke into the principal's car with a coat hanger, popped the brake, and we towed it to someone's house to hide it. The whole town thought we'd disassembled and reassembled the principal's car on the roof, and no one had any clue how we pulled it off. Then the next day we put his car back. How's that? Now that's a prank."

"Sounds like real braking news," said Lisa. "It must have been the torque of the town, huh?"

Stacey's mom threw her head back and positively *howled*.

The game was called Clawmaggedon. Quarter already deposited, waiting for her to smack the START button, Stacey instead held her phone and stared at the blank e-mail she'd opened. She tried typing: *Listen, I'm about to see your mom in New Canaan. I was wondering about you . . .*

And she quickly deleted it, the letters vanishing one at a time and then in wordly chunks.

She tried: *How have you been? So I'm in New Canaan because Bethany managed to track me down . . .*

And deleted it just as fast.

She tried: *You fucking cunt, hope you've had a splendid nine years . . .*

And deleted that as well.

She set her phone aside and slapped the START button. She crept the joystick to the corner as the timer began. There was one prize no one could ever get, these big stuffed lobsters that dwarfed the other toys. They were too big to grasp. The claw's pitiful tripod digits would close around the blue fur (like the lobsters were choking) and barely budge the behemoths. The only person she'd ever seen lift one out of the scrum was Rick Brinklan, who'd been preternaturally skilled at the game. He used to get a prize from the pit to the chute nearly every time for Kaylyn.

Rick had been the subject of one of her early fights with her brother, Patrick—although Patrick never really fought. He presented very cogent arguments in as agreeable and pleasant a manner as he could summon. He was polite and kind in his argumentation. She'd decided not to come home for Rick's funeral or parade. She'd stayed in Springfield for the summer, already researching teaching-abroad opportunities for when she graduated in a year, and the truth was she didn't feel like she still knew this person or owed him anything. More importantly, at that point in her life, she wanted to avoid the people she might see there. It was hard to describe to her brother when she finally did come home for Thanksgiving break.

"We weren't that close."

"You knew him from the time you were in sixth grade," he scolded in his reasoned, nonjudgmental way.

"It's just death, Pat. We'll all be there soon enough."

They were in his kitchen, and she remembered he was making her and the girls each a peanut butter and jelly sandwich. Her nieces ran amok in the living room, spazzing out over some kind of pink plastic toy with blaring, tinny speakers. As soon as these words left her mouth, she felt terrible about them. When she'd first started dating Ben, Rick had welcomed her to the group in his own Rickly way: by making it a running joke that she was too pretty, too smart, too good to date a "bubblegum airhead like Harrington." He got a lot of mileage out of that, and it wasn't so much that it made Stacey laugh as it made her feel comfortable around all of these older kids.

"What I want to know," said Patrick, "is what you did with my kid sister." He spun the top off the Sam's Club tub of peanut butter.

The arrogance of a wannabe academic humming sub-audibly beneath her every sentence (not to mention a burgeoning wish to hit back at her oldest brother), she did what most undergrads do, which was to pass off the very last thing she'd read as her own idea.

"It's like there's this simultaneity of the years 2003 and 1258. In 2003 we invaded Iraq, which kicked off the destruction of Iraq's museums and archives and all the looting of priceless pieces of art and artifacts in the aftermath. Which isn't that different from 1258 when

Genghis Kahn's grandson rolled with his Mongols into town, sacked the city, and destroyed the archives of that same civilization. For Iraqis, 1258 and 2003 might as well be one generation removed."

Cribbed from Dimock's *Through Other Continents*.

Patrick frowned like he was gravely concerned for her sanity. "What's your point, Stace?"

"People have other ways of looking at things." *Besides through Christ*, she did not add. "Like there's this idea of Deep Time. So the sacking of Baghdad in 1258 is right there in the historical memory of anyone living between the Tigris and Euphrates Rivers. Until 2003, when it all happened again. Then our government—which knows or cares about none of that—sends this kid from New Canaan, Ohio, and he's patrolling streets that probably existed in some form all those centuries ago."

Patrick slathered peanut butter across wheat bread, examining the knife's sworls skeptically. "Stace, what does that have to do with not coming home for the parade?"

In the back of Vicky's All-Night Diner, a waitress banged out of the kitchen carrying a full tray, and the blue lobster slipped from Stacey's proxy grasp, gripped between a pink elephant and a normatively colored killer whale, stuck in a quicksand of its peers. She decided to forgo the lobster and focus on a more malleable character, a purple pig the size of a softball. By the eye test, it seemed the pig's proportions would fit the spindly claw much better. She pressed the red button on the joystick, and the claw dropped. She hissed victory through her teeth as it lifted the pig skyward.

Then Clawmaggedon issued a broke-ass mechanical-clunk fart, and the lights of the game went dead. The claw slipped opened, and her piggy dropped right back into its plush prison.

"*What the fuck,*" she hissed without hearing herself. And banged plexiglass.

"It does that."

It was the scrubby kid, bearded, unwashed, and holding a plastic bag with a Styrofoam container of Vicky's to-go.

"They might give you your dollar back," he said, nodding to the two waitresses, now occupied. "You know, if it means that much to you."

"Just wanted that pig," she declared, slapping the plexiglass again. She kept her back to him to indicate that she did not feel like getting hit on right now.

"You're Patrick's sister?" At that, she turned to finally assess him. He had acne scars on his face and the yellow smile of a man happy to be working in a slaughterhouse or a prison. Crooked teeth and a tattoo of a cross on his arm, same spot as hers. "I was a year behind you in school," he explained. "And I go to the First Christian Church, so I know your brother pretty good."

"Oh," she said. "Nice to meet you—or see you again."

She wished for the game to fix itself, so she could turn her attention back to it.

"Do you live here or—"

"No," she said quickly. "Just passing through."

He nodded. She gestured to the register. "Gonna get my dollar back."

"Yeah. Hey." He reached out and touched her arm, and she tried not to pull it away too quickly or obviously. "I just gotta say—your brother is one of the best things to ever happen to me. I know you probably get that a lot, but I was in a real rough place when I met him. He helped me get clean and helped me find Christ again."

Sure he did. Maybe she'd acquired the bad habit of academicizing her memories, of trying to render them inert with the books she read and the theories she considered, but she recalled the days of her early twenties when her faith molted off like the dead skin of a snake. What a mystery everything suddenly seemed now that she was certain her dogma had been bogus. Creation, death? These were now free-floating, oppressively heavy possibilities. Where did one even begin to look? The answers she found were horrible in their lack of poetry. Socializing, organizing, family—all an adaptation to survive, accidentally sparking ingenuity, creativity, the creation of tools, and finally representations: codes, stories, art, culture. Experience distilled to essence. All she had believed as a child—all anyone believed, from the broken-hearted Muslim journeying to Mecca to her own devout family—was nothing more than the descendent of a hodgepodge shamanism, passed on, toyed with, whittled at, but ultimately the same nonsense. She wanted to ask this young man: *Because how else to explain the inexplicable, dude?* How to explain that we all show up to this party with no invite and no apparent host, and we can depart from it at any moment for no reason? The time she and Patrick had argued about Rick and Deep Time had been the same visit when she'd purposely taken Dawkins's *The God Delusion* into the open–floor plan living room to read in front of him. She kept her nose in it as he began preparing dinner, and when he finally asked what she was reading, she said the name of the book as if it tasted like a bite of velvety vanilla ice cream. Patrick only chuckled, half-amused, half-distracted, searching the fridge for something. *What a title*, he'd said. *Can you believe clowns like that? Scientists, I mean? They discover the quark or the gene and suddenly they decide they can write off what ninety-eight percent of humanity feels in our bones.*

For her brother's admirer, Stacey now put on a smile like a dress two sizes too small. "That's awesome. Yeah, he's great."

"Sorry to bother you, I just . . . I go to that church, and he's always talking about you actually. It's so funny running into you, but boy, you look just like him."

"Yeah, we get that a lot."

"He's just such an inspiring guy." He clearly wanted to say more, but she didn't let him.

She didn't care about the dollar but went to stand by the register. She waited until she saw him get in his car and back out into the square. Before she could find a seat in a booth, though, the door chimed. Her breath caught. Bethany scanned the diner until she spotted Stacey and gave a tepid little wave. All the years since she'd last seen Lisa's mother descended. The space between herself as an adult and as a child threatened to collapse, and she hated the rising pressure of the cold lump of fear that she thought she'd rid herself of long ago. How familiar, how endlessly reclaimable it felt now.

When Stacey was a child, she very much believed in Hell.

It kept her up at night, the sheer staggering bigness of suffering for eternity. She clutched the blanket over her head and wondered what that suffering would be like. She'd had pneumonia once as a little girl and abstractly recalled the pain that radiated from her chest down to her toenails, but even that seemed insufficient to that which was described. Heaven, conversely, was of little concern, the specifics always muted, uninteresting. Jesus was there, sure, but more importantly, it was the place you went that was *not* Hell. Pastor Jack ("Call me Pastor John. Johnny. Jack. Just don't call me late for dinner!") broached the issue as this regrettable addendum that he, unfortunately, was required to address. He didn't dwell on it; he wasn't much for fire and brimstone, but that made the instances he did bring it up all the more unsettling.

Because they were Grover Street Elementary peers and went to church camp together every summer, she was best friends with Tina Ross for a long time. As a girl, Tina was part of the reason she worried about Hell day and night. Tina could describe it so vividly: the sensation of burning alive, spears and knives run through you, demons taking out their sexual frustration on the damned. She had no clue where Tina got all this, but during sleepovers, she would describe it to her as clearly as if it were the Wyandot Lake water park (one of the few places for which the two young girls had the layout completely memorized).

"But it won't be us," Tina assured her. This was when they were maybe seven or eight, cocooned in the blankets of Tina's bed.

"But what if it is us?" she persisted. "We can't possibly do everything right."

"Sure we can." Even that young, Tina was already becoming gorgeous, and it was no secret at Grover Street that all the boys liked her. She reminded Stacey of a Siamese cat, her wide cheekbones giving her face the shape of a heart. She had flawless, seductive skin—some ancestor having added a dash of bronze. Maybe it had to do with envy, but she felt like Tina never lost an argument, certainly not about their faith. "We've accepted Jesus," Tina said. "We believe in Him, and we do His work. The only people who are in Hell are the ones who are supposed to be. They get their skin cut off in big strips and have hot needles put their eyes out over and over."

Tears came crawling to the corners of Stacey's eyes, and she wanted to tell Tina to stop but couldn't. She needed to know. Tina's dad ended up having to take her home that night when she refused to sleep with the lights off. A few nights later, Stacey's parents had Pastor Jack over so he could issue some corrections about what Hell meant and to reassure her that she had nothing to fear. The entire time, she could only picture Tina's descriptions.

When they got to high school, the two girls had the goal of taking over Fellowship of Christian Athletes. Stacey never attained higher office but Tina became secretary when she was just a sophomore. The school's largest extracurricular club met once a week in the cafeteria. It hosted speakers, shared stories, and prayed for various things (sick family members, sports victories, the usual). Members had locker signs with large crosses and Bible quotes (Stacey recalled only Lisa's: Paul's take on Romans 5:8, *I loved you at your darkest*). You didn't even have to be an athlete to attend. Every once in a while a troublemaking parent would protest the use of school property for religious organizing, but New Canaan was the wrong community in which to pick that fight. It wasn't until her senior year when she was agonizing about Lisa that Stacey heard the Sexual Purity Policy on the ministry leadership application form: "Neither heterosexual sex outside of marriage nor any homosexual act constitute an alternate lifestyle acceptable to God."

Tina, who colored the cross on her FCA locker sign pink and soon took up with the football team's co-captain, led the group in stridently, unapologetically earnest prayers. She wanted you to know the love of Jesus Christ so badly it made her ache at night. By high school, not only had their friendship withered and vanished, but for the first time Stacey had doubts.

It was hard for her to pin down when it started, but she remembered very well what Ben had to say during a double date to Columbus with Rick and Kaylyn.

"We're not Catholics," Rick said, in regards to Kaylyn being on birth control. Stacey had been plotting to do the same herself, but the thought of broaching the topic with her parents was semi-horrifying. "Premarital sex is one of those sins you can definitely get forgiveness for when the time comes. Jesus probably spends half his time rolling his eyes and saying, 'Yeah, yeah, premarital boning. Got it. Forgiven. Let's keep it moving.' " Rick was joking but not.

"Or it's all total horseshit malarkey, and you can have all the sex you want," said Ben, gazing out the window at the flat expanse of cornfields, barns, and country homes that peppered the drive south to Ohio's capital. Rick was behind the wheel, and his eyes fixed on Ben in the rearview mirror.

"Better be careful talking like that. A lightning bolt might hit the car, and I don't wanna get taken with you."

Ben sniggered. "If that's how it all works, maybe we should get God some Prozac or something."

"So wait." Kaylyn turned around and leaned all the way into the backseat. She never wore her belt. "You're with Ashcraft? You don't believe in God at all? Like, no God?"

"Him and Ashcraft believe in each other's buttholes," Rick chimed in.

"Bill's wrong about almost everything ever except this," said Ben. "I'm not saying there's no way, no how *not* a God, but the way they tell it to you? Like there's this omniscient dude watching us CIA-style and—you know—doling out rewards and punishments based on obscure, occasionally incoherent moral programs . . . Pretty dumb if you think about it."

Rick gave him a stupefied look. "Lightning is definitely striking you, Harrington. Stacey, you hearing this?"

She felt the clammy-palmed sensation of being asked to choose a side. This was early in her relationship with Ben, and all three of them were older, more popular, ready to judge her answer. She wanted to melt into the gray fuzzy material of the backseat.

"I don't know. I guess it's Ben's choice what he wants to believe."

"Yeah, it's just your eternal soul, dude. No biggie." Rick pushed back the Cleveland Indians hat on his skull and scratched at his hairline. "My question, I guess, is why not just believe anyway? Better safe than sorry, right? You pray a little, go to church enough, get right with God no matter what—and then what do you got to lose, Harrington?"

"That's Pascal's Wager, Brinklan. Someone already thought of that."

"So? Doesn't make it not true."

Ben shook his head, hair slipping across his brow, and he tossed it off with a buck of his head. "I'm saying this guy Pascal thought of that idea in like the seventeenth century. If that's all you got—better safe than sorry?—I'd start worshipping every other god you can. There's a long list of people out there who might be right about their god instead of yours."

"Jesus, please don't strike my car," Rick said to the roof. "Just because my sinning friend is in it. Wait till he's outside to get him."

They moved on to other topics, but that thing about Pascal sat with her. Later, at home, she looked it up and couldn't believe that Ben was right. She'd had this same theory, this wager, put in her head by Pastor Jack in different form, as the airtight case for why it's best to believe past all doubts and skepticism. For the longest time she'd thought it bulletproof. Many years later, she found herself unable to stomach her teenage naivety.

Even as an adult, Hell would return to her on occasion, unexpectedly, with violence. Like when her oldest brother sat her down in his kitchen and tried to save her. Patrick and his wife, Becky, had an unambiguous position about her "lifestyle," which they never brought up when the rest of the family was around. This began in 2005. After she came out to them, they were unfailingly polite and loving in the moment and then began to forward her the most offensive material one could possibly send a gay family member: the hard-core electroshock-the-fag-outta-you websites and "therapy" centers operated in Evangelical circles despite increasing ridicule by the mainstream.

"I'm not trying to hurt you. Or be cruel to you." Patrick wanted to know what she thought about seeing one of these therapists. "I love you. I'm concerned for you."

What she wanted to say—*If anyone other than you sent me a link to "therapy" like that, I'd set their fucking car on fire*—dangled on the tip of her tongue. And it stayed there. Becky had left the room on purpose, off pretending to fold laundry in the basement.

Stacey's nieces, Jamie and Elyse, were in bed. After dinner she'd played with them, their blinding blaze of adorable so acute, she knew she'd never risk estrangement.

"There's nothing to be concerned about," she told him. "This is just the way it is."

"It's the 'No Exception' clause, Stacey," he said gently. "You can't call yourself a Christian and then pick and choose which parts of it to follow. You commit to following Christ in every aspect of your life."

Her brother Matt was home when she came out, while Patrick was not, and sometimes she thought this explained the difference. Other times, she wondered if Pat's three years on Matt actually amounted to a generational separation on this issue. When Patrick, the primogeniture, became an adult in the late nineties, he hadn't known a single gay person (probably because they were all still in the closet). Then again, Matt had always been the family hellion—drinking and sneaking off with girls from the time he was in eighth grade—whereas Patrick and Becky actually *had* waited until their wedding night.

"I want you to take a look at this," he said, sliding the pamphlet across the kitchen table. It had a picture of a man and woman on a hike, holding each other's waists, staring into each other's eyes with the stupid smiles pamphlet people give each other to demonstrate true commitment. "Just look it over."

Both of her brothers inherited what Lisa called Mr. Moore's "Squaryan" looks: tall, chiseled, boringly handsome. Pat hadn't changed his haircut since he was ten: a helmet of stiffly gelled hair combed to the side. Fatherhood never softened his physique. Like Stacey, he was tall, athletic, and he still worked out, according to Becky, every day. He had virile, vein-bulging arms and looked impossibly hale and healthy. For some reason this made Stacey's surety flutter. Like, *Look at him. Maybe I have strayed.* And she felt her ancient fear of how long eternity could be.

"All you need to know for now, though, is that you're my sister and I love you." He beamed that resentment-incinerating smile. Then he leaned over and hugged her fiercely. These "recommendations" of Pat's had always been their secret. She had never told her parents about any of it.

"Stacey. Thank you thank you thank you so much for coming."

Before Stacey realized what she intended, Lisa's mother was hugging her, smelling like a room after it's doused in cleaning products and scrubbed. She received the embrace awkwardly, tried not to reciprocate, but found herself unable to be rude enough to pull away. This woman she hadn't stopped dreaming about for nearly a decade.

"Would you like something?" Bethany asked as they sat.

"I'll just have a Diet Pepsi. I still have an hour to Worthington after this."

"That's where your parents are now?"

"Yes."

"And how about your brothers? I see Patrick sometimes."

This was what she wanted least: to play catch-up like they were old friends.

"Patrick, Becky, and the girls are still here, and Pat just got a promotion at Jeld-Wen. Matt's in Columbus. He teaches high school PE and coaches the baseball team."

"That's wonderful. And you're back in school at Michigan?"

Bethany looked old, and even though it had been almost a decade since Stacey had seen her, this aging went beyond time's standard punishment. This was more than just ignoring the Revlon eye cream. She'd gained weight that stretched at her emerald blouse and the high waistband of her jeans. Her makeup cracked around wrinkles that had spread deep into her face. The droop beneath her chin waddled when she spoke. The flesh around her eyes was tumid, swollen as if from the scrape of tears. Her hair, the same highlighted, immobile bowl from high school, was the only part of her that seemed unchanged, and therefore it stood out. It looked like a wig.

"Yeah, for a doctorate in literature if everything works out."

"You couldn't go to OSU like a good Buckeye." She grinned. Stacey didn't respond, in no mood to fake like she cared for the ridiculous small talk people milk from a college sports rivalry.

"How are your parents?"

Working the zipper of her left boot up and down, feeling the satisfying click of the teeth, eased her pulse.

"They're fine. Dad's happy at the new job and Mom's back working a few days a week for an accounting office." In truth, her father had not been happy when Buckeye Mulch closed its New Canaan location, and he settled for a transfer that paid nearly fifteen thousand dollars less. Her mom had to go back to work, and he did not expect to retire for at least another ten years, but what was the point of bringing this up.

The waitress came, and she put in her Diet Pepsi order. It was a Coke establishment, so she settled. Bethany ordered non-caffeinated tea with lemon.

"What were you doing before Michigan?"

"I worked overseas for a long time. First, I was in Croatia teaching English, then I took a year to travel around Europe."

"Oh wow."

"After that I moved to Ecuador to do the same. Then when I got my acceptance letter from Michigan I spent six months traveling around South America."

Bethany smiled and nodded along. Stacey savored revealing how much she'd seen and done while this woman grew old in the same town where she was born.

"That's wonderful. That sounds really wonderful. And you got a tattoo." She pointed to Stacey's forearm. "What's it mean?"

"It's from a poem."

"Oh."

The waitress brought her Diet Coke and Bethany's tea. When she left, Bethany sipped, delicately replaced the cup in the saucer, folded her hands, and said, "I suppose you want to know why I asked you here."

She waited, arms crossed.

"First, I just wanted to say that . . ." She fidgeted with the straw in her water. "I don't want to drag up old things. We don't need to talk about old things. But I do want to say I'm sorry for all that happened with you and Lisa back then."

"You're sorry for what happened between us?" Her heart quickened, and her blood felt thick and fast. She heard Patrick saying, *Hell is real, Stacey.* Followed by the phantom scent of his Pine-Sol–smelling cologne. "Or you're sorry for what you did? How *you* acted."

Bethany closed her eyes for a long moment, as if in prayer. When she opened them, she said, "I'm sorry for the way I behaved. Like I said, I do not want to drag up old things. But yes, you girls didn't deserve . . . the way I reacted to everything. Those old things, though—that's water gone under the bridge."

She wanted her to call them *old things* one more time, so she could summon a satisfying fury.

"Fine. Water under the bridge. Apology accepted. Glad we cleared all that up. Now we can just be some gal pals gabbing at Vicky's, I guess? Great."

She hated how she sounded, shrill and emotional and vicious, but after nearly ten years, there was a speech much more cruel trying to clamor up out of her from some dark hole, reaching for daylight. It was all she could do to keep this from metastasizing into a wail of accusations and tears.

Bethany gnawed a fingernail. She could see the ragged cuticle and all the tiny, nibbled wounds. The highways of blue and purple veins on her hand.

"And I'm sorry. I am. I've had so much time to think, Stacey. You don't know how much I've prayed about this. Years and years. I know the way I reacted—I know you girls weren't—I got this from her last month."

As if just recalling it, she reached for her purse and pulled out a postcard, the corners worn from handling. Stacey stopped playing with her boot's zipper and took it from her. A picture of a gondola-like boat docked in front of temples with tiers like birthday cakes and sharp, needlelike spires rising into mauve twilight. She flipped it over and immediately recognized Lisa's looping cursive scrawl. Her handwriting rang of who she was: wild, unpredictable, devil-may-care letters.

"It's why I wanted to see you. She doesn't write much. But enough that I know she hasn't given up on me. And now at least I know where she is. I know I haven't done everything I can to say I'm sorry. To get her to come home."

Took a two-week trip to Bangkok. Beautiful city, beautiful country, beautiful people. Strange, but the pollution makes the color of the sky here remind me of home—or maybe I just stole that from a Harrington song ☺ Have been thinking of you. Hope all is well. Permission to turn my room into a hot tub/party spa.

—L

She felt a sting behind her eyes and quickly handed the postcard back. "I don't know what this has to do with me."

"Yes. I . . ." Bethany took a moment to sit up, her eyelids in a hummingbird flutter to keep back her own tears. "I know she left for many reasons, and even though she writes me—not very often, but she does—she keeps talking about how apologizing isn't what she wants. But she never says what she does want."

"Maybe she's not interested in forgiveness," Stacey said. "Maybe she doesn't want to come back and never will."

"I've considered that. I have. But . . . you see, she has been back. The last e-mail she sent, Alex told me he checked something called an IP address. Do you know that?"

In her stomach, she felt ripples of nausea, of insects scuttling over one another.

"Yeah, of course."

"Right. So he said this e-mail—I think it was the summer of 2011—it was sent from a computer in Ohio. At the New Canaan Public Library. She came home and left without telling me. I wrote over and over to ask her why, but she never e-mailed back. Then finally, I get this postcard from her—finally she writes to me . . ."

The sting behind Stacey's eyes grew sharper. She wouldn't have been in the country then, but Lisa never so much as reached out to ask.

"I keep thinking . . . I keep telling myself that she'll come around. That's what Bob keeps saying. But it's been nine years since she left. Ten years next summer. And I don't know what else to do. I've tried everything. I lie awake praying until I'm exhausted all day every day. I just want her to come home to me."

Her voice cracked on the last few words, and Stacey could see how this particular mode of crying had impacted her face, gouging specific wrinkles into her mouth and brow, around her eyes. Stacey tried to hold on to what she'd carried for so long. She wanted to spit on her. Ask her what she'd do if Lisa brought home a real butch dyke. Nine years spent loathing Bethany for her cruelty, for driving away someone she'd loved, and she sprang a couple of goddamn tears, and it all went melting away.

Because I know exactly how she feels. And suddenly her bitterness was directed elsewhere.

"I guess I don't understand what you're asking me for, Bethany."

"Just . . ." She pinched the knuckle of her index finger hard, like she might rip it off. "I don't know. Just write to her. She might listen to you. If you tell her how sorry I am, and how badly . . ." Her voice cracked again in that discomfiting pre-sob way. The waitress passed from the kitchen and darted a curious glance in their direction before minding her own business. "Just tell her how badly I miss her."

They sat in the booth for a while longer, Bethany dabbing her eyes with a napkin, Stacey staring at the table. Finally, Stacey said, "I'm not in touch with her. I haven't spoken to her since . . . I don't even know." This was a lie. She knew the time stamp on the last e-mail Lisa ever wrote to her because she'd just looked at it: 4:54 a.m. EST, September 2, 2004.

"I'm not asking you to move mountains, Stacey. But I know she still cares about you. If you talk to her, she might listen."

She put her hand on Stacey's. How quickly contempt can dissipate when faced with the pathetic humanness of another person. You see inside them for even the briefest moment and suddenly empathy blows through. A dark sky cleared by a hard rain.

"I can't promise anything. But if I do talk her, I'll tell her what you said."

She was not great at staying friends with people. Her family was her only constant, and she was one of those lucky/unfortunate women who was best friends with her mom since the moment she learned to speak. Other than that, whoever Stacey was dating tended to be her most intense friend until that relationship ran its course, at which point she was back to square one. It was surely a lousy way to organize her friendships, but she seemed incapable of adaptation. Natalya, an artist of indeterminate income and reputation with whom she spent a month living in Lithuania, asked Stacey when she knew she was gay. Young Lithuanians are a gorgeous people with a preponderance of neck moles, and Natalya had a line of them down the left side of her neck and one near her nipple on her otherwise milky and objectively incredible body. Most of Natalya's art was zombie-related: massive canvases filled with hordes of the living dead shredding the flesh of terrified men and sultry women. Natalya's zombies were overtly sexual. They ate the genitals first. The clothes of their victims always seemed to come sluicing off mid-portrait. They had disagreements about what the popularity of zombies signified (Natalya thought it was the suffocation of sexuality, the fear-mongering of the dominant culture that sought to eradicate non-normative sexual practices; Stacey, of course, maintained that it was a metaphor for pandemic, resource scarcity, and ecological collapse). Natalya claimed she knew her destiny as a sexual being when she was just a small girl, that she drew pictures of her female friends and watched them while they slept. Stacey found this impossible to understand because she truly had no clue.

There was a Goth girl two grades ahead of her, marginalized even within the school's marginalized population. She wore baggy jeans and Slipknot T-shirts, dyed her hair black and red, had a face full of piercings by age fifteen, and coated herself in white makeup until she had the complexion of a mannequin. Bloodred lipstick and the eyeliner quantities of a comic book villain. A bit overweight but still pretty beneath all her attempts not to be. Stacey could no longer recall her name. It was in the second-floor bathroom, just the two of them, when she was coming out of the stall as Stacey was walking toward one. She knew in the back of her head that this girl had noticed Stacey noticing her. That sometimes Stacey stared at her for reasons that were inexplicable to her at the time. She looked

Stacey up and down and sneered, "Want me to eat your pussy on the toilet, Stretch?"

Stretch, Stacey supposed, because she was tall.

Of course, she reacted with horror, turned a deep shade of pink that must have still been on her face when she got to class because her music teacher, Mr. Clifton, asked if she was all right. That night she masturbated for the first time in her life, and wouldn't you know she was in such phenomenal denial about herself that she didn't put two and two together until years later.

Then there was Kaylyn. Before things began in earnest with Lisa, when they were dating the three boys, and they were all just friends, Kaylyn was the pure, unchecked, blood-tingling crush she chose to never acknowledge. If eugenics experiments became commonplace and were led by a bunch of horny, scrotum-petting midwestern boys, Kaylyn would be their product. Long and slim, trash-sexy, she was always coiled around something, serpentine in her movements. At lunch, she'd pull apart her sandwich, eat the turkey, and then scrape the mayo off with long, lascivious strokes of her tongue before throwing out the bread. On the floor in Lisa's basement, writhing in her own stillness, her dirty blond waterfalling on the carpet as she lay with her head propped on her hand. At a dance, arms draped around Rick's industrial shoulders, hips swishing while he stood stock-still and enjoyed it like he was at a strip club. Even at her desk at school, she sat in such a way that her body seemed to melt over it. Stacey would study her face and try to understand how she plucked her eyebrows into these slim, skeptical arches; wish for the sprinkling of freckles and crystal eyes. She never felt entirely comfortable being alone with Kaylyn. At first she thought it was because she was older, desired by the entire school, but really Stacey was a part of that mess of desire. She wanted to feel different pieces of Kaylyn to see if her fingers might evanesce into those parts if she gripped hard enough.

"Stace." Kaylyn beckoned her to hang back. They were on their way from the locker room to the court for a game against Mansfield Senior, arch nemesis of Jags volleyball. It was Stacey's first game on varsity, and she had so much raw energy, she thought she might be able to break a nose with her spike if she got the right set. So when Kaylyn slipped a little blue pill into her palm, smiled, and bounced her dirty blond eyebrows, she already wasn't thinking clearly.

"What is it?" Stacey asked her.

"Adderall, darling—nothing wild."

"What's it do?"

Kaylyn laughed. She had her hair pulled into a tight Dutch braid, so sturdy it looked like you could use it to climb to a castle keep. Stacey had a couple inches on her, but Kay had the most penetrating green-eyed stare. She vivisected you every time she glanced your way.

"It gives you hallucinations of spiders crawling all over your skin." And Stacey's face must have gone dumb with shock because Kaylyn burst into bright laughter. "Jesus, Moore, it's for concentration. It's an ADHD med. It'll help you focus out there. I wouldn't poison you. Although I admit, one time I did feed Jess Bealey an ex-lax–laced empanada on Mexican food day in Spanish. Slut had it coming, though."

Stacey so did not want to take that pill, but Kay's eyes were on her, waiting, and her palm seemed to draw it up to her mouth of its own accord. That game, she regretted every moment on the court, where she felt jumpy and wired and three times sent the ball sailing over the heads of Mansfield and into the crowd.

Yet for all her devilish qualities, there was subterranean delicacy to Kaylyn as well. Stacey saw it on the rare occasions she needed a breath from her inhaler, which she hated doing in front of people. In their last game of the season, Kaylyn got a vicious asthma attack. No one could find her inhaler, and they had to stop the game. Lisa and their coach rubbed her back while the team tore apart the visitors' locker room. When the inhaler was finally found (on her seat on the bus), Kaylyn wrapped her lips greedily around the device and depressed the canister with her thumb, but she still looked terrified. Like maybe despite the medicine, her next breath still wouldn't come.

It wasn't until after Kaylyn graduated in '03, along with Rick, Ben, and Bill, that Stacey came to think of her differently. She asked Lisa if she thought she'd visit Kaylyn in college.

"Not likely."

They sat cross-legged on the carpet in her room, looking at Lisa's books. She pulled and piled them, agonizing over what to put in Stacey's hands next. *Gaia* still sat on her shelf, unnoticed.

"We grew up in the same neighborhood, then played volleyball, and then our boyfriends were gay for each other. But I don't think we have anything in common."

"That actually sounds like the definition of friendship, Han. Like long-lasting, maid-of-honor-at-your-wedding friendship."

Lisa flipped her hair back in an exasperated gesture. "You're kind of a nag, you know that?"

"Just curious. Seems like you and Kay and Hailey went from dudettes to enemies and none of you even knows why."

"Dudettes," she repeated, smirking. "With Kowalczyk, it's different. That was stupid freshman chick shit because she was being a total monster to Danny." Lisa and her Rainrock Road club. Her loyalty to Dan Eaton had no explanation, no comparable situation in her life, and no limits. She simply loved this goofy neighbor kid and was as protective of him as of a three-legged puppy. "With Kaylyn, you know . . . Trust me. She's two-faced. So like Bill used to win over my stepbrother by buying him packs of basketball cards—when Alex was that age where it was all he cared about. Not to mention he worshipped Bill, loved watching him play and all that. For his birthday, Bill bought him this expensive card, you know, supposedly worth fifty bucks or something ridiculous. This Shaquille O'Neal rookie card. And this became Alex's total obsession. He had this fishing tackle box that my stepdad gave him, and he kept all his favorite cards in it, but this Shaq card he kept in a hard plastic case in his pocket. Took it everywhere. Then one day it goes missing, and he was, like, freaking out. Crying, screaming at us, the whole thing. So even though he's a shit, I helped him look for it, and we tore the house apart, but it never turned up. Anyway, like a year later I was at Kaylyn's house spending the night—I think you might have been there—we were in the living room hanging out, and I wanted to change into shorts. So I went to her room and was looking through her drawers for a pair. I'll admit I got kind of snoopy once I opened the top drawer because she had all these little knickknacks under her clothes, lots of strange stuff. But then I found this little sandwich bag with some pieces of cardboard inside, and as I was looking at them, I realized it was my brother's Shaq card. She'd shredded it and then kept the pieces. I never told anyone. But from that moment on, I just never trusted her."

"She stole your brother's card, and that's why you don't talk anymore?"

"No. That's not at all what I mean. I mean she's not— You don't really know Kaylyn, Stace. You just don't. Like there are issues at play. Alex's card is just a good example."

Stacey didn't believe that this story was anything more than a cop-out. Lisa was a bad liar, bad at masking whatever hurt boiled inside her, but she didn't take it any further. Kaylyn was gone anyway, and all Lisa was saying was maybe that was for the best.

Leaving Vicky's All-Night Diner, Stacey walked Bethany Kline to the same beige sedan she remembered from high school, the fender dinged, a hubcap missing. Bethany hugged her again.

"Thank you so much for seeing me," Bethany breathed into her ear. "Even if you don't end up writing her, thank you for doing this. I know it couldn't have been easy for you."

Stacey started to say something, stopped, and just said, "Yeah. I will think about it."

Bethany squeezed her hand and gave her a weak, hopeful smile. In her car, Bethany reversed into the square and gave Stacey a little wave before heading west, back to her house on Rainrock Road. Suddenly Stacey felt the tension she carried, her whole body coiled with some evolutionary pressure. She tried to release it, to picture foul water draining down a sink. The conversation had been nothing she'd expected yet everything she should have anticipated, and now one thing rang in her mind: *Lisa had come home.* She'd been back to New Canaan.

She still had to deliver her letter, just a short walk from the square, but there she was: hesitating, and when she realized that hesitation was possibly guilt or pity or remorse for what she'd written, she loathed herself. To decide if this letter was something she wanted truly or just selfishly. *This fucking town*, she thought.

New Canaan, sclerotic in every capacity. Slow to adapt to manufacturing's flight to the far-flung corners of the Orient, to the progressive urges of a demographically shifting nation, and obviously to the tolerance of anything but heterosexual behavior. Bethany had simply reacted to her world, the closed circuit from which she came. Yet it was so strange for Stacey to see her broken like this, to see the fight drained out of her. The woman who'd stood outside Kroger handing out pamphlets to support Issue 1 back in '04—how hard had it been for her to get over her own prejudices? Probably as hard as it was for Stacey's younger self to admit to everything it took her so long to admit to. You make someone your devil for long enough, and you want to hold on to that. There's something rapturous about hating another person, especially if you have a goddamned good reason. And had Election '04 not been during her first semester in college, wouldn't she have been right there beside Bethany, gathering signatures to get the "protect marriage" amendment on the ballot? Hadn't her own parents gone with Bethany to pass out a few themselves? Hadn't Patrick spoken on the issue in church? Stacey bought into the whole spiel back then. It seemed perfectly logical to her that people's perversions were the result of wandering from the path of Jesus Christ. Too many people had put down the Bible and replaced it with hedonism and false idols: celebrities, musicians, all the other monsters under the bed. Hell, her first vote was for the reelection of George W. Bush. She could still hear some of the rhetoric coming out of her mouth as a teenager. Not that she went on about it all the time, especially not once she started dating Ben, who was not religious and was the first person she ever heard articulate why he was not. It's a strange feeling: to be ashamed and embarrassed of who you used to be. Even with the excuses of youth, inexperience, and influence—her church, her parents, her older brothers, her friends, almost everyone she knew—it still made her deeply uncomfortable to think of herself back then, who she might have hurt without knowing it.

You only get one childhood, one chance at formation, and Stacey would carry those lessons with her long after she'd ruled their conclusions bogus. Such lessons came conjoined at the heart, Siamese twins, to the dizzying sensation that settles in when a person of faith comes to understand that, after all this, it's logical that only darkness awaits.

She pulled out her phone. Before she could think too much about it, she wrote: *Hey. Back in The Cane thinking of you. Let me know what you're up to.*

And hit Send.

* * *

In Croatia, Stacey met a scientist giving a lecture at the University of Zagreb. She was finally reading *Gaia* at the time, when she saw a flyer on campus advertising a lecture on ocean heat by a professor of thermal and fluid sciences from Berlin. Hilde was in her midforties, with bags under her eyes to mark those years, but she was still striking, as tall as Stacey, with blond hair pulled back into a tight bun and sharp, V-shaped eyebrows. She wore neon-pink Nike running shoes during her lecture. Scientists in her field were gathering new data on ocean temperature using the "Argo float system" and now, she said, the trick would be to reconcile this data with the measurements taken previously by the inferior bathythermographs. When she looked up from her notes, her eyes kept finding Stacey. She needed only to wait for a few minutes following the talk before Hilde approached her. Stacey spent the next four nights in Hilde's hotel room.

"You are quite the conquest for me," she said in her lightly accented English. The sexuality of the German accent never got enough credit in Stacey's opinion. "An American coed is the hardest kind of cunt to eat, but also the sweetest. My father once said that."

Stacey burst out laughing. "What did you just say?"

Grinning, Hilde explained, "We are a very bohemian family." Propped on her elbows in bed, Stacey was staring at her and got caught. "What is it?" Hilde asked.

"Nothing," said Stacey. "You remind me of someone I knew once."

Hilde had wanted to be a dancer until she tore her meniscus, lost too much time, and had to give it up for ocean science. She bought Stacey expensive meals and cocktails, and they saw Zagreb together. She stank of cigarettes always, and to this day Stacey could not smell cigarette smoke without thinking of her. Beyond her sexual prowess, Hilde was impressive in every way—traveled, intelligent, fascinating. There was no subject she didn't seem to understand in its minutiae, from the architectural design of Zagreb's opera house, the HNK, to the Greek debt crisis. They were three of the best days of Stacey's travels in Europe. For the first time since Lisa Han, she was astonished again: by food, by her orgasm, by the hard spring wind, by the pleasure of painting her toes an azure blue.

"What were you doing at a lecture on ocean heat?" Hilde asked her at a café. "I saw you in the front row and pegged you for an American but also for a student."

Stacey showed Hilde the book she was reading. She did not mention the photograph she'd found still stuck in the pages: Bethany Kline, carrying Lisa in utero the day before she was born. She'd held the photograph for a moment, wanting to shred it and let the pieces fall in the wastebasket, but something stopped her. Instead, she went to the library where she pulled a book from the shelves at random and stuck the photo in its pages. The picture wouldn't be gone but neither would it be with her.

"But you in no way want to be a scientist?" Hilde asked.

"No. I think if I go back to school, it'll be for literature."

"Why literature?"

"I don't know. Probably because it interests me the same way ocean temperature interests you. The story. I once read this book about how literature was this vast conversation that mocked all the borders we normally think of: state boundaries, our own life spans, continents, millennia. That's why I like this so much." She tapped *Gaia*, sitting on the table between their cups of espresso. "It has this idea in it about how incomprehensible and ancient . . ." She searched. " . . . *We, this, us, it* is."

Hilde pursed her lips around a cigarette, the lines around her mouth deepening momentarily.

"Our birthright, then?" said Hilde. "Generations of imaginative, creative, scientific labor—this journey we're on, looking outward and inward. To our own psyche, our own subatomic structures, the heavens, all that?"

"Sure," said Stacey. "I don't know. I had a weird childhood. It took me a long time to consider any of this. I'm basically just a dilettante trying to sound impressive." And she laughed nervously.

Hilde took a long pull of her cigarette, releasing the smoke from the side of her mouth. "You do that a lot you know."

"Do what?"

"These self-denigrating comments. Especially as it relates to you being from your—how did you say? 'Bumblefuck' town? You should break yourself of that habit. You're here. You're curious about the world. You read widely. It doesn't matter where you come from. Neither does it really matter where you go. It's all the sex and sandwiches in between."

Stacey could feel her face turning as pink as Hilde's Nikes, one of which she twirled in small circles beneath the table. Hilde reached out and thumped *Gaia* with the two sturdy, sexy fingers that held the cigarette. "In this book, this man Lovelock talks about his job in London during the Second World War where he checked the quality of the air in the shelters belowground. Have you read this part yet?"

"I have, yes."

"So you understand the metaphor? Finding that vandals kept stealing the bolts holding the tunnel together in order to sell for scrap?"

"Yeah, of course. He was afraid the tunnel would collapse. Just because it hadn't yet, the thieves kept stealing the bolts. Figuring everything would be okay."

"That's right." She'd smoked her cigarette down to the filter and waggled the smoldering butt in the air before her face. "It's not that I disagree with you that literature can mock our human life spans, but I question whether there's any use left for what we call art or literature or culture—however you want to phrase it."

"How's that?"

"You follow your heart, pretty American lady." Hilde smiled. "Don't let me persuade you differently."

"But what do you mean?"

"I mean we are no longer cataloguing life with art, which is perhaps why art is failing. Life itself has become the final disposable, exploitable resource. We will do anything. Level whole mountains, erase whole species, relocate mighty rivers, burn forests to the ground, change the pH of the water, blanket ourselves in toxic chemistry. It took two million years for our species just to stand up and only five hundred generations to do the rest. Our culture is one of abundance, of entitlement, and basically little else. We've put our birthright at risk because we don't know how to control ourselves. Our lust."

In the years that followed, her memory of Hilde came with slices of imagined scenes: a bar's low yellow lighting, the underside of a bridge at night, a lace slip tossed over an antique metal screen, smoky whiskey stirring in a glass—but it would also come with that word *lust* used to describe not sexual desire but a remembrance of evil not yet done. Without understanding why, Stacey found her feelings hurt. It was in that very specific way from childhood when the older girl you love so much suddenly turns to you at recess and calls you stupid for believing a thing that before seemed so self-evident. "No such thing as the tooth fairy!" That kind of thing. They walked the streets of Zagreb on their last day together and Stacey couldn't think of much to say. Hilde had an early flight back to Berlin the next morning and woke Stacey only to tell her to sleep in. When Stacey finally did get up (too enamored of the plush hotel bed to not milk every last dream from it), she found a note leaning against a coffee cup.

Stacey,

Don't listen to an old, bitter woman. The heat in the oceans cannot stop literature nor joy! Here's some Yeats, lovely girl. Enjoyed our weekend together immensely.

And beneath this a snippet from a poem. An artifact she planned to hang on to.

The stoplights all burned green as far as she could see. She opened the passenger door of her Jeep and picked up the envelope with her letter. Sharp white edges pricked the pads of her fingers. She felt in herself the rebellion of doing the hard thing yet again.

She slipped the letter into her purse, ready to set off, but then, like an apparition, the zombie version of her freshman year homecoming date appeared before her covered in blood.

Jonah Hansen's sneakers patted the pavement, and as they approached, the dismembered horse clops of her boots mixed with these new percussions to nearly create a beat.

It wasn't the Jonah who had slipped the corsage on her wrist and then made a farting noise at his friends while all the couples' parents took pictures. It was Jonah grown up, buzzed head of hair going chemo-patient bald and seeming to bulge in a vaguely alien way with one of those ridiculous beards now popular in exurban America, the kind where the sideburns grow in a thin line down the jaw, connecting at the chin. It was Jonah with blood coating his nostrils and streaming down over his lips and chin, a cravat of dried crimson on his T-shirt. They both stopped and regarded each other. Tears crawled from his eyes, comingling with the ruins of his nose. He didn't say anything, so she felt it incumbent to acknowledge who each of them were.

"Jonah? It's Stacey. Stacey Moore."

He sniffed back blood and tears.

"Hey," he said, a noncommittal grunt.

"Are you okay?"

His eyes flitted evasively. She wondered if he had gotten jumped or hit by a car. "Yeah," he said.

"Your nose."

"S'fine."

She looked around the square to see what might be open. Of course, it was only the diner.

"Here, why don't we go into Vicky's? We'll get some napkins and ice."

He regarded her with suspicion.

"Didn't I hear you were a dyke now?"

Her laugh was loud and surprised. "That has no impact on my knowledge of how to stop a bloody nose."

He chortled, the blood rattling in his sinuses.

"C'mon," she said, and he followed her back in.

Senior year Jonah Hansen had all the wildest parties. His dad traveled a lot (although he was a local real estate baron, so that didn't make much sense) and his mother was a wraith, almost without presence (which usually meant a pill addiction). Jonah was popular by virtue of his family's barn, which wasn't a barn in the horse-and-hayloft sense but an enormous rec room decked out with a TV, surround sound speakers, a huge multi-couch seating area, pool table, and air hockey. In a factory and farming community like New Canaan, it was kids like Jonah who tended to command high social status, the "preps" as they were all called, and when you're a teenager and have never read Marx, you just think in this tautology: "These are the popular people because they're popular." Only in hindsight do you understand you could probably correlate the cliques of high school directly to each family's bank account.

Like Stacey, Jonah was a Grover Street kid, and his family went to her church. At a party in sixth grade, he dealt perhaps the greatest, most horrific blow to her adolescent self-esteem when they were playing Spin the Bottle at Ron Kruger's house. They'd already been through the first round of kissing without tongue. Someone suggested they leap to "feeling up," and Stacey was terrified but not enough to object to this new level of intimacy. On the very first spin, Jonah landed the bottle on her, and he said—she would never forget—"What? How'm I supposed to get a feel on those mosquito bites?"

Some of the girls gasped, some of the boys laughed, and Stacey sat mortified, smiled, and then allowed his hand to cup her training bra while they kissed anyway. She thought about this incident the rest of that year.

When Jonah asked her to homecoming freshman year, she'd angrily thought of that moment, wanting to ask him if her breasts were sufficiently filled in for him now. But your first homecoming is an event where you're already terrified of who will ask you, and she had it on good information that a rather unfortunate-looking boy named Amos Flood was plotting to corner her. Amos was acne-riddled, overweight, frighteningly sweaty, and to the previous point, poor. He and his cousins lived on a farm/compound and the parents were in jail or gone, the grandparents left to scrape for a pack of troubled kids. Stacey made the error of being kind to him in an eighth-grade home economics class, and she'd felt him longing for her ever since. To a freshman girl already petrified by the thought of stepping outside the boundaries, who had popular older brothers (one graduated, one on the football team) and was desperate to not be the weird little sister, Amos was unacceptable. Jonah at least made for a decent excuse to turn Amos down gently.

Her parents—especially her mom—did not like the Hansens.

Rarely an unkind word to say about anybody, she referred to Jonah's dad, Burt, as "the used-car salesman." When Stacey visited her folks after returning briefly from Europe in 2010, the Hansens had been a hot topic of conversation because her dad couldn't figure how Burt Hansen had not lost his shirt in the crash. It made no sense, according to her dad, because there wasn't a buyer left for all the housing developments Burt had financed over the last ten years, yet they'd heard from the Eatons that he'd just bought a new boat. Such was the way of the Hansens, though.

"Some people are just impervious to bad luck," her dad said.

It was from Jonah's homecoming party their senior year that Stacey pilfered a bottle of vodka from his stash. She and Lisa had gone stag, made a brief appearance at Jonah's, then slipped away to Lisa's house. They had to wait for Bethany to go to bed before cracking open the vodka, and Stacey remembered Bethany gently cleaning the makeup off her daughter's face. ("You look so beautiful the way you do this eyeliner, you'll have to show me that.") Even though all Stacey wanted was to go up to Lisa's room where the vodka waited in her overnight bag, and even though Lisa's constant carping had taught her to view Bethany as an odious old troll out to ruin all their fun, Stacey watched and thought about how mother and daughter looked, for once, at peace and in love.

When Bethany finally let them retire they put a rented tape, *Casablanca*, in the built-in VCR of Lisa's little cube TV. This had been a point of contention after it came up that Stacey had never seen it.

"Are you fucking kidding me, bitch?"

"So it was never on my radar, Han. Why, you gonna cry about it?"

Nodding furiously. "Yes, I might. If we watch it, I might."

"Naw. You won't. You don't cry. You're not capable."

"I'm telling you, I don't know what it is about that movie, but it, like, guts me every time."

"It's in black and white!"

"Your soul is a cake full of shit."

Stacey cracked up and felt a surge of an emotion she wasn't mature enough to identify.

As the movie began, she showed her Jonah Hansen's bottle. A red label named for a Russian peninsula. Lisa's mouth curled up in a wry smile. "Thank you, Jonah."

Beneath all Lisa's posters of bad-boy musicians—she'd gone to great lengths to frame Nelly's shirtless bod in white Christmas lights—they added the vodka to mugs of Sprite in drips and drabs and watched *Casablanca*. Stacey didn't care much for old movies. Something about the way they're staged, all the action and dialogue stilted and lacking verisimilitude. But Bogart and Bergman in that movie. Jesus. And sure enough, when the film began to wrap up, when the Nazis were closing in and Rick forces Renault at gunpoint to help Ilsa get away, she glanced over at Lisa and saw her biting the sleeve of her sweatshirt, cheeks shiny with tears. Then Lisa's hand moved under the blanket. Stacey's heart beat at her ribs so hard she thought Lisa might be able to hear it. Lisa's fingers laced into hers and held on for the rest of the movie, her thumb occasionally rubbing the knuckle.

By the time the movie was over, Stacey was drunk and not thinking about anything. She leaned over and kissed Lisa gently on the cheek. She gave her time to flinch, but she didn't. She tried it again on Lisa's mouth. Then her tongue, thick and wet and delicious, pressed against Stacey's. For once, Lisa didn't have a snarky comment.

Soon they were necking like the uncertain teenagers they were, unsure of what to do with their hands, how to transition further. She didn't think of anything while they did it. No shame, no questions, no worry, no fear, just the eager work of her lips, slivers of silk buds for her tongue and mouth to explore, pleasant in the way a man's lips just cannot be. It was strange, but Stacey could not recall the necking as viscerally as holding Lisa's hand as the movie ended. Nothing—not sex, not drugs, not waking on a train to the sight of dawn breaking over the Carpathian Mountains—nothing had ever been as exciting as watching the last part of *Casablanca* while she held Lisa's hand under that blanket. She could still remember the way their palms sweated together, feel the ghost of that moisture—and how it would cloud everything for the coming year and all the ones beyond.

The poet waitress got Jonah situated with a thick stack of napkins, a glass of water, and a baggie of ice. He worked two of the napkins up his nostrils and went about cleaning his face off with water. Because she felt bad about these free-of-charge services, she ordered another Diet Coke with no intention of drinking it. She had a makeup mirror in her bag that Jonah used to clean the worst of the dried blood from his face, but some of it clung to the black of his stubble and each hair got a murderous crimson shading around the follicle that he couldn't scrub out.

"Can I ask what happened?"

He made a scoffing noise in his throat. "Fucker sucker punched me in the bar."

"A fight, huh."

"No, like a faggot punched me when I wasn't expecting it."

"Why?" He rolled his eyes but said nothing, as though the answer was obvious.

"You know who I saw there?" he said. "Dan Eaton and Bill Ashcraft. Tonight's like a class reunion or something."

And she blinked at this hum of concurrence.

"What's Ashcraft doing back? Which bar?" Just hearing Bill's name, let alone that their ships had cruised so close on this night, awoke in her all the old resentments even though he'd had Lisa before she even knew that was who she wanted.

"Not sure. They came into the Lincoln. We had some beers. Guessed about The Murder That Never Was. Why are you back in town? Seeing your bro? Moving back to good ole New Cane?"

"Just passing through," she said. "I haven't been back in a while."

"Not fucking much's changed." His spittle leapt across the table on the f-bomb, some of it hitting her face in that chilled shrapnel way. She hadn't realized until that moment how drunk he was. His eyes lolled about in their sockets like the orbs were stumbling away from each other. His speech wasn't slurred, but it had that sharp certainty that the best angry drunks get right before they black out.

"Do you want to report him? The guy who did this, I mean?"

"Wouldn't give the motherfucker the satisfaction. He's a Brokamp, a food stamper, so jail's probably where he wants to be. Get-rich-quick scheme of the lazy."

"You should put the ice on your left eye," she said. "That's the one that's going to swell." He examined his face in the mirror, a face that when they were young had looked sharp and dashing, a strong, sturdy nose and a tough, resolute chin with a perfect dimple in the center. What kids fondly called a "butt chin." Now the face was well on its way to middle age with soft bloat growing around the jowls. When you reach your late twenties, you notice your peers beginning to go one way or the other. Some retain their youth effortlessly, others begin to take on time like water gushing into a breach in the hull.

He snapped the compact mirror closed and handed it back. "Remember we used to come here every weekend." He removed the napkins from his nostrils, pointed into dual thimbles of wet blood, and stuffed two fresh corners up each. "Time does fly."

It now occurred to her that Jonah, hanging around New Canaan all these years, woven into the fabric of the town the way he was, might have heard about Lisa coming back. The waitress returned with Stacey's second Diet Coke of the night. As she walked away, Stacey opened her mouth to ask him if he knew or had heard anything about Lisa, but he spoke right over her.

"I got a helicopter." The comment was sufficiently weird that her jaw closed. "Been doing real well. Making deals. Land development. And our house in Lake Erie. On South Bass Island. You and me can go there tonight. It's less than a half-hour flight."

How careful she was not to laugh in his face, the baseless confidence of his youth suddenly clownish.

"Wow, that does sound tempting."

"You can't be *all* lesbo." He grinned. "You got needs like any other woman."

"Don't I know it."

His mouth melted into a bemused smile. He ran each index finger along a sideburn, tracing the frame of his red-tinted beard all the way to his chin. She thought she could see the imprint of a skull on his cheekbone, almost like a stamp of two dark eye sockets gazing out from his cheek.

"Your brother know 'bout you?" he asked. "Wouldn't imagine Pat would take too kindly to your activities if he knew."

"He knows," she said coolly.

He sucked coffee through a straw. His eyes seemed to have grown more bloodshot, turbid as red smog. She took a small bit of pleasure thinking of how raging his hangover—coupled with a busted nose and two black eyes—would be tomorrow. "At's good. My folks tell me he's gonna be the new Pastor Jack when good ole Jack finally punches his ticket."

So strange after all this time, after all this steel grafted to her spine, how that old fear was still so immediate. Here she sat in Vicky's having flashbacks to high school, her stomach sinking like she was a teenager again, and Bethany had again caught her red-handed and her family had again learned the truth.

If she counted Ben Harrington as the first person to really sow doubt within her, then she had to credit Lisa for the next step.

The heady first days of any new relationship always have that new-toy excitement about them, yet with Lisa that glorious feeling of *new thingness* was amplified by the secrecy, the misbehavior necessary to follow through. On Halloween, only a few weeks after *Casablanca*, they were in Stacey's room, preparing their costumes. Only now did they understand the potential upside of what they were doing: their parents would never think twice if they disappeared for hours behind a closed door.

They were changing, and Stacey had her bra off, her hands involuntarily crossing in an X over her chest. She didn't even realize until Lisa pointed it out.

"You do that in the locker room too. You're afraid of your own tits, Miracle."

She blushed. She did not like to be naked. Did not like having anyone, even Lisa, assessing her breasts.

"I'm not a flaunter," she said. "Sorry I don't parade around everywhere with my boobs out."

"Like this?" Lisa reached behind her back and snapped off her bra. She was gorgeous, and she knew it. Stacey was about to say something more when Lisa took a handful of her hair, turned her around, and pushed her forehead against the wall, right up against her poster of the band Creed. She kissed down Stacey's neck, her back, and yanked her underwear down. Then she felt Lisa's tongue tracing a route from her clit up her ass and back. She did this until Stacey had to bite her own arm to keep from screaming.

Minutes later, she lay on her bed with her legs spread, exhausted, quaking.

"Who's the flaunter now, Moore? Put your pussy away."

"You're out of your mind," she breathed.

Lisa had on an old Jaguars cheerleading outfit, and she was busy covering it in fake blood, along with a sharpened dowel rod for a stake. "Buffy, the Asian Vampire Slayer," she called it. Stacey pulled her underwear back on and went back to assembling her costume. She had a hospital gown and a tank top under which she'd stuffed a small pillow. She smeared some of Lisa's fake blood on the gown and went about putting on zombie makeup.

"What a disturbing costume," Lisa said. "Like you got an abortion so you turn into a zombie?"

"This way I can just take the pillow out and be a regular zombie after."

Stacey was one of the actors for Hell House, where she would play the victim of an abortion before meeting up later in the night with Lisa and others at a party.

"I dunno. There's something fucked up about it. Leading kids through this showcase of ways they're going to end up eternally damned."

"It's just a haunted house," she said. "Not a big deal."

Patrick and his new wife, Becky, were in charge of organizing that year. Stacey hadn't particularly wanted to spend the first part of her night lying in stirrups, moaning for the spectators with a fake fetus in a jar bedside, but Patrick had pleaded with her to take at least one shift.

"Do you actually believe that?" Lisa pulled her hair into one pigtail and set about snapping a hair tie around the other. "Do you believe you're going to hell if you get an abortion or watch an R-rated movie?"

"No, not necessarily," she said, blushing. "It's complicated." Lisa rolled her eyes and decided her pigtails were uneven. She took the ties out and started again. "You're saying you don't believe in Hell?"

Lisa looked at her in the mirror. "Nope. Not even a little."

"You have that Bible quote in your room," she said stupidly, as if this was proof of anything.

"Oh, I'll put on a horse-and-pony show so I don't have to go to war with my goddamn mother. But c'mon, Moore, this stuff is bizarre. Hell House is whack. It's whackadoodle. Whackadoodledo."

"I didn't know that's what you really thought."

"Yeah, well, I guess we don't talk about it." She examined herself in the mirror, flipped her head around, and watched the pigtails twirl like pom-poms. "I'll tell you what I do believe."

She took Stacey's shoulders and looked her in the eye, serious as an aneurysm.

"There is a creator. He's just probably some pimply-assed geek masturbating while he watches us in this room."

Some of Stacey's anxiety retreated. She had thought Lisa was mad at her for taking part in Hell House. "Oh yeah?"

"Yep. I'm reading this book that says it's all but mathematically assured that we, us, this"—she flipped up her skirt so Stacey could see the orange spanks beneath—"and all human history is taking place inside a computer simulation."

"Yeah, I saw that movie with Keanu Reeves."

"This room, New Canaan, Ohio, Earth, Creed . . ." She smacked the poster. "This is all taking place inside a simulated model, which you gotta admit is even weirder than thinking there's a magic man in the sky watching your boner."

Stacey laughed, a deep *rat-a-tat* staccato.

"It's simple enough when you think about it. This book lays it out: Computational power has increased rapidly since its introduction, so rapidly that it's clear mankind is just scratching the surface of what's possible."

"Moore's Law!" she cried.

"Precisely. He says it's clear that at some point computing power will be so enormous that we'll be able to run simulations of anything, including the creation of a whole universe of conscious beings. But why run just one simulation? Why not run millions, Stace? And within these simulations, many of the beings we are simulating will at some point develop the ability to run their own simulations. The odds that we are the original biological entities who will create the very first simulation are small. Nearly impossible, actually. The odds that we are among the billions of simulations simulated by other simulators, merely the creation of other computer simulations, are extremely high."

"You're such a weird geek."

"Not that it makes any difference in how we live our lives," she promised. "We still have to treat people well, try to get laid, and we still gotta save the fucking whales, dude."

And yet later that night, lying in the fake stirrups, acting the role of forsaken abortion victim, who'd died of complications on the operating table, Lisa's bizarre story stayed with her, and she wondered why this theory was any less plausible than an outcome like eternal torture. It was the last time she ever let Patrick talk her into being a part of Hell House.

"Seriously, though, you should come back here and be with me," said Jonah, head weaving playfully. "Get down like we shoulda got down after homecoming. I'd make you happy."

"Would you now."

She guided her straw through the hole in the cylindrical ice and swizzled. An old man in a Navy ball cap began a coughing fit, his throat wet and horrid. He was horridly skinny and had a gruesome tattoo on his arm, a clown with a murderous smile. The man's skin was so brown and weathered, the image looked dehydrated, head-shrunken.

"Women need men, men need women," said Jonah. "That's as old as the Bible. And with me you get the added benefit of protection."

"Protection?" She was winding him up on purpose, but there was a freak-show quality from which she couldn't look away. Come see the geek. Come see the sword swallower. Come see the drunk proto-misogynist.

"This country's going between the rock and the hard place, proverbially speaking. We're about ten years away from fucking melt-down, mark my words. We got so much debt, we're drowning. And as soon as those bills come due, who you think they're gonna make pay? Not the parasites. Not the food stampers. It'll be the people actually making this country run. That's who the government will ask to bail them out. Then what happens?"

Her playfulness dissipated at this political millenarianism, and now she wished she hadn't asked.

"What happens is we got a narcotic in this country. We got welfare dependency so much so that it's—it's a narcotic. Now half the country's a drug addict and there's more and more starting to get in line for their handout. What happens is as soon as the balance tips . . ." He held his arm in a diagonal slash and then, like a teeter-totter, dropped it abruptly. "All those people just start voting more and more for themselves. That's what these whole Obama years have been about. That black man just gave his people what they voted for him for. And what part of the population is growing? It's not the white half, I'll tell you that. It's the drug addict part. And it doesn't matter if you get Obama out. If you impeach him or whatever. They're just going to vote themselves another Obama the next election because now there's more of them than there are of us."

"And the teeming hordes just get what they want, huh."

"What they think they want," he corrected. "But then all the businessmen who make this country run, who create all the jobs and the wealth, you think they're going to stick around? They'll take their factories and businesses to other countries or they'll go out of business all together. Just close up shop. It's already happening. Who do you think makes this country run?"

She pointed to their waitress, waiting for the Navy man to make up his mind about pie. "Her?"

"You know that's not what I mean. Why do you think the country's getting browner, huh? Why do you think all the Mexicans and Guatemalans and Haitians . . ." He began ticking them off on his fingers, his voice gaining righteousness. ". . . Indians, Cambodians, Nigerians, Kenyans, Angolans, Iraqis, Afghans, Vietnamese, Sudanese, Chinese—whatever—why do you think they all want to come here?"

She would have been impressed if Jonah had been able to name that many nationalities sober. She couldn't help but troll him back, all thoughts of asking him about Lisa vanished in the heat of this abrupt and unhinged political argument.

"Because the desert is expanding and the water tables are dropping and it's getting harder to grow food. So there's this mad dash to wall oneself off in Fortress America. Not coincidentally in the air-conditioned exurban housing developments you and your dad sell."

"Ha ha!" he cried, and the waitress looked up from her check pad. He jabbed the table for emphasis. "They're here 'cause they heard about the handouts. No one ever kicks you off. Get one baby born here, and you're set. You're American now, even if you can't speak the language, don't know the history, don't have any common cause with your fellow countrymen. You can still cash your check."

"What do you propose then, Jonah? If the barbarians are at the gate like you say?"

"There's stuff going down right now. Tonight, I'm talking." He all but glanced around to see who might be listening. Still only two bored waitresses and an old man at the counter waiting on his pie. "I'm not saying I got anything to do with it, but I might have given a few people a few bucks to grease the wheels."

"You're making no sense."

"Oh, but I am." He rolled his swollen, purple-filling eyes and ticked the next steps off on his fingers with a happy cadence. "These guys, they get their package tonight. Then in a few weeks they can go teach the parasites a lesson. Then you and me, we get to South Bass Island. My family's got a house there."

"You mentioned that." She tried to ask what he'd meant by the rest, but again he talked over her.

"And there are others. Phil Shackley, he owns the largest propane supplier in the Midwest. Kathleen Harden—she and her sons own about a million Subway franchises in the state. Jerry Mortzheimer, he's got a huge chain of earth-moving equipment. We're arming the island, bringing in resources. Guns, ammunition, food, medical supplies, water systems. We been talking about it ever since oh-eight. Now we have a place, when everything starts going to shit, we get to South Bass Island. Let everyone else out here eat each other when they run out of food stamps. And all the talent and business will escape, and then they'll be begging us, begging us for help, begging us for . . ."

He trailed off. Some fatigue seemed to overcome him during that speech, and he slowly lowered his head to the table. He gathered his hands as a pillow under his skull the way they had in high school classes. His eyes slipped shut. The two napkins jutted from each nostril like little crumpled flags. She forgave him his ravings because she knew how they likely helped: focus your rage, your

disappointment, your sorrow onto anything else. Allow the troubled, complex world to collapse into identifiable points of easily
rendered resentment. Cling to a satisfying fire and use it to hold
one's demons at bay.

After Lisa left in June 2004, Stacey kept trying to recall clues. The
problem was that she'd been so wrapped up in this enigma named
Lisa Han—especially the last months when they were really and
fiercely "together"—that she may have been semi-blind as to what
was going on with her.

That's what happens when you're taking a risk, savoring the
thrill of sin, writhing in the backseat of her mom's old Pontiac Sun-
fire, their shirts pulled off, Lisa's dangling from an arm, her eyes
grinding shut in concentration, tongue snaking out to glaze her
plump lower lip. All the places their old boyfriends took them to
get their pants off. Never the Brew because that's where the rest of
the high school would be. Lisa would clamp a hand over Stacey's
mouth, but her high, muffled cries would pierce that veil. All day,
every day—any amount of time that surrounded those fleeting encounters—panic lived like a hot stone in her gut.

Just before Christmas break 2003, they'd skipped the dance
after a basketball game and hit Wendy's with the plan to drive
around and pig out. She asked Lisa if they could talk about what
was happening, and the conversation did not go well.

"I always assumed I was bi," said Lisa, chocolate eyes studying
the road. "Never thought I would've done anything about it. But
c'mon, I wasn't best friends with Kaylyn all that time for her in-
sights on the human condition."

"Did you guys ever . . . ?"

"I wish," she scoffed. "Settled for my second choice."

From the driver's seat, Stacey threw a fry at her. "Shut up."

She picked it off her boob where the grease had stuck it and popped it into her mouth.

"Look, no offense, but who the fuck fucking cares or gives a fuck?" she said. "We're having fun. We'll keep it between us. No one'll know, and no big deal. I don't see what there is to worry about."

"Yeah, besides Romans 1:26, Leviticus 18:22, I guess nothing."

Lisa glanced at her, trying to gauge how serious she was, which was very. This was 2003, when the issue of gay marriage was everywhere, and every time it came up on a talk show or in the news, Stacey could feel herself growing hot, could feel the pit of fire Tina had spent their childhoods describing, and she'd make any excuse to leave the room. For as long as she could remember, Pastor Jack had served up at least semiannual sermons on the topic, and now, as it gained steam in the media, so did he. *Homosexuality is an abomination. That's not my word. That's the Bible's word. That's God's word. That doesn't mean we can't have compassion for those who stray from a righteous path. That doesn't mean we're not all guilty of sin in a multitude of ways. But that is the word of God, and it's our duty to abide by that in our lives. We treat sinners with compassion always, but we can never turn a blind eye to sin.* It wasn't like Stacey hadn't seen her mom nodding along in agreement with Pastor Jack, head ticking up and back in metronome rhythm while Stacey watched her from the corner of her eye. To this day, if she smelled the odor of her church, this scent of dusty library books mixed with citrus incense, a shameful heat would rise in her face.

She tried to articulate this to Lisa, who wouldn't have it.

"You need to get that stuff out of your head, dude. It's making you nuts. Take a break from feeling guilty over things you probably don't even believe in."

Stacey shot her a furious look. "I do believe."

Patrick had just been ordained as a part-time youth minister. During the party in the basement, he had thanked her: *My little sister, Stacey. One of the reasons I'm so excited about this. Your dedication and love for this church and for Jesus Christ has been a source of inspiration for me. It's been one of the great blessings of my life to watch you grow up and see what an amazing woman you're about to become.*

Lisa now met her gaze, and Stacey said something she hoped would hurt her. "I'm not you. I just don't think I'm like that way."

She hadn't even been able to say it. *I'm not like that way.* What a repressed dyke way to phrase your denial, to stay as far away from the actual word as possible.

Lisa threw up her hands, grin spreading. "So then stop going down on me, Miracle."

Even though she was driving, bombing along Stillwater Road in the pure, driven dark, Stacey wanted to reach over and smack her. It was the first time she'd ever felt that way about someone (though it would not be the last; Patrick and his wife would elicit that regularly). There was so much dismissiveness veined through Lisa's blithe attitude, but it sounded false, a whistle through the graveyard. Lisa couldn't stop fingering her locket, this dumb, cheap piece of jewelry in which she kept photos of various teen idols as a joke (the current half-ironic recipient was a singer from the group B2K, who'd replaced Aaron Carter). Her thumb and index finger worried it even as she tried to make a gag of this. Of them. She wanted to feel like she had control of this situation, and ridiculing Stacey's fear gave her that.

"Would you feel that way if your family found out?" Stacey asked. "Should I tell your mom?"

"Don't threaten me, bitch."

"Don't act like you're so above this then," Stacey snapped. At this, Lisa dropped the locket to her chest. Her eyes actually popped open a little, her whole posture subtly recoiling. "Don't treat me like I'm a joke to you."

Neither of them said anything for a while after that. Finally, Lisa slipped her hand over Stacey's, fingers skimming over the skin of her thin wrists. She said, "Only one verse I care about. What Paul said about the other Romans, baby. I loved you at your darkest."

They were both quiet for a while. Stillwater was the best road in the whole county—long stretches with no streetlights or homes or light pollution of any kind. The moon reflected off the thin sheet of snow covering the cornfields. Eventually, Stacey circled back into town. Stacey wondered if this conversation had been a bad idea, if she had spoiled what they had by letting Lisa see how afraid she was. Then, less than a mile from her house, as they passed the public library, Lisa pointed to it and said, "The first time I blew Ashcraft was on the roof there."

That surprised Stacey into laughter. "Gross."

"Really I'd have a hard time thinking of somewhere in this town I didn't blow him."

"Shut up, Han."

"It's true. My mom was always trying to get us to stay at our house so she could keep an eye on us, so last year during the Oscars, we watched it with her and Bob, and they're both so old they fell asleep before they even announced Best Actor. Bill and I went around the corner from the living room to the kitchen, and I sucked him off on the kitchen island."

"Oh that's disgusting! C'mon, Lisa."

Lisa had her window cracked, her fingertips holding the outside of the door. The night came in on the wind and black threads of hair blew across her eyes. "What, you never gave Harrington head? Poor guy."

"Of course I did."

"So? You didn't like it?"

"I didn't not like it. I don't know. I could take it or leave it. It was just a thing I'd do as long as we had a fair trade-off."

"Oh, well I love it. Turns me on." She shuddered dramatically, eyes fluttering. "I think I have a clitoris in the back of my throat."

Stacey brayed laughter. "Oh my God, where do you even come from?"

"What? That's Linda Lovelace. *Deep Throat.*"

"Huh?"

"The porn star. It's actually really sad. She wrote this memoir about how her husband beat her and like had her gang-raped and forced her into prostitution and pornography. Really terrible."

Returning her eyes to the road, Stacey said, "You're a really strange chick, chick." They were quiet again for a moment. "So wait, if you love giving head so much, do you miss it? Am I just totally not satisfying a need of yours? Is that what you're telling me?"

"Yeah. Well." She smiled, a cute little tick of her lips. "Luckily I have a clitoris on my clitoris too."

When Matt was a sophomore, Stacey still in eighth grade, there'd been a kid whom everyone suspected of being gay. Stacey couldn't remember his name, but she did remember hearing that someone beat the windshield of his car into spiderwebs of fractured glass. None of this was ever far from her mind that year, but the shame could never win out over the taste of Lisa. Her orgasm was never in the small, tight noises she made as Stacey teased her with her tongue—it was always in the silence, this moment when Lisa's breath caught and her nails dug into Stacey's skull, and reality felt impossibly taut, a wire stretched to the breaking point. Humming from the finger that plucked it.

She left Jonah with his head on the table. Passing the waitress—of the ample rear end, not the elderly poet—she told her to maybe call Jonah's dad. "He might have a concussion."

She wondered if she'd wandered into Vicky's not to meet Bethany Kline and marvel at how difficult it was to hold on to hate. Maybe Vicky's, from which she'd yet to escape that night, was a kind of supra-reality, an illusory space where so many of the spokes of her life crossed, her own Tel'aran'rhiod imbued with nostalgia, time, and interconnection.

She touched the envelope sticking out of her purse, but she had a new destination, and she would put off this final, horrible errand just a bit longer. If anyone knew Lisa as well as she did—that is, if anyone knew her at all—it was Bill Ashcraft. The thought of Lisa coming home and contacting him but not her was enough to send an old splinter of jealousy cruising through her vein like a sliver of bone on its way to the heart. Which was exactly why she needed to see him. Or maybe "confront" was the word. She checked her phone, but she no longer had Ashcraft's number. Other than the errant Facebook Like, they hadn't spoken in years. The Lincoln bar wasn't far from Vicky's, and she left her car in the square to walk.

She headed south through downtown, and the route brought her within view of the old steel plant, closed since the eighties when Fountain Steel decided it was cheaper to make tubular products elsewhere. Why the town had never gotten around to tearing down that ugly industrial boil, she never understood. It was like they left it alone hoping that someday whatever mechanized processes lay inside would simply start back up of their own accord. The plant and the abandoned middle school had been located precariously close to each other, possibly because some city planner wanted kids to get a good hard look at the best opportunity their town had to offer. Generations of students breathed the air from those stacks, while the plant's CO_2 drifted lazily into the atmosphere.

Where does a girl who's lost her religion go to find meaning? What replaces the hole that faith, cast off, leaves behind? Until her conversation with Hilde, Stacey had had no conception of how deep and aching this chasm inside herself was. Before that strange confluence of Hilde and *Gaia* she'd never really considered *herself* as part of any ecological system, and this came to astonish her later. How people walk through their lives nearly in a coma, unaware of the physical substrate that surrounds them. She considered the nights camping in Mohican with her family, Matt and Patrick getting yelled at for wrestling too close to the fire or throwing each other's s'mores in the dirt, and later the hiking and camping she would do in Croatia, Lithuania, and Switzerland; Ecuador, Peru, and Brazil. The natural world existed for her, as it did for most of the Global North, only as another theme park, a Disneyland. One of the luxuries of modernity was never having to consider how the asphalt from a parking lot could crush soil, disrupt a delicate system, banish a pocket of insects, birds, or small mammals to ruin. Or that this parking lot was merely a microcosm of something far larger and darker: a war on the living biosphere. People call it the Anthropocene, but a much better word for it is the Necrocene—a human-induced geologic age in which profit flows from exploitation and extinction with vast capital accumulation powering yet further devastation in a terminal cycle.

Back in the late 2000s while traveling through Europe, Stacey began to consider the implications of what she'd discovered since casting off her religious delusions. What humanity was doing to the biosphere at the moment—its obsession with the impact of a neutron on uranium or carbon-based fuels or fishing vessels that ripped scars into the ocean floor or its husbandry of every creature down to the honeybee—this fascination, this plunder, it could not last long. This dawning realization floated on the margins of literature. From Eggers's *What Is the What* to Adichie's *Americanah* to Collins's *Hunger Games*, modern authors had internalized it even if they weren't writing directly about it: the profound catastrophe the planet was undergoing.

She wanted badly to write about this. How humanity had created this overflow of prodigious breeders, masters, killers, and artists. How its narcissism could produce deities, literature, destruction, and dogma. How it nevertheless occasionally conjured fierce, unfathomably deep love. It made Lisa even more beloved in her mind and memory, raised her to the level of a prophet. What kind of seventeen-year-old picks up *Gaia*? Or for that matter reads about simulation theory or *The Book of Laughter and Forgetting*? Stacey hadn't caught up to Lisa intellectually until she was in her midtwenties, at which point she could only jealously marvel at her long lost friend. She'd known Lisa was more creative, aware, and curious than the next seven hundred people at their school combined, but it wasn't until many years later that the hidden depths of her friend's interior life came to shock her. There were only a handful of Lisa's margin notes in *Gaia*, but one of them stood out. In his epilogue, Lovelock asks the reader to consider the human sense of beauty, "those complex feelings of pleasure, recognition, and fulfillment, of wonder, excitement, and yearning, which fill us when we see, feel, smell, or hear whatever heightens our self-awareness and at the same time deepens our perception of the true nature of things." Beside this, Lisa had written, simply, the same quote she'd stuck on her locker and tacked above her desk back home: *I Loved You At Your Darkest*.

As the steel plant receded from view, and she took a shortcut down an alley, Stacey considered for the thousandth time that her preoccupations as a writer, a thinker, a consciousness, were simply a nebulous extension of Lisa Han's.

Steam hissed from a manhole cover, electric lines hung like jungle vines, and the Lincoln's dingy plastic sign came into view. Someone who agreed with Jonah had slapped a WRONG WAY sticker with the Obama logo on the stop sign at the end of the sweaty alley. Emerging onto the street, she saw a man standing hunched over the passenger window of an idling car. He too was familiar.

*   *   *

During their senior year together, she and Lisa grew so close that their other friendships ceased to exist. Lisa in particular had come to truly loathe her Elmwood friends, although that started back in sophomore year when Hailey Kowalczyk began dating Curt Moretti, the quarterback, and a friend of Stacey's brother Matt. He was a tall, truly stupid kid with a scimitar nose, hoop earrings, and one of those awful haircuts where the sides are shaved and his dark blond sat on the top of his skull like an oversized yarmulke.

Lisa tried to elucidate the falling-out for her once while they sat on a picnic table out by the softball field. It was the first unseasonably warm day of 2004. *Casablanca*, Halloween, Hell House, Thanksgiving, and Christmas break had all come and gone. Graduation loomed. Stacey had made the melancholy choice of Wittenberg University in Springfield. Lisa was still deciding between three or four schools. They could feel the road about to fork, and at first she thought this was what was bothering Lisa, but that turned out to be wrong.

"So Hailey lost her virginity to Curt Moretti? So what?" Stacey wondered. Not that she was advocating Lisa again become friends with the girl she called "Triple Threat."

"Danny's been my friend since we were little kids," she said defensively. "Hailey knew how much he adored her even while she was getting it on with Moretti. And I told her, 'Look, bitch, one day Danny's going to put on a little muscle, he's going to finally be able to grow facial hair, he'll get a better pair of glasses, and he's going to be killing it at like Cornell because the kid reads more than a librarian, and you're going to have Curtis fucking Moretti's little rat-faced teen mom baby to take care of.' "

Skinny and pale with freckles and a scrub of Irish-red hair, Dan Eaton was a sweet-natured kid—kind to the point where he could get trampled, even by his friends. The worst-kept secret of their class was that Danny Eaton had been in love—obsessed might be a better word—with Hailey for as long as he'd known her. Their junior year he'd finally, at long last, worn Hailey down, and they could be spotted in the halls, Dan doting. When Stacey heard he'd decided on the military over college, she was baffled: he'd worked so long to win her. Then to go put it all on the line in the very real stare-into-the-void sense of foreign military adventures—hard-won love wasn't worth that kind of risk.

"But so what? She dates Dan now," said Stacey. "She listened to you."

Lisa bit the sleeve of her sweatshirt and stared out over the rain-spattered grass. A morning fog had settled over the fields like their town was passing through the clouds. Lisa spit between her feet and at least appeared to think about this.

"Naw, she didn't listen to me. We barely say a word to each other anymore. And it's about more than that. She and Kaylyn—they've got this fucked codependent thing. You know Kay's back? Dropped out of Toledo. They've been hanging out."

"I don't get it, are you jealous?" She hoped the word *jealous* didn't sound as jealous as it did to her own ears. Whenever Lisa spoke of a person for whom she carried love, Stacey wanted to attach her mouth to her and siphon it off.

"Not exactly. Kay was always hanging on Bill when we were dating, always flirting with him like she didn't think I saw. But you don't understand, that girl is severely more fucked up than . . ."

"Right, your brother's baseball card or whatever." Stacey was angry—and fearful. Maybe it was irrational, but she wondered if either Hailey or Kaylyn had been with Lisa first. Maybe just a night like their *Casablanca* night, but it would be more than enough to make her crazy. For some reason, Ashcraft she could live with, but not another girl.

"No. Not that. I got ahold of this thing." She hunched forward, sitting like a guy with her elbows propped on her thighs, strands of oil-black hair falling in her eyes. Stacey had the urge to tuck them behind her ear, and it made her stomach queasy with longing. "I just know some bad shit about Kaylyn. It's been making me a little nuts . . . figuring what to do about it."

"What is it?"

"She's just a total psycho. That's all I can think about her anymore."

"What is it?" she asked again.

"It's a videotape. Kay and some guys from the football team. It's . . ." She hesitated.

"What?" she demanded.

"There's cocaine in it."

Understand at the time, this truly was amazing to Stacey. She'd never heard of such a thing in New Canaan. That anyone, let alone her once-close friend, had access to cocaine was beyond wild.

"Like they videotaped themselves doing it?"

"Something like that."

"So what do you want to do?"

"I have no clue." Lisa sniffed and stared out over the gossamer fog. Then she said, "Man, fuck her. Fuck Kowalczyk. Fuck Kaylyn. Fuck all these people. Four years from now I'll be drinking wine in Florence, and they'll both just be teenage bullshit I'll barely remember."

Almost four years later, when Stacey was home for Christmas her senior year of college, she went to her mom's gym and bumped into Hailey Kowalczyk in the locker room. They stubbed toes on their hellos, jammed fingers trying to find common ground for the brief time it took Hailey to change from nursing scrubs into workout clothes. Skipped over Rick Brinklan's parade, which Hailey had attended but Stacey had not. Hailey and Danny, she learned, had broken up, and she was now seeing Eric Frye. Then Stacey asked her if she ever heard from Lisa. It was all they had in common other than middle school basketball.

"We still write to each other every now and then. She's in Vietnam, working at some hospital running an English-language program."

"How is she?" Stacey asked with great effort to keep her voice even. A flare of that old irrational jealousy.

"She loves it. And I miss her. We kind of had our drifting apart in high school over stupid teenage stuff but . . ." She trailed off. "Want me to tell her you said hi?" she offered.

She was much taller than Hailey. She wanted to loom over her and say, *Why you? Lisa thought you were a fucking phony. Why you and not me?*

Then she was stuck on that bike wondering what Lisa could have possibly been thinking, and if she'd ever tracked down her dad in Vietnam, and of the complex transpositions of history that had likely brought Lisa's father from that country to Ohio and the daughter he abandoned all the way back to his ancestral home. In all of Stacey's travels to come, all her notions of wanderlust, she never dared tack her pushpin to Southeast Asia, where Lisa had chosen to make her life. Had she ever harbored any ambitions to do so, they dissipated after her heart was broken by that conversation with Hailey Kowalczyk.

A compact blue sedan idled in the shadows between the streetlights. At the passenger side, leaning in to speak to the driver, was a man who elicited memories of standing in the student bleachers holding Ben's hand and hurling classist chants at teams from towns far bleaker than New Canaan (*It's all right / It's okay / Y'all are gonna pump our gas someday*). Bubbling up from the depths of memory, his nickname for Stacey popped to the surface: "Little Moore."

Back when Todd Beaufort and her brother Matt were friends on the football team, all those intimidating older boys used to call her that.

Todd spoke to a figure ensconced in the dark behind the steering wheel. The face missing. Buried in shadow. Now he glanced her way, and she almost raised a hand to wave.

Todd had always been her favorite of Matt's friends, probably because when Todd came over to their house, he went out of his way to be nice to her. It was likely also how he turned his eye toward Tina. He ended up dating Stacey's childhood friend for the better part of high school, though by that point she and Tina barely spoke. There was a lot of gossip that the Todd-Tina celebrity dyad didn't end well. There was a reason she and Tina grew apart, however, and where others saw Todd as the villain, Stacey always saw Tina as more complicit. Sometimes being that beautiful, coveted girl at that age can almost be a curse (she thought of Kaylyn as well). Tina allowed herself to become enveloped by Todd and quit any activity that failed to bow to his wishes. She thought of the time as seventh graders when the two of them sneaked to the edge of the basement stairs to try to hear what Matt, Todd, Curtis, and their other friends were talking about. All they could hear, though, was the air conditioner and the occasional guttural guffaw of older boy laughter. While Stacey made new friends through volleyball, Tina hovered over her new love sycophantically, lost interest in anything else. When they finally broke up, grotesque rumors circulated about her, all of them ridiculous and likely fabricated by the football team, but they made Stacey wary. Tina made an aborted, half-hearted effort to reconnect with her, but by then Stacey had a new crew of friends. Tina retreated from the social scene, lost so much weight that people whispered about an eating disorder. Stacey lost all track of her after graduation.

Stacey lowered her hand when Todd glared her way. He looked

drunk. Not to mention fat and tired and old. Even more so than Jonah. He turned back to the car without noticing her.

She'd felt sorry for him then and felt sorry for him now. When she was a sophomore they'd been in the same study hall, and he'd asked her a question about algebra. He was studying for the SAT and absolutely needed a higher score so he could play college football. He showed her what he was having trouble with, a very basic $3x=15$, solve for x question. How was it possible that he'd made it to his senior year unable to do an equation he should've learned in seventh grade when she and Tina were still elementary school girls spying on him from the basement stairs? Stacey spent most of the study hall that semester tutoring him. He did eventually get the score he needed, although from the looks of things now, it hadn't led where he'd hoped.

He popped open the door of the car and climbed inside. When the driver pulled away, Stacey took a step back into the shadows of the alley. She wasn't sure why. She let the car go by and saw Todd Beaufort's bleary face beneath a red ball cap, cut through with a wounded, hopeless expression. She continued to the bar.

The Lincoln Lounge was one of those sad dips in the dunes of the rural-industrial Midwest: wood paneling reflecting dim bulbs and LIGHT/LITE beer signage. A few tables scattered around a dusky green pool table, and a TV playing West Coast baseball. Battered old men huddled over beers at the bar while a few younger ones clacked pool balls around half-heartedly. She'd gone to high school with the bartender, she was sure, but couldn't summon her name.

"Did you have a guy in here tonight," she asked the bartender. "Tall, black hair, cocky looking?"

"Have to do better'n that." She had a sharp nose that had looked prettier in her teenage days. Large breasts threatened to burst from the U-cut black shirt she wore, the cleavage vibrating in a gelatinous way as she poured whiskey and snagged the hose that dispensed soda.

"He was probably with Jonah Hansen?" Stacey tried.

"Oh. And Beaufort and all them?" She pointed her eyes at the door where he'd just departed and shook her head distractedly. "There was a fight, and they left a while ago now."

"Any idea which direction?"

She shrugged to indicate she didn't know. "You go to New Canaan?" she asked.

Stacey hesitated. "No, just trying to catch one of them." Outside, she felt a momentary chill and looked up and down the street before venturing farther. For some reason, she was sure the blue sedan would have circled the block, and the driver would be waiting for her, the passenger seat now empty. Like a hearse, all of this car's passengers only took one-way trips, and now the driver would be waiting to pick up another lost traveler.

She tried to remember if in that year between 2003 and 2004—in Lisa's bed beneath the covers or in her own basement, the blanket of rocket ships drawn around their legs and tucked beneath her bottom—if Lisa talked about leaving. Once, she expressed the thought to Stacey, but she dismissed it the way you dismiss such talk from a seventeen-year-old: as an idle fantasy, a wishful what-if scenario.

"If you could go anywhere, where would you go?" A dumb high school girl question like that.

Lisa traced her fingers along Stacey's belly, the tips grazing from her navel up between her breasts and then drawing cylindrical patterns.

"Springfield, Ohio," said Stacey.

"Seriously."

Lisa had felt far away all night. They'd eaten dinner with Stacey's parents and then retreated to the basement to "watch a movie," which meant jacking up the volume while they took care of each other and muffled noises in pillows. Even during this she could sense something troubling Lisa.

When Stacey didn't respond, not out of cruelty but because she was afraid of where this conversation was going, she felt Lisa's cheek rise from the nook in her shoulder.

"Hey, wake up. I'm like trying to . . ." She propped herself up on her elbow. It was hard to find her eyes in the dark.

"You're trying to what?" she demanded. "Ask me if I want to run away with you? We both know that's not happening. Why talk about it."

They were whispering even though her parents' room was on the other end of the house.

"When we started this, I thought it was funny," Lisa said. "I thought, 'Well, this'll be a good story for college.' "

"Glad I could be a good story."

"Stacey, shut up." Lisa blew a frustrated breath of mint toothpaste into her face. "Fucking fuck, I'm trying to tell you something."

She was quiet for a while, and Stacey waited.

"So. Okay. When I dated Ashcraft, we used to tell each other, 'I love you,' right? Which was obviously ridiculous—I didn't love Bill Ashcraft. I mean, yes, I cared about him. But I was not in love with him. The way I feel about you has been—I don't know— unexpected. And it's been different—and not because you've got a beautiful little pussy. Part of that difference is, you know, I love you. I'm in love with you. Whatever that means. Or whatever it is. Jesus Christ, I'm awkward."

This was February, the darkest month in the Midwest. There was thick, week-old snow outside and ice coating every surface. It caught all the light of the stars and glittered in shifting, restless arrays. It captured the errant glow of a streetlamp and reflected it, silver and blue, through the blinds. It had been about six months since *Casablanca*. Two months since they went shopping at a thrift store in Columbus and Lisa spotted a dress, white with blue flowers, and judged it Stacey's size, her style, her "swag." It was four months before Lisa would leave.

She continued. "Before all this started, all I wanted to do was get out of this town and get away from my mom and Bob and Alex, but now I'm thinking about leaving and what that actually means. Since we've been hanging out, I just find myself . . ." A pause. "Unable to stop thinking about you. Like totally incompetent about anything except wondering when I'm going to see you next. And I know"—she gestured to Stacey's naked torso to indicate the activities that went beyond friendship—"sometimes I treat it like a joke. But I don't think it's just screwing around. At least for me— like . . ." She kept getting lost, and Stacey could feel her face growing hot. "You're a crazy-gorgeous, dreamboat bitch, you know? If I was ever going to have a partner to travel the world with and help me raise Darkheart McStabababy it would be you."

Stacey laughed less at what Lisa said than at her inability to say anything sincere without injecting her particular brand of absurdity. And then on the next word Lisa's voice cracked.

"But really." She sucked on her cheek, which made a squelching noise. "It's because you lift my heart. You make me insanely happy to be alive. So I don't know what happens after this, and I know you still think we're both going straight to hell, but that's why you need to know. I'm fucking out-of-my-mind crazy about you."

There was a period of her life after she graduated from Wittenberg and started traveling in which Stacey tried to render this moment inert with both reason and irony. They were just children, she told herself, imitating emotions they didn't yet know anything about. That's why teenagers are in love with pop idols and think it would be fun to shoot bows and arrows in futuristic dystopias. She'd look at pictures of herself in high school—her button-nosed face and bob of blond hair, the way she slouched, perhaps because she subconsciously wanted to be shorter—and think, *Look at this awkward teenage baby! She can't feel anything real yet!* If she now heard a woman stammer on like Lisa had, she'd be embarrassed for her. So much Hollywood rom-com drippy bathetic nonsense. Yet the feeling she had back then always returned to her like a ghost; her face would go iron-hot and that pebble in her throat would exert its pressure. Because irony, distance, perspective would all eventually fail her—because that's the kind of shit you lived a lifetime to hear. And something only a seventeen-year-old actually has the courage to say.

She snatched Lisa's face out of the dark and kissed her. When their cheeks glanced off each other's, they were both slick. All dreams of the soul ending in a beautiful woman's body.

On the walk back to her car, she passed an older black man in shorts and sandals as he came around the corner. She recognized him as her high school music teacher. After the surprises of Jonah and Todd she was out of bewilderment to find Mr. Clifton snatching open the door of the Lincoln. It was clear to her why New Canaan wasn't the magical realist space she'd imagined, the same reason it always took her mother two hours to shop for groceries: in a small town you just ran into a hell of a lot of people you knew.

He didn't look Stacey's way even though she was the only person out on this bare rock of street. She called to him using the honorific in front of his last name, a habit difficult to break with old teachers.

He turned, let go of the door, face puzzled and assessing her blankly.

"It's Stacey Moore," she said. "Class of oh-four."

His eyes bugged in surprise, and finally the broad, familiar grin broke out. "Stacey Moore," he cried, hurrying over, taking her in a semi-awkward, hunched-at-the-waist embrace. "What on earth are you doing here?"

"Are you going in?" she asked.

He looked almost embarrassed by his need for a drink. "Felt like a night to get out of the house."

"Mind if I join you for one?"

Lisa got off easily and loudly. The night of Jonah's vodka aside, they rarely fooled around in Lisa's house unless they were sure Bethany, Bob, and Alex were out because all three rooms were clustered together at the end of the hall. There was an odd, musty smell to the place that had nothing to do with the tacky floral-print wallpaper, yet seemed related. It was a low, dark house with sticky surfaces and ugly shag carpet in the bedrooms. Stacey had never liked being there and knew Lisa felt the same.

When Bethany heard the cries coming from Lisa's room, surely she'd pictured a boy. Not Stacey Moore with her head between her daughter's legs, Lisa practically yanking fistfuls of hair out by the roots of her blond. They never so much as heard the floor creak. It was one of those button locks that you can pop open by sticking a penny or a paper clip in and turning.

When Bethany snatched Lisa's arm it made a sound like a single clap echoing in an auditorium. As Stacey scrambled to pull on her clothes, the panic was blinding. Bethany yanked Lisa out into the living room with an indifference to her physical well-being that seemed alien for a mother. Bethany threw her onto the couch, screaming, and not just with fury but with a panic of her own, like she was calling for help, trapped inside a flooding prison with the water bubbling up, and it amplified Stacey's fear. She followed them, and Bethany barked her into a nearby chair. Lisa was still naked, and she pulled an afghan around her torso. Face red, spit foaming at the corners of her mouth, Bethany could have acted in a B movie about a demon-possessed woman. It would have been funny except Stacey had never been more frightened in her life. *What do you think you're doing?!* was Bethany's refrain, but she wasn't employing it as a question. She wailed it into Lisa's face, clenching and unclenching her hands until the blood turned them purple.

Stacey tried to look at Lisa like, *Let's just leave. Let's go to my house,* but Lisa only stared at the floor, catatonic. In all the time she'd known Lisa, she'd never seen her like that. No quick retort, no rebellion, no fire at all. She just stared at the floor and accepted her mother's screams.

Bethany took Lisa by her ear and tried to yank their gazes together. "Look at me!" she shrieked, and Stacey felt the fear that precedes true violence. The breath in the moment before the knife pops the muscle and slides through.

Stacey blurted out, "We're sorry." Two frightened little words.

Bethany's head swiveled to Stacey, as if remembering she was there. She stalked across the living room, and Stacey hated how she shrank into the chair.

"Don't you talk to me. Don't you ever talk to me. Who are you? What are you doing here?" An adult had never laid a hand on her before. Her parents never spanked her brothers, let alone their daughter. She just had no frame of reference for it. So when Bethany snatched her hair in one hand and snapped her head back, she couldn't understand it. She remained limp, and felt her throat exposed, so much that she feared the woman's teeth.

"Who are you?" she repeated.

Then she clamped a thumb and index finger around Stacey's nipple, the right one, and pinched so viciously, she cried out.

"Stay away from her. Stay away. Stay away. Stay away." She barked that over and over, squeezing Stacey's nipple harder until the pain was a bright heat in her entire breast. And she just sat there letting her do it. She'd think about that for years. She was taller and stronger than Bethany. She could have smacked her, thrown that bitch across the room if she'd wanted. But adult Stacey would think of that later. Right then, she only knew she'd done something awful and irrevocable. This punishment was simply the beginning.

"If you ever come near my daughter again," Bethany hissed. "You will be so, *so* sorry."

Lisa had started crying silently, but still she didn't move. This was not even Lisa, Stacey would later decide. This vacant, idle-eyed girl was some reversion to a younger self, and the way Lisa sat, melted and melded into the couch, still haunted her.

Bethany's knuckles bore down harder. Like she was trying to rip her breast off. She leaned into Stacey's ear and whispered beneath the sound of her daughter sniffing back tears and the refrigerator gurgling loudly in the kitchen. "Go near her again, I'll set you on fire, you little whore."

Then she pulled Stacey from the chair by her hair and that savage grip on her breast and threw her to the floor.

On the drive home—after Bethany threatened to tell her parents if Stacey said a word about this to anyone—she had to pull over. She was shaking so badly. She couldn't complete a breath—a full-fledged panic attack. What it's like to understand your own death the moment before the darkness. She stopped on 229, just west of the retirement home, opened the door, and vomited onto the side of the road. Her vision glittered, and she tried to listen to the crickets and not pass out. To this day, she had dreams of lying immobile as that woman poured gasoline on her.

Bethany took away her daughter's cell phone, and Stacey couldn't even talk to Lisa at school. A handful of teachers knew Mrs. Kline or went to their church. The next week she and Lisa met in the library during lunch, away from the study tables, back in a quiet row of books. They sat on the floor hugging their knees together, like they were in elementary school. Lisa played at the fraying threads on her wrist, running her finger under them, plucking them like guitar strings.

"I'm sorry," she said. Stacey didn't reply. Her breast still had a dark blue bruise on it surrounding the nipple like a halo. "We need to be careful for a while."

"How long is a while? Because after this summer . . ."

Stacey would be in Springfield and Lisa in Virginia. Not the farthest distance two people had ever spanned, but at eighteen it felt like a continent.

Lisa looked at her, for the first and only time Stacey could ever remember, with anger. "She's sending me to a counselor."

"What kind of counselor?"

"What kind do you think."

Stacey didn't know what to feel. Part of her wanted to blame Lisa for just sitting there, for her cowardice, but who was she to talk. The relief that Bethany hadn't told her parents was total. The panic attack had subsided but not the image of her mom taking Bethany's call and bursting into horrified tears.

"You know I don't even know if she's my biological mother," Lisa said. "Her story's that my dad went back to Vietnam, but she doesn't even have a picture of him. For all I know I could be adopted. 'Han' might be some bullshit she made up. Shit, I've never seen the blood work." She picked at a scab on her hand, scratched away the gunky red crust like a lotto ticket. "All I know is I've hated her for so long. I figure you can't feel that for your real mother."

"This is crazy," Stacey whispered.

"Maybe it was." Then Lisa got to her feet and walked away. It was the last conversation they ever had in person.

Lisa left just before graduation. Stacey had to hear about what she'd done from Kaylyn. When she wrote to tell Lisa how furious she was that she hadn't said good-bye or told her this insane plan, Lisa wrote back, *It was too complicated. I knew it would be too hard unless I just left. I'm sorry.*

When Stacey wrote to ask her if she should save up money for a plane ticket, that after freshman year was over, she could visit her wherever she ended up, Lisa wrote back, *I don't think that's a good idea.*

Stacey felt shame that, at first, she was faking her own broken heart. It was complicated, but she was relieved Lisa had left. With her gone, Stacey's family would never find out. With the temptation of Lisa Han removed, she could get on with her life: go to college, meet a boy, marry, have children, be happy. She honestly thought this was for the best.

It was only a few months later, when she got to school, that the fury and the sadness and the hurt she'd sublimated began to bubble up. No eighteen-year-old is equipped to understand how love can inspire so much shame, so much self-loathing. Even after nearly a decade she could summon the anguish, like a rotting tooth you feel with each bite of a meal, once it dawned on her that she would probably never see Lisa again. She wanted one phone call, one opportunity to scream at her, to vent everything. But Lisa never gave her the chance. And this all led to darker thoughts. At first it was only the bereavement of a breakup and the anxiety of a secret, but that lonely first year at Wittenberg, Stacey tested the hanging rod in the closet of her dorm room. It was high and felt sturdy enough to hold her. If she got the length of the cord right, her feet wouldn't be able to touch the floor. That she'd considered this seriously seemed impossible now, but that was the corner she found herself in: so deeply terrified of what she would never be able to get away from or suppress, something her family would never understand. She'd have to choose between them and her sanity, and some days the rod in the closet felt like the easiest option. Especially now that the one person in her life who understood had left her for anywhere else, for distant lands and climes.

Mr. Clifton bought the round. They sat in a booth away from the pool table, and she caught him up on her story as fast as she could, answering backward. Yes, Columbus. Catching up with some old friends on the way home. Let the night get away from me. Michigan. Graduate school. Transnational Ecological Catastrophe in the Context of the Global Novel. An explanation of what that meant. All the while wondering—since she wouldn't have the time now to track down Bill—how to ask him about Lisa. Before his retirement, Mr. Clifton had been one of the most beloved teachers at the school. She'd only had him for the one music requirement, but it endeared him to her forever.

"You know, it's amazing. I'll never get over it," he said, sweeping a hand enthusiastically before tucking it back into the handle of his mug. "I see some of you kids I had in class years and years ago, and I can never believe the way you grow into yourselves as adults. Thirty years of teaching, and it still makes me want to cry tears of joy every time. It's really an incredible gift to be able to see that. Especially a young woman like you who had so much potential."

"Then it's probably okay to tell you that during your class I spent most of my time writing notes to Ben Harrington."

His laugh carried across the bar, and she imagined it filtering into the streets and out into the gloaming country.

"Oh my gosh. You were always so spicy, Ms. Moore. You were so terrific to have in class I would have let you get away with anything." His laughter receded as he remembered what this meant. "I'd forgotten you and Ben were sweethearts. I'm sorry. So much tragedy these last few years."

"Yeah, it's kind of unbelievable." In order to change the subject, she said, "I should also mention that I don't write notes to guys anymore. I came out."

"Came out?"

"You know, came out." For some reason she twirled her index fingers.

He brightened. "Did you now? Good for you, Stacey Moore. Good for the people around you." She thanked him. "Are you seeing anyone? How did your folks take it?"

"In between wonderful women right now, but yeah. My dad's just my dad—I could probably show up with a dead hooker in my trunk, and he would beam at my resourcefulness with a club hammer. But my mom really gets out there and tries to change people's minds. She's made it like a full-time project at her new church. I give them credit."

He really did look overjoyed by this. She decided he'd already had a few drinks tonight somewhere, but he was still such a heart-on-the-sleeve man.

She left out the part about her brother Patrick, although Mr. Clifton surely had an idea. Dread rippled through her, and she was grateful for the buzz of the beer.

"You know." He twisted his coaster. "My father once told me that it's on other people to let go of their fear and prejudice. And this was a man who had his shop burned to the ground because he tried opening in a white neighborhood in Cincinnati. It's their problem, he said, and that's on them. But he also told me that it's on you to give people a chance to change." He looked at her quizzically. "Dan Eaton was your class, right?"

"Yep. I heard he's home too."

"Take Dan's dad, Paul. When my wife and I first moved in next door, that guy looked at me like the whole world had lost its damn mind. That real estate lady didn't show me *this* crazy cracker 'Nam vet I was going to have to neighbor with. But I made an effort. Then again, I didn't have much choice because we were about the only black family for forty miles it seemed. But I heard it was his birthday and got him a bottle of whiskey. And then he made an effort. And then we were all just good. By the time Rosa passed away, there was no one . . ." He stopped, smiled into his beer. "Though obviously, these are different experiences we're talking about."

She raised her glass. "No way. Inspirational music teachers, issues of queerness and race—we're writing our own really condescending movie right now."

He laughed and cracked his glass into hers.

When she was home from college the summer after her freshman year she ran into Ben Harrington and his mom at Kroger (epicenter of New Canaan stop-and-chat time sucks). She and Ben decided to meet for lunch at Friendly's, the high school hangout chain rival to Vicky's. Stacey had only meant to catch up, to sit across from this old flame of hers and see how he was growing into the world.

"I'm writing weird songs," he explained, shy eyes darting. She was reminded that she loved how uncomfortable he was about his music and ambition. "My plan is to get five songs together that I'm really proud of and release an EP, and then hopefully get a full album within a couple of years. Part of my thing is I'm such a tinkerer. If a song's not perfect I stay awake at night biting my nails."

"You were always a worrier."

"Not when I was with you! And that's not flattery either—you just chilled me out."

"You're flirting with me," she warned.

His eyes were summer sun dappling off a dirty river. "I'm not trying to get you out to the Brew, but let me have a little flirting, Stace."

He did look impossibly handsome.

His skin had cleared up, and he'd grown his hair out and kept brushing the thick blond locks off his brow. She wasn't sure what clicked in her at that moment, but he just had this way about him, this quiet empathy, and before she knew what she was doing, she said, "I've got something sort of crazy to tell you," and spilled the entire story about Lisa. He listened, and as she got to the end, taming the conclusion, leaving out the part about the night Bethany found them, his face remained too even, his disappointment transparently subdued. He'd surely thought the Brew was at least a possibility, and there she was putting her guts on the table about the woman she'd fallen in love with.

"Holy fucking shit," he said, processing with a rapid flutter of his surfer eyes. "Does Ashcraft know?"

"No one does. I don't think Lisa's ever told anyone."

He'd always had this habit of removing everything from his pockets when he sat down. His wallet, phone, keys, and a small notebook lay on the table in a neat pile. The notebook was creased and handled to the point where duct tape held the binding together. He swallowed air trying to say something.

"Maybe I shouldn't tell you this, but . . ." While his friends had a way of keeping their inner selves ensconced under layers of jock masculine subterfuge, Ben had always been without guile. Quick to laugh and quick to cry. Sensitive in a way that would have left him exposed and vulnerable if he'd been anyone else in their school. When he left for college, he wept openly even though he was the one breaking up with her, and Stacey had to bite the inside of her cheek to get her eyes a bit misty so he wouldn't think her heartless. "I heard from her a while back. Or I guess I didn't hear from her, but she friended me on that thing—MySpace or whatever. Her profile said she was in Vietnam . . ."

"Sure. I heard something like that."

"But that doesn't make it any less fucked. She'll be back at some point."

Stacey shook her head. "I don't think she's ever coming back. And I don't care if she does." She twisted a napkin so she'd have something to do with her hands. She blurted out, "I told my family."

"And?" he asked, after she said nothing further. "I wouldn't even believe it if you told me your mom and dad don't support you."

"You know—Patrick, though."

"He'll come around."

She laughed without meaning to. "Yeah, it's just—"

At that point, she'd had what she now considered the hardest year of her life. She'd left for Wittenberg with this shock, this anger at the person she cared for most in the world. It made her feel the blood in her brain. She hadn't been able to understand that she was 1) depressed and 2) gay. That sounded absurd, but there it was. She'd spent a year with Lisa, and still she tried to date men when she got to college. Still she clung to this idea that Lisa had been a special situation, a fluke, a temptation now removed. Simultaneously, she was "losing her faith," not even realizing it was happening until she was deep within the throes of an antireligious conversion, understanding the infantile reasoning behind the fairy tales that girded the dogma of her ancestors. It created a sense of such loss, of mourning a thing she cherished, of flailing for something prescriptive to hold on to. When she stopped going to church there was a hole in every Sunday, and a tide of anxiety would come rolling in. So she sat around her freshman year feeling sad more or less all the time, getting a reputation as an ice queen, ignored by her roommate and uninterested in anything but old pictures of the people she missed. She spent one tortured spring day deleting Lisa from her life. Deleting her from AOL Instant Messenger, deleting the pictures of them from her computer, shredding the hard copies. All that stuff she should have been too old for.

She wrung the napkin and looked to Ben, wondering if she could trust him with this. "When I told my mom, we were sitting on the couch folding laundry. She was going on about something, and I was sitting there—" *Do not cry in Friendly's.* "Thinking about how I would wait until I got back to Wittenberg in the fall, and if I still felt this way. If I still felt like . . ." She swallowed her tears, but it did no good. "If I still felt like killing myself, I would be allowed to go ahead and do it." Ben didn't flinch at this; he held the blond stubble of his jaw and listened. "And then I was holding a pair of Matt's shorts and just thought, 'Are you kidding me, Stacey? Just tell her. If you're making a promise to yourself like that, you at least have to try to tell her.' So I did. I just said, 'Mom, I think I'm gay.' " She laughed and wiped at tears. "And then I corrected myself and said, 'I mean, I know I am.' "

Ben waited. "She didn't take it well."

"No, she did—I . . . There was this moment when I saw in her face—like she was trying to make a decision. And she could've gone either way, I'm sure of it."

Telling Ben this, she was basically right back in the moment. Dizzy and so short of breath that her apologies emerged in dry little heaves, like she'd just finished a sprint.

"I'm sorry. I'm really, really sorry," she kept saying to her mother.

When her mom started crying, tears pretty much exploding out of her eyes, Stacey truly felt like she might pass out. Why had she thought it would be a good idea to tell her? She should not have done that. It would destroy everything she had left. She would never be able to come home without this hanging between them. Her mom would never see her the same way, would never again be her best friend. And Lisa was gone. And now she had no one.

"How long?" Her mom wiped spastically at her eyes, open wounds that kept refilling. "How long have you thought this?"

"I don't know. A long time now. Years, I guess." For some reason, Stacey remembered camping and the time she fell into her own patch of pee. How hard they'd both laughed. She mourned to go back to that moment. She couldn't think of anything else to say, so she kept apologizing.

Finally, her mom's arm slid under hers, and she gripped Stacey's hand with the strength of a fever.

"No. Don't be sorry. I just can't believe you didn't tell me." She took Stacey's chin and pulled her face up so they were eye to eye. She'd never seen her mother so distraught, so sorrowful. Her bright blue irises, which she'd always thought of as a configuration of home, bore into her own. "I just wish you'd have known you could tell me." She palmed Stacey's skull, then her cheek. "You're my love, Stacey. And that love has no conditions, no exceptions, no matter what. Do you understand? I would *die* before I'd stop loving you."

There's something about hugging your mom that sends you back in time. Something about the detergent smell of her shoulder and the clean shampoo scent of her hair that reminded Stacey she had a long life ahead. So many things to do and see. She couldn't believe that all this time she'd let the dark gods of her neurons guide her so wrong. When Matt and her dad got home, she told them, and then they sat around on the couch for a while, teary and alive, laughing about how much they all loved one another.

"So it sounds like it worked out," Ben said very carefully. She reminded herself she was nineteen years old. There was so much more left to see.

"It did, but . . ." She shook her head because he wasn't getting it. She pointed to the table, jabbed her index finger to gain focus and control. "Lisa didn't do this to me. This is who I am and who I've always been, but I cared about her. And let me tell you, I could *fucking kill her* if I saw her right now. Because she left. I faced this down alone. I didn't run away. I didn't hide. Even though it terri-fied me to do it, I did it. And now everyone talks about how much courage Lisa had to go running off to the other side of the world? Fuck her. *I had fucking courage.* I had courage."

She retracted her finger and folded her arms. Ben sat back in the booth and looked out the window, glum on his pretty face like mud. "I realize . . ." He hesitated. To think about what would hap-pen to him. To think of him then: so beautiful and alive and her friend. "I realize this may not be helpful, but you've got . . . a good thing." He spoke each word deliberately.

"How do you figure that?" she wondered, almost angrily.

"You just said it. Your family's standing by you. You know when I last spoke to my dad? Last summer. He's down in Florida visiting my uncle while I'm here. Know why? Because we can't be in the same room together."

"You two always butted heads."

"No, you don't understand." He held his hands apart like he was cupping a loaf of bread. "I hate him. I hate him totally and completely. He is a small-minded, bitter man who's going to get liver disease and be dead within a decade, and you know what? I cannot fucking wait. I love my mom, I love my sisters, but I hate that man. He's poisoned everything I've ever done, and if I let him near me he'll poison whatever I try to do."

Because in those days she felt so close to bursting into tears all the time, it was unsettling to see Ben clear-eyed, motivated, and convinced of what he was saying.

"If you have people beside you in life who care about you, who love you, who you can count on—that's all there is, Stace."

"And you don't."

"No, I do! That's what I'm saying. I learned the difference. I've got Mom and my sisters, and Bill and Rick—if I can ever get them to talk to each other again."

She laughed despite herself. "You're counting your two douche-bag high school friends?"

He grinned, surely knowing what a torch his smile could be. "I consider them more douchebag high school *brothers*."

Then they were both laughing hard enough that other lunch patrons glanced over the tops of the booths to see what could possibly be so hilarious.

"Speaking of your neighborhood, I saw Bethany Kline tonight. Actually, that's sorta the reason I'm here. She wants my help getting Lisa to come home."

Mr. Clifton arched his eyebrows once. "Ah."

"Do you ever . . . Have you ever . . . heard anything from Lis?"

He took a long quaff and then licked the foam from his upper lip, now missing the mustache he'd worn for so long. "The inimitable Lisa Han." His eyes and lips searched for the right words. "Let me say two things: One, I have no patience for what Lisa did taking off like that. If Kim or J.D. pulled that on me, I would consider them cruel people. I would wonder if they could take into account human beings other than themselves."

She wanted to shout both *Yes!* and *But you don't understand.*

"On the other hand, I've lived across the street from Bethany since they moved in, when Lisa was seven or eight years old, and I know that woman has problems. She needs to see a therapist as badly as anyone I've ever met." He inspected a chip in his glass, scratching a thumb over the divot. "I wrote to Lisa maybe a year after she left."

Stacey's entire body tensed. "You did?"

"Sure. Just to say I understand why she did what she did, but that didn't excuse it. Her mother was on the verge of a nervous breakdown and she had a responsibility to call her, to try to work it out."

"Bethany didn't tell me that."

"I at least got Lisa to write to her, but . . ." He waved a hand to indicate how it ended there.

"Where was she?"

"About to cross into Cambodia, according to her."

She blinked back furious tears. Mr. Clifton could see this struggle, though.

"I take it you have not heard from her in some time?"

"No." She shook her head, swallowed, and swallowed some more. "It's not just her fault, it's mine too. I was . . . pissed at her. I didn't try very hard."

"If it makes you feel a bit better, you're not the only one. Lisa was always brash, impulsive, and I think she's completely miscalculated how much she's hurt the people who care about her. Take Danny. Those two were thick as thieves when they were little. He went and did three tours in the army. Three tours. Paul and I were supposed to get beers tonight, but Danny wandered off and didn't come home, so now Paul's back at the house waiting up. It's like even though Dan's the same sweet kid I've known since he was in diapers, he's not. Not really. It's not just his injury either." She'd heard of Dan's lost eye, torn from its socket in some botched operation pushing the pointless Sisyphean boulder that was Afghanistan. Maybe he hadn't suffered Rick Brinklan's fate, but there was something about the intimacy of an eyeball, the slick softness, that demanded it bear no injury in anyone's lifetime. "He's erratic," Mr. Clifton went on. "He's distant. He's about a million miles from the kid he was, and really, I'm coming to realize I always thought of him basically as one of my own. Now it's like talking to the ghost of Danny."

"Talking to Danny was always like talking to the ghost of Danny."

He appeared not to appreciate this gentle ribbing.

"No, not like this. He needed someone, and Lisa could have

been that friend to him. You know? If you do talk to her, please tell her I said that."

She felt an urge then. Because sitting across this table surface felt confessional. She wanted to spill everything about Lisa, about Bethany, about her final errand of the night. But something stopped her. Instead she drained the last of her beer. It wasn't the note she wanted to leave on, but it was late, an hour had gone by in a blink, and her mom and dad would both be waiting up. She told Mr. Clifton how glad she was that she ran into him.

"Just keep being yourself, Ms. Moore," he said. "The world needs souls like yours." She hugged him again, said good-bye. He turned his attention to the baseball game, and as she departed into the warm fluid of the night, she marveled at how many extremely decent people she'd known in this place. How much she'd taken them for granted.

She crossed from New Canaan's downtown into the nearest residential neighborhood. She passed her old church on the corner of McArthur and High Streets, where as a toddler she'd played in the basement, where she'd sat every Sunday of her adolescence. She remembered the First Christian Church as staggeringly tall, looming over the town, a fixture of permanence and strength. Passing it now, maybe five years since the last time she was inside, it was like seeing it through a new set of eyes. Fixed atop the twin wooden doors, the stained glass mural of Jesus on the cross looked like a cheap, garage-sale version of the epic mosaics she'd seen in old European cathedrals. The gray brick edifice was too bright. A sixties ranch home architect trying to pawn off a Gothic sensibility and failing badly.

She had to walk only another block. When Patrick and Becky went house hunting right after her niece Jamie was born, they decided on an old colonial-style near downtown because it was walking distance from First Christian. The porch light was on, but the home was otherwise dark. She took the envelope from her purse and read her brother's name one last time—as if she might have accidentally written another one without realizing. She stood beside his mailbox, letter in hand. Just staring.

When she told Patrick she was going to Columbus to see their parents, he'd, as usual, asked that she spend the night with him, Becky, and the girls.

You haven't been to see us in New Canaan in years. We always have to catch you at Mom and Dad's. There was good reason for this. At their parents' place, Patrick dared not bring up what she knew he wanted to.

The last time she stayed with them—not the kitchen conversation right after she came out, but years later, well after she thought he'd given up on his absurd notions of conversion—he'd cornered her after Becky and the girls went to bed. Sat her down on the living room couch. Put his hand on her shoulder. And he started crying.

"Hell is real," he said. "I know you don't want to hear that. But I have to say it." He tapped the corners of his eyes to staunch his tears. "I couldn't live with myself if I didn't try. Because, Stacey, you're playing with literal fire here. You're living a lifestyle contrary to everything laid out in the Bible. You're in *danger*. You have to understand that."

"Why won't you *stop* this," she begged, hating the tinny, pleading sound of her voice. She wanted so badly to get angry, but she couldn't. She just couldn't. She remembered too well how Patrick put her on his shoulders during the Fourth of July parade when she was little and nearly burned his hair off with her sparkler. When he let her hang out with him and Becky when they were in high school and Becky still filled her with such older girl awe. How when Stacey's team lost in the finals of their seventh-grade volleyball tournament, and she was so embarrassed by how hard she was crying, he hugged her, and made dumb joke after dumb joke that cracked her up despite herself. How when she, Patrick, and Matt got Monopoly for Christmas and played it to exhaustion, Patrick would always win, but he would also team up with her to make sure Matt finished last. He was her brother. She was helpless not to love him still. "Mom and Dad are over this. They're past it. Why can't you be?"

"Mom and Dad are doing what they think is right." He put his hand on her cheek. The wrinkles of a husband and father had crowded around his eyes. He was beginning to look so much like their dad. "And so am I. You can still change, Stacey. You can get help. There's still time. God can forgive anything if you allow Him."

She stood in front of her brother's home holding the envelope. She couldn't say on the phone—let alone to his face—what she'd written in this letter. It only occurred to her to pen it after she agreed to see Bethany. She'd say to Lisa's mother what she'd always wanted to say, and then she'd tell Patrick what she needed to tell him. She'd confront the two people who'd long made her ashamed for what she shouldn't have been ashamed of. She'd hurl at these two birds the same lethal stone. Yet she almost wanted to fail at this. To walk away. More than that, she wondered if Patrick would even hear what she was saying. She'd sealed the envelope before re-reading, but certain phrases came back to her, things she'd written to be as cruel to Patrick as he'd been to her. If she wasn't cruel, he wouldn't understand. He would not comprehend that his "love" for her was part of the reason she almost did something horrifically drastic as a scared, lonely eighteen-year-old. She recalled the line where she said he was part of the reason she almost hanged herself in her dorm room closet. No god could save a person from the responsibility of doing that to someone they claimed to love.

She opened the mailbox, set the letter inside, and closed it.

As she walked away, she pulled her phone from her pocket to text her parents that she was running several hours behind but instead saw the push notification for an e-mail. She slid it open. A chill rippled through her.

Hey Magical. Things are going well. Kiss the ground of The Cane for me. Let's catch up soon.

–L

Stacey wasn't sure what drove to the core of her aching and resentment and love for Lisa more: that after all these years all it had taken was one stupid e-mail, maybe not to hear Lisa's voice, but to at least see it alive on the screen—or that in the last decade Lisa had forgotten the nickname she'd bestowed on her, the one Stacey so wanted to hear again.

"We have our lenses, our goggles," Hilde told her at some point in their three days together in Zagreb. "We see our friends, our lovers, our home—all of it through this filter. And in many ways the impossibility of ever removing that lens, it's our defining trait as a species."

In 2011, Stacey moved to Ecuador to teach English while she applied to English graduate programs. Before she flew back to the States to begin at Michigan, she decided she wanted to see the world's greatest rain forest while it was still around. She flew first to Rio de Janeiro and then to Manaus, where the Rio Negro and the Rio Solimões split from the Amazon. Jet lag and an unpleasant reaction to the malaria pills made it a dizzying, mostly miserable trip. She felt hungover the whole time, in a perpetual state of soggy-headed exhaustion. On the tour she met a young couple, Nadja and Carlos, who were departing from the tour early, driving a rental car back to Manaus, and they offered Stacey a ride. She fell asleep in the backseat of their SUV, the jungle canopy blocking most of the sunlight from the lonesome highway that wound through the fringes of the jungle. When she came to, it was like she'd been dropped onto an alien planet. The rain forest was gone. They were driving along the side of a mountain, running parallel to a valley below where parched, sickly trees clamored from dry grass. Down in the valley, moving along a dirt road as wide as an airport tarmac, were thousands and thousands of cattle. The sun had fallen just to the horizon and a brown-yellow light filtered through the massive constellation of dust kicked up by the hooves of the animals. They were being corralled by two helicopters, which hovered above, blades beating the wind in a thudding, staccato percussion. The beasts moved like a river of flesh and leather, chugging over the land in loose formation, braying in fear or boredom or annoyance. Carlos was asleep, and stupidly, she asked Nadja what they were looking at.

She said it first in Portuguese and then translated. "Cattle ranch."

But this was only a ranch the way Noah's disaster was only a flood. This line of cattle stretched farther than she could see, brown and white, black and spotted, a ghostly noise rising from their collective voices, until they reached an enormous enclosure of aluminum gates and barbed wire fencing. The helicopters buzzed along like dragonflies, their opaque windshields grinning with the smugness of conquerors, certain that nothing could come along and sweep them away. Urine-yellow clouds wafted over the land, coating the draining day, the horizon ablaze with sickly brown light. Never in her life had Stacey felt so ill, the invisible scent that links us to our ancestors, to all living things right down to the lichen at the beginning of creation, rising through her lungs, throat, and nostrils like gorge. Watching that river of beasts was akin to watching a man try to bite off and eat his own tongue. In the years to come this image would never quite leave her. She'd think of those animals, and the reality of what was happening to her, to the people she loved, to her home, would become overwhelming. Occasionally this sensation would take hold of her heart and grip it with the loneliness of death, and she would wish for Lisa. Because when your waking mind is consumed at all times by wanton devastation, by oblivion, you have no choice but to dream of courage.

Now, driving through a dark Ohio night, remembering the collective moan of those cows, she thought of what she might say to Lisa. If she just bought a plane ticket. If she showed up at her door. Not with expectations but just to say thank you for what Lisa had given her. The girl who'd taught her to swear, to drink, to use a condom, to read weird, wild books, to explore this one irreducible, unquantifiable life. Without whom she never would have left home, never climbed down to the crater lake of Quilotoa, never tasted locro in Argentina with a group of Israeli backpackers, never stayed up all night on the streets of Vilnius with a gorgeous artist who painted only sex zombies, never explored a foreign capital with a woman who could explain to her its opera house and what carbonic acid does to the ocean's calcifying organisms, never thought to try to scrape her nails against the ceiling of her imagination and then claw past it.

Turning on to Stillwater, a shortcut to Highway 36 which would eventually lead her back to the interstate, she reached over and turned off her phone. She would wait until morning to write back to Lisa because the anxiety that had taken hold reminded her of that moment on the scarred edge of the Amazon, watching as that noxious cloud of dirt and shit and sun engulfed the world.

Coming over a hill, she was met with the harsh glare of headlights and slowed. The vehicle was still, pulled off to the side of the road so that its high beams angled right into her eyes, and this wrenched her from her brooding dream. As she applied her foot to the brake, she saw a figure standing beside this stranded car, arms above the head, waving, flagging her down. Her own headlights cut a hole in the dark, uncovering the pale ghost outline of a woman's face. There was a sheen of sweat on her forehead above a look of dismay, of dread. Stacey hesitated, but her hands took the wheel, almost without her consent, and guided the Jeep to the left so that it brought her vehicle nose to nose with the small blue sedan. Now Stacey could see a dark smudge on the woman's jaw that looked like a bruise or soil or soot. For the last time that night, the unnerving sense of a fated encounter descended upon Stacey Moore. Because she recognized the car. She recognized the woman. And she recognized the fear of stepping into a scene, a situation, a moment that in your heart you know is somehow utterly wrong.

DAN EATON AND THE MURDER
THAT NEVER WAS

On the drive back home to see Hailey Kowalczyk, the girl to whom Dan Eaton lost his virginity, probably his heart, and certainly countless games of driveway H-O-R-S-E, he got to thinking about Elias Wiman. Wiman was a nicotine/caffeine-addicted private who existed on a diet of dip, cigarettes, Red Bull, and Snickers, an emaciated, feral Kentuckian, who had a real chip on his shoulder about Ohioans, who he saw as effete snobs sticking their noses up at the real salt-of-the-earth south of the river. Despite this, he and Wiman became friends and had long, uninteresting arguments about what made their respective states superior. Take the night the two of them stayed up with Greg Coyle while Coyle waited to find out from his wife via Gchat if they were going to have a boy or a girl.

"You call your towns 'hollers,' " Dan objected. "I mean what *is* that? Russellville? That place was more scarring than anything we'll see at war." They'd had Kentucky immersion while living at Fort Campbell, home of the 101st Airborne. Wiman was from Russellville, an hour east. One visit was plenty for Dan.

"A holler," said Wiman, "means like 'down the road a ways.' It's a term of affection, you fucking snotty-ass bitch."

"I'm sorry but I got Eaton's back on this. Kentuckians all have sheep DNA." Coyle was playing with his knife, leaning back in a cheap desk chair to the point of spill. He'd thunk the blade into the plywood, twist, withdraw. Thunk, twist, withdraw. "You know why they can't teach driver's ed and sex ed on the same day in

Kentucky?" Coyle asked. " 'Cuz that poor fucking horse gets too tired."

This was in Hawija just as Iraq was spiraling into what some people called civil war. They'd agreed to stay up with Coyle because who could sleep anyway? After they lit up a bunch of insurgents that afternoon in a spectacular, invigorating firefight, the adrenaline was still there hours later. Dan half read a copy of *Theodore Rex*, trying to calm the thunder out of his blood while they waited for Greg's news.

"Can't wait till you got a hot little daughter. It'll serve you right," Wiman told Coyle. The new pastime was giving Coyle grief about a potential daughter. One of Dan's best friends since he'd gotten his platoon assignment, Coyle was a butt-chinned, all-American blond, California tan, muscled, and as breezy a guy as he'd ever known. He was also a total cad until he married a woman he'd been dating for only three months right before they deployed.

"I've just fucked so much nasty pussy in my life, it would be God's worst kind of justice if Melody's having a girl," he explained.

Without looking up from his book Dan told him, "I'm not sure that's how God operates."

"That *is* how God operates," said Wiman. His accent dripped. He wasn't so much playing *Grand Theft Auto: Vice City* as he was gunning down civilians and shooting rockets at the police vehicles that then pursued him. "Doling out justice, vengeance, retribution to pretty boys."

"Christ, where is she?" grumbled Coyle. He set the knife down, ran a hand over his buzz. He picked the knife back up, stabbed it into the plywood. Two weeks before he met Melody at the Cat West bar, Coyle claimed to have slept with a Tennessee Titans cheerleader. Dan tended to believe him because months after he fell in love with Melody, this cheerleader was still sending him graphic, close-up pictures of her vagina.

"Get. Some. Sleep." Sergeant Wunderlich emerged from the kitchen area with a spoonful of cereal crunching between his jaws, his T-shirt tucked into his sweatpants.

"Can't, Sergeant," Dan said. "We've got to find out if God will punish Greg for his loose ways."

"You ever stop reading, Eaton?" Wunderlich took *Theodore Rex* from Dan's hands to examine the cover. "Wasn't this a Whoopi Goldberg movie with a tee-ranasaurus?"

"Sergeant, I been meaning to tell you—and no offense," said Wiman. "But if you make us be in another video for your wife, I'm filing, like, a sexual harassment complaint."

Earlier that week during some downtime, Wunderlich had cajoled nearly a dozen guys from their undermanned platoon to be in the music video he was sending to his wife. This was like a thing in the war: soldiers choreographing and lip-synching. *To our horror,* Dan wrote to Hailey, *the song was Alanis Morissette "Hand in My Pocket."* Part of the dance actually involved putting one hand in the pocket of their ACUs while giving a peace sign with the other, hips swishing.

"That's what you fucking kids don't understand about love," said Wunderlich.

"You're like ten months older than me," said Coyle.

"You go trudging off to war every couple of years, puts stress on your marriage. You gotta find ways to be inventive, be surprising, so your wife don't suck off the mailman."

"Please, Sergeant. Your wife ain't got shit to do with it. You chose that song for you," said Wiman.

" 'Hand in My Pocket's' a fucking jam, Private." He slurped milk from the bowl, lapped the stubble that seemed to grow right onto his lip flesh, and shook his head defiantly. "I have no shame."

Greg coughed, *"Understatement."*

Sergeant Wunderlich was an interesting dude. Lumberjack

strong, he looked like a total badass, had civilian pictures of himself with a beard like roadkill strapped to his chin, had the tattoo of a skull on each shoulder (one with a knife jutting from the eye socket and the other with a rose clamped in its teeth). Yet he listened to music like a teenage lesbian. He had CDs from Lilith Fair. No one in the entire battalion could have told you what Lilith Fair was until meeting Wunderlich.

Wiman whistled air through his sandstone teeth. "Again, I don't mean to be combative, Sergeant. Just mean to point out that love be like some highly dubious bullshit Hollywood made up to sell us movies and diamond rings and shampoo and boner pills."

"Wow, what a fine philosophical rumination from a nineteen-year-old who smokes cigarettes while he's dipping," said the sergeant.

Dan laughed as Wunderlich returned his book. Seeing that this conversation was not ebbing, he marked his place with the photograph he used as a bookmark: him and Hailey in seventh grade.

"What it all boils down to, Private, is that no one's really got it figured out just yet." And for some reason, Wunderlich made a little lasso motion over his head and pretended to rope in Elias Wiman. Somewhere a few klicks away, a mortar exploded. No one even moved.

Coyle's wife never messaged him that night. After patrol the next day he learned about his daughter in an e-mail. Two weeks later, Wiman would be killed in a traffic accident. His driver saw a dead dog in the middle of Route Omaha and decided to go a different way. They'd all heard of insurgents hiding the bang in those rotting carcasses that flecked the Iraqi roads like spittle, but in this case, the driver ended up flipping their Humvee off an embankment.

If Dan let his mind idle for any amount of time, even mid-conversation, he'd see them again. Coyle. Wunderlich. Wiman.

Rudy doing a pencil sketch of the small sliver of Afghanistan's Hindu Kush that made up their whole horizon. When they pulled Elias Wiman out, there was no solidity left to his pulverized bones. He flopped onto the stretcher like a sack of sawdust.

Dan tried letting Wiman lay as he drove over the dips and rises of the Allegheny hills. Finally the oblate plane of Northeast Ohio came into repose. Down through the Mahoning Valley and a tinderbox summer, he passed his father's hometown, the city shimmering in the hazy sun as if it might vanish. Once over the hump of Youngstown, it was nothing but the rippling green spears of cornstalks, the trembling soy leaves awaiting the sweatless industrial harvest. The mile markers fell and the telephone poles bled tar. The sky went from a deep orange to a bruise of purple and blue, the clouds carved by shafts of biblical sunlight—here lighting a patch of cud-stuffed cows, there illuminating a fallen barn with Ohio's bicentennial logo flaking paint.

He avoided driving long distances as often as possible. His peripheral vision compromised and still, a year after the enucleation, having to focus extremely hard when judging depth, heavy highway traffic made Dan uncomfortable. And yet this excuse for why he so rarely went home sounded thin even to him. Now he had to at least cop to the beauty of it. The sky over the place you were born has a familiarity beyond how the clouds roll in or how the stars wink at you at night. The sky over your home behaves like that moment when, as a parachutist, you pull the rip cord and the heavens snatch you back. Even if you've traveled the world and seen better sunsets, better dawns, better storms—when you get that remembered glimpse of the fields and forests and rises and rivers of your home meeting the horizon, your jaw will tighten. The rip cord will yank you back from the descent.

The radio shuffled between talk and song and ad. To avoid thinking of Wiman and the others, he instead termited the details of his seventh-grade Ohio history class with Mrs. Bingham—this being where he first got to know Hailey. Seventh-grade boys have an insolent, smarm-soaked attitude about everything, but they all shut up for Bingham, the oldest teacher in the middle school. She had the physique of a snowman, capped with hair just as white, as grandma as it comes. She was utterly shameless in using Ohio's savage frontier history to hold their attention.

The first day she didn't even take roll. She just launched into a story of a Shawnee council of women called the Miseekwaawe-ekwakee, who, when they captured prisoners, might touch a certain white man, "To reserve him." The Miseekwaaweekwakee women would strip the prisoner naked and bind him to a pyre.

"And they'd roast him alive and cannibalize him," said Mrs. Bingham. She had a mellifluous voice, almost singsong in its lilt. Later she told them how women of her day had gone to elocution school, and her voice was particular in the way of that word: *el-o-cue-shun*.

Dan felt that hot panic of enjoying that class, of loving its lucid, gory stories yet wanting to remain totally anonymous and unremarkable to his peers. He was always conscious of Hailey, a simmering presence to his right, embedded in his awareness like a pleasant splinter. He hadn't known her at Elmwood because she'd been in a different class, with his buddy Lisa Han. Now sitting near her once a day every day, well, he chewed pencils into gnawed, pocked kindling.

"You should take it easy," was the first thing Hailey ever said to him. "You'll give yourself lead poisoning." He spent days puzzling out if this was disgust, teasing, or an overture. Assessing himself in the bathroom mirror, he decided—despite his hatred of touching his own eyeballs—to begin wearing contacts as often as he could stand.

Mrs. Bingham assigned them each a character from Ohio history that they had to live with for the whole year, leading to a grade-defining presentation. It had the aura of being the popular class, and it was where a short, shy kid, who couldn't help but raise his hand, learned to fit in. Dan got a reputation for knowing everything about history even though he was just reading the textbook like everyone else. He found it a page-turner. Because of this reputation, Hailey asked for his help with her historical figure; to Dan, it felt like some combination of winning the lottery and being punched in the gut. Tina Ross was widely regarded by the boys as the hottest girl in their class, but his crush on Hailey was a brushfire gone wild. On the bus she usually sat in the very last seat in the back with Lisa and Kaylyn Lynn where they hunched into one another and shared whatever peculiar secrets girls always traded. He lived for the days he ended up across from her so he could hoard stolen glances. When Hailey asked him for help on her presentation, he ended up reading every book with even the scantest mention of Simon Girty, this gritty, larger-than-life product of the Ohio frontier. His mom was driving him to the New Canaan Public Library every other day.

What began with her coming over after school so he could feed her details from his Simon Girty reading continued even after her presentation. They'd shoot baskets at the hoop above his garage or watch *Total Request Live* and root for their preferred videos to top the list (Hailey had a passion for Korn's "Freak on a Leash"). They'd sit at opposite armrests, as far as his living room couch would allow, but he could still feel her like a source of heat. One time his mom came in and snapped a picture of them ("I've got to finish out this roll—smile, guys!"), and that picture explained everything about the distance of memory. He remembered thinking Hailey extremely chic, hip, always dressed like a tomboy model, usually in her favorite Sheryl Swoopes USA jersey. But in that photo, she was just a dorky seventh grader with a ponytail, red-faced, a missing baby tooth in her embarrassed smile, jeans, and a black tank top a size too big. Gripping the armrest like he's afraid of this girl was a pale, scrawny kid with his dad's ginger hair, freckles like a bomb of cinnamon went off on his nose, and a big zit on his lip. Before he deployed, Dan took that photo from his desk and stuck it in the book he was reading at the time.

One day Hailey found his *Calvin and Hobbes* comic books, and he kicked himself for leaving them out. He still felt so much like a little kid, clinging to all the things he loved about childhood, while his peers, especially Kruger, Jarecki, and Hansen, were growing facial and armpit hair, stretching ever taller, their voices dropping through the basement. When Hailey picked up the comic, he wanted to snatch it out of her hands and run.

"I've heard of this," she said. "Is it funny?"

His shrug took his shoulders nearly to the top of his head. "No, not really. I mean, I got them for Christmas a while back."

"Can I borrow one?"

She did, and she ended up borrowing them all. They'd sit on the bus and pore over their favorite strips, cackling at Calvin's limitless imagination and capacity for trouble. In Hailey's favorite, Calvin was hammering nails into the coffee table when his mom comes running in screaming, "Calvin! What are you doing to the coffee table?!?" He quizzically looks at his work and asks, "Is this some sort of trick question, or what?"

Dan could still see Hailey, knees propped on the back of the bus seat, clutching her gut, her plump cheeks pink with laughter.

"You're totally Calvin," she said.

"How do you figure? I never get into trouble ever."

"Not like that. I mean, you're like wise beyond your years or something."

And he had the very not-wise-beyond-his-years reaction of: *I think I'll probably marry Hailey when I grow up.*

His own character in Mrs. Bingham's Ohio history class was General "Mad" Anthony Wayne, the man President Washington tasked with avenging a debacle, in which the U.S. Army lost 623 soldiers trying to capture Ohio from the Indian tribes. It was the worst loss the United States would suffer against any Indian force in its history and also a worse loss of life than any battle during the entire Revolutionary War, which he always thought said a lot about how nations go about remembering themselves. Wayne led an army of 3,500 back into Ohio.

"Little Turtle was the only war chief who saw the writing on the wall," Mrs. Bingham told them on the day she recounted the Battle of Fallen Timbers. She picked up a book from her desk. She took her eyeglasses, which hung from a beaded strap around her neck, and rather than hooking them around her ears, held them in front of the page the way you would a magnifying glass. "Little Turtle told the other war chiefs, 'The trail has been long and bloody; it has no end. The pale faces come from where the sun rises, and they are many. They are like the leaves of the trees. When the frost comes they fall and are blown away. But when the sunshine comes again they come back more plentiful than ever before.' " She snapped the book shut and let the eyeglasses dangle.

He tried to make a goofy face at Hailey, but she didn't return it. She hadn't come to his house that week or sat by him on the bus. A few days later, he saw pen-knifed into the rubbery green plastic of the bus seat in front of him *DE + HK* inside an angular heart. Scratched there by some enterprising wit.

"Everyone can tell you like her," Lisa told him as they walked home together. "Just some advice: Don't be so all over her."

He knew Lisa didn't say that to be cruel. He'd been eating her mom's cookies, drinking their Capri Suns, and wondering about her beautiful friend for as long as he could remember. Lisa was both his buffer and his conduit to the popular kids; she looked out for him. Nevertheless, Dan protested: he wasn't "all over" Hailey. They were just friends. They liked hanging out. But he knew that wasn't true. Hailey didn't like him that way, and now she had to put in her distance.

That night he went home and read about "Mad" Anthony Wayne. The encounter took place in a portion of northern Ohio near present-day Toledo, an eerie slice of forest called The Wilderness. A recent storm had felled hundreds of trees, and Wayne's army charged under, over, and through the timbers. The retreating Indians fell back to Fort Miamis, but the British spurned them (some might say "betrayed") and they had to keep running. They had no choice but to sue for peace. The Wyandot, Delaware, Ottawa, Miami, Potawatomi, Chippewa, and all the other mighty tribes of the Ohio territory ceded nearly all their land in exchange for goods. Beginning with the Treaty of Greenville in 1795, to paraphrase Thomas Jefferson, war would become mostly bribery. Whites would always view their boundaries with the Indians as a temporary arrangement until the moment they needed more land. In this fashion, the borders of Ohio were born, but the battle would continue over the course of the coming century. All the way to the glory of the Pacific.

From the exit, he followed State Route 229 past the endless bisecting county roads, the small towns cluttered into plots of two-story buildings, gas stations, volunteer fire departments, Jean's Ice Cream, Buddy's Tavern, Gary's Grocery, long spans of telephone wire, pickup trucks of every make and model carrying their loads. From the east, he passed the sweeping gloss of Jericho Lake with its ink-smudge homes on the other side. The sun drew down over the straggler clouds, vestiges of some long-dissipated low-pressure system now drifting lazily in a sea of dark cream. The rest of the drive was as familiar as finding his way through his childhood home in the dark, the way you know every corner, every doorway, how to angle your body around the dining room table.

And then there was what had changed. Zanesville Road, once nothing but fields, had vanished under pavement and parking lot. Gas stations, pet stores, tanning salons, Pizza Hut, AutoZone, Ruby Tuesday, Staples, Dairy Queen, Discount Tire, and finally a new crop of prefab homes, each one a clone of some original vinyl-sided patient zero. This was the strip that scotched away New Canaan's downtown, relocating all business, all jobs, to this stretch of off-the-rack strip mall, even as year by year the same gutted quality befell Zanesville Road.

Turning down Rainrock, he passed the old bus stop, the Klines' dark house, and pulled into his uneven slab of driveway beneath the basketball hoop, rusted and genuflecting over the concrete, where he and Hailey had waged countless H-O-R-S-E wars. He crawled from the stale odor of his car, stretched his limbs, felt them crackle. Dusk had settled to a purple velvet over the top of the nearby woods. His home sat almost completely unchanged: one story of white linoleum siding, rust-red shutters, and a basement level that grew out of the hill like a corn-fed rear end. The hoop looked worse than ever with pieces of the backboard chewed away, the rim bleeding rust all over the top of the net. The scars of Dan and his sisters could be seen on the scuffed and dented garage door, the quaint driveway lamp that had not one pane of glass left and the jagged root of a broken bulb still protruding from the socket.

Of course their neighbor Mr. Clifton was in his yard, flapping a hose around his flower beds. When he saw Dan pull in, he hastily shut the water off and crossed the lawn to greet him.

"Dan-Dan-Dan-Dan." He pulled Dan into a bear hug. "Dan, you're back."

"I'm back." He couldn't help but return a bashful grin at the enormity of Mr. Clifton's smile.

"Oh man, your parents didn't tell me you were coming home."

"Sorta didn't know myself until a few days ago."

"You look great!" Hearty slaps on the shoulder. Dan noticed Mr. Clifton studying his right eye. He was too polite to say anything awkward about how good it looked.

The Cliftons had been their neighbors for Dan's whole life. Their daughter, Kimberly, had been friends with the younger of his two sisters, Heather, and Dan's occasional babysitter. The hair had retreated to a ring around Mr. Clifton's skull with one kinky black patch struggling to hold territory on the crown. He'd shaved off his mustache. He'd never known him without it, and his lip looked bald. The wrinkles of his face seemed deeper, his smile still pure white in a pale brown face. Having Mr. Clifton for music class was almost like having one of his own parents. Dan got a C on a quiz once, and he wrote, *Dan! I'm sorry! Study!*

"How's Kim and J.D.?" he asked.

Mr. Clifton gave Dan the short version of his kids' various successes. "Feels like only yesterday your parents were paying Kim six dollars an hour because they thought Heather might push you off the roof. What about you, though? How's work? How's life?"

He tried to wrap everything up as concisely as possible: Good job in a civil engineer's office in Titusville. Basically glorified secretarial work, but still interesting enough. His boss was in charge of developing drilling projects across northern Pennsylvania, poking holes in the Marcellus Shale wherever feasible. Mostly Dan was in the office, but sometimes he followed him to job sites. He was learning a lot about drilling rigs and other gas infrastructure.

"Never thought it's where I'd wind up, and—you know—I still have thoughts about going back to school, but that won't pay the bills, and this does. Never thought I'd know so much about feasibility analysis, site layout, gas pipeline routing, grading, drainage, storm water management . . ."

"So you like it?" Like a salute, he put a hand above his eyes to block the setting sun.

"I do. Plus it gives me time to read. At this point, my apartment's just a bed and books stacked to the ceiling, you know?"

With a shudder and a rattle, the screen door of the house thwacked open, the storm door closing mechanism no match for the arm that threw it wide.

"Kid! Get away from that man. What'd I tell you about stranger danger."

Mr. Clifton guffawed, and Dan went to hug his father.

When his dad hugged his sisters he held them by the shoulders first, looked them in the eye as if deciding about how they turned out, and then wrapped them up like he wanted to kill their husbands for taking them away. With Dan, he always took his hand in a crushing shake. Then the other arm looped around the back for three hard slaps. Each pat vibrated his lungs.

"Cam!" Dan's father called. "The worst of the kids is home!"

As his dad shook hands with Mr. Clifton, because he literally could not converse with another man without a firm handshake first (even if it was a neighbor and friend of nearly thirty years), Dan could hear his mom racing out of the house, throwing the storm door almost as hard.

"You little stinker, come here." A fierce hug and about twenty face-peppering kisses later ("My little man, my little man!"), she pulled away. "You come home and go see Clift first? Before the woman who pushed your damn watermelon head out?"

"Cam, get off the kid. You're giving him an O-dee-pol complex."

The older Dad got, the more he looked like himself, handsome somehow, improbably, despite pits of old acne scars and a rough

Scots-Irish face leathering further and further. He needed to put more sunscreen on his scalp where the white fuzz had thinned down to the sunspots. Maybe his gut had swelled, but there hadn't exactly been a washboard there in living memory. His gold tooth, tucked in place of an incisor he claimed to have lost in a bar fight in Saigon, threw a dull shine over an otherwise browning row of teeth.

Mom had colored her hair a lighter, summer shade, and her aging was still a graceful retreat. In school, all his friends had given Dan never-ending hell about how hot his mom was. Above her blue top was an expanse of pink skin and one hard mole. They must have been up to see Heather in Cleveland. Mom loved to get sunburned on Lake Erie. She held his cheek, studied him, tears pushing at her eyes, and Dan felt guilty about not coming home more often.

Arms crossed, Mr. Clifton beamed at them. "How long are you planning to stay?"

"Just a couple days."

"Unless I kidnap him," said Mom.

"Here's the thing you gotta understand about Daniel," said Dad, putting a finger in the air. "And I tell this to Cam all the time: the point of having kids is to get them the fuck outta your house. Now I hear all these stories about kids coming back home to live with their parents. Back in my day, that's called panhandling. Bums do it."

Again, Mr. Clifton cracked up. There was a little kid element to the two of them, Dad always trying to get his friend to shoot milk out of his nose at the lunch table. Mom had once told Dan and his sisters, "Your dad gets his jollies pretending to be the toughest mother-effer in the world, but that's all it is: pretend."

Dad was a door gunner on a helicopter in Vietnam. He came home and married a girl fifteen years his junior (she was sixteen when they started dating). He'd always been a bit of a schizophrenic character, which Mom attributed to his inability to make up his mind politically. He still swore that the U.S. could've beaten back the Viet Cong and won that war had it not been for the media and the flower children. According to Mom, Dad voted Nixon in '72, skipped '76, went hard-core for Reagan in both of his races, then voted Dukakis over Bush in '88. He then proceeded to vote twice for Bill Clinton and twice for George W. Bush. He maintained that Clinton was "the greatest president of my lifetime" and was furious when Obama kept Hillary from the White House, casting outraged votes for McCain and then "Pattycake" (which was his inexplicable nickname for Mitt Romney). First and foremost he was an old-school union guy. Retired now, for Dan's entire childhood he commuted up to Ohio Metal Working Products in Canton. His truck was still wallpapered with bumper stickers for the International Brotherhood of Boilermakers.

Dan spent his childhood wishing to be his father's son but by disposition channeled his mother: bookish, too nice for his own good, hearing from the other St. Vincent de Paul parishioners how sweet he was. It didn't seem possible he could ever be his father—a man who regaled even his daughters with stories of how he once fought a guy with a chain and a trash can lid in an alley (Mom called these his "tall Paul tales"). It took him a long time to understand what Mom meant about Dad being pretend. He was too young to see it when Mr. Clifton's wife, Rosa, passed away from cancer. To a young boy, the wonderful woman next door who stuffs you full of baked goods and comments on how handsome you're becoming every time she sees you is an invincible figure. Dan was very young, and she went very fast. He vaguely recalled the duality that fell over their little corner of Rainrock Road: utter sorrow and utter rally. Mom and Rosa had been young mothers together, and he remembered her trying to explain the death of her friend at the dining room table. Dan, Betty, and Heather sat there while Mom's pretty face crumpled—the first time he ever saw her cry.

"Do you get what's happening?" Heather asked him afterward.

"Course," he sputtered, but he thought maybe he didn't.

At the wake, he spent most of his time with Kimberly and J.D.'s younger cousins, all of them chasing one another in backyard tag, not understanding that dividing their teams based on skin color was inappropriate until J.D. came out and integrated them. When he went inside, Mr. Clifton was telling a story about Rosa and had everyone laughing through their Kleenex. Dan asked his mom if Dad was pretending not to be sad. She said that, no, he was sad: "He just has a durable heart." And he saw how Dad took care of almost everything: coordinated with the caterers, the funeral home, directed family from Cincinnati who weren't familiar with the screwy rural roads. He helped set up and tear down, cleaned the whole house afterward, and was at Mr. Clifton's, Kim's, or J.D.'s side every spare moment. Later that week, Dan watched from his bedroom window—Dad and Mr. Clifton sitting on the porch, passing what he thought at the time was a cigarette. Dad put his arm around Mr. Clifton's shoulder, and he could see his babysitter's father shaking. They ate many dinners with the Clifton family that year. Dad cracked jokes, and Mr. Clifton could still laugh like life had never cheated him.

Night edged over the heat of the day. The sweat clinging to the small of his back finally began to evaporate. Mom returned from the house with beers. She carried them out, two in each hand. Rolling Rocks, of course.

They stood in the driveway by the hoop, sipping from the emerald glass.

"You keep missing the ruckus, Dan. DEA raided that little shitbox motel by the square," said Mom.

"The Cactus Motel," Mr. Clifton offered.

"Folks running heroin out of it! Unbelievable." Dad slugged back the Rolling Rock. He used to only drink Budweiser until those commercials with the frogs came out. He'd said, "Welp. Can't drink moron beer," finished the rest of his Budweiser that night and, as far as Dan knew, had yet to touch another.

"I'll tell you, they need to clean that shit up. The last two years the DEA's been up here 'bout five times," he said.

"Meth," Mom said knowingly. "That's the one that makes getting your coffee at Dunkin' Donuts suspect."

"The skin and dental issues alone," said Mr. Clifton.

The three of them went on like that for a while as the first fireflies arrived from whatever netherworld they inhabited while the sun was up. In the year since he'd been out of the army, Dan had learned to stand by and let others do the talking, but with these three it was actually enjoyable. When you come back from deployment and you hear people blathering about stuff that doesn't quite have the life-and-death immediacy of running your fingers around your friend's body to check for unseen blood, you drift off quickly. You learn to turn the volume down on people's frequencies. He'd had a friend, Everton Cleary, who'd blown out both eardrums. Occasionally, Dan wished that had been his Purple Heart instead of the eye.

"Clift, come for dinner?" Mom asked, brightening. "We're doing pot roast."

"Already ate, Camille, I'm sorry."

Dad rolled his eyes. "Well then just come and drink my fucking beer—Jesus Christ."

Mr. Clifton looked at Dan. "I get the dinner invite near every night."

"Yeah, but Danny's home," Mom whined. "We need to catch up."

"And hear if he's getting his knob polished by anyone special," said Dad. Mom slapped his gut. He chortled.

"That's disgusting, and I *do not* want to hear about that." She winked at Dan. "Unless she's smart and pretty and I'd want her to give me grandbabies to smell."

He couldn't help but laugh. He was always surprised he didn't grow up to be funnier—maybe the gene skips the youngest.

"I can only eat a little something," he said. "First off, I'm picking up Hailey after work and we're getting dinner. Then for seconds—and I keep telling you guys this—I'm a vegetarian."

Dad reeled. "Jesus have mercy, what did I do wrong."

"No pot roast?" said Mom.

"What about brawts? They got those little flecks of peppers and jalapenos in 'em."

"Not sure you understand what vegetarian means, Dad."

"I'll give you some money. You can run to the market and pick something up." Before he could object, Mom ran inside and returned with a twenty from her purse. He continued to protest that this wasn't necessary, but he was preaching to nonbelievers. Ruth's Market was a small operation, but it was walking distance. As he set off down the street, Mom called him back.

"Wait wait wait! Just one more hug." She held him even tighter and longer this time. "My little man. Good to have you home." And over her shoulder he rolled his eye and the matching prosthetic for the men's benefit. Dad rolled his back at him. Mr. Clifton beamed. "It's good you're seeing Hailey," she said.

When he rounded the driveway he took a final glance over his shoulder and saw Mr. Clifton following his parents inside, hands tucked in his pockets. Mom and Dad slipped into the house, bantering. Mr. Clifton stopped to stare at the glowing blue evening, the smile on his face like the lonesome North Star.

Dan watched the last streaks of ashen light winnow away to the west. Walking down Rainrock, he passed Lisa Han's house again. Everyone else on the block had a paved driveway except the Klines. The delta of gravel still spilled into the road. It had been that way since he and Lisa were at Elmwood, and they'd skid out on their bikes.

The house sat at the end of the street, forlorn, the lawn browning, a testament to how the world never works out the way you think it will, let alone the way you want it to. He and Lisa exchanged a few e-mails in which she excitedly described her travel plans, and then she stopped responding. She had been his best friend for a time, like him a compulsive reader, and simply an easier companion than the guys who made up the punishing social web of adolescent boyhood. She left books she thought he'd like in their mailbox. Even though she was bound for higher social strata, bound to date the star basketball player, Lisa never dropped him. She made it her mission to yoke Dan into the network of New Canaan's popular kids. Even when Lisa and Hailey had their falling out, her loyalty never faltered. She also never made him feel bad when he forgave Hailey for Curtis Moretti.

He turned up the side of SR 229, heading past the woods where he and Lisa used to climb trees and come home with poison ivy. His tennis shoes felt too soft, each piece of gravel transmitting through the sole. He missed his rough-cut, full-grain tan leather boots, army-issued, where you could step on a piece of razor-sharp rebar without feeling it.

Like that, he was thinking of his time rooming with Greg Coyle in Italy. Greg, who would boredly thwock a tennis ball against the wall whenever Dan tried to read. One time when Coyle just wouldn't quit, Dan started to read to him the mystery of the Phaistos disc, explicated by Jared Diamond in *Guns, Germs, and Steel*. Discovered in an ancient Minoan palace on the island of Crete in 1908, the disc, a piece of otherwise unremarkable, unpainted baked clay, was the oldest example of printed writing in the archaeological record, dated to around 1700 BC. The printing on the disc perplexed archaeologists because the signs bore no resemblance to any known writing system, and the next example of such a technological innovation in printing would not appear until 2,500 years later and on the other side of the world, in China. It would be another six hundred years after that before such technology reappeared in the West, this time in medieval Europe.

"Plus it's still never been deciphered," he told Greg.

Coyle cocked a blond caterpillar eyebrow and said, "No big mystery there. Aliens, dude. Gotta be."

When they stood for inspection, Dan, like everyone, would get ripped, maybe because he'd stored his compression bandages in the wrong place or always tried to get away with not wearing the side plates of his body armor (those heavy, awkward five-by-five bastards). Greg Coyle, no matter how goofy he was, never got ripped, was always on point. Coyle, who referred to everything as a "MacDougal." A bore snake, pliers, a target at the range, military-age males, MREs, ops, battalions—they were all just MacDougals to him. To the dismay of the whole company, within weeks of their deployment everyone was saying it.

"We're getting those new up-armored MacDougals next month."

"These powdered MacDougals—goddamn! Better than Mom's homemade MacDougal."

"That other MacDougal was getting rocked by IEMacDougals,"

They landed in Iraq in 2006, when the country was no joke, but that joke worked right through rocket attacks and EFPs.

The second thing Dan did after he got out and visited Rudy in the hospital was attend Brent Della Terza's wedding in Austin, Texas. A lot of his friends from Iraq were there, guys he hadn't seen in a while because they'd gotten out after two tours. Badamier, Lieutenant Holt, Cleary, Wong, Doc Laymon, Drake in his wheelchair, "Other James" Streiss, now with two robot hands. They of course got drunk and began referring to everything as a "MacDougal," annoying the hell out of those piqued Texan bridesmaids. Decent, churchgoing women who had never seen soldiers cut loose. How hilariously stupid they could be. In his buzz, Dan found himself wishing to return to 2006, to be back on patrol with his friends.

He stopped to pull off his shoe and empty it of a pebble.

The remnants of the day backlit a distant cirrus cloud. It looked like a knife with a serrated blade. As he slipped the shoe back on, he heard a car approaching from behind and stepped farther off the berm. The headlights swept up the hill, stretching his shadow ahead. When it zipped by, he felt a rough snap of wind.

With an animal shriek, the car—actually a pickup—suddenly locked its brakes, and the whole creaking, rumbling pile lurched to a stop. Brake-red flipped to reverse-white, and the truck's tailgate cruised backward. He gave it a wide berth as it pulled beside him, window already down. He felt that tension: the sense of heightened alert that never leaves an infantryman. As his gut tightened, he read the lone bumper sticker: THIS MACHINE MAKES FASCISTS next to a television crammed with the logos of Fox News, MSNBC, and CNN. It wasn't like he knew who was in the truck, but he had that sensation only the French had given a name, the one of a life already lived.

The truck braked hard next to him, and the driver leaned across the bench seat.

"Eaton? What the fuck?"

As if he'd summoned him by thinking of Lisa. Her old boyfriend, Bill Ashcraft, looked every bit as strutting and cocksure as he had in high school.

"You swinging dick," said Bill. "You drop off the face of the earth for a decade and think you can ignore me. What are you doing?"

Dan forced a chuckle. How nervous it sounded to his own ears. "Home, visiting."

Bill swept back greasy hair, the color and shine of black leather, and his jaunty grin seemed to live in every corner of his face, from the squint of his dark eyes to the hard line of his jaw. It was a face he'd envied as a kid—handsome in a knowing, unconcerned way. He wore a wrinkled plaid shirt with checkers of violet and green, and half the collar had flipped up, though he didn't seem aware of it. Even in the tepid light, he looked like he had a few years of hard living behind him. Like high school Bill Ashcraft left out in the elements too long.

"Same. Get in, man, we gotta go see what's what."

"Can't. Heading to the market to pick up some stuff for dinner—"

Ashcraft let out a booming, farting blast of air from his lips. "Eaton, *fuuuuuuck that.* The devil didn't put you and me on this hard twilight road so you could buy your fucking grandmammy groceries. Get in the car. We need to catch up before civilization's wearing its crown of thorns."

Three tours and Dan still felt the stratifications of high school. The pressure to be liked by the basketball team's greatest ball hog.

"I can't, man."

Ashcraft's eyes cranked and crackled. "Fuck you, Eaton. You show up in my life after ten years and think I'm gonna just let those cute little apple butt cheeks strut away while I have to watch? Get the fuck in the truck, motherfucker. We're getting a beer."

He reached over, popped the door handle, and threw it wide.

Dan wasn't even completely inside when Ashcraft whipped back onto the road so quickly that the force shut the door for him. He realized he'd left his cell in his car. He snatched for the seat belt.

"Where're we going?" he asked, smelling whiskey.

"What? The graveyard. Where else? Christ, look at you, Eaton. I missed you, kid."

Freshman year, Hailey persuaded Dan to try out for the basketball team. Because his dad was six four, Dan spent his youth hearing from everyone that he'd grow, but he never breached the sixth inch of his fifth foot, and the only time he spent on a basketball court was in his driveway with Dad or Hailey. Yet during his doomed tryouts, Bill Ashcraft, the rising star, was unusually decent to him. He didn't think Bill even knew his name, but from the first three-man weave through every scrimmage, he encouraged Dan, helped him with plays, called out loudly when he did something well—as if he wanted to make sure the coaches all heard. He was the quintessential jock in a lot of ways: cocky as hell, drank like a river after a thunderstorm, smoked pot like a human bong, and in a lot of ways he was the exact opposite of that stereotype: cerebral, knowledgeable, and, as Lisa promised Dan again and again, weirdly kind.

"So get at me," Ashcraft said, eyes leaving the road. "Where's life?"

"Titusville, P-A. I work for a civil engineer at a gas drilling company."

"Jesus! You traitor to humanity! Okay, what else?"

"Not much. Got out a little over a year ago."

He glanced at Dan, his eyes caged and questioning. Only now did he see how raw and red. His breath reeked of booze.

"Had enough of our bullshit imperial wars?" Only Bill could say this in a way that somehow wasn't antagonistic. It was actually sort of refreshing. You tell people you served and your hand was always sore from the enthusiasm of their grip, but they took the tax cuts and were happy to forget about both conflicts between election cycles. At least Bill stuck to his guns.

"When you're over there," Dan said, "you're not really thinking about the politics."

The truth was, he'd been exposed to way more antiwar sentiment in the actual military. His second tour when a guy named

Josie Burlingame complained of PTSD, Command Sergeant Major Hoskins told him to get the sand out of his clit, so Josie "accidentally" shot himself in the calf and joined Iraq Vets Against the War. In Afghanistan, Sep Marshall had them all watching conspiracy documentaries about the military-industrial complex. He would go on and on about how Woodrow Wilson sank the *Lusitania* to get the U.S. into World War I and George H. W. Bush helped assassinate Kennedy. The boredom of war gave people time for all kinds of weird hobbies.

"When you're over there you're just hoping your dick doesn't get melted?" Bill offered.

"Yeah. Something like that."

Over the course of high school, people had grown to really despise Bill Ashcraft. There was a big kerfuffle after 9/11 when he tried to wear provocative T-shirts denouncing the war. His entire bearing was bull elk in rutting season. Wet nostrils always flared. It ticked Dan off as well, especially as he began to settle on what he wanted to do after graduation. He talked crap behind Bill's back while cheering him on during basketball season, but that was the whole school, and teenagers tend to do whatever it takes to reach a perfect equilibrium of noticed but *not* noticed. After Dan's failed tryout, Bill would still talk to him, say what's up in the hallway, ask him what he was reading. Even while feeling flattered, Dan would snake away. Then one morning his sophomore year he was walking from the parking lot to the school, feeling that persistent panic of the first period bell somewhere nearby in time, and he saw Bill doing the same hustle. There were only about a dozen people in the parking lot when a beige sedan pulled beside Bill—and then about a dozen paintball pellets exploded off the kid's head and torso before the car tore away. The shots took him to the ground, covered him in neon splatters of yellow and pink. When he turned over, Dan could see tears streaking his face, a mess of paint in his hair. He was dressed in a shirt and tie for game day. No one in the parking lot moved to help him, including Dan. Bill was sobbing, crumpled from the pain. Later, when Dan would see men writhing on the ground from real gunshot wounds, this memory would come back to him because—at least for the first moments—it looked so similar. Finally, Bill got up and hobbled to his car. That night he didn't score a point and the Jags lost by fifteen. Dan remembered him chucking a pass into the crowd and Coach Napier pulling him from the game.

Bill slapped down his visor and pulled what looked like a folded piece of paper stuck into the side of the mirror. "Take a look." He handed it to Dan without saying another word. Unfolding it, he recognized the brute size of Rick Brinklan first, the way his huge shoulders occupied a room's horizontal axis. It was a homecoming or prom picture. From the looks of Hailey's dress, it was junior year when she wore a tight-fitting strapless number made of reflective white material. She'd looked beautiful that night with her hair twisted into a bun on top of her head and sprouting a collection of small white flowers. She was yanking Dan into the photo. He looked about twelve years old, his face a mess of red acne, hair a crisply gelled lawn, dark and wet. Hailey, still slim from a teenage metabolism and basketball practice six days a week, had her mouth and face brightly agape in a coming smile, as if she'd wandered into her own surprise party instead of homecoming. He noted the other characters in it, mostly Bill's friends, and handed the picture back to him. "Crazy," was all he said. Bill replaced it in the visor.

"I don't know why I still have that," he said. "I took all the rest of my high school shit to the dump when my mom had me get rid of a broken recliner."

Bill now reached into the slot on the door and retrieved the nearly finished bottle of whiskey Dan had sniffed out. He took a swig and handed it over. The road blew by through the headlights.

To change the mood, Dan said, "Now I understand why you're driving like garbage."

"I resent that. I'm one of the best drunk drivers New Canaan's ever seen. I don't hit pedestrians, I obey red lights, and when I hit a deer—" He smacked one palm off the other so that it rocketed loudly away from him, the truck twitching left and right as the steering wheel went unsupervised. "There's nothing left of the biggest buck except antlers and deer jelly for a hundred and fifty fucking yards." He swiped the bottle back from Dan. "Shit, if you can't drive these country roads loaded on cheap whiskey what's the point of being from Ohio? What do you do on the weekends?"

During his pro-drunk-driving rant, he must have noticed Dan weaving his head back and forth, a dumb technique the docs taught him in rehab to help get a more complete field of vision. Cats do the same thing, the docs told him.

"You all right?" he asked.

"Yeah," said Dan sheepishly and forced his head to be still. "So what have you been up to?"

"Lust. Addiction. Revolution. All the shit makes life worth living."

"Yeah? And where've you been doing that?"

"Anywhere you can dream. Loo-eez-ee-ana currently."

"Never been."

"Depressing as shit. That's why when an old ghost from my past comes calling, wants to pay me a couple thousand bucks to mule some package from New Orleans to Ohio in a day without popping too much acid or getting busted by the pigs"—he shot Dan a knowing look—"I'm down."

Dan assumed this was malarkey, but then again with Bill Ashcraft, you never knew.

"You just here to see the 'rents?" he asked.

"Not really. I came back to see Hailey."

"Kowalczyk?"

"Yeah."

"Y'all still keep in touch."

"Not really."

"Babes, huh, Eaton? It's why I keep a sleepwalker's hours."

Dan let that one hang. Bill pulled from his whiskey and passed it to him again. The sky angled like a carnival game, deathwatch blue, while a single oil tanker of a cloud passed overhead. They drove over shadow landscapes into the paling west.

Dying was something he thought of every day, while at the same time keeping it buried in the heart. *How scared do you get?* Hailey asked him after he came home from tour #1. He honestly couldn't answer. He did get scared, especially when the chaos got going, when bullets were flying and he got a feeling like only an anorexic housefly could navigate through them. But he just put that away and did his job. Before his first deployment he often wondered if he'd freeze up. He never had any kind of gung-ho attitude about war. He was everything the old women called him: quiet, sweet. A nice Catholic kid. But he discovered he was good in combat. By the end of tour #1 he had a reputation that Greg Coyle called "Danny-on-the-Spot." He could be calm and do what he had to do. Sometimes he'd recite the Lord's Prayer. It helped him flow with the moment and focus, but that was about it. Bravery wasn't a real thing, not as such, but his friends thought he was fierce, and they thought he was brave. And Dan had never seen himself that way before.

During tour #2, he found himself two Humvees back with Macy Gray stuck in his head because when they'd left for patrol that morning Sergeant Wunderlich had been singing her hit single in the shower. One second, Wunderlich's tune was banging around

Dan's mental jukebox and the next he was watching a fireball shoot out from under his sergeant's Humvee, the EFP coming up through the bottom. A geyser of dirt and concrete rained down on the rest of the convoy. Almost everyone made it out of the vehicle. James Drake lost both his legs above the knee, Kyle Nickel an arm, James "Other James" Streiss both his hands, and they all had severe burns, but they got out. Drake ended up in the BAMC complex in San Antonio where they treated the most critical cases. Nickel committed suicide in 2010. Streiss moved back to Nashville and seemed in great spirits about a career in country music when they spoke at DT's wedding. But it was Wunderlich, one of the weirdest, most popular sergeants in the company—maybe even in the entire battalion—who they all saw burning inside the vehicle. His body was already cinders by the time Dan got a look—just the shape of his Kevlar and his face on fire, the flames and smoke lapping him up like he was a log in a campfire back in Ohio.

That might have been the moment Dan was done. Hailey had already made her feelings clear, and Wunderlich's death really rocked him, rocked all of them. For weeks, every time they were outside the wire he was so keyed up it felt like sleepwalking, and everything—the homes, the mosques, the reeking open sewers, the dust, the head scarves, the Humvees—it all began to tremble in his vision. He'd stare at something or someone for too long and begin to wonder if it was even real. At night he'd try to listen to the sound of his own breathing, but he'd get this feeling of all his past lives, between the scorpions and the sun, gathering.

At Wunderlich's service they listened to him get eulogized by the army chaplain, his helmet and dog tags hanging off a rifle bayoneted into the ground over his boots. Before they send you off to battle, the army makes you fill out this little blue book, which includes whatever music you want played at your funeral. As soon as the chaplain finished up, the beat and the guitar riff started up, and they all kind of looked at one another. Dan watched Coyle's face light up in amazement. And as soon as Alanis sang *I'm broke but I'm happy, / I'm poor but I'm kind*, they all roared. Coyle sat beside him with his hand over his mouth just bawling with laughter. They all stood to dance, one hand per man in a pocket, peace signs wagging.

He'd figured Ashcraft was joking about the graveyard until they pulled onto Dryland Creek Road.

The hill rose like the curve of a breast, and at the top were the cemetery gates. Ashcraft piloted the truck through the grave markers. He pulled off to the side and angled the truck so that the headlights spilled across a certain set of footstones. He cut the engine and seized the nearly empty bottle of Jim from the door. Dan followed him across the grass, snaking between the graves while Bill stepped right on them. Dan had this long-ago memory of his father gripping his arm as a child, lifting him by the bicep away from the grass. "Don't walk across them," he'd said.

He asked why not.

"Because if one of them was your kin, you wouldn't walk across it, would you?"

Dan remembered thinking that these people were dead and gone and well beyond caring, but even as a little boy he knew better than to challenge his father on such matters. To this day he avoided walking on graves, and not because he thought lifeless boxes of bones held any sway or say on the mortal world.

The glare of the headlights created tiny shadows in the letters of the stone marker.

RICHARD JARED BRINKLAN
CPL US MARINES
NOVEMBER 4, 1984–APRIL 26, 2007
BELOVED SON,
LOST IN SERVICE TO THE COUNTRY HE LOVED

Bill stood over the grave while Dan kept to the side. Bill unscrewed the cap of Jim and let it drop to the ground. Tilting his head back, he took a large gulp, then another. He passed the bottle to Dan, and he took a quick hit. Then it was back to Bill, who turned it over and splashed the remaining liquid across the grass. He held the bottle with his index finger stuffed in the open neck, looking mildly annoyed. It was almost the look you'd give a vending machine that had failed to return your quarter.

"I wonder," Bill said. "If you could really break it down. How much money he made for Bechtel or KBR? Like who got the richest off this dead asshole from Ohio?"

Dan wouldn't humor him. "How'd you spend the wars, Ashcraft?"

"Protesting."

"Yeah, how'd that work out?"

"Not too well now that I think about it."

After a long time standing at the grave, watching him grim-lipped and catatonically quiet, Dan asked, "How often do you come out here?"

He shook his head. "First time. My mom had to e-mail me a map."

"Ben's buried here too, I guess."

He shook his head. "Nah. They scattered the ashes at Jericho."

They stood for a while longer.

"Wanna go to a bar?" Bill asked.

Your worries are simpler as a kid.

Dan thought about the weak smile Hailey gave him before she told him she was going to homecoming with Curtis Moretti, the soon-to-be starting quarterback. He'd asked her to go the week before and she had put him off with a *Let me just see what all the girls are doing*, referring to Lisa and Kaylyn. His stomach didn't sink so much as it crashed through to the basement. He went to homecoming with plump, agreeable Jamie Eakins, and was hyper-aware when Hailey and Curt disappeared from the bannered and ballooned cafeteria early in the night. Lisa had been getting rides to and from school with Bill, so he didn't see her as much anymore. She came over one night to put a book in Dan's mailbox and he caught her outside.

"I sort of have to know," he explained.

Lisa shook her head against the brisk autumn wind and kicked at brown leaves piled along the curb.

"Danny." She crossed her arms and glared at the ground. "Fuck Hailey. Seriously, fuck her. She doesn't know what she's doing."

"What's that mean?" His befuddlement was genuine.

"Hailey had sex with Curt after homecoming." Dan so loved her for how distraught she looked when she said it. He was surprised Lisa had it in her to tell him.

He searched for something adult to say. "I see." Then Lisa surprised him by wrapping him in her arms. "It's okay," he said, laughing. "Whatever."

"I'd punch her in the vagina for you." They both laughed, and this time his was less forced.

"Where we headed?" he asked Bill, sweeping away this stark, unhappy memory.

"I'm thinking Lincoln Lounge."

"I can only stay for a bit. I'm meeting Hailey after she gets off work."

Bill threw up his hands and took his time putting them back on the wheel—a couple of seconds Dan spent willing them to come home. "Just humor me while I kill time before this thing."

"You look like you could use some sleep."

"Sleep's for people who don't know about coral bleaching and drone assassinations. I don't sleep without earplugs, a blindfold, and about five Diazepam."

"Just keep your hands on the wheel. I didn't survive Anbar and Kandahar to become part of the New Canaan Curse in a car wreck."

"There's no such thing as curses." Fireflies thronged in the head-lights. "Only shitty luck and forces of political and economic sur-render. That's how they get good, sweet kids like you to give their eyes for democracy." He pointed to Dan's skull. Most people didn't even notice the prosthesis. The docs had this way of attaching the implant so the blood vessels grew into it, as well as the surround-ing tissue and muscle. Then they pegged the porous implant to the prosthesis, this little almond sliver that matched the bright hazel of Dan's real eye. It moved in the socket like a real one, and usually no one could tell unless he let them know. Maybe Ashcraft had heard, though.

"Sure," Dan said, snorting a laugh.

"Hey. Question. Why's everyone call that guy Whitey again?"

He understood he wasn't actually asking about Whitey's nick-name.

As far as Dan could remember, Eric Frye was one of the only black kids in their school. It wasn't like he endured all kinds of racist abuse, but at some point, it was noted that he had not tried out for the basketball team, knew nothing about rap music, and was otherwise quiet and smart (his dad was an orthodontist; his mom taught at Grover Street Elementary). Someone started calling him "Whitey" behind his back and it stuck. The military taught you that nicknames were inexplicable. Hell, in Iraq they called a guy "Sig" just because he once messed up the Iraqi signal for "halt." Sig's real name was Anthony, and soon there wasn't a soul left in the army who called him that.

"Ah fuck," said Ashcraft, zipping around an Amish buggy, saved by the reflective triangle on its rear. "Had no idea. I was calling him Whitey the whole time I knew him."

"He never said it bugged him." But Dan knew better. By no means had he and Eric been best friends, but when he heard about Hailey marrying Eric, Dan's first thought was, *How could you do this to me? I was like the only person in school who didn't call you that ridiculous name.*

Bill took them through the old part of town, past the big colonial homes, and they reached downtown New Canaan. Every place needs fuel to run the engine. Like much of Northeast Ohio, once there had been real industry here. Rubber was king in Akron, Youngstown had steel. Post-World War II, it was the region's honey, practically dripping from the mills and into the maw of the national economy. Then the rest of the world began to make non-unionized steel. New Canaan was one of the minor places that bore the aftershocks of deindustrialization. Maybe not the way Paul Eaton's hometown of Youngstown did, but nowhere in the Midwest really escaped. Businesses closed, people left to find jobs at malls and big-box stores. DUIs, teen pregnancies, domestic disturbance calls, suicides, and assaults all spiked. New Canaan didn't fare as poorly as some places. In the mideighties, two different companies opened manufacturing facilities in an industrial park to the south. A screen door manufacturer and an auto parts plant. Developers figured out that they could sell the town as an exurban retreat from all the cities that were going to rust. But the smokestacks of the Fountain Steel plant were still visible just west of downtown. Shuttered for as long as Dan could remember, his parents talked about its closing the way you talk about a death in the family. Maybe with even more bitterness because with its closing came betrayal. The way they'd reference that Fountain plant—which had only been responsible for some seven hundred jobs—it reminded Dan of the first time he saw a lethal wound in battle. Everyone gets their virgin taste: How it feels to look at such a thing. How when it dries, these heinous skeins of crust and dirt will cling to shredded, serrated flesh.

Ashcraft parked in a slanted spot beneath the tacky glow of the Lincoln's sign. Music beat in the middle of downtown's shallow pulse. Past the crummy bar with the nonsensical Abe Lincoln motif, Dan could peer down Hudson Street and see the scrapyard. Beyond that was Allied Waste Services, the water treatment plant, and the power station. All the places towns try to tuck into a corner to keep the Main Street America façade shining.

"One pitcher," he told Bill.

"Five," he said, hopping out of the truck.

"Two."

"Fine. Seven pitchers, and that's it."

During tour #3 in Afghanistan, Private First Class Rudy Jamirez enjoyed mocking Dan for "just how shithouse Northeast Ohio actually is." Rudy, the son of Nicaraguan immigrants, was from a scrubby town in western PA not that much different from New Canaan. Even though he was Dan's subordinate, he also became his fastest friend in a kid brother sort of way. Maybe it was a nerd thing. He loved graphic novels and went on long disquisitions of what he considered the classics: *Watchmen, Y: The Last Man, Sandman, Miracleman, From Hell*. But they truly bonded over *Calvin and Hobbes*.

"Bill Watterson," Dan told him. "Ohio's like a factory for talent and brilliance and guts."

"You got Watterson and Harvey Pekar," he countered. "That's it." Only a few inches over five feet, strong, and stocky, Rudy wore a military buzz on a bucket of a head and had small, protruding curlicues for ears. He had this tattoo on his shoulder of a medieval knight, and beneath it the words *Sí Se Puede*. He was tough, irascible, funny. He reminded Dan of kids he'd grown up with. Even after he finished Ranger school and moved up to sergeant first class, when he really began to feel the weight of his responsibility toward the guys, Rudy would be the friend he'd look to, much like Greg Coyle, to keep him sane.

Dan schooled him: "Uh, LeBron James? The Black Keys, Chrissie Hynde, Steven Spielberg? John Brown spent his formative years in Ohio."

"Christ, don't get you started on Ohio. You're a fucking walking Wikipedia entry."

"Johnny Appleseed. Ever heard of him? Ohioan."

They were sitting with a bunch of guys at FOB Lagman, harvesting time before they had to go back to the Hindu Kush and not get a shower for who knows how long, watching *Black Hawk Down* on a projector screen. Everyone who served in Iraq or Afghanistan saw this movie a dozen times, but they had nothing better to do so they talked through it, savoring the A/C while they could. Rudy changed the subject.

"You know the problem with war movies? They never show how funny the army is. It's always drama-this, eyes-squeezed-shut-crying-that, but c'mon, dude, the army's fucking hilarious."

On-screen, a .50 gunner took a bullet in the neck. Fake gore exploded into the camera, dousing the lens. *"What's his status?!"* Commander Tom Sizemore demanded, while Staff Sergeant Josh Hartnett, stricken, held the dead man in his lap.

"See?" said Rudy. "That's fucking funny."

They'd be humping up and down mountains on patrol, skittering over loose shale that broke ankles, trying to look everywhere at once for Taliban or farmers earning a buck by popping off shots at Americans, and the second they got back, Rudy would grab someone by the collar and scream, *"What's his status?!"*

Rudy had a point, though. There's probably no funnier profession than the military. You can spend five hours arguing about something totally bizarre. On tour #2 in Iraq, Della Terza and Josh Packard got into a two-day debate about who they'd Fuck, Marry, and Kill: Harry, Ron, or Hermione.

DT: "Ron is the obvious Kill. Put him in one of those Shiite torture basements for all I care. Then marry Harry, fuck Hermione."

Packard's rebuttal: "You're an idiot. Marrying means you get to fuck all the time anyhow. You marry Hermione, kill Harry, and fuck Ron."

Coyle's two cents: "Trust me, marrying does not mean you fuck all the time."

Packard: "Fucking Della Terza. You fucking beshitted moron. Ron's butthole's gonna be the most satisfying. That's what all the books are secretly about."

The two of them actually got pretty heated about this. Lieutenant Holt had to enter the fray and give them both a time-out to cool down. Years later, at Della Terza's wedding, Dan brought this argument back up, which didn't seem fair because Pack was in jail for firing a gun off at the Iowa State Fair and thus unable to defend his point.

"I don't care what the fuck Packard thinks, I still say I'm right," Della Terza muttered, and he threw an ice cube at one of his new wife's bridesmaids.

Something about the mix of tension, the specter of death or grave injury, and being around guys for whom nothing is off limits—but Dan had never laughed harder than during deployments. It's what he could never explain to Hailey: You'll never be closer to human beings than in combat. Not your parents, not your wife, not your kids. That sense of duty you leave with—the one toward God and country—evaporates in the murky realities of Baghdad or Kandahar. What's left is your duty to your friends, your brothers. It's what Rick Brinklan would describe when they ran into each other in Iraq. Even after only months, you feel like you've known these guys for millions of miles of a hard, dark road.

* * *

He and Ashcraft had barely crossed into the sweet chill of the A/C, eyes working with the dim red light and HDTV glow before a boisterous greeting bellowed through the evening crowd.

"Holy faggot-fucking shit, look at these two queers!"

Jonah Hansen had gone seriously bald. A PacSun hat tilted back on his head, the bill nearly vertical. The visible follicles looked so thin, each like a pore with a blackhead. To compensate he now had a chinstrap beard outlining the contours of his jaw. He was drinking with Todd Beaufort, also ball-capped and battered. Sun-fed face with a slaughterhouse smell to him, looking depleted and fat under his Buckeyes hat.

Beaufort greeted them with a jerk of his head. When Bill saw him, his face made all kinds of buried calculations before returning to its default expression of bemused distance, of riding above the storm and laughing downward at a world of jest.

"Tee-Bee. Five-Six," said Bill. "How you doing, man?" They shook, and it came with a stir of awkwardness. Jocks sizing each other up long after their moment of relevance.

"Remember Dan Eaton?" Jonah said. "My class."

"Hey man, how's it going?" Beaufort shook his hand, and Dan was sure it was the most they'd ever interacted.

"Of all the dive bars in all the Midwest, you two go and walk into mine," said Jonah. Dan started with his hand out, but Jonah wrapped him in his arms.

"C'mon, dude, no need for a welcome parade," said Dan, laughing.

"Nah, it's just you look good. All in one piece, man. That's all you can ask for."

They pulled up stools, and Jonah poured the rest of their pitcher into two opaque plastic cups. He ordered another from the bartender, Jessica Bealey, class of '02. A cheerleader who was rumored to have scored a thirty-two on the ACT by filling in bubbles at random. She didn't seem to recognize either Dan or Bill. As she walked away, Jonah looked at her behind skeptically and said, "That thing's gotten chunky as Campbell's Soup." He had a pointed, serpentine tongue that frequently slithered out to taste his lips.

"We're celebrating. I just bought a helicopter," Jonah declared.

"A helicopter?" Bill could cock an eyebrow like he was throwing a knife.

"I fly it to our place up on South Bass."

Bill looked pained. "How in the fuck?"

"Real estate. It's been rocket fuel lately."

"Real estate," Bill sniffed. "There's a fucking depression on. There's no real estate."

"Just gotta know how to play the game, dude. Everyone's got chips in, so play the right cards and know when the other guy's whistling bullshit."

Jonah had always been given to speaking like that. Back in the early eighties it was Jonah's dad who came up with the idea to market New Canaan to retirees from the cities, and Burt Hansen went on to make a killing. He claimed credit for helping to bring the auto parts plant and the screen door factory that began New Canaan's short-lived renaissance. Dan's mom had this expression about the Hansens: "You can feel the devil meddling." Burt Hansen kept fetish porn videos in an unlocked cabinet in their barn, which doubled as a glorified rec room. In sixth grade they gathered around the TV out there and Dan got a disturbing first blush with pornography, "barely legal" women enduring abusive, violent treatment. He also distinctly remembered Burt hovering over him while he and Jonah worked on a project about the Underground Railroad for history class. "Just remember your white skin," he told them, to Dan's great and enduring discomfort.

"Not shit," said Beaufort when Bill asked what he was up to. "Working Cattawa construction." He sipped bored beer.

Jessica returned with shots. "For the reunion, you stank old Jags!" She beamed at Todd, who didn't even look up.

They slammed back tequila and replaced the shot glasses on her tray.

"To hope and change!" Jonah's knee jittered away, and he kept playing his hands on the table's surface like a drum kit. "Assume you're feeling pretty good about that now, Ashcraft."

Bill's smirk was his home. "Oh, is this an Obama conversation?"

"You wanted socialized health care, an open door for all the aliens, and an end to America's Judeo-Christian foundations. Am I mischaracterizing?"

"We're both pissed, but I'm assuming for different reasons. See, I *don't like* the oligarchic corporate state and necrotic ideas like market fundamentalism. For which I see Bee-O as a caretaker. You're just pissed 'cause some black people ended up marginally better off."

Jonah shook his head sadly. "Everyone wants their food pre-masticated now, cradle to grave. You been to Columbus lately? If you send your kid to a school there, it's going to be half-Muslim, no question."

Ashcraft brayed with laughter. "The fuck's that got to do with anything?"

"Here's the problem with you liberals, Ashcraft." He stuck one drunk finger in Bill's face. "You're really only about the sanctimony. You got this club for right-thinking people, and all you care about is being able to control the way we speak and what opinions we're allowed to have. In college I had this girl blow up at me for saying 'colored people' instead of 'people of color.' Thought she was going to have an aneurysm 'cause I reversed two stupid words. But that's what liberals are: thought police. So they want to protect a religion like Islam, one that treats women and homos like shit and doesn't even respect free speech—so you can't even be consistent there. But when it comes to Christians not wanting guys with dicks in the women's bathroom? Hell, put those backward hicks on TV and ridicule them! Call 'em bigots! Chase 'em with pitchforks! Do liberals care about the economy being shit, about jobs leaving, about how no one can make it in a business or how much it costs to move to one of their precious cities on the coasts? No, of course not. They care more about the rights of illegal aliens than they do about the heroin those aliens bring in that's killing every last person we know. Or no—you know what they care about? Not calling those people 'illegal.' I'm sorry, they're 'undocumented.' They'll hold a protest over a word. But they're not protesting for Curtis or Ben or anyone else ODing, are they?"

Jonah was frothing; the beery sluice of his spittle fell on Dan's cheek. Bill looked less amused, especially at the mention of his dead friend.

"We're all just trying to hold our ground against the deluge, Jonah. Whatever makes you feel better."

"I'll tell you what would make me feel better." He did the thing where he looked around and pretended to care that he was about to say something offensive. "Just one eensy-teensy little bomb in one of those mosques in C-bus. Not while anyone's there or nothing but like during the night. Just enough to make these Satanists think twice before building another temple."

"Ah, a scholar of Islam right here in the Lincoln Lounge."

Jonah laughed. He'd always loved needling the Liberal Terror of high school and raised his glass in a cheers. "Wanta cig?"

Ashcraft tapped cups. "Obviously."

Dan demurred and Todd said he'd just had one. Even in the army, Dan hadn't picked up a smoking habit. His mother had implored him one too many times to never take up the addiction that had taken his father forty years to quit. On his way out, Jonah walked up to a pretty, pudgy girl at the bar and pinched her flab. She bolted upright and swiveled to him. He said something, grinned, and continued on his way. A bald guy in an Oakley shirt, who'd been ordering from Jess, caught the end of it. Must have been her man (though he looked like he could be twenty years older). Dan felt like he recognized him from town rumors. The guy glared after Jonah with drunken disgust until his pitcher arrived.

"I don't remember people arguing 'bout politics back when we were kids," said Beaufort. "It started at the millennium. Before that I don't remember anything besides the president liked getting hummers."

Dan plucked at the small red hairs growing out of the pale knot of his knee.

"So what brings you back to town?" Beaufort asked.

"No reason really. I'm seeing Hailey tonight."

Beaufort gave him a long, considered look. His teeth were square, nicotine-dark nubs. "No shit. You still in love with that trick?"

So he knew more about the situation than Dan would have expected. Curt Moretti had been one of Beaufort's best friends. An errant memory of watching their group grilling out in the snow before a basketball game, Todd picking up Hailey and spinning her in circles while she shrieked laughter and then, when he put her down, she stuffed a handful of snow in his face. Hailey's year with that strutting moron Moretti was the worst of Dan's adolescent life. While it felt silly now, he recalled thinking how effortlessly cool Curtis looked. He had this stiff skullcap haircut, a heavy Adam's apple, and a nose like a hawk's beak. Each ear pierced with a gold loop earring. Dan thinking he could never manage this combination of style and hardness. Daily, he wished for something terrible to befall Moretti while Moretti looked through him like he didn't exist. He probably knew Dan only as the short kid who slunk away from Hailey's locker whenever he approached. It made him feel like he'd never left seventh grade, and he often wished Curtis Moretti dead.

"Ancient history," he assured Beaufort.

"God, I remember y'all back in the day. Curt used to hate any time she even mentioned you. Gotta admit, though, you looked at her like an ice cream cone in the desert." He picked something out of his beer and flicked it to the floor. "She's still got an ass like a bomb went off."

That Todd or Curtis had even noticed Dan was shocking as hell. That his longing for Hailey had been obvious and threatening made him feel some combination of pitiful and powerful.

"So'd you see any shit over there?" Beaufort asked.

"Not sure what that means."

"Shit. Blood, death. You kill anyone. That kind of thing."

"I'm not that in to talking about it."

Beaufort poured himself more beer while he thought on this. Of course Todd Beaufort would fall into that camp. Most men who never serve do. He'd always worn blank dog tags, some inscrutable statement about his badassedness, and Dan could see the chain now. Even before the wars, he was emulating behavior many civilians would come to follow: wrapping themselves in the theater of war, pretending at honor and sacrifice without actually bothering with either of the two. Flag and bumper sticker patriots without any idea of just how gruesome the business of it could be. How rancid, wet, and sticky it was.

"I thought about joining. Even got as far as going to sign up for the National Guard. But I failed the physical."

"That's tough."

Greg Coyle once called the National Guard units "steroidal farm boys looking to work out their feelings." Dan wished for any other subject besides the military. Hell, he wished for Jonah and Bill to return and start talking politics again.

"Looks like you came through all right, though, Eaton."

No point in explaining his prosthetic. While in recovery he'd met other guys who chose an eye patch over the prosthesis—even one dude who wore a bull's-eye instead of the piece of acrylic that perfectly matched the living iris. Dan's looked too good, even down to the orange tint that ringed the pupil. So much so that occasionally he'd look in the mirror and forget. The only hint a small clump of scar tissue near the zygomatic bone like a flesh parenthesis. Sometimes he'd even go a couple days and forget about it. Wait to be reminded by a nightmare of his long-gone right eye, free of his skull, a jellied lump in the dust.

When he got home from deployment #2, after the VBIED that convinced him to reenlist, he ordered a book from Amazon about a Union colonel name Marcus Spiegel. He'd resurfaced in Dan's memory, a vestigial lesson from Mrs. Bingham's long-ago Ohio history class. Maybe he was looking for reminders about why he was doing this, and Spiegel provided a template.

A German Jew who immigrated to Ohio after the failed German revolution of 1848, Spiegel married a farmer's daughter and when war between the states broke out, he saw it as his duty to fight for the country that had given him this second chance. It was a reminder of patriotism's bewitching promise, how the achievement of a common goal can inspire disparate peoples to do mighty things. Spiegel began the Civil War as an anti-emancipation Democrat, steeped in the prevailing racial attitudes of the day. He quickly rose to the rank of colonel and received command of his own regiment—the 120th Ohio Volunteer Infantry. As he and his men battled farther into the heart of the Deep South, fighting through Virginia, Mississippi, and Louisiana, his perception of what the Union was fighting for changed.

"Since I am here, I have learned and seen . . . the horrors of slavery," he wrote from the Louisiana bayous to his wife, Caroline, the daughter of the Ohio farmer with whom he'd made his American family. "You know it takes me long to say anything that sounds antidemocratic, but . . . never hereafter will I either speak or vote in favor of Slavery."

It must be a shaming, damning, beautiful moment to understand such a thing. To have your heart changed.

Dan thought of how he felt before he left for basic training. The anticipation. The itch. He watched *Saving Private Ryan* over and over again. He read massive tomes about the Civil War and World War II. He tacked patriotic musings to the corkboard in his room, which were still there to this day: *Those who expect to reap the blessings of freedom must, like men, undergo the fatigue of supporting it.* That was Thomas Paine. And Lincoln: *I like to see a man proud of the place in which he lives. I like to see a man live so that his place will be proud of him.* Because what was he going to be? The quiet, skinny bookworm who nevertheless finished with an unspectacular GPA, who never stood out, who was the wallpaper of everyone else's young experience, a face in a yearbook? Dan came to dream of himself as Spiegel. Selfless, determined, bound by a higher cause.

So he returned to Spiegel's story and was still reading about it by the time tour #3 began in Afghanistan. The very first patrol a child walked up to him and asked, "You got girlfriend?" He wore a small white hat and one of those long shirts that looked like pajamas. They were doing good there, Dan was sure of it. The kid pointed to his M4. "Bang, bang, cowboy," he said. And the sun dripped over the brown hills, the nearby clay homes, their new up-armored Humvees.

Two years into the war, Colonel Marcus Spiegel wrote to his wife Caroline: "I have seen and learned much. I have seen men

dying of disease and mangled by the weapons of death; I have wit-
nessed hostile armies arrayed against each other, the charge of infantry, cavalry hunting men down like beasts." And yet, he said, he
would never stop, never falter, never back down from the "glorious
cause." They were fighting not just to save the Union, he wrote, but
to expand the reach of freedom.

Spiegel never made it back to Caroline. His regiment was am-
bushed during the Red River Campaign in Louisiana following the
successful siege of Vicksburg. Most of his men were taken prisoner,
and Spiegel was mortally wounded by an exploding shell. Just one
of 35,475 Ohioans who gave his life for the Union.

"I'm having a boy," Todd Beaufort told Dan. "Me and the mom, we
ain't together. Not my decision." He pushed his hat back to scratch.
Hints of gray rested on his head like ashes. "Told her I'll be there
for the kid no matter what, but she don't believe me yet. Not that
I exactly blame her."

Nothing would change Dan's opinion of the guy. He knew the
kind of hick-jock shithead he'd been in high school, and yet the
echo of Greg Coyle soured Dan's stomach.

I hold her, Coyle had said, *and I swear I feel the fucking weight
of eternity.*

When Bill and Jonah returned, the former was folding a piece of
paper into his breast pocket. "Guy's a delivery service," Jonah told
him. "He'll meet you wherever, hook you up with grade A shit."

On his way to the bathroom, Jonah said something to the same
paunchy, nose-ringed young woman. The rolls of her chin contracted like the folds of an accordion when she jerked her head
back. Yet there was something striking and sexual about the way
she told Jonah to fuck off. He breezed by while the guy in the Oakley shirt stared him down with murder in his eyes.

It was a testament to Dan's hometown—maybe to all small towns—that so much of the history and pathos could accumulate in errant pockets on any given night. Looking back and forth between Beaufort and Oakley Shirt, the pieces clicked together. Dan's dad, one of New Canaan's preeminent gossips, told him the story once.

Oakley Shirt was actually a Brokamp, which was one of those families that had been in New Canaan for as long as anyone could remember, the family tree simply sprawled across the whole county. If the Hansens embodied one New Canaan dynasty, the Brokamps were its diametric opposite. Like the Floods or parts of Kaylyn's family, they were, according to Dad, "white trash that grows right out of the soil." This Brokamp was from the meanest branch of that line, a tributary packed with stories of domestic abuse, jail, suicide. He lived in a west-side motel and had spent much of his adult life in and out of prison. Todd Beaufort was supposedly his son.

"When we moved down from Youngstown, I knew him from around the bars. Real piece a work," Dad confided to Dan and Hailey on a drive to Columbus for a football game. "Todd's mom was kinda turning tricks at the time. Not like in the sense that she was standing out on the street corner or nothing, but it was well known if a man had fifty bucks on him and was willing to buy her drinks all night—well." Dan remembered his face growing fiercely hot as his father shared this story in front of Hailey (they'd only just started dating), but she was on the edge of her seat. "Brokamp was her frequent flyer, and that's most likely Todd's daddy. I mean, it don't exactly take a geneticals test to look at the two side by side. You'd see him at every one of Todd's football games."

Dad was right. Dan had always noticed Brokamp watching from near the concession area, arms crossed, stance wide. He never actually sat in the bleachers. He had a wildebeest build, a head as bald and shiny as the chrome knob on a truck hitch, and a nose that looked like a gnarled chunk of pink charcoal. He shared with Beaufort the same ruddy complexion and near-handsome Neanderthal face. The kind of face where the brow is heavy, but with youth it looks serious. On the elder Brokamp, it only looked cruel, a concentration-camp-guard quality to it.

And yet Beaufort seemed totally oblivious. He sat in the bar, not fifteen feet away from the guy, and it appeared to matter nothing to either of them. How frequently did these two not acknowledge each other in one of New Canaan's five or six watering holes?

With Jonah and Bill back at the table, the chatter began again, raucous and hearty. Spanning three classes of New Canaan High, they relived, they returned. Stories of sports victories and senior pranks and the teachers who'd been in the closet—all the last dredges of what they had in common. Dan had served three tours. Bill had traveled the world. Beaufort had flamed out on a college football career. Jonah had bought a helicopter. That history burned away as they attempted to reanimate themselves through stories of their roaring youth.

Dan listened but found himself drifting back to Coyle and the night their unit sat on a rooftop during the famed surge. The Baghdad suburb was quiet, an entire platoon having cleared and secured a few square miles. He and Coyle sat facing west as the sun set. They shared some beef jerky, talked about home, about war, cracked dark jokes. They talked about Greg's daughter, who was five months old. He only knew her from a computer screen. She sat in his wife's lap, a blinking lump back in San Lorenzo, California. Once an inveterate womanizer, now Coyle hung his head when he walked, his mind always elsewhere. This introspective aspect of him, this kind, complicated piece had taken over. And this was Dan's favorite night of the war, strange as that sounds. They talked about what they did to lie down at night. Greg would lift weights, play video games, mix sleeping aids with Boom Boom energy drinks for a tawny strung-out high, watch bootlegged movies and TV shows. He laughed because, "All you do, Danny, is read behind blast walls." It was the only way Dan could calm down. Hard to sleep when you came back from a firefight and all the screaming and the cussing and the percussion and the sweating still had your adrenaline at Mach 5. They talked about what it looked like when a person got shot, how a guy doesn't get blown backward the way it's sometimes depicted; he just kind of crumpled, like he was being deflated. Then there was twitching or sometimes perfect stillness—from life to no life. From existence to meat that dogs will pick at and shit out all over the city. Just like that. They talked about what it was like to kill someone. Decided it's not that they never thought of the wives and children and families of the people whose lives their bullets took, "But there's one of two outcomes: either this man will die or I will," said Coyle. And the exultation of winning this duel and walking away to continue living—it was a narcotic joy not even the pillheads of the Ohio Valley could understand.

"Violence solves nothing," Coyle joked, gesturing to the quiet streets below and smiled, dust trapped in his blond stubble. "Well, except for this whole MacDougal."

The pink sky turned purple then blue, writhing with the dust to create the most chilling pond of sky, cleaving around minarets and modest skyscrapers. Apaches and drones thudded and buzzed over the most crowded airspace on the planet, but still everything felt whisper-still. How breathless you can feel gathered together with your friend looking at some wild sunset.

"How could you not think about it?" said Todd Beaufort, and Dan blinked back into the moment. "Soon as it happened everyone was talking about there being a curse again."

"Blech," said Bill Ashcraft. They were talking about Curt Moretti's death by heroin overdose in '06. "No such thing as curses. We're all just dust to dust." He poured beer into his open vortex of a mouth and gargled with it like mouthwash. "People got a real problem with that. So they go about trying to explain it any way they can, adding up numbers so they get letters."

"Forget a curse. It's this whole mystery murder thing," said Jonah, wiping perspiration from his brow, his drunk ratcheted. "That's what we should all be paying attention to."

"What murder thing?" Dan asked.

"Awww sheee-it," said Jonah. "You've been gone, Eaton. You haven't heard of The Murder That Never Was?"

"I admit my ignorance."

"I've heard of it," said Bill, nodding. "Got enough dead friends to've heard of it."

"Lotta bodies to consider," said Jonah.

They were all drunker than Dan, and he did not appreciate the cavalier nature of this conversation.

"What is it?" he repeated.

"New Canaan's greatest urban legend," Jonah explained. "Someone got murdered, and someone did the murdering and somehow it all got swept under the rug."

Bill rolled his dark eyes. "And I heard Tony Wozniak got big into Satanism and cut off his own dick. Doesn't make it true."

"Where'd the rumor come from?" Dan asked. "The murder, not Wozniak's dick."

Jonah looked at him like he was mental. "Who the fuck starts any rumor? That's what makes it a rumor."

Fair point. Rumors were cheaper than tears. The point was never veracity. When everyone in a community has lost someone they care about people go in search of an explanation.

Ashcraft blew air through his nostrils. "Shit, a lot of people got murdered, sure, but if it happens in a war zone, it gets classified differently."

"S'all bullshit," said Beaufort. He glared at his beer.

Jonah flippered a hand around. "A curse, yes, that's bullshit. But the murder? Bet on it."

"Wasn't Curt. He was sitting right there on his stoop for everyone to see," said Beaufort in a way that made Dan wonder if he'd been right there, maybe shooting up beside his buddy. He imagined Beaufort coming out of his high and finding Moretti with vomit on his chin and no pulse. He had to admit the image gave him a nasty bit of satisfaction.

"ODs, blown up in Iraq, who the fuck even knows what else," said Jonah. "Either of you guys been to Fallen Farms lately? Bet the Flood brothers have at least a couple bodies buried out there." He laughed by himself.

"This is a grim conversation," said Bill.

"Grim like a lizard," Jonah agreed and fingered something stuck in a molar. "That's why I totally buy it every which way. Shit like that doesn't just pop up outta thin air. Somebody had too much to drink, let a little something slip, and then it entered the grapevine. Psychos walk among us, man, trust me."

"There's no such thing as psychos." Everyone looked at Dan at the same time. Jonah was raising his blood pressure, similar to how he'd wake from a dream of smoke and metal fragments. Occasionally Dan felt like civilians had no idea about either bad luck or grace.

"Uh, yeah there is," Jonah asserted like a second grader explaining that ghosts are real.

"Remember Mrs. Bingham's class? Seventh-grade Ohio history?"

Jonah gave him a baffled shrug. "I guess?"

"She talked about the massacre at Gnadenhutten—remember that?" Blank stares. "During the Revolutionary War, American soldiers, they led a bunch of Delaware Indians into two killing rooms like they were cattle or pigs, including thirty or so children. And while the Indians kept on singing and praying and kissing each other good-bye, one by one the soldiers beat their heads in with a common cooper's mallet. So a couple of months later the Indians captured an American commander, this guy William Crawford. First they scalped him clean to his skull. Then they cut off both his ears. Then his nose. He was still alive, *begging* to die, when they stripped him naked. Then the women of the village took turns burning his body with firebrands, so the flesh slid right off. There was this white man with the Indians named Simon Girty. A guy raised on the frontier, who spoke the Indian languages and fought alongside them against the Americans. Still, he was white, so as Crawford's being tortured, he pleads for Girty to shoot him. All Girty had to say was, 'I have no gun.' "

Bill tore apart pieces of a napkin, let the snowflake bits fall to the floor. Beaufort sat with his back to the man who might have been his father. Finally, Jonah said, "Gross, Danny! What the fuck's your point?"

"Point is . . ." His eyes flitted up and back down. "We lack a whole lot of imagination about violence. We want to chalk it up to 'psychos,' whatever that means. It's a notion that feels safe. It's comforting. But shit like My Lai or Auschwitz or Gnadenhutten—that's not aberrant. It happens because of what we all have in common. How frail we are. We're insecure, we're greedy, we want a promotion at work, we're afraid of the guy in charge—that's the stupid, mundane bullshit that makes people do terrible things to each other."

The four of them were quiet, looking at the table, except Bill, who glared at Dan with what could only be described as a kind of jealous affection. Jonah hopped up from the table.

"Not that you aren't a real ray of sunshine, Danny, but I got my chance with this filly." He nodded happily at the young woman Brokamp had left alone, either for a cigarette or the bathroom, and Jonah made tracks to sidle up beside her at the bar.

Beaufort had his thick arms crossed, and his gaze was impossible to read beneath the bill of his Buckeyes cap.

"Shit, that's spot-on," he finally said. "That's really spot-on. You get into a shitty place, you might do all kinds of stuff that don't make sense. Man—" He pulled the bill of his hat farther down on his head, as if retreating beneath it. "There was a time I couldn't get through the day without about two hundred milligrams of Oxy and a couple of benzos. Couldn't face the world, just a total slave to it."

This revelation hung in the air, and Dan felt great pity for this guy who he'd always viewed caustically, one-dimensionally.

Dan offered, "My lieutenant, a guy named Holt. He needed painkillers for all kinds of things, and when he got out, last I heard, he went straight to being a full-blown addict."

Beaufort squeezed the plastic cup so that it crackled and kept sharing. "Got my first scrip for 'em when I separated my shoulder sophomore year on jayvee. Basically didn't stop popping until a few years ago. Hardest thing I ever did in my life was get off that shit. You're not yourself. You'll do evil, unbelievable things. And there was moments." He nodded his head, matter-of-fact. "Was a lotta times I wanted to eat a whole bottle and just have done with it."

He reached for the pitcher to pour himself another. Dan had the sense he was about to say more.

There was a meatpacking thunderclap and a sharp cry from the bar. Their heads all whipped in time to catch Jonah, reeling back, blood gushing between clawed fingers as he clutched his nose. Brokamp, back from the bathroom, gave his hand a shake and closed it back to a fist. Jonah stumbled and slid to the floor.

No one in the bar moved.

"You got balls, fucker." Brokamp grabbed Jonah by the shirt and hauled him to his feet, muttering, "I know you. I know you, fuckface bitch."

Bill stood, knocking his stool back. He hovered just out of the guy's reach. "Fuck off, man! Leave him alone."

"You want this too?" Brokamp asked. He got his knuckles righteous again, his arm pistoned, and Jonah's nose exploded. He drew back the fist. Doused in brown-crimson, it looked like a brick, and he wore an enormous metal band on his ring finger that probably had traces of other people's blood in its grooves. Dan made no move to help and instead gripped the edge of the table as if anchoring himself. Because at the sight of blood, his instinct was to grab this man's skull and try to break it against the bar. He could already see what it would look like when his head opened up. Dan had seen such things many times. The girlfriend watched from her stool, disinterestedly, drunkenly, twirling an earring between thumb and forefinger. No one in the bar looked ready to break this up, maybe because they could feel what Dan felt, the electric buzz of tragedy on the way. He thought of Rudy, whose own father was killed in a drunken altercation. Guy takes out a knife over a stupid disagreement that he wasn't even a part of, and there you go, no more Rudy's dad. *Happens all the time*, Rudy had said. *Go look in any city paper sometime, Eaton. Every Sunday go look in the paper. People get drunk; they think they're invincible*. Beaufort now stood but made no move to intervene, and Dan wondered if the look on his face was that of a coward, like he'd seen among the insurgents—people who were willing to visit violence upon others as long as the odds were weighed endlessly in their favor. Or maybe he watched the man who might have been his father with total disinterest—maybe even a bit of drunken glee that he was at least getting a free show. Jess Bealey clawed through her purse, probably looking for her cell phone. The frantic but unsurprised look on her face told Dan this guy wailing on Jonah was a problem client, that she'd been here before, and yeah, he just might kill Jonah if someone didn't pull him off. Because the unemployed and underemployed came in here, drank away a disability check, and then went look-ing for an excuse to wail on anyone, to open up some cheek flesh. Brokamp had unrequited revenge in him, and he would take it out where he could. Here was his chance to feel like he could hit back. And when he drove his fist down a third time, the sound Jonah's nose made was the crunch of dry cereal stomped to dust underfoot. He went limp.

Jonah had tossed his pack of cigarettes on the table—Virginia Slims—and now Dan drew one, put it to his lips, and lit it with a Harley-Davidson Zippo. As Brokamp ordered up his arm again, elbow cocked, Dan slid from the stool. Took a step to within an arm's reach.

Dan said, "Hey, man," and Brokamp looked up. His expression was delighted curiosity. Who would be dumb enough to interrupt his lovely moment?

"He's good," Dan said. "You made your point."

Brokamp let go of the fistful of shirt. Jonah oozed to the floor, trying to cup the blood from his ruined nose.

"Man." Brokamp's voice was a whiskey whistle. "I'll take your pride too if you want." Breath heaved in and out of his barrel chest. His face and skull were sweat-streaked, the bright pink of a crayon.

Effete smoke drifted from the moon-white Virginia Slim. Wor-ried he would cough, Dan didn't inhale. The Backstreet Boys' "I Want It That Way" played on the jukebox.

Dan nodded, thought about how best to put this. Maybe this would work, maybe it wouldn't.

"Whatever you say, boss. Only so you know, I got a particularly high threshold for pain."

Then Dan took the lit cigarette and stuffed the burning orange ember in his eye.

Someone in the room gasped, a sound that seemed to come out of the walls.

He ground the cigarette into his prosthetic for a moment, ashes between eyelashes, lids wide so as not to singe them, and then let the butt drop to the ground.

The girlfriend's expertly shaped eyebrows shot up. Brokamp's face fell, like he suddenly glimpsed sobriety and hated what he saw. He looked worn out. Ready for bed. Todd Beaufort barked a short laugh. Dan blinked away smoke and debris.

"*I never wanna hear you say / I want it that-a way.*"

Bleary, Brokamp said, "Fuck this configuration." He looked to his lady friend and cocked his head at the door. Jonah whimpered, blood puddling on the hardwood.

The woman hoisted up her top and threw back the remainder of her beer. She bopped off the stool in a dainty move and stepped around Jonah. Wobbling on her heels, fat pouring from the undersides of her midriff-exposing top, she took her man's hand and led him to the door. On her way out, Dan heard her ask him, "I thought you couldn't smoke indoors no more?"

Instead of responding, Brokamp stuck his ring finger deep into his mouth, seeming to forget the blood on his hand. He wet the finger and then tugged the ring off so he could clean it on his shirt.

When they were gone, Jess Bealey ran to Jonah with a bar towel. Beaufort tried to hoist him to his feet, but Jonah slipped and sat back down. Bill looked at Dan in total awe.

"Well, fuck me, Eaton!"

Jonah sat in his blood, eyes wet, and took the towel from Jessica. His nose called to mind Marjah after Operation Moshtarak.

"Just a stupid bar trick," Dan said. Picked up from a guy named Benny Steidl, who'd also suffered an ocular penetrating injury. He'd been fitted for a prosthesis before Dan and was flying through the PT vision training when they met. He took Dan out to a bar near Ramstein Air Base and told him to watch his flawless pickup move. He put out a cigarette on his eye for a table of middle-aged

German women, and they lost their minds. *Works almost too good*, Steidl told him. Last Dan heard, Steidl was having an affair with a married gal.

"What a night," said Bill giddily. "These ten-year reunions should be a doozy." Laughter floated in the ponds of his two real pupils.

Jonah composed himself by unraveling into a drunk, ranting fury. Crimson blood drying to rust on his T-shirt, hat knocked from his head and forgotten, he took three shots of whiskey in rapid succession, then stormed out of the bar barking about his helicopter and the evils of taxation.

"He gets like that," said Beaufort.

"Should we go after him?" Dan asked.

Beaufort gave him a puzzled look. "Then we gotta listen to him."

Dan told Bill it was time to go. He pulled something from his pocket. Dan saw it was a small electronic timer. He glanced at it and said, "Yup. Let's boogie." They exchanged good-byes. Dan noticed Bill's pained handshake with Beaufort, as if both men wanted not to touch the other's disease.

"Can I ask you something," Dan said to Bill once they were on the road. "You got a problem with Beaufort?"

"Do I have a problem with Beaufort." He considered this. "Nah, not really. No more than anyone else. I think that kid got about what he had coming. Maybe not. Rick had beef with him once, and he dragged me into it. Beaufort just reminds me of how this town sucks you in. Keeps you doped on its own mythology. And I've always felt more sorry for him than anything else. When we were smoking outside, Jonah told me he had double-digit concussions before he quit in college. Said he sometimes forgets simple things. He has panic attacks. You heard him talking about his pill problem. All that for fucking high school football and two years in a shitty small college program? Fuck."

From the passenger seat, Dan watched the town of his birth recede into the valley below. Like a constellation fallen to earth.

"And how are you still buddies with Jonah?"

He batted a hand. "Oh, the guy's an Agenda 21 loon to be sure, but, you know . . ." The hand trailed to the ether beyond the roaring window. "He's my tribe. Gotta defend the tribe. Everyone's friends as kids. You don't know what makes you different yet."

"Still, he's like your arch nemesis politically speaking."

"Jonah wore a jersey with my name and number on the back to games. He stood front and center and got 'MVP' chants going when I was at the foul line. He knew my politics. I sure as shit didn't make it any secret. But whenever I see him, we find a way to let it lie."

Dan was silent for a moment, wondering if he wanted to challenge Bill on this. The beer helped make that decision.

"Did you and Rick ever let anything lie?"

Bill blew out a breath and sat in silence for a long time. They went by the Walmart, and Bill watched it as they passed. It was lit up like an army base, so bright it might be visible from space. "I'd like to burn one of those stores to the ground just once. Just watch all that *shit* inside go up in flames or melt in cool, fucked-up ways. Like how do you think an LCD TV melts? Probably burns in lots of awesome colors, right?"

Dan said nothing. Waited. Bill turned off Zanesville Road, bombing along 229. He knew the guy shouldn't be driving, Bill's adrenaline mingled with his drunk and maybe some other substance. His fingertips barely grazed the wheel, scooting it back and forth, alarmingly casual. His gas light had been on the whole time, but Dan wasn't about to say anything. With some luck, the truck would die, and he'd have to call someone for a ride.

"You know what your problem is, Eaton," he said. "Other than you wasted the best years of your life fighting for elite profit while those bastards fucked the rest of us dry."

"Yeah, do tell." In Bill's drunkenness he missed Dan's venom.

"Your problem is your good nature, bro. Hailey—you fucked that up so bad. No wonder she married Whitey fucking Frye, man."

Dan rarely got angry with anyone, but Ashcraft was goading him, probably because of what he'd just said about Rick. Dan stared out the window as they rocketed by the backlit pines and a yard scattered with stripped engines.

"Yeah, and what's your problem, Bill? You're such a perceptive student of the human condition, how about you?"

"My problem? Oh, I don't know. Substance abuse mostly. Also all my fucking friends are dead or won't speak to me." He hiccupped. "But most stupid of all—and here's my real problem—even though I know there's nothing left but to stand in front of the tank and let it mow me down, I still believe in the old myths. I still get drippy for meeting at Seneca or marching in Selma or rioting at Stonewall. I can't give up this idea that if you can get enough people to stand up, then you've got a power you cannot suppress or repress or contest. And I'll probably chase that funny fantasy until my fucking liver melts and my heart explodes."

"Yeah, or maybe you're so wrapped up in your own bullshit that you can't see the forest for the trees. Maybe your problem is you're no different than Jonah."

Ashcraft threw him a savage glance. "C'mon, that's a false equivalence. And don't spout clichés, Eaton, you're smarter than that. Or do you wanna sit here and say you never questioned what you were doing on your two tours."

"Three."

"Whatever."

Bill took the turn off 229 into the drive of Eastern Star Retirement Home. The sign was lit by halogen floodlights and an American flag rode above. His truck lurched up the drive and into the parking lot. The grounds had lights pointed at the brick, as if to keep at bay the dark of the surrounding woods, trying to convince the observer of a sense of warmth. He parked the truck in the shadows where a screen of pines shielded them from the road. Windows down, crickets screaming. They were buried in the dark, but he could see Bill's face contorting.

"I got a feeling the only way left is the way of the knife, way of the gun, way of the bomb." He snickered. He was worse than drunk, on something else Dan couldn't figure. "Hard to see the truth and not want to immediately burn your eyes out. I was trying to explain that to Rick before he left—or not explain so much but belittle that stupid, stubborn asshole that he wasn't fighting for his country or freedom or democracy or anything else. He was going to war so an overstretched superpower could flex nuts and maybe pump a few million more barrels per day onto the world oil markets—that's what I told him. And I was *so fucking right*."

He closed his eyes and rested his head against his arms on the steering wheel, the plastic creaking. Dan almost told him the story just to piss on him.

During the surge on tour #2, as their sector was quieting down, they pulled an absolutely terrible mission of escorting supply trucks to Camp Baharia. Not normally their purview, their captain had volunteered them. Guys grumbled but no one had the kind of energy necessary for mutiny. The drive to Baharia meant an hour-plus on open highway, exposed, heading toward Fallujah—not known as the sweetest getaway from western Baghdad. Of course, that was the mission that went without a hiccup. They could've watched movies on laptops.

In Baharia, he was lounging against the side of a blast wall, enjoying a rare cigarette, when he saw a muscle-bound guy coated in tattoos bench-pressing without a spotter. When he let the bar slam down, weights rattling, and sat up, Dan recognized Rick Brinklan.

"You embarrass me, man," he said, walking over to Rick. His head snapped to Dan like he'd heard the pops of AKs. "I put on some biceps since I joined, but look at you . . ."

"Eaton." He gave Dan a sweat-soaked hug, then rubbed his gray USMC tee in his eyes to clear the moisture. It must have been 110 degrees. "Don't let me give you a boner, dude. Get home to Hailey."

He'd heard Rick was 2nd Battalion, 1st Marines—Dad must have told him—but he never imagined running into him. There were at least a dozen or so kids from New Canaan serving, but what were the odds? He and Rick spent that afternoon smoking and walking the perimeter of the blast walls, listening to the sounds of small arms fire in the distance. Rick's battalion had had a staggering number of casualties on this deployment, including the previous day.

"PFC Slopes. This surfer bro from Florida—real nice guy but a total airhead. When I helped him do his taxes he asked if he could deduct his stereo system 'cause it helped him get amped for battle. He was like mystified when I told him that was ridiculous." He smiled in the grimmest possible way. He had small, tough eyes, but with all the added bulk his face looked bloated. His trapezius muscles were like suspension bridges coming down from his neck. The claw mark tattoo Dan remembered from high school now had neighbors all over his back, torso, and down his arms. He was like an old-timey steamer trunk slapped with erratic stickers. The only part of him inkless was from the neck up, as per military regs. How tough and leathered Rick looked now. Dan had once written a history paper for him, after Lisa begged him for help on Rick's behalf. Apparently Rick was floating with a C in his history class already, and anything less than an A would make him ineligible to play football. "He's all equations," as Lisa put it. Dan did it because Lisa asked and because he liked writing history papers. Rick thanked him by buying him a six-pack, though Dan never actually drank the beers.

"EFP?" Dan asked him now. "We're getting them every day."

"Yeah, E-F-buttfucking-P," Rick said, taking a drag. "I get there and the door was hanging off. Dragged Slopes out and tried to do something for him. He had blood coming out his nose, mouth, his ears." Rick used his smoking hand to palm his entire face to demonstrate the extent of the damage. "I got his helmet off and a piece of his brain just *splats* out onto his MARPAT. He had this wound on the right side of his head, and it was like his brain was trying to crawl out. His eyes were all bugging." He tapped his cigarette. "It was pretty grotesque. I got him sitting up so he wouldn't get blood in his airway and started doing finger swipes. Got him wrapped from head to shoulder in Kerlix, but he might as well have been dead when I found him."

"Were you guys close?"

"He lived until morning. We went out and pink-misted some haji for it, so . . ."

Dan didn't particularly feel like reliving every combat death and traumatic casualty right then and there, but he understood the need to process the stuff that had just happened. He thought of watching Sergeant Wunderlich's face on fire.

Rick didn't seem much interested in talking about New Canaan, but Dan had to somehow change the subject. Of course he ended up having to explain about Hailey.

"Y'all are done?"

"I told her I was thinking of signing up for another tour. She didn't take it well."

Dan expected more pushback—the kind Mom, Dad, and his sisters had all given him—but Rick only nodded.

"Yeah, I'm thinking about becoming career. I fucking hate it over here, but it's better than back home. No jobs, everyone's on fucking drugs. Can't believe I was thinking of going to OSU and then starting a family in New Canaan. So I get it. You might share blood with your family, but you sure as shit didn't shed it with them."

Exactly. Because how easy had it been to let go of her? He tested the subject of Kaylyn. The way Rick pretended to shrug it off, he could tell he'd gotten his heart good and broke. Rick had never been much for hiding how he felt. As transparent as glass and possibly as fragile.

"For the best," said Rick. Someone had left a dust-coated forklift by the perimeter, and they stopped in its shade. Rick put one boot up against the machine. Dan had a memory of standing near Kaylyn when Rick made a heroic run in a football game. Her shriek had been the loudest. *Get it, babe! Getitgetitgetit!* Until her voice hit a pitch like a fire alarm.

Rick ashed his cigarette. "I can't believe I proposed to her. Turned out she was a total whore." He shook his head and looked at his hand to examine a fingernail, black and probably soon to fall off. "Total psycho dick-chugging whore."

Dan had never heard someone use the phrase "psycho dick-chugging whore" with so much evident remorse. If Kaylyn had walked down from the FOB right then, he'd have bet his paycheck that Rick would have fallen into her weeping.

"Just wish I hadn't thrown the damn engagement ring into the woods. Could use the cash now." He smiled his gritty grin.

When Dan was back home on his eighteen-day R&R, he and Hailey had gone to Nashville only to have the fight that ended it. She made no secret that his deployments were breaking her. She didn't like the wars, didn't like him participating in them, absolutely loathed the president. When they talked by Skype or Gchat, there was no joy in it. She hated him doing what he did too much.

They had the final conversation in her apartment in Bowling Green. She hugged herself and told him if he signed up for another tour, she was done.

"I want to start my life." She bobbed her shoulders matter-of-factly, strands of auburn hair piled around her thick pink cheeks. "Not sit around playing army girlfriend or, worse, army widow. I said I would wait for you one tour, and that became two, and now you're telling me it could be three or four? No. That's not what I agreed to. It's not fair to ask me to do that." He could feel the ill-lit kitchen, the buzzing fire in the bulbs. It sounded like she'd been rehearsing that speech. "Don't fucking kid me, kid: You're choosing Iraq over me, Danny."

All he said was, "It's a weird transition being back. You can't turn it all off, especially for just eighteen days." In the years that followed, when he'd have imagined arguments about their children, Dan would think of what he could have done differently in this moment. But she was right. He was happily, knowingly, gladly choosing the army over her.

"Well," she slapped her hands on her thighs. "Then maybe it's time not to worry about it anymore."

Flying back to Baghdad, he realized he wasn't even hurt. He was relieved. And when he landed back in the desert, when he got his M4 back in his grip, when he got shot on his second patrol, the bullet catching him in the vest so that he didn't feel like he was hit in one spot but across his entire torso and that sliver of air between body and armor billowed up and out across his throat and face, he felt more at home than he had the previous eighteen days in his mother's gaze, in his father's humor, in Hailey's arms. Home is a roving sensation, not a place, and for a large chunk of his life, the feel of that bullet to the chest, that was home.

Rick grabbed one of his buddies to take a picture of the two of them before they headed out. He had an old Jaguars football banner that they both held up, the snarling beast exploding through a fifty-yard line.

"Surge buddies!" he cried as his friend snapped away on the digital camera.

As Dan prepared for the nerve-tingling drive back to Baghdad, Rick gave him a burned CD. "I got it on my iPod, so you can keep it."

He read the title: *Slow River*.

"Oh shit," he said. "This is Harrington's album."

"Yeah, man. Not sure what you're into, but dude's got chops." He laughed. "We were having beers when I was back after my first tour, and some shit I said ended up right in the lyrics. I always busted the kid's balls for being such a fag, but it's pretty great. You'll recognize so much of The Cane."

Dan burned *Slow River* onto his own iPod. Before bed, he'd read or write and listen to all twelve tracks on a loop. Something about it just unwound him, and he'd come to think of the title track and "Cattawa" to be as essential as any other piece of his gear.

A couple of months after that, Rick took a sniper's bullet on a dismounted patrol. One clean shot through the temple. Of course, Dan couldn't make it home. Nor did he care to since Hailey would no doubt be there. Mom sent him pictures of the parade and clippings from the *New Canaan News*. Joni Ashcraft wrote the story. It quoted two of New Canaan's football coaches, several teachers, and Rick's father, Marty. It was hard for Dan not to imagine what his own parade might look like.

You called me Bullfrog, Harrington sang on "Cattawa." *You warned me about these chains / If I was a weatherman I could believe / Only the darkest storms reveal the finest rains.*

"And the way everyone, even the Left, would venerate them. Picking their noses and talking about *the troops*. Like we were over there in the desert churning out heroes—all that macho bullshit that gets idiot fucking kids to go and die every time."

Bill kept going, and Dan let him. He'd heard worse.

"Rick was one of them," he said. "And so when he got his head blown off, you know what I fucking did? I didn't cry. I'll never cry for him. We weren't making heroes; we were making dead boys and invalids and occasionally monsters. Turning eighteen- and nine-teen-year-old kids into rapists and murderers. And even you guys who came back expected a parade like the saps you were when you went. Nobody gives a fuck now." He spat these words and then choked on the leftover saliva. "So no, I didn't go to his funeral, the parade, or fuck-all anything, and I sure as shit won't cry for him." He sniffed and wiped his eyes with a shirtsleeve. "This doesn't count. This is a drunk, drugged thing."

Dan wanted to leave, but Bill wasn't done.

"We had this huge blowout fight before he left. I mean, I told him what I thought. I told him I thought he was getting played, and we almost beat the shit out of each other. But that's not what it was even about."

"What was it about?" Dan asked, mostly because Bill wanted him to.

He looked at the vivid dusting of stars overhead. "I was fucking his girlfriend."

"Kaylyn?"

He nodded. A teardrop of snot hung from his nose.

"You were dating Lisa, though?"

A quick, bitter laugh. "Well, yeah, that's kinda the point of cheating. If you're gonna fuck over one person you care about why not make it a hat trick."

"Did Rick know?"

"I don't know. Probably."

He couldn't find a way to assimilate this.

"The thing about it was . . ." Bill wagged his finger at the night. "I knew it. Even before he left I knew it was going to happen. Not like a pure psychic premonition or anything, but . . . Jesus, I just fucking knew it. And when I heard . . ." He sucked in a long breath. His voice cracked. "When my dad called me and told me, all I could think about was how much I fucking hated him." He sobbed the last few words. "How glad I was that I'd hurt him like that. Because *fuck* him. That selfish fucking piece of shit with his liberty and freedom and God-and-country idiot fucking bullshit. Fuck him."

He put his face in his hands and hunched forward. He folded into himself like a snail and stayed there making soft noises that bloomed around him and competed with the crickets.

"Goddammit," he barked, punching the steering wheel hard enough to make the whole dash shudder. His sobs made him sound even younger than when Dan had known him in high school. When you really weep, you always sound like the child you ultimately still are. "I want all those years back. I want out of this fucked parallel universe we're all living in."

Dan thought of walking a dirt road, the twilight still sweltering, training the sights of his M4 on laughing children. Ashcraft wanted to see conspiracy but only because it allowed him an explanation and a way to lay blame. All history was cyclic. And these cycles beget us, even if we didn't understand them as we live them. Cycles of politics, cycles of exploitation, cycles of immigration, cycles of organization, cycles of accumulation, cycles of distribution, cycles of pain, of despair, of hope. The only fallacy, Dan figured, is the notion we've never been here before. But he'd carried that sensation in his chest his whole life—like he'd lived this already. Like he knew this moment a thousand years before he was born and would know it a thousand years after he died.

Dan popped open the door. "See you, Ashcraft. Can't say it hasn't been interesting."

Wiping tears from his cheeks, Bill gave him a little two-finger salute. "Been real, Eaton. And be sure to be on the lookout for the spirits tonight. Trying to steal your light."

His truck stammered and chuffed as he pulled away. Dan had this furious, forestalled sensation he wanted to be rid of. It was like trying to express the word *love* in a time before there was speech.

The receptionist desk was empty. Dan started down the antiseptic hallway, sharp white bulbs throwing uniform light across the pebble-colored carpet and walls of listless, institutional pistachio green. The alcohol gave everything a surreal quality—a sensation of bright faux-cheerful catacombs. He found a few nurses gathered at a desk, all mauve uniforms and hair in buns. He could hear the music from *Seinfeld* leaking out of a room down the hall.

"I'm here to see Hailey Kowalczyk," he said. "I mean, Hailey Frye."

One of the buns looked him over and left to find her.

You can always remember a person's face but not their presence, not how they fill a room. Not how they move or think or how they weave a conversation. Green scrubs swishing, one hand swinging a clipboard, she looked thicker in the hips and breasts. Her hair was much darker, the shade of yellowing autumn leaves, held back from her high forehead in a no-nonsense bun. She smiled and there was still that bulbous quality to her cheeks, like two rosy tangerines. The closer she came, the more each of her features felt like its own vortex into the past. The slim bridge of her nose widening at the nostrils, which she flared with every expression, every smile or frown. Inflating then deflating. No ridge at the top of her ears where the cartilage ended like a disc. Her eyes the color of a blue flame. Her grin kept spreading wider and wider.

"Danny." Her steps picked up and she tossed the clipboard at the desk where it barely caught the ledge and rattled to rest.

"Hey, pal." Which immediately felt like a stupid way to address her.

Her arms fell around him, and he tried to let himself just be there, standing with her, but there were too many vast unspooling histories. The three nurses watched.

He waited for her to let go. When she did, she needed to wipe tears from her eyes with symmetrical swipes of her index fingers. "Sorry," she said, more to the other nurses than to him. "I haven't seen this guy in a long time." She laughed at herself. "You look so good!"

"You look so good."

"Hey. I know I'm fat, you lying shit. I'm working on it."

"Shut up, you look great. You—" He forgot what he was about to say. "I worried I was late. I left my cell phone in my car, and then I ran into—" He stopped because the night was a long, strange story that might take a minute. "I got a ride here."

She waved this away. "You're fine. I'm just getting off. You still want to get dinner?"

"Of course."

"Want to see her first, though?"

"That was the idea."

She looked to the nurses, who were studying them with a smoke-screen of indifference. He wondered how much they knew about him. She told them she was taking him to see a patient.

"You shouldn't wake her," one of the nurses said.

"She told me to," Hailey said, some kind of ice between the two.

He followed her down the halls where he could hear the television sets mix with snoring, snorting, and mumbled dream speech. They were both silent, and he could feel the flux of miles and years and other measurements.

"Is this awkward?" she asked.

He looked at her. "No. Of course not."

"It is. What do people even talk about? It suddenly occurs to me that I have no idea what people talk about at all ever."

"Movies?"

"Danny, I haven't seen a movie in like four years."

"World events?"

"How about *Dora the Explorer*? Do you keep up with Dora?"

"Can't say I do."

She couldn't stop watching him. Dan knew she was looking at his eye. He kept her on his left, as he always did when he walked beside people so he could see them, and he could feel her leaning to glimpse it. "You really do look good. I like your hair longer . . ."

"I'm just bad at remembering to get it cut without someone barking at me to do it."

She slipped her arm through his.

He followed Hailey into the room. Dark except for a bedside lamp with the adjustable bulb pointed at the ground, the room was a jungle of ferns and other potted plants and flowers. There was also an enormous stack of books that centipeded up alongside the dresser, reminding him of his own Titusville apartment. The woman in the bed appeared to be dozing, but when Hailey put a hand on her arm her eyes slid open immediately.

"Mrs. Bingham," she said. "Look who I brought."

A misremembered dream from the night before rose, unbidden, some scenario where his captain was begging him to shave, but employing that dream logic where the electric clippers wouldn't turn on. Then in the dream, he looked up, and he was alone, back in the frigid winter of the Hindu Kush. A land unchanged since Alexander the Great's armies had forged across the same terrain. There were flurries coming down from a gray sky, little stars of snow that melted on his tongue. He could see for a hundred miles in every direction, from the burlap plains to the peaks and ridges that looked like bones breaking through the skin of the earth.

Afghanistan, deployment #3, made Iraq look like a trip to Cedar Point amusement park. Afghanistan was an ugly, cruel divot in brutal mountains. During a major operation in Marjah, he found the bones of a toddler in a field. They were wrapped in a shawl, not buried, but very old. Like the body had been out there all winter. They looked like seashells. He couldn't figure out why these people hadn't buried their dead. Maybe they didn't get a chance. Maybe the child was alive when someone put her out there. He'd get in arguments with this Evangelical kid from Georgia, Specialist Brody Van Maanen, who wanted him to leave Team Catholic. They talked a lot about God, about the morality of war. Dan asked him what he would do with the farmer who told them the Taliban had forced him to plant an IED they'd found. The Taliban threatened to kill his whole family if he didn't do it. "What do you do with that? Where's the moral true north on that one?"

Brody looked at him like he was an idiot. "Well, the farmer's not a Christian, dumbass."

That night, trying to kill some tedium, he watched Rudy sketch by the light of a small reading lamp. He remembered it was a full moon because the moon had never looked bigger than it did in Afghanistan. So big you could see the ruins on the surface.

Rudy drew comic book sketches, one-image stories with no dialogue and no title. Black-and-white drawings of Titusville, Nicaragua, Afghanistan. He would soon do an impressive rendering of Vicky's Diner after he visited, and his sketch of the train tracks running over Oil Creek in Titusville captured that minor view of the world down to the riverside grit.

"If only you had some stories to tell," Dan said.

Rudy scrubbed a pencil eraser furiously against his notepad, getting that gunky buildup of graphite and rubber strands. Dan was so bored. His mom had sent him a crop of new books, but he was burned out on reading. Instead, he threw rocks into a pot he'd set between their bunks.

"That's the idea, though. The whole story's in the one image."

"I realized the other day," said Dan. "That I stopped praying. I haven't prayed in like a year."

Rudy flicked some eraser gunk from his sketch with the back of his hand. "You been at this too long, Sergeant. Prayer's not like an active thing. It doesn't work like you check it off like a duty. My mom says prayer is, you know, ambient. The spiritual are always doing it." He looked up at Dan. "Why? You feel like you need to pray for something? You jerking off too much?"

He wanted to tell him about Hailey. He wanted to tell him about Greg Coyle and Iraq. That panic wasn't urgent but it was there. Like when a phone rings and rings and no one moves to pick it up.

Finally, he said, "Brody really is obnoxious, isn't he."

Rudy continued shading in a mountain. "I'll say this: I'm definitely jerking off too much."

After he got out of the army for good, Hailey tried to get in touch with him. She sent bombardments of e-mails and Facebook messages. She asked if he needed help because of the injury. When he didn't reply she eventually gave up. Then she wrote to tell him that she'd gotten a new patient at Eastern Star. A stroke and other accumulating health problems had convinced Mrs. Bingham's four children that it was time. Dan couldn't figure why he responded to this message and not the others, but he sent back his best wishes. Mrs. Bingham wasn't all there anymore, Hailey replied, but she'd asked after him a few times. Out of her nearly fifty years of teaching, she still remembered Dan Eaton as one of her favorite students. He should come visit her, Hailey said. She'd get such a thrill out of it. Dan told her maybe the next time he was in town. Another message arrived. Again, Hailey said Mrs. Bingham would love to see him. *And I'd love to see you too*, she wrote. He ignored it. It wasn't until she wrote that Bingham didn't have that much time left that she hit that central cortex of guilt and grief and nostalgia that commands people to face the things they'd rather not. So with most of the muscle fibers of his being protesting about walking among these graves and ghosts, he did it anyway.

"Well, Mr. Eaton, hello," said Mrs. Bingham, rheumy eyes popping from sleep to joy in an instant. "You came."

"He came," said Hailey.

"It's great to see you, Mrs. Bingham."

"Mad Anthony Wayne," she said. "One of the best Wayne presentations I ever had."

Gone was the elocution-school way of speaking, replaced by a slow and precise slur. Her hair was now bone white and so thin he could make out the moles on her scalp. She looked gaunt; her face an unhealthy plum, the blood looking congealed beneath the skin, and the right side drooped so the eye, lips, and cheek seemed in the process of sinking into quicksand. She took his hand in both of hers, the fingers pointed off like the gnarled knots of a tree branch.

"I'll also say . . ." She patted his hand and drew a deep, laborious breath. "I was surprised how well you did when you were doing all that extra research on Simon Girty."

He felt his blush as he laughed.

"She won't stop giving me hell about that," said Hailey. "I told her I did all the writing on my own—how am I supposed to help it if you suddenly got interested in Simon Girty?"

"You're so wonderful to come see me," said Mrs. Bingham, still holding his hand. "I keep telling Hailey my mind is not what it used to be—I used to be able to tell you any important date in the last five hundred years of Western civilization. I used to be able to do all the presidents and vice presidents. I could even tell you what my children's names were most of the time—" This mined another laugh from them. "But I still remember every student I loved and every one that was an awful little shit."

Hailey faux scolded her. "Mrs. Bingham."

"No, you're not supposed to say that when you're teaching, but middle schoolers can be some supreme turds, and I remember every one of them. But I also remember all my favorites, and you two were on that list. Daniel likely at the top."

"Don't play favorites," Hailey warned. "Only one of us here feeds you."

Mrs. Bingham worked at taking her breath. "Hailey tells me you work in Titusville."

"That's right."

"Edwin Drake and the town that started the oil boom. Bet you get a kick out of that."

"Yeah, I think I've read every book written about it at this point."

"What are you reading right now? I just got this wonderful book—" She pointed to her bedside: *1491*. "It's about the Americas before European discovery with all this new research." She let go of his hand to raise both of hers and indicate the ecstasy of a great read. "Oh, it's just fascinating. Hailey reads to me because my eyes get tired. What did you say you're reading?"

"I've actually been rereading some Ohio stuff. Andrew Clayton and this historian Rob Harper."

"Oh!" She put a hand over her heart. "My life was worth it. End it all now, dear." She closed her eyes. "Put the pillow over my face."

"Stop," said Hailey. Then to Dan, "She always says that. When it's meat loaf night she says that."

When she opened her eyes again, it seemed like more of a task. Her breath came with such difficulty.

"I'm glad you're back, Daniel. That's so much to be proud of. So much pride. You know my husband was headed to the Pacific when Harry Truman dropped the two atom bombs. I always said, you can mourn the devastation, you can mourn all the loss, but I would still thank him for it to this day. That kept my man out of combat, so he could come home and meet me."

She took a tissue from her bedside and held it with only the tips of her fingers, delicately, as if feeling a ball of skin.

"I'm so proud of all of you who served. Though it doesn't surprise me, I'll say. I had you pegged for some kind of hero back when you were in my class. You were a good, decent boy on his way to becoming a good, decent man."

How he'd come to hate this part of it: the gulf between how people thought of him and how he felt about what he'd done. It brought all the dread back in one vivid constellation: Wiman, his lip pregnant with dip, as he threw an old man to the ground and shattered his arm; Daniel Imana grabbing an ANA soldier and forcing him through a door, telling him to get the fuck in there because these men were their human shields, and some booby trap bomb ripped this guy's entire chest out; backing over an Afghan hut in an MRAP and later finding a whole family inside. What happened after their Humvee was hit on Highway 1, and he crawled out with his M4 ready. He could put that stuff away better than most— except when people got starry-eyed and dreamy about, as Homer put it, where men win glory.

He put his hand on Mrs. Bingham's to steer her away from heroes. "I'm glad I got this chance. And I think you know you were my favorite teacher by about a mile if it was a footrace."

Her eyes slipped closed and back open. "Oh. Well. When you're in the storm of it, you're mostly just hoping that you're not screwing up all the kids too bad."

Toward the end of seventh grade, when Hailey stopped coming over and all the boys had started to feel the itch of impending summer, the class reached the industrial boom part of Ohio history—a unit far less exciting than frontier gore—so Mrs. Bingham told the story of her family, beginning when a German immigrant named Heinrich Mundt arrived in Ohio in 1877 to soon become a fiery organizer for the Knights of Labor at the Cleveland Rolling Mill Company. She showed them an ancient copy of the Cleveland *Plain Dealer*, with a quote from her grandmother, Ada: "If the police try to break up the strike, the women will charge first. And then the men will come and kill every policeman that comes out here."

"Which gives you an idea of what my grandmother was like," she'd said.

She led the class on a tour of the Great War, Prohibition, the labor disputes that rocked the industrial Midwest, how her father was run over by a train after stumbling onto the tracks while drunk on the eve of Pearl Harbor. How her widowed mother moved the family to Toledo and found work at the Willys-Overland Motors Plant building a vehicle called the Jeep that helped the Allies fight and win two wars at the same time. Forty-five years old with four children, she went to work six days a week welding together pieces of a vehicle that would roll into Berlin four years later.

"My own life and times aren't quite as interesting," she said. "But when I say that my mother was my hero, I do not say it lightly. There were many times when she could have given up, when it might have gotten too hard for anyone, but she shut up and then put up, as they say. So that's my family's story, that's my Buckeye blood, but let me say one more thing. I tell you this story only to try to explain to you that the world you see today and the world you will see at the upper span of your long lifetimes—well—it will amaze you. The changes you will experience, the chances you will have to shape those changes—I just cannot stress how astonishing and astounding and joyful an opportunity it will be."

Thirteen years old, he walked around for weeks thinking of those words, feeling the way you do when you're outside with your friends and it starts to rain, but you're too far from home to run for it. So you just get soaked and marvel at why you don't do such a thing all the time.

They left Mrs. Bingham to fall back asleep.

Before changing out of her scrubs, Hailey poked her head into a few rooms, brought ice water for one resident, elevated a swollen ankle for another. She moved with that graceful, Haileyed confidence he remembered only now that he saw it again. When she was twelve her mother was diagnosed with osteosarcoma, cancer of the bone in her leg. For two years while her parents were absorbed with tests, treatments, two surgeries, and many rounds of chemo, Hailey took over the household responsibilities. She'd make dinner and clean most nights, pack lunch for her two younger brothers, coordinate rides to school and all social outings, and pay bills with her dad's checkbook. They were a tough family. Her dad used to say to Dan that if he had to get stranded on a desert island with one person, "It would be my daughter. She was born with steel-toed boots and knows how to put one foot in front of the other." She could do it all: sports, school, partying, helping to save her mother's life with her calm and collected takeover of the home front. "Triple-threat Kowalczyk. The strong carry on," as Lisa used to say.

"Wait, who gave you the ride?" she asked as they climbed into her car. She'd changed into jeans that stretched to their limit against her rear, maybe a size too small, and a sky-blue top with spaghetti straps that exposed the tan of her shoulders and dual cream-white swimsuit lines from a day spent in the sun. Not that she had dressed up, but she looked fresh, and in his ratty beige cargo shorts and a long-sleeved gray baseball shirt (purposely pulled from drawers that morning to prove he didn't care), Dan felt an ancient self-consciousness that dated back to morning bus rides. Agonizing over freckles and acne and the coils of red hair he couldn't get to rest properly on his skull. Admittedly, he'd chosen to put in one contact rather than wear his glasses the way she'd encouraged him to back in the seventh grade.

"Bill Ashcraft, of all people." And during the drive into town, he told her the story of running into Bill on the road, the visit to Rick's grave, finding Hansen and Beaufort at the Lincoln, and how that all played out. She laughed, she cringed, she laughed some more.

"That's a hell of a night. Not sure how much more adventure you can fit in."

"Maybe a round with Vicky's mechanical claw to see if I can win you a stuffed animal."

"We're not impressed when boys win us stuffed animals anymore." A fractional tic of her mouth. Amusement and nostalgia in its becoming. "It's 2013—we got the vote now."

That was the moment it came over him. The sense of finally seeing her after all this time. It was a bullet going off in his chest. How hard he'd tried to forget that his heart had always been a loaded weapon with her.

After he and Hailey broke up and Dan was back in Baghdad, Greg Coyle decided he couldn't do another tour. Yes, Greg did need the money. His mother was having health problems and wouldn't be eligible for Medicare for another five years. She couldn't work, she was living with his wife, and they had a mountain of medical bills. Dan was leaning toward re-upping even though he could feel a darkness following him around, keeping tabs, trying to decide if it should touch him.

They were back from patrol, stripping off their gear, when Coyle broke the news that he was getting out, that a buddy from home had promised him a job selling equipment for fire trucks. "He says they'll have me the moment my boots hit American soil."

Out came his earplugs. Off came gloves and boots. Dan needed a new pair.

"Fire truck equipment? You'll pay your mom's bills with that?"

"Shit, that's probably a medical bankruptcy situation anyway."

Off came his elbow pads, kneepads, throat protector, ammo mags. He felt like throwing his gear at Greg's frosted-blond head, a piece at a time.

"It's really Hanna," he said. "I can't be away again. I'm missing her whole childhood."

Coyle had gone from the self-professed "biggest pussy slayer in the entire U.S. Army" to the most nerve-racked father of the institution. His bunk was wallpapered with pictures of Hanna. He'd taken to building toys out of wire and soda cans, little figurines to show her over Skype.

"I get you," said Dan.

Off came his groin protector. Some guys didn't wear it, until Badamier's injury, and they heard he'd have to pee through a catheter the rest of his life.

"It's just." Greg removed his compression bandage and knife and now clutched each in a hand, staring at them. One to open a wound, the other to close it. "It's just. Man. It's like I get home and I hold her, and I feel everything. I swear I feel the weight of fucking eternity on me."

They had that conversation roughly nine months into the deployment. They were close to going home.

*　　*　　*

Vicky's looked like Vicky's. Nothing within or without had changed since he'd last ordered a slice of pie there. The few patrons at this hour looked haggard, drawn down. The speckled red plastic material of one of the stools at the counter had burst and a puff of foam protruded. Clawmageddon was OUT OF ORDER. They took a seat in a far back booth, and when the waitress came by with menus they barely needed a glance.

Hailey asked, "Do you want to see a picture of her?"

He said of course, and she zipped it up on her iPhone.

"How old?"

"She just turned four a month ago."

The little girl had a wide nose and slim eyes. A squashed infant's face that resembled her father's features, though the skin was much lighter, dosed with Hailey's pallid Polish ancestry. Curly black hair pushed out from the edges of a tiger costume packaging her head, and she stared at her mother's camera with slim-eyed mischief, mouth slightly agape as if to ask a question. Maybe all little kids looked sort of the same, but she reminded him of Hanna Coyle.

"You love it? Being a mom?"

She bobbed her head and some of the hair piled in a bun spilled; she went about cramming her dark blond back into the hair tie. "I do. I really do. Happened a bit more quickly than I'd planned, but once I was holding her . . . Things I always cared about or thought were important suddenly fell exactly into perspective. You get this feeling like . . ." She finished, snapping the hair tie into place, and puffed out her chest. "Emma Will Rule All of You One Day."

"Emma," he repeated. He handed the phone back. "She's beautiful."

Hailey's thumb slid across the screen, toggling through a few more images. As if to remind herself.

"I know. She's freaking unbelievable. Probably the smartest, most beautiful human being to ever live—and that's not my opinion. That's science."

He turned his water glass in slow spirals, dug into himself in order to ask the next part. "My mom told me you'd gotten married. Then she told me you had a daughter. I never got the story, though—I mean, with Whitey."

He didn't know why he used the nickname. He didn't mean it to be cruel, it just sort of slipped out. She rolled her eyes, annoyed but not offended. "Jesus, what is it with that? You know even his friends still call him that? Because he didn't listen to DMX in high school?"

"Is that how it started?"

"Who knows. But Jonah or Kruger or someone starts calling him 'Whitey,' and now it's a dozen years later, and even the other teachers call him that? I'll see you in hell, all of you." She hesitated, picked up the pepper and held it in her hand like a lucky talisman. "It's not like anyone would ever accuse New Canaan of being this liberal, happy-go-lucky oasis, but I can feel people looking at us and Emma sometimes. And then my mom and dad . . ."

"I can't imagine they'd have a problem? That doesn't sound like them."

"No it's not—and they don't. It's just when we first started seeing each other, they sort of went out of their way to treat him well. Like they bent over backward to make it clear that they don't care that he's black, but sometimes they can be so, so awkward. Like they buy magazines if Michelle Obama is on the cover and leave them on the coffee table."

Dan snickered at this.

"Anyway . . . I don't know. Eric and I were just friendly. I never thought of him that way. But I was back in town working, and he was back subbing at the high school, and we started seeing each other, and I got pregnant. It wasn't till then that I, you know, sort of figured out I wanted to have a family with him." She swallowed. "And I was in love with him."

"How'd it start?" he asked immediately. So they could blow by what she'd just said. She looked at him, probably wondering if he really wanted to hear this.

"When Rick Brinklan died, they had a parade for him." Dan stared at the condensation on his water glass. "Everyone was back for it. Our families ended up by each other when the coffin came through. Dad's friends with Marty Brinklan, and I hadn't seen him that upset since Mom's cancer. Afterward, Eric and I went for a drink and had a good talk—Eric's just a really . . ." She hesitated. He could feel her gaze the way you feel a fire if you put your face too close. "Decent guy. It's funny, in high school I thought his eyes were too close together, but it's the stuff like that you end up falling in love with."

"That's good," Dan said. "You sound happy."

Maybe her smile was rueful. "I am."

The conversation stuttered. He'd feared it since he first saw her. That his jaw would clamp, and the heft of whatever he felt for her would hold it closed like a counterweight. One of Hailey's skills was changing the subject, though.

"You know what I can't wait for? When Emma gets old enough that I can start getting her into *Calvin and Hobbes*. Hence the tiger outfit. I'll tell her she went as Hobbes."

"You ever read them still?"

"Are you kidding? I have all the books on a shelf by my toilet."

He barked a laugh.

"Only— Okay, here's the thing." She leaned in to reveal the embarrassing. "*Calvin and Hobbes* changes when you get older, especially after you have your own kid. I think because it's this really . . ." She paused, searching for the right words. "This specific, acute rendering of childhood and everything that childhood's about. Just all the hope and friendship and wonder of being a kid, but also some of the sadness and the loneliness. You know?"

Of course he did.

"So sometimes I'll read it, and I'll just . . ." She laughed brightly. "I'll start crying. It's silly as hell, but I'll get to the strip where Calvin's railing against the condominiums being built in the woods where he plays or the one where he's putting himself in the transmogrifier, and it doesn't really matter the subject, I'll just be *moved* by it. You know? And then I'm sitting on the toilet, holding *Calvin and Hobbes*, getting all teary . . ."

They were both laughing, and then her hand shot out and grabbed Dan's.

"No! No! And I can't let anyone ever know that! Promise to take it to the grave."

"What about the raccoon story line?"

She pulled at her cheeks until the pinks of her eye sockets shone wetly. "Oh God the raccoon! When Calvin's talking about death and he tells Hobbes, 'But don't *you* go anywhere.' That's like rip-my-heart-out, leave-me-sobbing-in-the-corner *Calvin and Hobbes*."

It was how she made him laugh as a thirteen-year-old. It's why he dreaded the moment when they'd have to get off the bus at Rainrock Road and part ways—because he knew there was a finite number of those bus rides in this one precious life.

Their waitress had what looked like blood spots on her apron and an uneasy-making bruise on her arm that he saw when she set down their plates. Hailey voiced her displeasure at splurging on a burger while he forked at a salad. Vicky's menu didn't offer many options for vegetarians. She cut her burger in half, and asked him what his days were like. "Tell me about your life while you eat your dainty little salad."

He told her of Chesapeake Energy; visiting the rigs; the difference between horizontal and non-horizontal wells; his boss, a jocular, high-spirited former Pitt baseball star turned engineer, who called him "D.E."; his apartment, a one-bedroom in a two-story unit on the west side of Titusville, overlooking Oil Creek (and the less scenic Morrison Builders Supply).

"Maybe I'll come visit sometime."

"Not a lot to do in Titusville. Nearest movie theater's about a half-hour drive."

She gave that twitch of a smile, hard to read now, and bit off a gnarly chunk of beef.

"Seeing anyone?" she asked, mouth full.

"Not right now, no."

"Seen anyone lately?"

He felt the old frustration, born when Lisa told him about Curtis Moretti, now curdling in the light of her husband, her child, her new life.

And like that, he let it go. Like he'd always done.

"I don't have a lot of time for dating. I'm always helping out with Rudy."

"Your mom told me, yeah." She poked at her fries. Her face gleamed with grease and compassion. "How do you help out?"

He didn't give her the whole story. Just the aftermath and Rudy's injuries. His mother, Yunely, worked at the Titusville Quality Inn as a housekeeper. She didn't speak much English and needed a lot of help dealing with Rudy's injuries, talking to doctors, and navigating the VA. When Dan arrived back stateside, he visited Rudy at the polytrauma unit in Richmond, Virginia. The doctors told Yunely no way, no how would he make it. He had severe burns and had been shot in the head, just above the right ear. The bullet had torn across his frontal lobe and exited the other side. That the medics had kept him alive at all was something of a miracle. But Yunely refused to take him off life support. Dan had enough high school Spanish that he didn't need the hospital translator to understand *Dios encontrará la manera*. God will find a way.

Burns had seared away most of the flesh on his chest and left arm. To prevent life-threatening infection, the medics had needed to close those wounds right away, washing away charred flesh with light streams of warm water and then beginning grafts immediately. The burns on the right side of his face required a much more difficult procedure. The doctors cut a strip of skin from his shoulder, peeled it back, and let it grow onto the ruined part of his face. This odd pink bridge looked like a giant tongue lapping at his cheek. It would be fourteen more surgeries until the skin took. The grafts contracted into thick scars and pulled at the tissue around his nostrils and right eye. Like pinched plastic.

Yet the burns were not why the doctors didn't hold out much hope. The bullet had done severe trauma to his brain. They gave the technical explanation, but this meant as little to Dan as it did to Yunely. Parenchymal hemorrhage and edema. The only thing he really understood was that they'd removed a large piece of his skull to allow his brain to swell. All Rudy had was skin between mind and world.

He thought Yunely was just being a mother. Dan knew his own mom would have to be dragged away by about fifty cops before she let the doctors take him off life support. Yunely and Rudy's father had come from Nicaragua to join family in Pittsburgh and to escape the rampaging of the Contras. She had an immigrant's tirelessness, the quiet ability to accept and assimilate whatever new obstacle descended. He thought it would be his job to convince her to let Rudy go—at least that's why he told himself he was in Richmond. Then he finally saw Rudy. His good eye, the one that had escaped the burn and wasn't buried in a stretched plastiscape of skin grafts, landed on Dan and widened. Rudy couldn't move, but he made a sound deep in his throat, a grunt of recognition, Dan was sure. He took Rudy's limp palm and held it. Beneath the carnage of his face he could see what Yunely saw, that Rudy was very much alive inside.

After the cranioplasty, when the doctors fixed a prosthetic piece to his skull, Yunely persuaded them to release Rudy to a rehab center in Pittsburgh. Dan followed, living out of a dumpy motel on the south side, all thoughts of returning to school abandoned. The rehab center had little success. The bullet had destroyed whatever part of the brain sends signals to the rest of the body. He couldn't move a finger. Noises would bubble up from his throat, but it was hard to tell what these articulated, if anything. Since he couldn't keep his trunk erect, he had to be strapped into his wheelchair, head held in place with the same type of setup as quadriplegics. After three months, though, the therapists did make one advance they considered significant. When Rudy arrived he still couldn't swallow. The therapists used electric nodes to zap his throat. To trigger muscle memory, they explained. After months of patient work, they taught him how to use his cheeks and tongue to drink through a straw and swallow. Dan picked up Yunely in Titusville every Thursday on her day off. This was the arrangement they'd worked out so she could keep her job and spend her spare time at Rudy's side. That Thursday afternoon, when the therapists held up the flex-straw of his plastic mug and Rudy took it with his lips, his cheeks going concave as he drew the water, Yunely shrieked. Like Rudy had thrown a touchdown at the Super Bowl instead of sipping liquid. Her voice flowed in a dense, indomitable waterfall as she gripped her son and kissed his ruined face. Then she went around the room hugging the therapists, weeping onto their sleeves, and the women looked so unembarrassed for her, so genuinely happy to have been the cause of this display. Finally, Yunely held Dan, her head barely reaching his chest. *Dios enviaron a su amigo. Su hermano.* God sent you to be his friend. His brother.

Rudy went home, and Dan found a job in Titusville. The gas boom had begun. Companies were cracking into the Marcellus and Utica Shales like an enforcer bringing a baseball bat across a car's windshield, spiderwebbing the rock to release the prize. He moved into an apartment down the road from Yunely and Rudy, and they worked out a schedule. Rudy still needed twenty-four-hour care, and the endless list of tasks included dressing him, changing his diaper, managing the feeding tube, and checking and treating problem sores. Dan would arrive after he got off work and stay until Yunely came home at midnight. During the day, the VA paid for a nurse. Carly, sullen and quietly truculent was first, but then came Annette, a vivacious old Jamaican, who called both Rudy and Dan "Boy-man." Between Dan, Yunely, and Annette, they managed. There were still moments of real fear. When Yunely worked a late shift, he usually spent the night at the house and would hear Rudy making these desperate, keening moans in his sleep. They had the power to put a dream in Dan's head the moment before they woke him. He asked Yunely how often Rudy had nightmares. He thought she said once or twice a week, but she may have meant those were the rare nights he didn't dream.

Rudy had come a long way from when the doctors considered him a corpse in suspended animation, but it was relative. He could move his head, lift a hand every now and then, look at Dan's one eye with his one eye, but that was his range. His progress seemed to promise so much more, and yet after those first months of rehabilitation he'd hit a wall. Yunely still thought he would be the same again, someday, but it was hard to see how.

Meanwhile, Dan learned how to have a conversation with a friend who had no voice. They watched a lot of movies—he never expressed interest in picking them so it was a lot of Dan's Net-flix queue, a lot of historical documentaries with a *Hot Tub Time Machine* thrown in now and then. They watched Ken Burns's *The Civil War* all the way through twice. He bought graphic novels, held them before Rudy, and read to him.

A few weeks ago, Dan had been reading to him from the Frank Miller classic *The Dark Knight Returns*. He came to a panel where Harvey Dent was flashing back to his eponymous facial injuries. He felt Rudy stir, and Dan looked up. With great effort, Rudy lifted his arm—the one where the burns had just missed the knight and *Sí Se Puede*—and his hand hovered over the illustration, index finger attempting a gnarled effort to point. His eye met Dan's. The left corner of his lip, which managed all of his ability to express, curled up. A movement Dan knew to be his grin.

"Uhn," he said.

Dan burst out laughing, and Rudy stayed like that, smiling, for the rest of *The Dark Knight Returns*.

"Do you ever see Kaylyn?" he asked.

They waited on the check, and Dan picked at the cold chits of fries from Hailey's plate.

She wiped her fingers on a crumpled napkin. "Not really."

"She's around, though."

"Sure. She never went anywhere. We don't see each other that much. She was still a barfly up until she got pregnant." A grim smile.

"Pregnant?"

"Yeah. So there's that." She closed her mouth, looking oddly troubled.

"Bill told me something tonight." Maybe it was in poor taste to gossip, but bringing this up didn't seem any worse than watching

Hailey's face go limp as he related the story of Rudy. He told her what Bill had said about him and Kay. Hailey barely looked surprised.

"You knew?"

She flicked at the napkin and watched it spin and tumble on the plate. "Yeah, I knew." She closed her mouth. Her teeth clicked together. "Kaylyn called him her 'pity fuck.' Bill had been after her for so long that she thought . . . Well, I don't know why she ever did anything she did, but I've got theories."

"Such as?"

"It was all like a game to her. It was her way of being able to get to Lisa if she ever needed to."

This sat poorly in his stomach. His most persistent memory of Kaylyn was when she'd lost her inhaler in the eighth grade (Dan in seventh), and he'd seen her in the hallway heaving breaths during an asthma attack, a teacher rubbing her back and telling her to breathe while Kaylyn's face brimmed with panic. "That's twisted."

She chuffed a humorless laugh. "Hardly the most twisted thing Kay has ever done. She hangs around real fucked-up people now. She hasn't had a job since she quit waitressing, so she makes money any way she can . . ." She trailed off.

"How 'bout Lisa?"

She gave another humorless laugh. "No."

"She's gotta come back someday." He felt a surge of longing for his long-gone friend and fellow bookworm. He missed her dearly wherever she was.

"Maybe," said Hailey. He could feel the night going blank. Hailey preparing to return to her other life. The waitress brought the check. He took it before she could offer to pay. They sat there for a while waiting on the change, looking like a still life painting to anyone passing by the window.

*   *   *

He could never explain it to Hailey or Mom or Heather or Betty. Not even Dad. Why he wanted to go back. Why even after he was healed and discharged, he couldn't leave Rudy.

It was tour #2 in Iraq, September 22, 2007, thirty-five days before they would go home. They were doing a dismounted patrol just south of a mosque where they usually took small arms fire. When muzzle flashes and tracer fire erupted, they were ready ("Got some MacDougals on the rooftop and in the alley," Coyle had warned). Cleary laid down fire with the .50 from the gunner's hole, Della Terza with the SAW, and it didn't really feel like much. They'd encountered way worse. And then Dan saw a boxy white car coming their way, the kind you saw all over the roads of Baghdad. All he remembered was the driver's beard peeled back in the smarmy grin of the about-to-be-martyred. Della Terza went cyclic and the VBIED detonated well before it reached the convoy. But they were building those things with a lot of frag: ball bearings, nails, feces, ceramic shards. The post-blast buzz filled his ears until the world he knew returned: the smell of hot, ripe shit, and the rubble plinking and thunking off his helmet. When he saw someone down, he didn't think it could be Coyle. He thought Coyle had been standing to his right, on the other side of the blast, but for some reason he must have gone to the lead Humvee. Dan could see the explosion had blown both front tires, shattered the windshield. He ran, splashing through engine oil.

He got to Coyle first, before their medic, Sasha Laymon. Laymon was one of the best sixty-eight whiskeys Dan ever worked with. He had lightning hands and an intuition for unseen wounds, but when he got to Greg Coyle, he knew Laymon's gifts wouldn't matter.

His friend had been torn in half, Coyle's left leg completely gone and a wound going up his midsection so deep he could see hot blood boiling up from primal, interred pockets, spilling into light it was never supposed to see. His left arm was pulp. Part of his face and scalp were burned. You wouldn't even know where to start with the Kerlix.

Yet he was conscious, shivering all over when Dan got to him, kneepads skidding across asphalt. Coyle was trying to look down at himself to assess the damage. Dan pushed him down. Cleary slid into the dirt beside him, ripping his headset off.

"Hold on, man. Lie still. Let Doc work on you. You're fine," said Dan.

Laymon shoved Dan out of the way so he could start on the— (*On what? His leg? His guts falling out?*)—damage. Coyle was still trying to get a look. He'd thrown up on himself. Bits of eggs from an MRE that morning peppered his stubble. Dan held his trembling shoulders down, but Coyle was surprisingly strong. He managed to crane his neck up far enough.

"Oh fuck," he said. It sounded like he'd just taken a look at his taillight after a fender bender.

Dan shushed him. "Just lie still, dude. You'll be fine, man. You're going home."

Several Bradleys and MRAPs from another patrol had surrounded them, and their squad came hustling over, edging in around Laymon. Lieutenant Holt called in a medevac. They all told Coyle lies because they knew that's what they would want to hear.

"You're good, dude," said Cleary.

"It hurts like hell, I know, but you're heading home," said Wong.

"You're gonna see your family. Hero time," said Della Terza.

"Fuck," said Coyle, staring at the sky, tears and blood in his eyes. "Fuck."

Slowly their palms came in. Dan gripped Coyle's good right hand, his fingers fierce and alive, and he put his other hand on

Coyle's vest, over his heart. Della Terza's hand came to his midriff. Wong's to the other side of his chest. Cleary put a palm on his forehead like his mother checking his temperature. Other hands, from the rest of the unit, found him, encouraged him.

"We love you, Coyle."

"We're right here, Greg."

"You got this, dude. You got this."

"*Fuck,*" Coyle hissed. Blood streamed from his ear.

They gripped him. Tried to hold his soul to the earth. He blinked tears; his whole body trembled uncontrollably, his eyes filled with panic.

"You're going to be with her," Dan said. "You're going home, bud."

Their hands spiraled around him like the spokes of a wheel. They held Greg until well after he was dead.

Dan wrote letters to Coyle's family that night, one to his wife and mother and another to Hanna. The superstition about the short-timer dying made them all crazy, but everyone who died had a daughter, a son, a wife, a husband, brothers, sisters, parents. Everyone was about to get out. Everyone was on his or her way home. He thought about the moment when a soldier is dead but his family doesn't know. They're going about their lives while this awful information exists, but they don't have to live with it yet.

Their last month ground on. A few days later, Della Terza got an e-mail from Coyle's wife saying she wanted a chance to talk to some of the guys from Greg's unit. They gathered around a laptop, Danny, DT, Cleary, Wong, Laymon, Drake, and Melody Coyle appeared to them on the janky video call, freezing and pixelating at various moments throughout the conversation. Dan had seen her before. When Coyle would call, he'd sometimes lift his computer and have them say hi to each other. She looked rail-thin, like she hadn't been eating. Her cheeks were sunken, her elbows knobby.

Hanna, the daughter, bobbed on her lap, smacking and drooling on a Thomas the Train. Seeing them, Dan wanted to hurl grenades at the continent of the sky until it all shattered and came crashing down.

"Say hi, Hanna!" Melody waved Hanna's pudgy arm, and the oblivious baby gargled happily. "Say hi to Daddy's friends." She smiled at them. "I just wanted to catch y'all in the same place at the same time just to say—you know, to say." Melody dragged that last word out in her Kentucky drawl and then hesitated. She was no longer the beautiful girl Coyle had met at the Cat West, who danced like a wild woman to dirty music and hooked up with him the first night they met in the backseat of her car. That girl had been dragged through motherhood and the loss of her husband. She looked exhausted.

"How you doing?" Della Terza interrupted. "Is there anything we can do for you?"

"Oh, I'm fine. Greg's parents have been great. It's hard being out in California, so far from home for this, but—but the reason I wanted to talk to y'all is I thought it was important to let you know how highly Greg spoke of you. He really loved you guys. He loved working with you, living with you, being friends with you. He just raved when he was home about how he'd met the very best people of his life over there. I thought it was important I got in touch and told y'all that."

Melody managed to say this with dry eyes, while it hit them each in the solar plexus. Dan let a breath escape his chest, somewhere between a sob and a sigh, and he could feel his friends do the same.

"I'm sorry. I didn't mean for it to be like this." Melody took her index finger and tapped a single tear under her eye. It melted away. "I've already done all my crying. I'm exhausted by it. But me and Hanna just had to call and let you know how much Greg loved you." Dan had been standing behind DT and Cleary, peering over their shoulders. "Danny?" When Melody said his name, they all looked back at him.

"Yeah?" He wiped his eyes. He could not bear to look at her.

"Greg left you something."

"Oh yeah?"

"Yeah. His surfboard."

Dan laughed. "I'm from Ohio. We don't have an ocean or a wave for a thousand miles."

"He left a note with it." She picked up a scrap of notebook paper on the desk in front of her, and Hanna tried to slap at it. She read, " 'Danny, just in case, I leave to you my most prized possession. Get some sun and get your nose out of the books. The Phaystoss disc, bro, that's aliens. It's solved. I told you.' " Dan burst out laughing. They all did. Their lives took place in such a claustrophobic sliver of space between suffering and laughter. "Whatever that means," said Melody.

He was laughing so hard, crying at the same time, Melody had to call for his attention.

"Dan. Greg said he'd never met anyone as smart and stand-up as you. He really considered you one of the best friends of his life."

That was the night Dan knew he'd absolutely re-up. He'd let Coyle down, but he wouldn't let that happen again, not to anybody he loved. And it came back to him: He could feel his friend's blood on his ACU, his hands, his face, the chaplain washing him with Catholic comfort, and he knew he'd be back. Until they kicked him out or carried him out, he'd be back.

The car seat in the back of Hailey's Camry was coated in Cheerio dust. She started the car but didn't put it in gear. She stared at the steering wheel like it had poetry written on the plastic.

"I told Eric I'd be home late anyway."

"H-O-R-S-E?" Dan suggested.

"And embarrass you for the millionth time? Wanna just drive for a while?"

He picked at his thumbnail and almost said no. "Of course."

Pulling out into the square, she took Main Street past the Cattawa. As they neared the river, the streets were deserted except for a lone figure stalking away from the bridge. He had his hands tucked in the pockets of a hoodie, baggy jeans, and a head exploding with crazed dreadlocks. The kind of figure that made you glad you were cruising by instead of walking past during an abandoned hour of night. But when just enough of the headlights spilled over him, Dan recognized the face and wished he hadn't. He forgot the name, but he was a kid from their high school, a couple of grades older. What he recalled most acutely was that he used to come to school in hand-me-downs and Goodwill clothing onto which someone—probably his mother—had attempted to stitch an A+F logo, Abercrombie and Fitch. Dan remembered this distinctly because once, at lunch, Kaylyn had dared Hailey to go over and compliment him about his "fresh threads." And Hailey had done it. After that, the two of them never let it go. They sniggered about this lonely skateboarder, who never bothered anyone, for a full year. It reminded him of the entire period in high school when she was dating Curtis, when the maintenance of her status seemed to be all that mattered to her. They blew past this kid, now a man, and he vanished into the gloom.

He'd once read an amateur interpretation of the writing on the Phaistos disc, a claim that it was not a geometric theorem, a prayer, or a war cry but a love poem. According to this random person on the Internet, the last line read: *And they will join us in our home these children and dogs. And I will do anything, have no fear, face any obstacle for and with you.*

Headlights setting the course, Hailey glanced over at him. "We should go out to the Brew. For nostalgia's sake."

He felt that suggestion in the pit of his stomach. "Sounds like a plan."

They drove with the radio loud, beneath the satellites that delivered the beat, hawked insurance, and carried the cellular signals that ran the world.

The clouds had parted, and the road angled with the river. The trees hung over the Cattawa, lurching across the water like old men with curved spines. During floods, the river could rise halfway to the treetops, and it would run muddy and viscous on its way to Lake Erie. The Brew used to be a stretch of weeds overlooking a dirt cliff face. A handful of teenagers generations before them figured out you could maneuver a car down an old hunting trail and park in the grass, which quickly became dirt or mud as more people discovered the spot. After a drunk couple drove into the river, the county put up a knee-high guardrail and called it the Cattawa Scenic Overlook. Kids never stopped calling it the Brew, likely named for the way the water foams as it comes around a bend (or maybe after all the beer drank there). It was supposed to be the place the country songs were written about, but from what Dan had heard in the last few years it had become a sewer of pills, pipes, and needles. Hailey crept them up to the rail, flipped the lights off, and killed the engine. The slice of moon sparkled off the water and gave the leaves on the tops of the trees an incandescent sheen, like all the thousands of wandering fireflies had been mashed into a paint and spread across each tiny canvas. The outline of the woods, wet and stark against night's blue-black pool. Stars and moon all swimming out there in the infinite. It made him think that if he could stretch his vision far enough, he could see to the end of it all, where the universe simply trickled back to God's eye.

They listened to the throaty voice of the river below. The ticking of the cooling engine.

Finally, Hailey said, "I'm glad you're here."

"Me too." He wondered if this was true.

"I had to lure you with Mrs. Bingham."

Her eyes had the shimmer of an ocean at dawn. Time and memory surged. Brilliant and violent.

"Why don't you ever come back?"

He didn't know how to answer this. He stammered about how even coming back for a night—less than a night—he'd run into too many people they'd grown up with.

"It's so hard. Just. To not look back," he tried to explain, feeling numb, feeling dumb. "I'm doing my best to keep moving forward, to keep happy. That's hard when I'm here."

Hailey's brow crumpled into agony, an expression he remembered from when her mother was diagnosed. Or when he told her he might re-up.

"You left," she said softly. "And you took my heart with you, you fucker."

He stared at his hands, laced together over bare, bony knees.

"You're never *ever* far from my thoughts," she went on. "And I hate that."

A contour of starlight put her profile in repose. He wasn't sure how old you have to be before you know what you feel is not infatuation, that you are not merely dreaming up an idyllic thing; you understand the world differently because of this other consciousness bound to yours. He'd mourned her every moment he'd known her.

"You know," Dan said, "I think we live these costume pageants with very little control and then fool ourselves into believing we have agency. That's how I feel about us. Mostly, it was out of our control."

"Danny." His name seethed through her teeth. "Maybe you need help. From what your mom says . . . Maybe you're not okay."

There was a simple wood cross hanging from the rearview mirror. It dangled from a piece of fraying twine. He reached out and rubbed the smooth grain between his fingers.

"I'm not PTSDed, if that's what you're asking. I have nightmares sometimes." How solid the cross felt. How he ached for its conclusions. "But I'm over checking the roadside for bombs. I can sit through a fireworks display. Mostly . . ." He hesitated then tried on a smile. "Mostly my heart's just broken. But that happens to the best of us."

"Danny." She shifted, took his face in her hands. Her fingers ran over the scar by his eye, and she looked into his prosthetic like it could possibly see her. A barb uncoiled in his throat, and he felt tears push at the edges of his eye. Something so deep and so awful tried to rise up then. He felt it battering from below, screaming, and he let go of the cross. It bounced and twirled on the twine. He had to get out. Like the Humvee on its side, fire clawing in the box, he had to get out.

Hailey called after him as he threw open the passenger door and practically fell out of his seat, scraping his hand against the gravel as he caught himself. She called again.

He walked to the rail at the edge of the overlook. He heard the driver's side open. He gazed into the water, wondered about the fall.

"Danny!" Hailey screamed. "Stop."

He stood hovering at the edge, looking at the cluster of dark rocks over the drop. The Cattawa murmured by in its river's whisper. Hailey snatched his wrist and pulled him to her. "Stop it. I'm sorry." She wrapped herself around him, tight enough that he could feel her heart thundering against her breastbone.

Then the cool of her fingertips grazed his cheek. She pushed him back on the hood and in doing so broke some dense spell. She slipped her tongue into his mouth, climbed onto him, fumbled at the belt until his shorts dropped to his ankles, clattering in the dirt, and the summer night wasn't nearly as warm. There was the contrast between the skin and the core. She gripped his shoulders, his hair, the muscles of his chest, her hands with memory. He bit the salt of her nipples. She was sweet, slick, sorrowful, and he thought of how time folded in on itself when that bomb erupted beneath him or that bullet connected with his armor. How everlasting those moments could feel. As if he'd lived them billions of years before when the oceans first rolled and lightning first raged and the course of all life was plotted in the murk. Of course, you only ever get a moment, and what lingers after is nothing but threnody, a chilly song for the dead.

When he came, it all returned: the hard give of the Toyota's hood at his back, the stickiness of their sweat, the bugs flying in and out of his ears and nostrils, mistaking these warm, wet places for home.

She lay back on the hood for a moment, touched herself. She gathered his semen onto two fingers and then tasted it the way she had when they were young.

They dressed in silence. Then they were back sitting on the hood, watching the night again. Hailey sat cross-legged. Her jeans had a smear of dirt on the knee from when she'd kicked them to the ground. She held his palm in both of hers, and her thumb absently caressed the back of his hand.

"I'm sorry," he said.

She looked at him like he was stupid. "Why? I'm not."

"Your family."

"Is still my family. This doesn't change that." She traced a finger along his palm. "If you had any idea how much I've missed you . . . You have to understand that, right? I just don't see how you couldn't."

"You gotta walk on with it." He thought of how to say this. "Every mistake. There's no doubt in my mind that if you knew. If you knew what I've seen and done . . ." She closed her eyes. A tear crawled to the corner of her nose, where it hung. "You wouldn't be here right now. And you wouldn't have just done that with me."

"*Stop*. Just. Please stop." She gripped his hand in both of hers, wedding band and engagement ring grinding into his knuckle. "You don't think we all carry something that makes us less than we were? That we'd do anything to take back?"

"No. I don't." He pulled his hand away, hugged his own knees in, and thought of those he'd killed, the ones who'd deserved it and the ones who hadn't.

He thought of the sudden pressure in his eardrums when the bomb went off beneath the wheels. The screaming pain in his skull and how the world abruptly went half-dark. Three tours. He gave his youth to the dust of those theaters. An eye, some skin, blood, and hair, and his ability to walk more than a few miles without a crippling pain in his knees and an ache in his spine that made him feel seventy years old. On tour #3, the day before the incident on Highway 1, he was reading about Ohio's place in the Civil War and came across a quote about a Union general: *At the sight of these dead men whom other men had killed, something went out of him, the habit of a lifetime, that never came back again: the sense of the sacredness of life and the impossibility of destroying it.*

"You hold the goddamned war over my head just like you did when you came home the first time," said Hailey. "You hold it over my head like I'm a child. Like I don't know what it's like to have ruined something. You're not the only one."

"Please." He felt the heat rise to his cheeks and forehead; an angry sweat bloomed from the pores. For some reason wanting to scream at her about Curtis Moretti, some dead pillhead who would never stop making him feel like a fourteen-year-old bed wetter. How the hell could all this still be so fresh and painful? They were children when any of it last mattered.

"Fuck you, Danny. I'll tell you something." She looked away from him. Back toward the Cattawa. A lock of dirty blond had escaped and now hung over the high expanse of her forehead. "What I said about not seeing Kaylyn. That's not true. I've seen her plenty."

He waited. She bit into a fingernail, and then began peeling it off. She'd always had the nails of a boy, chewed and ragged. When he watched her come out of the game in the brief minutes her coach could afford, her backup would turn the ball over and clank shots while she took apart the cuticle of every finger.

"She's been a mess lately. Like more of a mess than ever before. I took her to a rehab clinic in Columbus a while back, but who knows if that'll take. It's not all I've done for her."

"Okay. So she didn't keep the baby?" he guessed. Thinking Hailey's big secret was that she'd driven Kaylyn to an abortion clinic. Hailey looked at him like he was an imbecile.

"Everyone keeps it here. How do you think half our friends got to the world?" She pulled the nail all the way off and looked for another one. He could still feel her body on him, all the flab she'd added, from stress, pregnancy, age. It didn't make her any less attractive, but more human, more herself. "Kay just keeps getting into trouble, just stupid, terrible trouble. So she cut deals with Amos Flood and Kirk Strothers and all those redneck nuts they hang out with."

"Who?"

"You know, Fallen Farms. We called them the Flood brothers in high school."

"Right, okay." He stammered, tried again. "What does that have to do with anything?"

She looked at him, annoyed. *I'm getting there.* "She was buying them guns and other things their parole officers wouldn't be happy about. I told her she was going to end up in prison over it, but they paid her. She's never thought five minutes ahead." She used a forearm to swipe at her cheeks, hot and bright with sex and pain. "She's just always been my friend, and I've always done things for her or because of her. She's always had this power over me, and I know you don't want to hear this, but that's part of the reason I ended up going out with Curtis and doing everything I did with him . . ."

Dan shook his head. "You're right, I don't want to hear this."

"But you should." She swallowed. "I wasn't ready. I wasn't ready to . . . to do what I did when I did. And so Kaylyn did her part. At this party, she got me drunker than I'd ever been in my life and took me to the bathroom with him . . . I barely even remember it."

He had the urge to clamp a hand over her mouth or dig up Curtis Moretti's bones and use a hammer to smash them to dust.

"And I didn't blame her," Hailey went on. "Never occurred to me to blame her. I always did what she wanted. You think you had it bad? Girls, man—teenage girls can be so . . . *fucked up*. It's like they suddenly understand that boys think they're hot, and they just go insane with power. Kay used to call herself my older sister, and I believed her even though she was just a user. A manipulator. She was this agent of chaos I could never get away from. And still can't."

"Why?" A bitter tear crept into his eye, and he blinked it away. "Why would you tell me this now? And you want to blame Kaylyn for—"

He shut his mouth. With the anger, with the frustration, came a dark adrenaline.

"It was more than that. Kaylyn—I felt responsible for her."

"That's absurd."

"Before her parents lost their house and moved off Rainrock, there was . . . She got attacked. When she was eight and I was seven, she got attacked by her cousin. Her sixteen-year-old cousin."

"Attacked how?"

"How do you think."

He chewed on the inside of his cheek, scraped away the flesh with little pinches of his incisors. Through the trees in the distant hills, homes glittered, practically as tiny and gone as the stars. He could hear the mournful low of a far-away cow. He dreamt of walking through the woods to that farm and then he could just keep walking. Over the fields and barbed wire fencing, over the county highways and the old bridges and creeks. Just keep walking until he didn't remember or care about anything.

"I didn't understand what happened exactly, but I was the first person who went to see her after. My parents told me something really bad had happened to her, and it would cheer her up if I would be with her. And I remember so vividly . . ." She paused, eyes shimmering again. "I remember she asked for my Barbie's dress. This sequined dress for my Barbie that she'd always really liked. She asked me for it while we were playing, and I gave it to her. And she kept it. And it didn't seem like anything bad had happened to her at all. I remember thinking, she seems fine. She seems fine, and maybe she made the whole story up to get my Barbie's dress. But obviously I got older, and I understood it better and . . . It made me love her. And it made me afraid of her." She laughed happily. "And then one day, she really did go too far. And she got a person hurt."

She wiped her nose where the tears had collected. Dan waited, but she seemed incapable of saying more. For no reason, he suddenly felt like turning his head and checking the woods around them. His eyes had adjusted to the dark, yet the shadows seemed to have expanded.

"There were rumors about this videotape of Tina. Tina Ross. You remember that?"

He shook his head. He'd heard rumors of Tina—most of the school had. But never anything about a videotape.

"Doesn't matter. Only point is that Todd Beaufort really didn't want people to get ahold of this tape. And Kaylyn, she came strolling back into town after she dropped out of college and decides—I don't know what she decides. She decides life's not interesting enough, I guess. So she told Todd that she knows someone who's got a copy of this tape. She told him they were going to use it to ruin him."

"I don't get it. What does she care about Todd?"

"Her and Todd." She laughed again, the sound so high and bright. "They're old, old fuck buddies. She was his first in middle school."

Dan thought of the rumor he and the guys had argued over in the bar that night. He recalled the hoary, threadbare quality of Todd Beaufort's face, its coat of fleshy skin.

"Was it going on while she was with Rick?"

"I don't know. Maybe. All I do know is that Todd did something that she didn't expect. Or she claims she didn't expect it. I'm not sure what she wanted to happen or thought would happen. One night she comes to me and tells me . . ." Hailey was quiet for a beat. She sucked back her tears, and what she said next was as hard as winter stone. "She claimed she found out who had a copy of this tape, and she told Todd, and Todd stabbed some poor kid to death over it. And I believe her. She was there, and she said she tried to stop him, but she couldn't. And then she helped him. She helped him get away with it."

The moment was like a tumor, surgically cut out of time. If, while one day helping Rudy to the bathroom, he hopped up and started tap dancing, Dan couldn't have been more shocked. If Wiman or Wunderlich or Coyle showed up at his door in their dress blues with their eyes rotted out and grimly told him, *Psych. Gotcha good, Eaton*, his skin couldn't have crawled colder.

"Hailey." He took a breath of the fecund soil-sweet air. "Are you joking with me right now?"

She hocked snot back into her throat. Her head vibrated from side to side in a trembling affirmation that no, she was not joking.

"I never told anyone. I know I should have, but I couldn't. I've never said anything. By the time she told me . . ."

"Who?" he whispered. The river, in motion, the color and texture of hardened lava.

"Doesn't matter," she said. "Just . . . Someone who got a copy somehow. Kaylyn swore she didn't know what he would do."

He felt like he'd stumbled into a blizzard. And when he found the words again, it was like the wind had blown them back in his face.

"You need to tell this to someone. You need to tell this to . . . I don't know, Rick's dad."

"No, I don't." Her breath quivered. "And not just because it might make me an accessory after the fact or something like that. But it's settled now, Danny. No one knows any better. And if it came out . . . Everyone's better off if this—if this stays buried."

"Tell yourself that," he said. "But I can't."

"Yeah, you can."

"How do you know?"

She smiled like she'd smiled at him not long after he heard she'd hooked up with Curt Moretti. Like he was some stupid little kid who would never know better. She put a hand on his cheek.

"Because you still love me."

The wind picked up. Rumors, it turned out, were purposefully indistinct, shifting, shimmering. Maybe they were more about erasure than they were about revelation. Muddying a great sin so that no one knew what to believe.

"See? You lovely, beautiful, crazy boy, you see, right? It's not just you who's had to live with shame and pain and disappointment and the certainty—and I mean the fucking absolute certainty—that you're going to wake up one day in Hell."

She lowered her head to his chest, and more by instinct than by cognition, his arm wrapped around her shoulder. How could Eric and Emma go their whole lives without sensing this in her? For that matter, how had he? Yet carrying a secret like this, Dan understood, was like having something alien siphoned into the blood. One learns to live with it in the pulse. Compared to what he'd done, whatever meager bit of violence she'd accomplished felt less than meaningless. She knew he wouldn't tell because he knew what it was to carry a piece of fixed doom. She knew he'd walk until the earth burnt away for the last moment of her escaping smile. The history had already been written. What is history but an adjudication of memory. And what is memory but a faithless rendering of all sex, death, justice, murder, prayer, greed, hope, mercy, and love. Memory was as molten as the soul.

Better to let it all lie; let it continue Never Was-ing. Sitting there in the night with his arm around her, smelling the coconut in her shampoo, he retreated to thinking of the angel looking backward upon the ruins. Rudy had once said that killing people was funny. Not because murdering another human was funny, he assured Dan. No, killing was an act of bottomless cruelty. "What's hilarious is how people are killed over such dick-trifling matters," he cracked. "And then we go and call that civilization."

After Dan woke up in the hospital at Bagram with his right eye gone, the first thing he managed to read was an essay. Someone had brought his personal items, including his Kindle. He couldn't sleep, he couldn't eat, and he didn't want to talk to anyone because every time his doctor came by, the man insisted on repeating, like an incantation, that none of what happened was Dan's fault. Dan wanted to say to him, *Imagine*. Imagine it had been your call to take Highway 1, the Kabul–Kandahar Highway, the ISAF money hole in the south of the country, which you knew had been nothing but a graveyard for American soldiers. So you thunder over brown countryside, past the village of Najuy, and you don't even recall the sound of the EFP going off. One second you're casting about for the enemy, checking the second Humvee in your rearview, the next your vision is dark, your ears are bleeding, and the world has gone airborne. The explosion turns the vehicle in incomprehensible spatial directions, and it feels like you're in a Black Hawk falling out of the sky. You come to trapped inside this burning box, and you hear screaming all around. You feel absolutely no pain—only heat, and that sensation of time slowing, each second stretched to a dazed minute. Your door is lying against the asphalt of the highway. The screaming's coming from behind you, and you understand that your vehicle is on fire. You can see a bit of sky the color of cool milk. You struggle out of your harness but people are in the way. Everyone's in the way and it's getting hotter and you can feel the fire blistering all around you and the smoke is thick as drapes. You've got your eye on that slice of sky, and all the panic you've felt since you started this journey, practically all the panic you've felt your whole life, it descends upon you. There's a body in your way. You feel your M4, and then maybe accidentally, maybe not, you pull the trigger, and warm gore splashes over your face, but now there's a path. Nobody in the way. You scramble toward the milky light. The screaming is no longer your problem. So you push aside remnants of a shredded man, step on a screaming other who can't get out of his harness, and crawl out through the gunner's hatch into the sun and the sweetest air you've ever breathed. You're not on fire, but you're sizzling, smelling burning ACU cloth and blood. The agony in your skull begins to dawn on you. One eye is nothing but a gray-red fog, yet with the other you see bits of flesh and bone clinging to you, and in that second-by-second way you understand these are parts of what once was Daniel Imana. The men from the tail vehicle fan out, scanning the ground for another bomb, but what you focus on—in all this smoke and fire and chaos and crying—is children from a nearby village gathered, watching, twisting sandals in the dust. They're standing there laughing at you and your friends burning alive in the box. Your unit, your guys are all about to be dead and you can hear shrieking and, you think, the snap of bullets, and these little bastard orphans of Najuy are laughing about it. Even in your haste to escape, you held on to your M4. And you think you see a triggerman through the thin trees, about forty meters off the road, clutching something rectangular in his hand, maybe a phone, certainly grinning in the pale dust. The grin of the man, years ago, in the VBIED that killed Coyle. You raise your weapon at the threat, at the laughing, and sort them all out with about twenty rounds, which hack bits of bone and hair skyward. You make sure this group of kids falls in your line of fire, and they go down so easily, so serenely, and now there are all these little bodies, maybe five, maybe more, and a lot of very clean-looking blood. Very red, very wet. Now you realize maybe you were premature. The vehicle's on fire, but it's not, like, ablaze. Sep Marshall managed to get Brody's body off him and push his way out despite a gristly wound in his abdomen. Jody Picarn approaches from the tail vehicle, screaming at you. He's trying to get Kerlix to your face, your eye, but you brush him off. Steve Otterman wields a fire extinguisher. And there's Rudy, on fire a little, shot in the head of course, but Otterman manages to put him out, and the others, they manage to get inside, to slice through his harness with a combat knife, get under his shoulders, and haul him out while you, the numb idiot that you are, stand watching. Sep Marshall, wound and all, drags him away from the wreck. Everyone is looking at the kids and the dead guy with the phone—who turns out to just be a teenager. You call in the CAT Alphas. Then you get tired and lie down and wait for the medevac. A part of you is sickly impressed with how the enemy orchestrated all this. They got you good this time. You figure your life is over, but the investigation will clear you easily. You saw a threat in the cell phone boy and removed it from your section. The bullet Rudy took to the head—a 5.56mm piece of U.S. hardware—it turns out that came from extra ammo carelessly left in the rear cooking off in the heat. And lying there in the dust, head buzzing from the burning fuel, the wind smoldering with black smoke and ash trailing to a seared pink twilight sky, you understand that something's gone out of you, the habit of your lifetime. Any notion of the sacredness of life or the impossibility of destroying it. You go over to what's left of your friend, sit down, bleed from your face, and wait for some rescue.

Days later, Dan Eaton lay in the hospital, head wrapped tight, wondering about swallowing a bullet and how soon he'd be allowed near a weapon. So he tried to read with the one eye the doctors were letting him keep, and for whatever reason, instead of a book he opened this essay he'd downloaded to his Kindle months earlier. The author wrote it in France in 1940, just as the Vichy government was handing over Jews to the Gestapo. He finished writing just before he escaped the collaborationist government, only to commit suicide in Spain a month later. With his newly acquired monocular vision, Dan struggled, word by word, through the unsettling conclusion that one cannot look at the treasures of his society without feeling horror. Because when we look at history we only empathize with the victor, an empathy that benefits the current ruler. This ruler comes from a long line of those who've stepped over the stricken body of the one who came before, each an heir to a long line of violence and power. So the spoils of resources and culture get carried along in a direct procession, and it becomes difficult to contemplate any document of civilization as anything but a document of barbarism. The inevitability of progress being such a hopeless fantasy. Progress, the author warned, is ephemeral. The notion of progress lies in each successive generation's "weak Messianic power." How each one considers itself the conclusion of history: all who came before were fated to live and die so that it might triumph. Dan smiled through bandages and tears because he remembered a *Calvin and Hobbes* strip about that very idea. The author had a different vision: he owned a painting by an artist named Paul Klee called *Angelus Novus*, in which an angel seems to hurtle backward, wings spread, eyes fixed, mouth agape, and his description of the Klee painting was something Dan had never been able to get out of his head, his memorization hopelessly accidental: "This is how one pictures the angel of history," the author wrote. "His face is turned toward the past. Where we perceive a chain of events, he sees one single catastrophe which keeps piling wreckage upon wreckage and hurls it in front of his feet. The angel would like to stay, awaken the dead, and make whole what has been smashed. But a storm is blowing from Paradise; it has got caught in his wings with such violence that the angel can no longer close them. The storm irresistibly propels him into the future to which his back is turned, while the pile of debris before him grows skyward. This storm is what we call progress."

Hailey Kowalczyk took them the long way home. To get from the Brew back to Rainrock Road, you can either take Stillwater or 229. It was a night to drive with the windows down, and they were still a mile away when they began seeing red and blue hues, like extraterrestrial spacecraft reflecting off the night sky. They said nothing as they drew closer, and the lights pulsed with greater and greater urgency. Cresting a hill, Hailey slowed the car. A lunch-box ambulance and three patrol vehicles, sturdy SUVs with *New Canaan*

Police Department spelled out in yellow italics along the sides, blocked the road. A cop was taking yellow police tape from the fence on one side of the road to a stake on the other.

"Wreck?" said Hailey.

It wasn't, though. They pulled to within twenty feet, headlights illuminating the scene. There were two cars outside a gate: an old, battered Jeep and a small blue sedan with both its driver-side door and trunk open. Spray-painted on the gate were the words THE LORD HAS HIV. Beyond that there was a long field followed by miles of woods, and he could see more blue and red strobing from the depths of those woods, along with what looked like dozens of flashlights crawling over the black skin of the field.

A uniformed officer approached the driver's side. Hailey, who'd not been wearing her seat belt, quickly pulled it across her lap and clicked it home. Bald and heavy, he leaned into the window. His name tag said OSTROWSKI, and Dan remembered him from long ago.

"You'll have to go back," he said.

"What happened?" Hailey asked, seemingly unconcerned about being seen this late at night with a man who was not her husband by someone who surely knew who she was.

"Can't help you. Gotta turn around."

The lights pulsed eerily, flickering on and off in the pitch-black hills, jerking and colliding in near silence, except the rattling of nearby sycamore leaves.

"Is that Marty Brinklan?" Hailey asked. Rick's father wore an improvised outfit of sweatpants and a pink polo shirt. He still had his mustache, though the hair there and on his scalp had lost any last hint of gray and was now white as a cumulus cloud.

"Turn around, ma'am," said Officer Ostrowski. There were huge beads of sweat on his upper lip and tracing paths down his pink scalp. Even from the passenger seat, Dan could smell him. He stank of something deeper than body odor. Dan would have called it fear. "Go back the other way. Take 229."

Ignoring him, Hailey called out to Marty Brinklan. He was talking to two other officers, and at the sound of his name, he shielded his eyes and looked their way.

"Hey! I said turn around," Ostrowski demanded. "I won't warn you again." But Marty was already there. He touched Ostrowski on the shoulder and motioned for him to step back. Ostrowski did so, reluctantly.

"What's going on?" Hailey asked again.

Marty looked into the car, first at Dan, then at her. He still had the same cold, tranquilized expression Dan remembered. A stony face always held in leathery reserve.

"Hey, Danny," he said.

"Hello, sir."

He thought he saw the look in Mr. Brinklan's eyes. The one Dan had seen in Rudy's mother and in Greg Coyle's wife, Melody, when he met her briefly at the memorial in California. Maybe it was all in his head, but he saw it nevertheless: a look of selfish, guilty anguish. *Why couldn't it just have been you? Why him instead of you, you miserable stranger?*

"Wherever you're headed, you need to find another route."

"Can you at least tell us what's going on?" Hailey demanded.

Marty Brinklan looked back at the scene—the vehicles and a dark puddle on the ground—running his fingers over his mustache, deciding.

"I can't have you driving through." He took a long look back at the field, like he was trying to articulate something awful. "We're just hoping we find this individual alive."

Hailey began to say something else, but Dan finally grew impatient with her. "Hailey," he said. "We'll just go back and take 229. Come on."

"Do that," said Marty. He looked at the boy who'd come home from the war. "Good seeing you, Dan."

"You as well, sir."

He walked away, and Dan thought of standing over his son's grave that night. As Hailey reversed and began to make a U-turn, he gazed back across the field. Two flashlights clashed like swords and then struck off in different directions. Particles of dust and wind filled their beams as they searched restlessly over this strange insomniac night.

In his driveway, beneath the basketball hoop where they'd first played H-O-R-S-E in seventh grade, kicked at the autumn leaves, and danced around their blossoming crush, Hailey kissed him. He ran his fingers around the skin of her eyes and wondered if she would truly be able to live within her own exile. The way he did. Then again, maybe this was right. Maybe her sins would fit like a key in the lock's tumblers of his own. In the distance he heard murmurs of thunder. The horizon crackled with bursts of golden lightning behind clouds the size of mountains. Fat droplets of rain began exploding across the windshield, one at a time, their compatriots surely not far behind.

Involuntarily, his lip curled in a smile. "Calvin hammering nails into the coffee table," he said. "I loved how much you loved that one."

"Is that some kinda trick question or something?"

He said good-bye to Hailey in his driveway, and it was the last time he ever saw her. In the moment she pulled away, he felt what lay deep behind his eye, like a television left on day and night. He watched through the vision of others: He saw himself grow into a man as if he was his mother. Through Hailey's eyes, he saw his ancient, hopeless longing. He looked through Rudy and bore witness to the snowflakes of Korengal and later the way his skin bubbled on the bone. He looked into the desert sky through dirt and blood and tears and bile as Greg Coyle, and he saw his daughter in the falling murk. He stared into the shredding wind of paradise, hurtling forward even as he could only look back in this one fixed direction, pissing tears for all the vanishing debris.

Names and faces went by like vapor. Ashes and bodies Dan Eaton would hold close until his last moment.

Tina Ross and the Cool at the Edge of the Woods

After she snapped her fingers next to Cole's ear and put her palm under his nose to make sure he was still breathing and she hadn't overdone it with the G, Tina left him curled on the couch and drove back to her hometown. She spent most of the trip thinking about love.

The highway from Van Wert to New Canaan was a pristine stretch of Ohio asphalt, wide and unpocked and always empty. A road she knew well. It was so familiar to her that the sights along the way—a billboard reminding in stark, towering black and white that JESUS IS REAL, a McDonald's sign with the light in half the arch burnt out and never replaced—served as markers of distance. She'd made many trips on this highway, spent so much of her adult life crossing back and forth between these two places she knew. A few years back, Van Wert had gotten some of those wind turbines, and when she hit the road they were blinking in unison, blades slicing quietly in the night. Gary, her boss, lived near one of the farms where the turbines had gone up, and he swore the steady, almost-not-there hum of the blades gave him headaches and nosebleeds, but she liked them anyway. They were like something out of a movie about aliens or spaceships, each with one glowing red dot hundreds of feet in the sky, burning on and off in the dark.

The stereo in Cole's Chevy Cobalt had been broken forever, so she drove in silence, but that was okay. Normally she hated being alone, but now she had to be. She had to think about all of this very carefully. What she would say.

Tina once had a theory about love, which was that you can only have—really, truly—one love of your life. You could be in love with more than one person. You could let multiple men have sex with you. You could even come to care about a certain person more than that one love, as she had with Cole. But in the end, you only had the one Love of Your Life. For most people, that love happened early.

The summer before her freshman year at New Canaan High School, she and her friends got wind that the football team had made a list of the top twenty hottest freshman girls. According to her friend Stacey Moore, Tina had been number one (Stacey had been eleven). Hearing this had filled Tina with that adolescent heat that quickens the pulse. The boys looking impossibly giant and handsome. Unlike those in her class, they looked like men with real muscles, thick bristles of cheek-scraping facial hair, and halos of worldly confidence. New Canaan was a small town, so you kind of knew who was behind the list.

That summer, she and Stacey rode their bikes out to the football field and watched from behind the fence while the team endured two-a-days. She knew who he was—everyone did—but that was the first time she really took him in. Number 56. She wondered if he remembered her from the handful of times their paths had crossed at Stacey's house. They'd mostly hid in Stacey's room, too embarrassed by youth to be anywhere near Matt Moore or any of the older guys. Now at the field, on the brink of beginning high school, she watched him. Those football pants made some of the heftier boys look comical, the flab of their butts slumping over thick thighs in little pooches. But 56 had the legs and thighs and butt of a statue. She watched the way he carried himself on the field. She knew nothing about football, but he looked like the leader, calling out to everyone around him, pointing, making signs with his hand, cocking his helmeted head and crying out like some ancient warrior leading men to battle. She didn't take her eyes off him until Coach

Bonheim himself came over to tell them to get lost, his Appalachian drawl thick as motor oil. "My boys can't concentrate with a gaggle of girls giggling at 'em."

The rest of the summer she thought about almost nothing else. In church, during dinner, hanging out with her friends, Number 56 was never far from the front and center of her mind, ready to be rolled around and absently obsessed over like a hard candy on the tongue. And her place as number one on the list? He had to have voted for her. She could only speculate that the other guys followed his lead in this the way they did on the field.

It was a two-and-a-half-hour drive to New Canaan, and through the dark summer night, the headlights of the Cobalt showed the way. She kept her eyes peeled for deer. She'd hit a deer a year ago, and the Cobalt still bore the crumpled scar on the fender. She'd smashed the brake when she saw the glossy reflection of its eyes on the roadside, but instead of hightailing into the woods, the terrified doe leapt back into the road, and she clipped it. Coming home from a long shift at work—and after Gary had screamed at her for knocking over a row of pickles, the jars shattering into a mess of glass and reeking brine—she'd been picking at the spot in her hair, digging out the roots with the blade of her fingernail, when the doe bolted. She got out of the car to assess the damage, saw the smear of blood on the headlight, the damage she'd done to Cole's car, and then the deer scampering into the woods with its hindquarters pulped and broken in some grotesque way she only glimpsed briefly. She sat on the cold ground and wept for a while.

She absolutely could not afford to hit a deer tonight.

Glancing in the rearview mirror to check on a car overtaking her, she met herself now, almost ten years removed from high school. There weren't many lists she'd top these days. She tried going to the gym on her day off, but it cost ten dollars, and she'd get on an elliptical for a little while, get discouraged, leave, and feel guilty for a week. It didn't help that Cole kept sweets around the apartment (he had frequent cravings for Cool Ranch Doritos and Little Debbie Swiss Rolls), yet she was the one who gained the weight. He never added a pound to his stork frame no matter what he ate. They didn't have a scale, but the last time she'd weighed herself at the gym, she'd been a dismaying 154 pounds. She'd never weighed that much before.

Cole had bought her a bike for her birthday the month before. It had sleek red and yellow colors and intimidating gear knobs.

"So you can ride to work in the summer." Cole was great at that: understanding whatever was making her anxious or sad and finding a way to encourage her. She had yet to actually take it out, but she promised herself when she got back home she'd start.

Cole was an example of how you could grow love like a weak flower. If you gave it enough care and attention, you could create happiness from the most sickly of bulbs. They met not long after she started at Walmart. After her dad lost his job when Dave Kruger's medical supply store went out of business, her parents moved out to Van Wert. She went with them. That was right after graduation, when she really needed a change of scenery anyway, what with her eating troubles and the pricks she had given herself. Her dad's cousin Bishop worked at F & S Floor Covering and helped get him a job as a floor salesman, showing off carpet, tile, stone, laminate, hardwood, and the rest. Her mom got on part time with the YWCA janitorial staff, and Tina, without much of an idea of what she should do, had walked into the Walmart and asked for an application.

She'd been working for a month as an associate and only noticed Cole because he seemed to always need something from her register. He'd come through wearing the uniform of the Tire &

Lube Express technicians to buy a pack of Little Debbies, a Snickers, a fishing magazine and ask her how her day was going.

"Fine." She tried to keep it to one-word replies.

"We're really backed up. Looks like you guys are too."

"It's always like this."

One thing she learned quickly was that Walmart wasn't a slacker's job. She never had fewer than five people waiting in line when she worked the register, and Gary always assigned some additional stocking when the line finally went down. But complaining about the grueling pace was how she made friends. It felt like they were all in the trenches together. Her best friend at work was Beauty, who usually worked the same shift. They traded trashy true crime books and, on particularly stressful days, shared a cigarette out by the loading bay.

"He likes you, you know," Beauty told her. Beauty was black and lived up to her name. She had rich dark skin and elegant movie-star features. She also had a jealousy-inducing figure, a black girl's round butt that all the guys at work stared at without trying to hide it. Tina once saw Gary throw an elbow into the ribs of a young associate and nod at Beauty's behind as she passed. Beauty never reacted or let on like she was aware of this. She had a boyfriend in Afghanistan—a sturdy, handsome farmer's boy she'd gone to high school with—and they were getting married when he got back.

"Who does?" Tina asked.

"Cole."

"Who's Cole?"

"Cole, in the Tire and Lube Express."

She had to describe him in detail before Tina put it together. The boy who kept coming by her register. Rail-thin with slumping shoulders, no chin, an Adam's apple like a turkey, and several overlapping teeth.

"I'm not into it." She'd been admiring Travis, who worked in the electronics section. He had a wedding ring but also the bulging shoulders of a former athlete.

"Cole's sweet," said Beauty. "Girl like you needs to recognize sweet more."

"Would you recognize sweet if that was the guy who was sweet on you?"

After she went with Travis to the dark side of a strip mall parking lot, and then he never looked at her again, she started to see Cole differently. She could tell from the way her coworkers shut up when she walked by that Travis had told at least a few of the guys, and Cole stopped coming by her register. She ran into him in the break room and expected him to avoid her. Instead, he licked at his weak, embarrassed smile, and said, "I really like that new way you do your makeup on the eyes. Like how the lines come off and make your eyes look a little Chinese."

This was so awkward, so dopey, and so genuine that at first she thought he was making fun of her. When his smile faltered and he forced it to beam again, she understood that he'd heard about Travis. That this comment was his marble-mouthed way of telling her that he was okay with whatever had happened, and he didn't blame her; he just couldn't come by her register anymore in case she had an obsession with a married man. At least this is what she inferred.

She went to the Tire & Lube Express the next day.

"Would you want to come to church with my parents and me this Sunday?" she asked. After stumbling through an explanation of how he worked Sunday but not until the later shift, his neck suddenly bright red and splotchy, he said yes.

So they met at her church (her mom and dad giving Cole their intrigued handshakes; Cole in full tie and jacket, dressed for a wedding instead of the Sunday sermon, his rigorous explanation to her father of what he did as a Tire & Lube Express technician, "That means anything, sir, from tire changes, oil service, battery service, but I'll also stock shelves, or run the cash register. Often-times people will want to buy their groceries at the same register if they're getting an oil service."). The sermon had been about per-sonal responsibility and community responsibility, how Jesus had instructed us to be kind and compassionate to our fellow man. Taking care of one another was the responsibility of the church, that's what it was there for.

Her dad's head bobbed along to this, as did many others'. He was going on about it a lot at the dinner table: "Governments should protect their people, not try to balance everyone's wealth so that it's perfectly equal." Tina remembered this well because all the talk at work then had been about how they'd have to lay people off or cut their hours if this healthcare thing went through.

Cole sat beside her, hands in his lap, staring straight forward. His nervousness radiated off him like heat. She and her parents went for brunch at Bob Evans afterward. Her mom invited Cole, but he had to work. "Thank you for having me," he said. "I had really a good time." He gave Tina a hug, the sweat on his hands dampening her bare arms.

She passed the turnoff for Lima and worried about what time it was. The clock in the car hadn't worked for years, but she knew all the new phones tracked their own locations, so she had to leave it behind. She calmed herself. As long as she got to New Canaan before the bars closed she would be on time to catch him.

She hadn't known how to go about it back then. Just seeing him in the hallways was nerve tingling, flustering, crazy making. His eyes took a beat in her direction, as if he'd been aware of her the entire time and decided at the last moment to turn them to her. She quickly adjusted her gaze down, and it was all she thought about the rest of the day. Her biology, English, and health classes might as well have been taught in the Spanish she didn't pay attention to either. She never would have approached him. That's not how high school worked. Fifty-six was at the top of the hierarchy in a universally recognized way. He was being recruited by Division I colleges. He had a way of speaking—a baritone ripe with earned authority—that made everyone understand he was to be paid attention to. He carried his books in this particular nonchalant way, palmed from above rather than with his hand curled beneath them like everyone else.

At the first dance of her high school life, she waited at the fringes of the floor along with the other freshmen, all but the bravest too uncertain to wander into the forest of upperclassmen that crowded the dark cafeteria, the light swimming and flickering like in an aquarium. Stacey's parents had only just begun allowing her to buy makeup, and Tina helped her out in the bathroom.

"This is the best cheap mascara," she said, stroking Stacey's lashes with jet-black Maybelline Great Lash Waterproof, hoping that her awkward tomboy friend wouldn't hover beside her all night (heck, maybe she'd even get asked to dance, God forbid). Tina followed up with Almay liquid liner. "And this'll keep it in place if you start sweating."

The Jaguars won 29–7, and it seemed as if 56 had done well (at least he'd clobbered the other team's quarterback three times, leaping to his feet and screaming in triumph loud enough that the sound washed all the way to the back of the bleachers where the freshmen found space). The football players came streaming into the cafeteria after the first hour, showered and wearing street clothes. A different boy asked her to dance each slow song, many of them upperclassmen, and she accepted while watching the door. She was dancing with Conner Jarecki, a boy in her grade, when 56 came in wearing khakis and a white wifebeater. His shoulders, chest, and arms were on full display and looked like armor clicked into place beneath his skin. Each time a slow song came on she watched him and waited until he'd made his choice before allowing another boy to take a turn with her. He danced with a few girls she recognized, the popular upperclassmen, including the bubbly, curvy Jess Bealey, who didn't own a top she wasn't spilling out of. Tina grew increasingly frantic as the night wore on. Of course he wouldn't ask her. He didn't know who she was. The franticness turned to fear, the fear to hurt, the hurt to disappointment as one of the chaperones announced the last song. And then, like she had psychically willed it, he pushed through the crowd to her.

Dan Eaton had approached to ask for the last dance (she was wary of Dan, who'd fixated on Hailey Kowalczyk in such a way that most of their class tittered about him behind his back), when a sturdy branch of an arm caught the slight, skinny boy in the chest. "I got this one, bud."

Then 56 had his hands on her hips, and she placed hers around his neck, though she could barely reach because of the height difference. The song was Seal's "Kiss from a Rose."

"You're Tina. Little Moore's pal."

"I am."

She felt the heaviness of her lashes. For the first time in her life, she felt the word *sexy* about herself. Her eyes were at his chest where two dog tags skittered on a chain around his neck. He was never without them. Now she saw that each tag was blank on both sides.

"Aren't these supposed to have your name or something?"

He looked amused, as if it was a silly question. "Why? My fate hasn't been written yet."

He had his hands low, his pinkies creeping down just far enough to rest on the rise of her bottom. He held her very close, and she could feel it against her abdomen, pressed just beneath her belly button. It wasn't hard, but it was undeniably *there*.

When the lights came on signaling the end of the dance, they parted.

"Strow's having some of the guys out to his place for a bonfire. You wanna come?"

She did. So badly she did. Her mom was outside waiting to take her and Stacey home, and there was literally no way on Jesus's good grand earth she'd be allowed to do this.

"I can't. But do you want my number?" This was 2000, before everyone carried cell phones. Her stomach ached for a pen—maybe someone had a locker in the cafeteria.

He waved her away. "I'll see you at school. We'll figure it out."

For the entire weekend, she was sick with worry that he hadn't meant this. She had numerous phone conversations with Stacey until they could get together for a sleepover Saturday night. They pored over the results of the first dance. Hailey Kowalczyk of course had gotten approached endlessly by Dan Eaton, though she wanted to dance with the quarterback, Curtis Moretti. Stacey claimed to have gotten attention from Jonah Hansen, Ron Kruger, and a cute sophomore, Ben Harrington. Tina assured Stacey that she'd grown pretty decent boobs over the summer, and Ben surely noticed. Stacey had also noted that Lisa Han, who Tina didn't much care for on account of her hyper-foul mouth, had danced several times with Bill Ashcraft, whom Tina had once liked. And in all the spinning and tumbling of high school courtship, Tina attempted to segue back to her dance with 56, which seemed to her the much more interesting development. She told Stacey about 56 pressing it against her. Stacey said, "That's like the worst-kept secret in school. My brother says they see each other's dongs in the locker room, and all they do is compare."

Tina barked a laugh. "Boys are messed up."

"We should go back to throwing mud at them." Then Stacey gave her a side-eyed glance. "You should be careful, though. I know him some through Matt. He only wants one thing from you."

She hated Stacey intensely for that comment, the way you can hate only a close friend so acutely. Shortly thereafter, she turned her back and pretended to sleep.

On Monday, 56 found her between classes and asked her out for ice cream at Friendly's. The anxiousness then transferred itself to what to wear, how to do her makeup, how many pimples would appear between now and then. She lied to her parents about who she was meeting and how she would get home, and her mom dropped her off ("Guess Stacey and them all aren't here yet. It's okay, I'll just get a booth."). Then she went around the corner to stand beneath the awning of a dentist's office (William Ashcraft, DDS) and waited until she saw his huge black truck pull in.

They sat across from each other with dueling glasses of ice cream sundae.

"Want my cherry?" he offered. "I don't like 'em."

"How can you not like cherries?" she exclaimed, taking it from his red-stained fingers. "That's the best part. That's why they say 'the cherry on top.' "

He was grinning, admiring her. "I like some cherries, just not these cherries."

"Oh, so you like the ones with pits still in?"

He laughed hard at this, but she didn't understand why. "That's right. The ones with pits."

He took a large bite of his ice cream, his tongue volleying it into liquid.

"My friend didn't think you'd actually ask me out."

"What?" He swallowed a huge gulp of vanilla and fudge. "Why not?"

"She said you could have any girl you wanted." She amended Stacey's comment. "So why a freshman?"

"Your friend sounds jealous."

Yes, Stacey was jealous. That was so obvious to her now, sitting across from him with his letter jacket, black and patched with his football letter on the breast. His hair gelled into tiny, neat spikes over a heavy, severe brow. His smile that curled half of a thick, lovely lip. Who wouldn't be jealous of her?

"This is going to sound stupid," he said. "Promise you won't think I'm a creepy dork."

As if there was any way she could think this.

"Last year I stayed over at Matt Moore's house and the next morning I went with him and his family to church. Which was your church."

"Really? I never saw you there." Oh, but she had. Now that they were older, she cursed Mrs. Moore's new rule forbidding anything resembling a coed sleepover.

"Naw, we were in the back, but I had this view of you the whole time, and man." He rubbed his eyes with the heels of his hands. "I was just like, 'That's the most beautiful girl I ever seen in this town.'"

He was blushing, which made a similar heat rush to her face. She looked down at the melting suds of her ice cream and tried not to smile like a mental patient.

"Alls I knew was I had to be single when you finally got to high school."

He laughed loudly at himself, his face grew a shade pinker, and she finally looked up to admire the jagged horizon of his top row of teeth.

She noticed the gas gauge dwindling. She had enough to make it to New Canaan and could get gas on her way back but . . . so many uncertainties lay on the other side of that. Like if she'd even be coming back. Better to do this menial task now, have the full tank, and be prepared for whatever happened between her and 56. She pulled off the highway into a Pilot station, reached for her debit card (mindful there was only $73 attached until the end of the month), and thought better of it. She had $14 in her wallet, enough for about four gallons. She rummaged in the change drawer and put together another $2.84. She put every last cent into the pump, giving the gas nozzle tense, spurting squeezes to land on $16.84 exactly. She tucked one of Cole's ball caps onto her head, went inside, landed the money on the counter, said, "Got it exact," and breezed back out. Perhaps it had been a bad idea to stop. She now regretted it, but love would keep her going. Love shoved aside second thoughts, regrets, fear. She had to do this. She had to see. No matter what it meant for her parents or poor, wonderful Cole.

It had been difficult to learn to love him. In the weeks after he came to church with her family, they'd meet for lunch in the break room. Their conversation would be stop-and-go as they cast about for suitable topics. It was hard to look at his elongated, alien-shaped skull, the thin brown fuzz above his upper lip with one hairless vertical line, a scar from a cleft palet surgery he'd had as an infant.

"Do you like carrots?" he asked, holding a baggie of slimy baby carrots.

"Not really. They have no taste."

He nodded and pretended to pay enormous attention to snapping a Ziploc bag closed, folding it up, and putting it back in the plastic Walmart bag he always brought his lunch in.

He aroused nothing in her, and she often found her mind wandering to any of the other men she'd been with. (Though it had been almost a decade, one in particular cast his ever-present ghost over her desire.) He asked her out several times, but she made excuses.

"He's awkward," she explained to Beauty. "And it looks like God put the teeth in his mouth drunk."

Beauty's head whipped back in laughter, and then she slipped quickly into a pout.

"Not nice, Teen. He's sweet. He just hasn't had a lot of girl-friends, and the one he had—Sarah Wiloxi?—she wasn't nearly as pretty as you. He's just intimidated."

They were hidden in the bedding aisle, taking their time restocking. The store was as empty as it ever got, and Gary had the day off, which meant everyone was moving at an unafraid half speed.

"He just doesn't do much for me, you know? It ain't like I need him to be Luke Bryan, but he's just—argh, he reminds me of a big, tall bird. And he's got that gross scar on his lip." She shook her head. "I dunno. I was thinking of going out to the bars this weekend. Just seeing what's out there with the fish in the sea situation."

Indeed, that weekend she found herself a sturdy boy in a camo Budweiser hat who might not have been Luke Bryan, but at least when she got around his beer gut there were strong arms and a broad back she could cling to, really wrap herself around. For a few months, she went on to see Darren of the camo hat (he never went without it, she realized, because he was covering a rather oddly clean bald spot on the top of his head). Maybe everything would have turned out differently with her and Cole if her dad hadn't taken a fall on the ice following a winter storm in early 2010.

He was coming out of F & S Flooring late, and someone must have missed a spot with the salt in the parking lot because her dad caught a slick piece and took a fall, shattering his hip. The lot was technically not on F & S property, so no insurance, no workman's comp, and the surgery alone pretty much wiped out her parents' savings. Credit cards took a bite, and their lives became defined by interest payments and medical debt. Then there was the issue of caring for him once he got out of the hospital. Her mom had to cut back her hours at the YWCA to be home—and Tina had to be there whenever her mother wasn't.

Her dad, always fiercely independent, hated this, and it made him a difficult patient. Every four hours or so he'd have to go to the bathroom (though she suspected he held his bladder out of stubbornness sometimes). He also needed to be fed, helped to the shower seat, and his pill regimen enforced. She did physical therapy with him, extending his leg in different directions, yet even these slight movements made him grit his teeth, sweat, and mutter rare cusses. He'd never looked so old to her, shuffling along with his walker, jowels looser, the last of his hair vanishing from the top of his head to reveal dark, pulpy liver spots. One time when both she and her mom had no choice but to be at work he wet the bed, and when Tina found him, he was furious, not at her but for some reason at the doctors, who he was convinced had botched his surgery, which was the reason he still couldn't walk.

"Those incompetents butchered my leg," he raved, slapping his water off his nightstand, scattering plastic mug, lid, and liquid across the floor. He'd calmed down only because this unusual rage had brought her to tears while she stooped to clean up the ice.

Suddenly, without her dad's hours and her mom working half as much, her parents were in serious trouble. Their church rallied to help. They brought food, raised money toward the bills, and put together a volunteer sign-up sheet for people to stay with him so that her mom could go back to work.

But after a couple months that goodwill began to dissipate. People had worries of their own. You could see that plainly enough on Thursdays when the church provided to anyone who came—not just members—a free hot meal. She'd gone a few times with her parents in the years since they moved to Van Wert ("It's just nice to take one meal of the week off the grocery list," her mom liked to tell her dad when he was insistent that they didn't *need* to go), but lately the church rec center had been getting ever more crowded. So crowded that the line sometimes went out the door. She and her mom went each week and brought a plate home for her dad until he could manage to get there using his walker. But one hot meal a week wasn't enough, and Tina took on extra shifts, worked as much overtime as she could (although she was sure Gary was going into the computer and rounding down her hours). They made too much to apply for an EBT card, but her dad would never have allowed his family to take government handouts anyway. Van Wert had a food pantry where she could sometimes help her parents stretch paychecks, but even with extra dry cereal and Oodles of Noodles, they were overwhelmed.

One day she went outside on her break to smoke a cigarette without Beauty as her partner in crime (something she did rarely) and cry (something she did frequently). Cole must have spotted her and followed. He found her trembling with the mitten portion pulled back from her glove so that the digits were free to hold the cigarette.

"Everything all right?" he asked from ten feet away, like he was afraid to approach any closer.

She wiped her face and snorted back snot.

"It's fine. I'm just a bit on the stressed side. My dad and all. Can't wait to get my raise." She laughed without knowing why. In April she was due for another $1.07 an hour. "It'll make a big difference."

"Look, if y'all need help, I'd be glad to help out," he offered. "We got sorta different schedules, you know? I could, like, come over and help out your dad when you and your mom are at work. That way maybe you could pick up more hours?"

She sniffed, looked up at Cole. "Really?"

"Sure, it wouldn't be no problem. I really like your dad." Said as if they'd met more than that one time.

For some reason this made her cry even harder.

"I mean, I don't have to."

"No." She sobbed, then sucked it all back in, wiped her tears with her jacket sleeve. "No, it's just that's really kind of you, Cole. Everyone's been so kind."

And that was how Cole began spending a lot of time at their house, the little two bedroom on Jennings Road. He'd sit and watch sports with her dad, help him to the bathroom, bring him news-papers or magazines, refill his water. One of the worst things about the injury was that her dad clearly needed the company. He hated being dependent on others, but Cole gave him an excuse. He could see it as just guys watching sports. Cole also brought over a lot of food. Casseroles and noodles and homemade burritos and salads and fried chicken and mac and cheese. Tina went from opening up their refrigerator and finding nothing but some butter, jam, and a dwindling loaf of bread to constantly finding Cole's leftovers.

"Cole, you cook all this?" her mom asked him. "Not so bad for a boy. Let alone a bachelor." Her mom had never looked at 56 this way, with genuine surprise and fondness.

"It was just me and my dad after my mom died, so we learned to cook together," he explained.

Tina knew how much it was probably costing Cole to do this, but at least her trips to the food pantry became less frequent.

When she slept with him, it wasn't necessarily as a thank-you. She'd started to think maybe there was something to what Beauty had said. There was something attractive about a person so selfless, so relentlessly decent, who clearly cared about her so much that he made her family the first priority in his life. Her parents went to the church's Thursday night dinner, and she told them she wanted to skip to go see a movie with Cole. Instead, they went to her house, and he saw the ugliness of her stomach for the first time, heard her feeble explanation about a childhood accident while climbing a fence. He wasn't nearly as bad in bed as she would have thought, and after kissing him that night, she stopped noticing the scar on his lip.

*   *   *

After gassing up, she kept on straight to New Canaan. The closer she got, the more she experimented in her head with what she'd say. She wanted so badly for it to be perfect, and now she'd spent weeks, possibly months (but really, years), thinking of what she'd tell him. Still, nothing seemed entirely right. How do you describe love, though? It was a totally ungrippable idea. A slick bar of soap you had to snatch out of the air with one wet hand.

They'd spent so much of the first part of the relationship just trying to figure out logistics. His mom wasn't a problem, as 56 pretty much did what he wanted, when and where he wanted, but *her* parents were strict. Her mom especially did not like the idea of her dating a junior, and Jerry Ross always followed his wife's lead on such things. She wasn't allowed to ride in his truck; she could only see him at school, dances, or other gathering points (Vicky's Diner or Friendly's being the most likely hangouts). Her mother had just two moods: playful and severe. Around 56, she only showed the latter. Tina ended up lying a lot. Stacey mostly covered for her.

The first time he drove her out to a deserted strip of road, he took off most of her clothes in his truck. She stopped him right before it appeared he would take off all of his as well. This put him in such a surly mood that after he dropped her off that night, she lay awake panicking that she'd screwed things up. The next day at school when he casually put his arm around her shoulder, she could have sobbed with relief.

She decided to make the complicated simple: She was in the Fellowship of Christian Athletes and told her parents they were starting a Bible study group in the evenings. That way she and 56 could take off after he got out of practice. She knew she was not the first teenager to think of such a scam, but it did surprise her how well it worked.

By dating him, she shot up the social ladder. She met him at his locker and enjoyed the glares from girls three grades above.

They walked to every class together. He came by her study hall and lingered until Mrs. Northup told him to buzz off. She imagined them as celebrities. If the school paper (*The Jaguar Journal*, a black-and-white glossy distributed in the cafeteria once a month) covered gossip, their picture would have made every issue. (And in fact, it did make one: The *JJ* always had a photo collage of images from around the school culled by the photographers. These usually included sports, assemblies, but also candid shots; November's issue featured a large, nearly half-page image of her and 56 holding hands while walking down the hallway. Taken from behind, it showed their heads turned in profile, her laughing, and he with that wonderful half grin. She bought seven copies of that issue. She put four untouched in a box in her closet and cut the pictures out of the rest. One went above her dresser, another in her locker, one inside her notebook.

At the sixth game of the season, Kaylyn Lynn found her beforehand and said, "You can't stand in the freshmen section when your boyfriend's a star. C'mon."

She regarded the older girl, who wore an orange sports bra over her small breasts and had *Go Jags!* written across the tight muscles of her stomach. She wore her hair in cute pigtails and had fingermarks of paint, one black, one orange, under each green-grass eye. Kaylyn was almost a head taller than her, and maybe because she was a year older and seemed to already intimidate even the senior girls or maybe because she and 56 were such good friends, Tina found herself both flattered and unnerved. They stood in the front row, and Kaylyn pointed at Rick, standing with his back to them, Number 25.

"Look at him," she said. "I've got a thing for butts in football pants. Even the fat kids, you know?"

Tina agreed but felt no more at ease. Fifty-six had a history with Kaylyn. Before they began dating, she'd seen 56 at Kaylyn's locker after school, the halls empty. He'd stood too close to her, and Tina couldn't help but strain to overhear him say, "Summer makes you dirty blond" and Kaylyn reply, "Not dirty enough for my taste."

It wasn't the questionable comment so much as when 56 reached for Kaylyn's hair and rubbed a strand of it with his thumb and forefinger like he was testing the consistency of soil.

"Problem is," she told Kaylyn, clearing her mind of that image. "I don't know a thing about football. Like I barely understand what Todd even does."

Kaylyn laughed. Her teeth were nice except for one Dracula fang that crowded out its neighbor.

"I gotcha here, Tina. So he's the middle linebacker, which is sort of the leader of the defense. He's like a jack-of-all-trades, so he roams around and can call a blitz and go after the quarterback, whatever he thinks is best. Your boyfriend," she explained, "is a really freaking good middle linebacker. He already has the school record for sacks and tackles, which is why he's getting recruited and part of the reason the team's five and oh."

Tina nodded, though much of the explanation flew over her head. Yet this became her identity. She was 56's girl, and thereby staked her claim to the first two rows of the bleachers next to juniors and seniors. She felt mature there, adult, knowledgeable about the world in some new unquantifiable way.

She loved how everyone referred to the guys by their jersey numbers and quickly adopted the practice. She made a shirt with his number and last name across the back and threw dagger eyes at Jess Bealey, the cheerleader responsible for making his locker signs and baking him cookies and brownies before games. (They were just friends, 56 would say, and she'd worry about all the female friends he seemed to have.) It was her introduction to this exclusive club, this new world. His best friends, Ryan Ostrowski, Curtis Moretti, Matt Moore, and a few others, formed a kind of athletic elite. They got away with drinking, toilet papering houses, egging cars, always something. At the pep rally they introduced one another on stage, each to a rap song, each with a dance, jerseys tucked haphazardly into baggy jeans. She felt like an intricate part of the spectacle unfolding in the bonfire's glow.

Once she understood more about what he did on the team, she found him even more appealing. She'd watch him on the sidelines. When the weather turned cold, steam would rise from his hot, sweaty head. In the game, he'd look to the one coach on the sidelines (the defensive coordinator, this was called), take a signal or wave it off, expressionless beneath the helmet, yet still expressive in the tics of his head and hands. Then the play would commence and it was like watching jujitsu, the way he tried to snatch apart the opposing player's hands, feint, or slip his grip in some manner. She began to see that he was quicker and stronger than almost everyone he played against. Often he'd get right past the other team's player, and then it was like watching a wolf in an open field bearing down on a rabbit. In the sixth game of the season, against Marysville (at that point the twenty-fourth ranked team in the state!), he had one truly amazing moment. The center hiked the ball, and instead of clashing into the other team's player, 56 duped his matchup by sliding back, which caused the Marysville player to go tumbling forward. Fifty-six leapt over him, smashed aside another defender, and then there was nothing between him and the Marysville quarterback but grass. The QB tried to retreat (drop back, was the term), tried to throw, but 56 was so fast. He hit him with a spectacular plastic-crunch of pads, lifted him off the ground, and hurtled both of them through space. The whole stadium heard the hit, and a collective gasp and groan went up from both sides of the bleachers. The ball came out, and Stacey's brother Matt (No. 44) scooped it up and ran it back for a touchdown. Fifty-six jumped up screaming, muscles flexed, beating the air with his fists as his teammates slapped his butt and helmet. The QB left the game with a concussion and New Canaan won 28–14. From the bleachers, Tina screamed and jumped and smacked her hands pink while she thought about how she was falling in love.

When driving into New Canaan from the west there's no sign to greet you the way there is from the north. There's only the farmland giving way to clusters of homes until you reach the first stoplight on SR 229. You followed that into town, past a massive grain silo, the empty steel factory now three decades abandoned, the old middle school shuttered since '96 and entombed behind barbed wire fencing to keep inquisitive kids from running through the ruins. The Little Caesars and Donatos Pizza sitting side by side, Le Nails, House of Hair, A-Plus Insurance, Wendy Bakerfield Attorney at Law.

She'd brought Cole here to show him her hometown shortly after she agreed to temporarily move into his one bedroom. This living arrangement had not been an ideal situation from her parents' perspective, but at that point the rent for the house on Jennings had become too much of a burden. Moving into a smaller place saved her parents so much money, and Cole had become family to them anyway. "I suppose your generation does things a little different anyhow," was her mom's final word about it. So she moved into Cole's one bedroom in a little development five miles east of Van Wert.

She drove Cole out to the park in New Canaan, the town square, the baseball fields, the high school. She was incapable of articulating how alive this place had seemed when she was young, how much energy you could feel here. She could only see it through his eyes now: a dingy town getting dingier. Nostalgia shielding the rest.

"That's the football field." She pointed to the ring of fence and bleachers overseen by bleach-white stadium lights. As a child, the place had looked like it could hold the Super Bowl. The jaguar mascot burst through a wall, snarling, muscled arms with razor claws extending for prey, looking the way 56 had when he swallowed up that Marysville quarterback.

How to explain to him the town's sadness, the tragedies. By the time she left, she'd held in her heart the notion of a curse, the one the town whispered about. At that point she and 56 had been broken up for well over a year. He was playing football for Mount Union, destined to flunk too many classes and get into the trouble that he did. She weighed around eighty-eight pounds, her eating problem having reached its apex. She kept seeing herself in the mirror; she'd always understood how pretty she was, blessed with strong cheekbones, a slim, delicate nose, long lashes, and smooth, smoky skin framed by raven hair. And yet her body never stopped looking grotesque to her; she pinched the flab around her belly, arms, and thighs; she skipped meals or ate a bag of chips for dinner. She'd also gone too far with the pricks.

Then that sensation of a curse began to be borne out. When Curtis Moretti died of a drug overdose, she found herself envying him. What a relief it would be to no longer be afraid and hurt all the time. The same fate later befell Ben Harrington. Rick Brinklan was killed in Iraq, and New Canaan had a parade when his body returned. Though her parents and Rick's had known one another since they all went to New Canaan High School themselves, Tina missed the parade. How could she explain to Cole that it followed them all, that sadness somehow born in their high school days that could reach out and touch any of them at random. She had this image of Christ swimming through the chaos of life, trying to protect all these people who deserved mercy, and yet these oily tentacles kept slipping past Him, carrying away all the people He wanted to give sanctuary.

Tragedy wasn't entirely why it was so hard to come back to New Canaan. After she drove Cole past the high school that day, she took him out to the overlook where the Cattawa River flowed, a spot popularly known as the Brew, where her classmates had sometimes come to drink and where she'd sometimes made love to 56. She'd felt guilty next to Cole, but she wanted to return to all the memories so badly, even the ones that throbbed, that brought so much shame. Looking out over the steady murmur of the river, the setting sun turning the clouds pink, draping that soft, wonderful color over all the leafless trees clamoring at the sky, she began to cry.

"What's a matter?" he asked.

She wiped her eyes. "Nothing. It's just always been so pretty out here. Just sometimes I miss this place so much."

She thought she'd want to be left alone with this thing only she could understand, but when he reached out and took her hand it felt in sync with the shiver of the sunlit water.

She checked The Office, then Honey Buckets, grew nervous. She reminded herself that there were only three bars he really ever went to, and his routine was so ingrained it would serve as a sign from God if by coincidence he had not gone out to drink tonight. He stayed, usually till close, nearly every night after he got off work at Cattawa Construction. Finally, she spotted his truck parked across the street from the Lincoln Lounge. In high school, when the truck had been new it looked like the gleaming transport of a futuristic military. Obsidian black with chrome door handles and a cap for the truck bed that kept the rain, leaves, and snow out. A lift kit gave it a bulked-up look, like the vehicle had been chugging the same protein shakes as its driver. Over ten years later the cap was gone and the truck was covered in a film of dust that gave it a sickly gray color under the streetlights.

She parked a ways down the street beneath a lamp fortuitously burned out. She felt safe in the shadows. Her mind worked furiously trying to puzzle out what she'd say. She turned off the dome light before she opened the car door.

After her parents finally agreed to let her ride with him, he began driving her to school, to the movies or the diner, to Ryan Ostrowski's place. So much passed between them during their time together. Memories wonderful and not as wonderful. They spent the day that became very famous just driving. This was the day when classes stopped and all the boxy TVs affixed to the corner of the ceiling in each classroom got turned on, and the whole school watched as the towers burned and collapsed, that expanding cloud of cancer-gray smoke blooming through the city streets, turning all the fleeing faces to ash, coating the visible world. It had all felt very far away to her. New York City was a bright, colorful set in TV sitcoms. Terrorism was nothing she had ever considered before. She'd gone to an emergency service at church that night with her parents where Pastor Jack said that wonderful line that offered so much clarity ("In this moment of profound grief for our fellow countrymen, this will seem odd, but today I'll paraphrase not Paul the disciple but Paul the musician: God makes His plans, and sometimes that information is unavailable to the mortal man.").

Afterward, her mom dropped her off at Stacey's, and then 56 picked her up down the street. They spent the evening traversing the square downtown as they sometimes did.

"I say we bomb those faggots back to first principles," he said. "Whoever it is, China, Iraq, doesn't matter. Just turn their country into a fucking crater."

He drove slouched to the right, his elbow propped up on the center console, his hand in an L with the index finger on his temple, thumb thoughtful on his chin. His left hand guided the steering wheel with all the loose nonchalance of how he held his books in the hallway.

"It's so crazy," was all she could add. They were all unprepared for how this would unfold around them. Bill Ashcraft told someone that if Americans had to live like some of those people do, we'd probably want to fly planes into buildings too. Bill always said stuff to provoke people, but this would be the time he went too far, when his addiction to attention manifested as an easy way to wound the people around him. After all, they were still children by every measure, still reeling, in shock and mourning. She was glad when 56 knocked him down in the hallway. How frightened he'd looked, unable to even get up until a teacher came and rescued him.

"Why not use the nukes too," 56 reasoned. "We got 'em for a reason, right? Put down a nuke on Mecca, and then the Arabs have an example set for them. It won't be more clear what happens when you try to fuck with the most powerful military in the world."

He looked over at her when she said nothing. He fingered the chain to his dog tags, drawing thumb and index along each little ball bearing.

"You wanna go out to Strow's place tonight? The guys are out there."

She swallowed, kept her gaze steady. "Not tonight."

He kept looking at her, eyes flitting back to the road only momentarily. "I want to go out there."

"Well." She pondered a less obvious way to phrase it, came up with nothing. "I don't."

The square, abruptly awash in American flags wafting lazily in the breeze, glittered with light. Drivers laid on their horns in solidarity as they circled the town's heart.

"That's fine, but we're heading out there soon. Maybe this weekend."

When she didn't respond, he returned to his previous line of thought.

"People without the Christian faith don't view the sanctity of life the way we do. They think it's disposable, which is why they can do the suicide thing. Don't even realize it's a sin, that's how fucking backward they are. Maybe we can convert some of 'em, but I doubt it."

She'd never say anything, but in the months that followed as the news filled with images of the men who did this, she'd think maybe people had it wrong. Maybe it was about being Muslim or hating America, but also maybe not. Maybe it was about the need to lash out at the world, to make someone listen to you and see that you are there.

They ended up going to Ostrowski's place that weekend.

For the rest of the month as the news reported on anthrax and color-coded alerts, military recruiters set up tables in the cafeteria, and he took the pamphlets. A few of the other seniors on the football team simply began the sign-up process right there.

"It's tough because I've got this skill," he explained to her. "I'm a hell of a football player, and this's been my dream since I was a little kid. I'd have to give it all up."

She understood, and she felt for him with that mourning ache you feel for someone you love so much. When he didn't score high enough on his SATs the first time, she'd seen how it rendered him helpless, how it made him so angry and sad, he was like a boy again. It made her care for him unfathomably. If the worst happened, and he couldn't get a high enough score to play college ball, maybe the military would be another, better place he could make his mark. Of course, she didn't want him to go fight in a war, but she knew he would be a hero. His bravery was practically written across his brow. He had something great inside of him.

They spent Halloween evening playing with his dogs. He and his mother—a bear of a woman with a considerable gut and close-cropped blond curls—had a feverish love of dogs. They adopted them rapid-fire, kept some, and tried to find others homes. He hated that the New Canaan pet shelter wasn't no-kill.

"They put down any animal that doesn't get adopted in seventy-two hours," he told her. "If it's got so much as the sniffles, they'll put it down even faster."

They adopted a new dog almost every month and then made phone calls and put ads in the paper to try to place each one. They only had enough room on their property to keep so many. Plus, the dogs would sometimes attack one another. She loved watching him with the animals. That night they sat in the vast, yawning expanse of backyard, which, compared to the wee double-wide, was the main event: grass and forest and those beautiful Ohio hills rising to the dawn and stars. They fed the dogs, threw tennis balls and sticks and toys, watched the pups sprint after them in an excitement that didn't have a human parallel. Like they knew they'd been saved.

That evening she found Symphony with burrs in her hair, and he grabbed a pair of scissors to cut them out.

"You think she'd learn better by now." He snipped into the dog's coat and brought out yet another small barb tangled in fur. "Swear she runs into that patch every time we let her out back."

She watched from beside him, holding the scrawny mutt gently with two hands, rubbing the poor girl under the jaw. She was the newest of the strays, some timid mix of Australian shepherd and cattle dog, according to 56. Something bad had happened to her. She trembled every time a human got near her and had horrible scars on her snout.

"Maybe she's trying to run away," she suggested.

"Can see the fence right there." He gestured to the back of their property where wood posts and welded-wire field fence enclosed three acres. He finished cutting the burrs out and fed Symphony a treat. The dog took it with deference. Let it drop to the ground and sniffed hesitantly before picking it up.

"Good girl," he whispered to her, scratching around her head and neck. "You're such a beautiful girl."

It was cool outside. Fall trying to break through summer. The clouds huddled around a setting sun so that the sky looked like pink cupcake frosting. They talked about what life would be like in just a few years when he went pro. The things they could buy. The worries they could forget forever. The house he'd build his mom. The dogs that would bound across their enormous property. He'd use his money when he made it to the NFL to open a no-kill pet shelter in his hometown. And then open them everywhere and save all of these beautiful pups.

She waited in Cole's Cobalt a long time. She'd brought nothing to do, no magazines or crossword puzzle to occupy her. That was fine. She stayed in the dark alone with her memories. She imagined the whole span of her life like it was a world of fireflies trapped in a jar.

When the door banged open and 56 stumbled out, she almost didn't recognize him. She'd seen him only from a distance in the last few years. She'd seen the weight he'd gained, especially in the belly and face. His jaw had gone round and fleshy. His stubble now covered a pouch beneath his chin. She knew that he still went to the cheapo gym out by Bluebaugh Auto Body where he benched and squatted, but all that muscle now had a heavy coating of fat. Tonight he wore a red Buckeyes hat that had dirtied and faded to a crimson rust. He moseyed on to his truck, excavating keys from his jeans pocket.

She turned the key in the ignition. It revved and then sputtered out. Her skin went cold with dread. The battery was old and the engine cranked sluggish, but it always turned over. *Not now*. She looked back to 56. He tottered slightly. She expected him to get into the truck before he noticed, but as he sifted through his many keys, she saw him catch sight of the tire. His cuss rang out through the quiet. She tried the ignition again. It wheezed, struggled, and failed. *Wait ten seconds. Don't panic.* But panic was all around. She found herself praying as she tried it a third time.

Fifty-six bent down to examine the wheel, and just as he was pulling his cell phone from his pocket, maybe to call a buddy for a ride, the engine caught and turned over. She put the Cobalt in drive and her foot to the accelerator.

Her heart thundered in her chest. Memories winking in and out in the jar.

She thought—she didn't know, but she thought—it had something to do with the day in the black depths of a midwestern winter her sophomore year, his senior, when Mr. Clifton, the music teacher, stopped her after class. She could see 56 waiting for her down the hall as students scurried to the next period. He had his eyes on her when Mr. Clifton shut the door.

"I just wanted to speak with you very quickly, Tina. Hope you have a minute."

"Sure. I have chemistry, though."

"I can write you a note."

He motioned for her to have a seat in a front-row desk. He sat beside her, folding his hands. Mr. Clifton was probably the most adored teacher in the school. He was funny and warm, and he took a direct interest in every student, knew everyone by name, knew their sports and extracurriculars. His voice reminded her of a middle school vocab word she'd never forgotten: *mellifluous.* When it flipped from a rich baritone to a high peeling laugh, it was a sound of extraordinary pleasure to the ear. The tone of this kind voice troubled her now, though. She had no idea what he might want.

"You date Todd Beaufort on the football team, right?"

She nodded. "For a year now."

"And that's going well?"

"Of course. It'll be hard when he goes away to school, but it's only two years, and I'll probably visit every other weekend."

He nodded, stared at her.

"I heard some . . ." he began and then stopped. His teeth worried his lower lip. "I heard some pretty outlandish stuff from a student. In regards to you and Todd. I won't go into the details, except that my position almost requires me to inform the higher-ups of . . . of what I heard if it's true."

She frowned. "What did you hear?"

Mr. Clifton looked extremely uncomfortable. Beads of sweat had popped out on the high part of his brow where the hair had receded. He swiped at his mustache.

"Does Todd treat you the way he should?" he asked.

"Of course."

Mr. Clifton nodded. He opened his mouth, but was cut off by the *snick-snack* sound of the classroom door unlatching. Fifty-six stepped into the doorway, still holding the knob. His eyes assessed them the way they would an offensive line: quickly, expertly.

"Everything good in here, Tina?"

"Excuse me," said Mr. Clifton. "We're having a conversation. Please shut the door."

"What all about?"

"It's okay," Tina said, but neither of the men seemed to hear her.

"A private one," said Mr. Clifton. For the first time since she'd known him, she heard anger in his voice. "Shut the door, Mr. Beaufort."

Fifty-six kept his eyes cool, indifferent.

"Another day not that long ago, Mr. Clifton," he said, "and you wouldn't dare talk to me like that."

Mr. Clifton bolted from the student desk. "Excuse me?" He took two steps and put his face inches from her boyfriend's. "What did you say?"

He was a great deal taller than Mr. Clifton, but he turned his gaze to the side anyway. "Nothing."

"No, why don't you repeat that, Mr. Beaufort? Repeat that to me right now."

Number 56 shook his head back and forth lazily. "Can't even remember what I said."

The two of them stood like that, nose to chin, for a moment. Tina pictured him in his pads on the cold sideline and could nearly see the steam wafting from his skull. Finally, Mr. Clifton said, "If you want to play Friday, get out of my sight right now." He slammed the classroom door in her boyfriend's face.

When he sat back down, she smiled apologetically. "I'm really sorry. He's just protective. He cares about me, so he gets worried."

Mr. Clifton nodded but appeared not to be listening. Instead, he stared at the surface of the desk. He looked up at her.

"Tina, I'm going to tell you this one thing, and then you can go. I heard something distressing, but perhaps it was not from a source that would prove very reliable. All I will say is that when you're dating anyone—but especially with Todd—you need to make sure he's respecting you. Understand?"

"Of course. I do. And he does." She smiled to show that she meant it. "He's just protective."

Mr. Clifton grilled her awhile longer, increasingly desperate to hear her disparage 56, but he finally let her leave. A few weeks later, with the awful year of 2001 having flipped forward, 56 told her, "We're done." One day they were fine—she ate dinner at his house, they played with a dog named Winnow in his backyard, he drove her home—and then the weekend passed and he never called her. When she finally got him on the phone, he only had those two evil words to say. After her stunned silence, tears, and protestations, he realized her secret fear. He said it right out loud: "It's like, how can I marry you after all that shit I've seen you do?"

Nearly a dozen years later, it still made her breath catch in her throat. His cruelty. He barely looked at her in the halls when they got back from break.

A year of her life cut off like a guillotine came down and severed her neck.

He began seeing that awful skank Jess Bealey, who, every time Tina laid eyes on her, made her want to scream. Tina spent weeks holed up in her bedroom struck dumb with grief, a constant panic coiled in her chest, unable to comprehend how he could drop her so casually and instantaneously. Had Mr. Clifton told Principal MacMillan or Coach Bonheim something? Had he threatened 56? Had 56 seen Mr. Clifton prying into their love life and decided she was more trouble than she was worth? She asked these questions endlessly and in circles, obsessed with finding an answer but afraid to leave her room, to talk to anyone at school, to accept her mother's reassurances that this too shall pass, to approach the love of her life and ask for an explanation, though in her dreams they still sat together in his truck and looked out over the Cattawa, the water like scrolls of gold in the autumn sun.

Pulling alongside him, the window rolled down, she tried to call out. Her breath caught and hitched in the back of her throat. The residual terror due to the Cobalt's faulty engine still rippled through her nerves, and the words became a choked cough. Fifty-six turned around on his own when he heard the car stop at his back. He still held his phone, index finger poised to dial. He'd crouched to examine the tire, and he turned to her with one knee on the ground, his boot scraping at the grit. He wore a short-sleeve plaid shirt, the top three or four buttons open over a white tank top, and when headlights washed over them, she could see a meat-yellow sweat tint at the collar.

"Hey," she said, pushing her voice to as bright and jaunty a note as she could manage. "I thought that was you, Five-Six. Whatcha doing?"

It was hard to read his face because the eyes were a bit bleary and his expression was so neutral. Still, there was none of the joy or surprise she'd hoped for.

"Hey, you." He snorted a laugh. "Of all people. Fucking tire's flat," he muttered, looking back at it. "Think some grab-ass prankster let the air out."

"That sucks." She glanced around the street, still empty in all directions. "Need a ride somewhere? Thought I'd do a nightcap."

"You got booze?"

"Course."

He laughed softly and shook his head. Then she caught him glancing at her chest. Just a flit of his eyes, an assessment. One thing about her weight gain was that a portion of it had gone to her breasts. She'd worn a tight black shirt and a bra that pushed them to his eye.

"Yeesh. Why the hell not." He pocketed his phone and reached for the passenger door. He crashed into the seat, which protested his girth. He grabbed hold of the handle above the door and skipped his seat belt. She pulled into the street, amazed at how easy that had been, thinking ahead to what she would say now, how this might possibly go. When she checked the rearview, she saw a tall woman in a pretty summer dress come slinking from the alley to the street. She wore high black boots and had a cute purse slung over her shoulder. Her gait looked familiar, the way she carried herself. To Tina's dismay, the woman watched them drive away.

She let the air out of his tire only because she saw no other way to be alone with him. He wouldn't have gone with her if she just walked up to him and said she wanted to talk. He didn't work like that. She'd tried many, many times in high school. *Grow up*, he'd hissed by his locker. *Mine ain't the last dick you're ever gonna have in you.* Words that made her panicked and ill.

At some point crying wasn't quite enough. That's when her eating troubles began. When she looked in the mirror she saw a fat, ugly, slutty little child that a man bound for the NFL could never be attracted to, let alone love. "Shorter women have trouble keeping the weight off their hips," her mother explained, herself a squat, rotund woman, once pretty in old pictures but now suited in middle-age flab. She could already see the advent of her mother's figure in her shape. This got better only when she mostly stopped eating.

It wasn't until 56 graduated, though, and it became very real that he was going away and would not be coming back to her, that she really started with the pricks. "Pricking herself" was how she thought of it, but her instrument was not a needle. A box cutter from her dad's tool kit, rather. A few months after it disappeared her dad finally noticed and ransacked the house looking for it.

"Just go buy a new one," her mother suggested.

"Why? I have a perfectly good one. It didn't damn well dematerialize. It's around. Unless you put it somewhere."

"That's right, I hid your box cutter to gaslight you."

It had a bright orange grip. The blade was about an inch wide and could extend four inches from the handle. You pushed the black button with your thumb to pop it out, and then the button pulled apart to lock the blade into place at your preferred length. It was the only weapon the men had used to take over those planes and fly them into the towers, and this seemed to lend it a certain power it otherwise could never have possessed. This was a tool that changed history overnight. A little blade like this had toppled those two incredible buildings with perfect Hollywood symmetry, rained ash and fire and gray dust across the capital of the world. She liked holding it in her hand and marveling at this. Eventually, her dad bought a replacement and forgot about it.

She began on the back of her thigh. First, she'd clean the blade with cotton balls soaked in isopropyl alcohol and stand naked with her back to the mirror in her room. Watching over her shoulder she'd press gently at first, then more firmly, and draw the blade over the back of her thigh until blood trickled down. She liked doing it there because in class the next day she'd have to sit on the hot, secret filaments.

Then the backs of her thighs began to get too messy and she moved to the inside, cutting right up to the V near her groin. This was okay for a while. Then she needed more and moved the pricks to her torso. Drawing the blade along her rib cage, she explored the contours of the bone. Her body became a map, a serpentine sketch of scars in different stages of healing. Old pricks faded to thin pink and white lines while newer flesh, raw and red, could still bleed through the bandages she applied. She collected the used ones in a plastic bag in her closet and only threw them away at school.

They made her promise to stop after one of the pricks went too far.

"I was thinking of going to the Lincoln to get in a drink before it closed, and there you were," she told him. "Small world, huh?" Fifty-six hadn't said anything since he got in the car. She had to begin the conversation somewhere. "I was in town tonight picking some stuff up from my parents' storage locker and figured I'd see if anyone was out. How 'bout you?"

"Just getting on after work." He sounded tired, so worn out.

She wondered how much he'd had to drink. "You still over by the Indiana line?"

"Yep. Van Wert."

"Huh."

She waited for him to say more, but he only nodded. He seemed very far away, which rubbed her wrong. Her left heel jackhammered the car's carpet. "I'm thinking I might want to get into trouble tonight." He looked over at her, and she flashed a bright grin. "I mean, the kind of trouble we used to get into."

A shy smile finally lit into his face, the one she recognized from high school: half a lip curling up—only gone was the confidence, the daring. She saw the stainless steel ball-chain necklace, but he now wore the dog tags tucked into his shirt.

"Yeah?"

She shrugged. "If you don't mind."

Approaching a red light, she braked and reached into the small compartment in the driver's side door. She pulled out two airplane bottles. One Jack and one Jim. "Start with a little whiskey? You want?"

He slapped his thighs and lurched forward. "Not at all how I saw this night going."

She unscrewed the cap on the Jack, his preferred brand, handed it to him. "Cheers."

The glass necks made a small *tink*, and they both tipped the bottles back. The whiskey struggled down the thin neck. Air bubbles replaced the liquid, gurgling up. She wasn't much of a whiskey drinker and couldn't help but cough at the burn. He swallowed in three bobs of his throat and dropped the bottle to the floor.

"Where we going?" he asked. The light turned green and she eased forward.

"I don't know. Figured we could just drive out to Stillwater. We used to hang out there sometimes, remember?"

He rubbed the red-blond stubble of his cheek and directed his gaze out the window. "Of course. Had us some fun for a while, didn't we."

She forced a smile to prove it had been fun.

"Who were you at the Lincoln with?" she asked to change the subject.

"Just a buddy from Cattawa. Him, me, and Strow were at Honey Buckets earlier, but Strow had to go on duty for the late shift. He's a deputy now, you know."

"He drinks before work?"

"Ha, just a couple. Then ran into Hansen at the Lincoln and a couple of dudes from around your year. Like they were having a reunion thing. Of course it led to trouble." He snorted. "Always does, I guess."

Now that she was sitting beside him, hearing the smooth boom of his voice, breathing his tangy musk of sweat and dirt, she sensed something different about him that she'd never been able to put her finger on while watching him from afar. He sounded exhausted and much older than his twenty-nine years. She knew things hadn't worked out the way he'd hoped. He'd gotten into some kind of trouble and lost his scholarship to OSU before he even took a class. After signing on at Mount Union, he'd redshirted, had a lackluster two seasons where he had to keep sitting out due to injury, and then tore his meniscus his junior year. Each time she heard of yet another one of his setbacks, she thought of him after he bombed the SATs or after the one time she'd asked where his father was: that hideous, hurt scowl. His certainty that he'd get to the NFL (which became her certainty) was matched only by the panic that he'd never get out of New Canaan.

He was laughing about how Jonah Hansen had gotten in a fight. "Not much of a fight. Jonah got his nose busted and ran off. But

Jonah's got that coming to him and then some. Acts like he owns the town 'cause of his last name, but I'll tell you— Wanna hear a secret?"

"Sure."

"The Hansens—Burt and Jonah and all of them—they near about lost it all in the crash. The reason they're still making money is they're cooking crank and running pills in some of their properties."

"Really?" The Jonah she'd known in high school was self-assured but bland. Preppy and swagger-loaded. The idea of his straitlaced father cooking meth sounded ludicrous, and yet it had been a rough few years. People hung on any way they could.

He gave her a knowing look. "From what I hear they got two or three houses—send it all over the state. Then Jonah acts like he's some whiz kid with money. Like what? You think what you're do-ing's any better than the Mexicans selling black tar? Prick."

"That's nuts."

"Yep."

She took a left onto Stillwater Road. The gaps between the houses grew. The lights of New Canaan receded. The dark country spread before them, lush farmland and summer-green forest awash in night.

"You still see a lot of people from school?"

"Not really. I guess anyone who stayed around. Strow and Jonah. Jess and . . . and Kaylyn. This place—man, what a shithole it's got to being. Jess's mom works for a dentist, and she says people come in and get teeth pulled just to get the Oxy scrip. If they can't get that they'll buy heroin. Nigger bullshit you can't get away from. I was hanging out at Fallen Farms for a while, but had to cut that out."

"Fallen what?"

"Amos and Frankie and their cousin Kirk and all them? Their

grandma owns the place, and she's totally deaf and blind, so they have parties and we go shooting sometimes. Those guys are turning into friggin psychopaths. Getting loaded and stocking up for World War III out there. And this one time, we were shooting at bottles and Amos missed with a whole clip, didn't land a single round, and so he tosses the gun down and Kirk just—" He made a quick motion with his hand, drawing a two-fingered pistol and using his other hand to mime chambering a round. "He just puts his Glock right to Amos's forehead, screaming at him about throwing a gun."

"Oh my god."

"I ain't been back since that little incident. Don't even like seeing those guys at the bars anymore."

He looked at his thumbnails, one of which had an enormous blood blister, like the surface of a deep purple marble. Tina interrupted him. "Can I ask . . ." All that time on her drive to think about what she'd say and here she was, mouth as dry as the drought that summer. He looked at her expectantly, tenderly. She thought of sitting in the stands wearing the T-shirt with his name and number. Decorated with glitter glue and stars you could iron on. "Do you ever think of me?"

He snorted a laugh, and the sound made her ache.

"We had fun. It was high school, though. You were what? Fifteen when we started? That's not, like, true love, Tina. That's high school."

"I was fourteen," she whispered.

"How come . . ." Whatever tenderness she thought she'd seen was gone. His eyelids had fallen. They hovered halfway open, fluttering. "I'm sorry, but high school was high school, Tina. Nothing more."

"It was more than that to me."

"Jesus." He shook his head. "I'm sorry if you thought that."

A lump formed in her throat. "For a year I did whatever you wanted. Everything you asked."

"What you want me to say?" His eyes, red and engorged, shimmered. "Lotta shit didn't go as planned. Or didn't you notice?" His speech slurred. *Din you.*

"I loved you. Really. I still do."

"Girl, you got no idea. You got no clue." She wasn't sure what she heard in his voice, but it sounded almost like loathing—the way he'd hissed at her the one time he spoke about never wanting to meet his father. "You're lucky to have gotten as far the fuck away from me as possible. Everything I ever done, everything I ever touched. It's just led to the next worst thing."

He pulled at the purple nail, looking like it was held on only by the slime.

" 'Bout to have a kid, you know. A son."

She tensed at this, all her muscles twitching at once.

"Not sure how the hell I'm gonna do it. I get . . . headaches. Like so bad I can't see or think. Tressel, back when he was recruiting for the Bucks, told me I was the hardest hitter he'd ever seen, and guess I'm paying for it now. I was a headhunter. I brought the violence. And I wouldn't give it back for anything. It's what I loved. But now every few months I'll go through these times where I just feel like I'm losing my goddamn mind. Like my whole life's been a bad dream."

The road carried them on. Fifty-six slumped farther into his seat, his voice drifting.

"I did . . . bad things, I know. It ain't like you know what you're doing when you're that age. You just do stuff. And no one's ever told you what it means, so why do you care? You don't. You just do it."

His eyelids slipped closed, opened, fluttered, and his words turned to scrap and debris. He ended by muttering something about "All the blackmailers coming after me"—nothing but nonsense trailing to sleep. Then his eyes slipped closed and his chin slumped to his chest.

Tina let the tears come then. She rolled down her window so the sobs wouldn't echo in the confines of the car.

At the edge of the city limits, there was a stretch of woods that ran all the way to the end of the county and a town called Morova (which itself was little more than a string of houses, a gas station, and a few churches). This was what Tina always thought of as Deep Ohio. These were the places where you got some hunters during the season, some kids playing war in the summer, and occasionally teenagers sneaking off to play with each other. But those cases were rare. Mostly it was the earthen depths of comingled tree species, a loamy scent, and floodplain grasses dotted with the inky purple of great blue lobelias. She remembered it because 56 had taken her here when the Brew was crowded. There was a turnoff for a dirt road about ten miles out on Stillwater. This road had a fence with a NO TRESPASSING sign fixed to the gate. Rather than a padlock, whoever owned the road simply left a metal spike in the latch to keep the gate closed. Fifty-six had shown her this. Tina left the car running, hopped out, and pulled the bolt. She noticed someone had spray-painted THE LORD LIVES over the sign.

He snored softly from the passenger seat, breath whispering in and out of his nostrils. Her fingers slipped beneath her shirt and found the scar on her stomach, palpated it the way she did when she felt like screaming. The ridge of flesh a reminder, a relic, of the prick that went too far.

Her senior year, she'd been in her room carving into her belly. Cutting into the fat forming the spare tire around her waist that never went away no matter how much she starved the creature. She was in her bed, under the covers with a flashlight, the way she liked to do it: holding the light with her left hand and cutting with her right. She'd made a pretty good gouge into this spot on her abdomen just above and to the left of her belly button. She hated looking at this flesh, this pudge. She hated the way it amassed around her torso. Hated the way she could pinch it. She began digging the blade of the box cutter deeper. The fat swallowed the steel. Then she felt a pop as it pierced the muscle beneath. The pain was unbelievable. She nearly cried out, hissing the sound into her hot bed tent. Clenching her jaw, she pushed in deeper. Then she began sawing. But the blade kept getting stuck and she had to start over. Blood bubbled up, flowing over her stomach and staining her hand. The pale yellow sheets caught the blood running down her torso. That stain grew and grew. She kept cutting. It seemed the more she cut, the more her ruined stomach looked irredeemable to her. The scar would be hideous, so why not keep going? Why not take out this entire part of herself? And anyway, she knew about pain. She knew about bleeding. She managed to cut half her stomach apart before the agony wailed and she along with it. Which brought her mother running. She woke up in the hospital.

They called it a suicide attempt even though that was not what had happened. She hadn't been trying to kill herself. Nevertheless she stayed in the hospital for a week, and a woman came and talked to her for an hour every day.

This woman, Dr. Marsha, had an ugly bob of red hair, that kind of old-lady red that looks nearly purple. She had a withered face and wore bright red lipstick that sometimes got on her teeth. She sat by the hospital bed and badgered Tina about everything. Her mom, dad, school, boys. Once she hit on 56, she never let up, made Tina tell her everything. Every last detail.

Tina eventually asked, "This can't get him in trouble, right?"

Dr. Marsha stared at her. She had this annoying habit of not answering questions. She'd sit and stare at you until you said something else.

"What I'm telling you can't get him in trouble?" Tina repeated. She hadn't told Dr. Marsha Five-Six's real name, but it wouldn't be difficult at all for her to figure out. The New Canaan hospital was the tallest building in the county but ultimately just as small a community as the rest of the town. She could probably ask any nurse with a kid in the high school who Tina Ross had dated her freshman and sophomore years.

"This won't go beyond anyone but us," Dr. Marsha said carefully. "But let me make something clear to you, Tina. And I'd like you to really listen to this, okay? You're eighteen, you're an adult, but hear what I'm saying." She tented her fingers, flexed them against one another. "What you're describing to me . . . This boy and his friends raped you. Even if you think some of the encounters were later consensual, what you're telling me is that you were drugged and raped."

How she hated this woman.

"You don't know. This isn't— It's not the way you're making it sound."

"Tina. Honey. Listen to me. What happened to you—at least the way you're telling me this happened—is not acceptable. In your heart you must know that."

She'd nodded only because she had wanted Dr. Marsha to leave her alone. She promised she'd tell her parents, but she never did. After she went home, her mom reverted to the parent she'd been years earlier, doting, nervous, terrified of the fragility of the only child God had given her. Her dad wouldn't let her drive anywhere alone and gave her rides where they both sat in silence. She saw Dr. Marsha twice more before they found out her dad's insurance wouldn't pay for the visits.

When she thought of God she thought of him not as the risen savior but as a man. In the guise of Santa, her parents had given her a picture book as a child, the story of Christ's sacrifice. Beautiful illustrations of the garden of Gethsemane with violet and green vines twisting into a coal-black sky and tears of blood crawling down Jesus's brow from where the thorns bit. The picture she studied the most, though, was of Jesus in the moment before the Crucifixion, after he'd laid down the cross and stood at the crest of Golgotha, Roman soldiers and a swimming blue sky at his back. The illustrator had rendered this moment with such care, but most surprising was the expression on the young man's face. It wasn't determination or anger or love or any of the other likely candidates she would expect from the immortal, stirring tale of his last long walk. It was fear. It was an unsettling realization when it dawned on her that the Son of God could feel fear. Could feel alone.

While she dated 56, all her friends from church and school became afterthoughts at best, strangers at worst. Senior year, she'd tried reconciling with Stacey. They spent an afternoon after church walking through town, talking about why they'd stopped speaking.

"You got to being his groupie." Stacey reached out and tucked a strand of Tina's hair behind her ear. Her fingers felt so pleasant as they drew down the back of her earlobe. "You became somebody else, and I didn't care for that girl at all."

It was difficult for her eighteen-year-old self to hear that and not grow defensive. Her best friend from childhood, whose house she'd once practically lived at on the weekends, who had the revolting and incredible ability to fart whenever she wanted, which she deployed to hilarious effect, whose brothers she coveted because she had none of her own—Tina simply couldn't love her anymore. She'd become extremely close with Lisa Han, Tina's least favorite person in high school. Vulgar, know-it-all, and cruel, Lisa stalked the halls with an unmistakable arrogance and swagger. Maybe Tina had dropped her friend for 56, but in turn Stacey had chosen such an odious replacement, there was no chance of repairing the friendship.

"Are those rumors true?" Stacey asked her abruptly. "About you and him and the guys on the team?"

It was the same panic she'd felt with Dr. Marsha. The same fear. She glared at the ground, hating that she could not meet Stacey's eye, and therefore hating Stacey.

"Of course not," she said. "It's dumb rumors he started just to hurt me. So no one else would date me."

Of all the things she regretted, lying to Stacey was close to the top. It was impossible to not wonder if things would've turned out differently if she'd had courage in that moment.

Six years later when she met Beauty, it was like coming up for air. Her first real best friend since she was a ninth grader. Beauty spotted her reading a book about Lizzie Borden at lunch on her second day of work and said, "You've gotta let me borrow that."

"You'll have to ask the library. It's theirs."

"Then let me know when you turn it in. I can't get enough of that stuff—it scares the crap outta me."

Beauty had a funky sense of humor, an ability to leave Tina gasping for breath over some absurdity. She called the Walmart regulars "the village bizarre." It meant the people who came in frequently but only to push a cart, gab, blab, and gossip with whoever they could manage to run into, and who left after only buying a six-pack of pop. (In their dullest moments at work, Beauty did an impression of a character she called "Mr. Raithenth," which was just her crossing her eyes and asking Tina for some raisins with a lisp. "Uh, excuthe me, Mith. Where can I find the raithenth?" It never failed to bust her gut and occasionally have her in tears.)

And maybe it had been Beauty, a few years earlier, who first laid the kindling for an idea. Tina had been complaining about sleeplessness. She was working sixty-, sometimes seventy-hour weeks, her dad had just broken his hip, and she was so anxious trying to fall asleep, fearing the exhaustion she'd feel the next day if she didn't, that she'd stare at the ceiling for hours in a self-fulfilling loop.

"I can get you something to help," Beauty told her. "My cousin in Dayton makes G."

"What's that?"

"G. Liquid G. People take it at raves and stuff. The right amount's like a really good sleeping pill and too much is like a date rape drug, so just be careful."

Tina turned these words over in her mind for a long time before giving Beauty the go-ahead. She experimented on herself at first, and the stuff did help her sleep. Then later, she tried it on Cole. It came in mini Ziploc bags of white powder. She was trying to think of a place to hide it where her mother would never clean and went rummaging through her closet. There was a box, still untouched from when they'd moved to Van Wert. Among the junk, she found the four copies of the *Jaguar Journal* she'd saved from freshman year. Beneath those was the picture book story of Jesus. Creased with wear, the covers fell open automatically to the page she'd spent so much time studying as a child, the one that began to teach her what kind of courage it takes to overcome true fear. What kind of love. She placed the baggie in the page and returned the book to the box.

Two miles down the dirt road, there was a turnoff into the woods. This wasn't where 56 had taken her, but she'd noticed the road from the occasions they'd parked in the field. About a year ago, on one of her increasing number of visits back, she'd taken a drive to see where it went. She followed it now. After creeping through the woods for about five miles over leaves, branches, and the crunch of caked mud, fried crisp by the summer drought, the path finally terminated in a small clearing carved out of the forest like a bowl. The woods fell away, and she cruised across the tall grass to the opposite edge of the clearing. She parked the car and shut off the lights. Then the engine. Outside, the crickets chattered, and the fireflies made the night sizzle. She took a moment to breathe in the air, to watch the stars, so bright out here in the country, an indecipherable map to somewhere better.

There'd been stars like this on the night it all began, the same stark, clear, cloudless sky. Maybe that was wrong, but it helped her remember why she was here now. Because she owed it to herself to return to all the corners of her memory where she rarely ventured.

She'd plotted it so carefully, her first time. As dictated by her young theory, Love was giving the person you cared about something you'd never given anyone else, the one thing only you could give him. During the winter of her freshman year, after football season had ended, she constructed an alibi involving FCA. Fifty-six had the perfect idea: his friend and teammate Ryan Ostrowski (No. 63) was throwing a party to celebrate their 10–2 season, one of the best finishes for New Canaan football in a decade. He basically had his own place because his dad was long gone and his mother drove a truck that took her down south for weeks at a time. The team was getting a keg from the brother of Jake Levy (No. 16), and most of the upperclassmen would be there. Fifty-six said that Strow had promised them the basement guest room.

At school that Friday, she spent her entire day composing. The contents of that letter were mostly lost to time, but she remembered explaining how dear he was to her, how much she loved him, and how she couldn't believe she was so lucky that they had somehow ended up in the same continent, country, and small town, in the same high school, born in the same wonderful age. How God must have planned for them to meet and fall in love. After going through three drafts, she carefully printed out the final version, folded it into a thick, tight triangle and taped it shut. She wrote 56 across blue notebook lines.

The party was more than she had expected. Everyone she could think of from the senior and junior classes was there, along with many sophomores and a scattering of freshmen. Red Solo cups cluttered every surface of the Ostrowski house, a humble little bungalow at the end of a dirt lane, far enough from the neighbors that it was unlikely they'd be bothered. The music was headache inducing, vibrating out of a car stereo and subwoofer rigged together in a complicated knot of electrical cords. Ostrowski greeted 56 with a high five and a one-armed embrace. Strow greeted Tina with the back of his index finger grazing her cheek and a Solo cup of warm beer. She sipped it because she didn't want to seem lame but planned to pour it down the toilet later. She'd always considered Ostrowski fairly gross. He was beefy, bordering on fat, with a shaved head and a little goatee overwhelmed by the pudge drooping from beneath his chin. His acne was total. Zits not only conquered his face, but you could see them through the hair on his skull, on his neck, even on the palms of his hands. She made her way into the dim recesses of the crowded living room, stood with her beer, pretending to be part of a conversation between a few juniors she barely knew. The loathed Jess Bealey was there, as were Matt Moore and Tony Wozniak. She recognized Kirk Strothers, the rat-tailed cretin who 56 had remained friends with even though Strothers had been expelled. He now sat on the couch in a daze, staring at Mackenzie Boylan's chest. Tina knew many of the faces, but not the people. She kept smoothing parts of her outfit, picking threads and hairs from her black pants, pressing at a wrinkle in her top, tugging her jean jacket so that it fit correctly on her chest. She had an urge to check her makeup in her compact but resisted. She watched as 56 moved from room to room and thought about the compact wad of her note pressed into her back pocket.

She eventually finished the beer and went to the keg for another. She spotted Kaylyn across the room. It was a friendly face, someone to talk to, but the stupid rumors—no matter how baseless they were—kept her from approaching. She didn't want to hate Kaylyn because of dumb lies told by people who were jealous, but the rumors at least gave her pause.

Around midnight, arm wrestling broke out at the dining room table. Jake Levy challenged Curtis Moretti (No. 8), the quarterback, and the crowd gathered to cheer and jeer. Their arms flexed, their wrists curled, their faces broke into dual sweats. Curtis had an odd face, she decided, sniveling and a bit rodenty, especially when he peeled a lip back in exertion like that. He shaved his whole skull except for a little cap of brown on top. He wore a tank top, so she could see all the muscles in his body go taut. His lat muscle jutted out from his side like a sleek tumor.

The night hammered on. The beer was making her light-headed and warm. At some point, she wasn't sure when, she went back for her third. Kaylyn approached her at the keg.

"Here, tilt the cup or you'll get all the foam," she said. Tina did so, and the golden fluid streamed down the side with only a small white cap. Kaylyn dipped an index finger in and stirred. "Party trick."

"Is Rick here?" she shouted.

The older girl bounced her eyebrows twice. "Nope. And wouldn't you know, I'm actually having fun."

"You don't have fun with him?"

"No, I do. Just not at things like this." She stirred her hand around the party. "He gets jealous about everything, especially the older guys. So stupid. Boyfriends are the absolute worst."

She tittered at her own comment and sipped. Tina did the same. "*You* look kinda miserable," Kaylyn observed.

"Oh, I'm fine." She looked around. Brent Brandon (No. 27) had gotten on one knee to take the hose end of a beer bong in his mouth. His neatly moussed hair had a loose strand. "It's just, like, absolutely crazy in here right now. We're yelling to hear each other, you know?"

"Welcome to the life of dating the team."

"Rick's a starter—he should be here, right?"

Kaylyn was so beautiful. Even now as she wrinkled her face into the expression of someone who'd just smelled rotten eggs, she still glowed. Her freckles added some lovely component to her fluorescent eyes, which reminded Tina of the smattering of green in the stained glass windows at her church.

"He doesn't get along with these guys. Your boyfriend makes him uncomfortable. He's sort of a closet nerd, you know."

"Todd?" she asked, confused. She was two years younger than 56 and often helped him with his homework.

Kaylyn laughed. "Nuh-nuh-no." She laughed some more. "Rick. Rick's a math nerd. He can do crazy calculations in his head. What I mean is he's like a secret brain. I guess that's why he hangs out with rich preps like Ben and Ashcraft."

These rumors about Kay and 56 simply could not be true, she decided. Where had she first heard them? Probably from Stacey, who was obviously jealous of her. If 56 was cheating on her, it meant Kaylyn was cheating on Rick, and that just seemed absurd. And yet the image of 56 and Kaylyn in the hall stayed with her, so that she could almost hear that gristly sound as his fingers kneaded strands of Kay's hair together.

She was roused from this unpleasant pit of jealousy by the sound of someone crying out, "Strow, no! Don't do it."

They both turned to see Ostrowski empty a twenty-four-ounce

can of malt liquor to the brim of the beer bong, held by Brent Brandon. He then took a knee. The crowd had differing opinions of whether or not this was a good idea.

"Back up, faggots," he told them.

By the time he sucked down half the liquid, Tina thought he would finish. He did in fact succeed, but the last of the foam had no sooner vanished than he was buckled over, hands on knees, vomiting like a garden hose when you put your thumb over the nozzle.

People screamed and stumbled backward to avoid the spray, which was hard to do given the pressure with which the liquid exited him. Watching it, Tina felt like she might hurl. People were streaming outside when Kaylyn grabbed her arm.

"C'mon, this place is going to smell like ass."

They pushed past all the revelry and found themselves in what must have been Mrs. Ostrowski's room. The bed was made, a flower duvet stretched over crisp sheets and half a dozen throw pillows. Tina sat while Kaylyn wandered over to the bookshelf, which had only books on CD.

"You're lucky," she said. "Todd's a good guy. He's going to be the biggest deal to come out of this place maybe ever."

"I hope so." Jealousy flared. What had Kaylyn done with him? She'd never asked 56 if he was a virgin. She hoped so but realized there was a chance he wasn't, maybe even a chance she was staring at the girl he'd given it to.

"My friend Hailey—you know her?"

"Kowalczyk?"

"Yeah, so she's like a little feminist, right? But you know it doesn't matter what your opinions are— If you can, you'll always date a football player."

"I don't know about that."

"I overheard these girls in the hall—you know, Goths and skanks, typical, just talking all this shit about fucking jocks, fucking preps, and it's like, you dumb bitches, you don't even know what those categories mean. You got that from every fucking tired, bullshit high school movie. You're just using that to make yourself feel better about your inability to actually talk to anyone and get to know them. It just drives me crazy."

It was strange hearing such volatile language come out of Kaylyn's beautiful mouth. She held a hand to her breast.

"Like I'm some rich girl? I don't fucking think so. My dad's been on disability since I was five. He walks around town looking for people who need their lawns mowed or their houses painted because if he gets a real job that check goes away. It all drives me crazy," she repeated.

Tina surmised that this was what it was like to be drunk: because all of this actually made a lot of sense. Kaylyn ran her fingertips—nails painted a bright pink—over Mrs. Ostrowski's audiobook collection, her long-haul-trucking companions: Tom Clancy, Joel Osteen, and Danielle Steel. Tina sipped.

"I don't think I've ever drank this much," she said.

"Ha, better get used to it, you ho. You want something so the hangover's not so bad?"

She did. Amid the bubbling anticipation of the night, she still feared her mother would know she'd been drinking when she got home the next morning from her "FCA sleepover."

Kaylyn groped in the coin pocket of her jeans and withdrew a small round pill. "It's just a vitamin, like B12 and stuff. It'll definitely make you feel better tomorrow."

Tina washed it down with a gulp of beer.

She looked like she might say something else and then stopped. Tina felt watched by her. Something passed through her stare, a look of judgment or spite she thought at first, but then it was gone. "You're really beautiful," Kaylyn said.

"Thank you. You too."

Kaylyn lay down beside her on the bed, stretching across the flowers. She propped her head on a hand.

"Do you like traditions?" Kaylyn asked.

"Depends on what you mean by that. Like going to church?"

She laughed. "Oh my god, you're so cute. No, I mean like outside that stuff. Rituals."

"I've never really thought about it."

"I love traditions. Anything that lets people celebrate or remember something that binds them."

Tina sipped her beer.

"Like I heard about this one school in New York, like a prep school where rich kids go. And not just rich kids, but like *the* rich kids. The kids whose parents have more money than they know what to do with. The boys have this thing where they divvy up the freshman class, and they all get assigned someone. And then they spend a month just making that kid's life a living hell. Beating him, making him eat nasty shit, making him wipe his ass with pinecones."

Tina grimaced. "That's disgusting."

"Yeah, but when they're seniors, those kids get to do it to the incoming class. It's a way they bond. Something they never forget and can take with them all through life."

"I'll stick with church, thank you."

Kaylyn threw her head back, and when she laughed, Tina could see the boxing bag in her throat vibrating, and the one tooth trying to push past its neighbor. "You're hilarious."

She wanted to throw out the rest of her beer; she felt gross.

"C'mon," said Kaylyn, hopping off the bed. "Let's go downstairs."

"Why?"

" 'Cause that's where the party's at."

Kaylyn led her to the basement. It was a dim wood-paneled

space with a low ceiling and carpet the color of bathwater. The furniture all looked secondhand, cobbled together from the Salvation Army and yard sales. They were alone down there. A case of Busch Light, half-empty, sat on the coffee table along with a bottle of vodka. Tina took a seat on the couch. The music still thumped upstairs.

"I'll be right back," Kaylyn said.

Tina was left to think about how gross she felt. Like she needed to poop. Kaylyn was gone for a long time. Eventually, she heard the rowdy sounds of 56 and his friends descending the stairs. It was an odd crowd. Fifty-six in front, followed by Ostrowski with a bit of vomit still staining the collar of his shirt, then Brent Brandon clutching the bannister because he was clearly wasted and having trouble staying upright, then Jake Levy, Curt Moretti, and Stacey's older brother Matt. She felt extremely awkward when Matt's gaze fell over her since she knew him from eating breakfast in his kitchen, from spying on him and his friends with Stacey in order to gain access to their older-boy secrets. Matt, Brent, and Curt were arguing about something very loudly, but she only really saw 56, so she smiled. He gave her the same expression right back. She felt dizzy—not like she was dizzy, but like she was *watching herself* feel dizzy.

"Where you been, babe?" he asked.

She nodded to Kaylyn, now descending the stairs, brushing a strand of hair from her face. Her pink fingernails were curled around something, a box.

Fifty-six collapsed onto the couch next to her, his eyes a bit bleary but still handsome. "We had to go outside. The smell was just—" He fake-gagged.

Brent Brandon stumbled onto the carpet, sat cross-legged. "You guys said I was second. I *got you it*, so you said I was second."

Ostrowski punched him in the shoulder and told him to shut up. Kaylyn continued down the stairs, and as Tina watched her descend, she could see her feet making ripples in the carpet and the surrounding air, as if she was tapping water with her toes. It wasn't a box she held—it was a camcorder. Fifty-six asked if she wanted another drink, but his voice sounded like it came from another room. The ripples glided out in concentric circles from Kaylyn's slender feet. They made the air shimmer in tones of violet and a deep midnight blue.

That was the last thing she remembered of the night.

She woke naked on the couch hurting in ways she'd never experienced and would never forget. Her head ached, but her privates screamed. It felt like someone had jammed something barbed and rusty far up inside her. There was a sheet under her and the stains were rust-colored clouds. She couldn't breathe through her mouth, and it took her a moment of confusion to realize something was clamping her lips and face together. Stretching the skin painfully, she peeled away a piece of shiny gray duct tape. Dumbly let it drop to the floor. She looked around at the mess of beer cans and clothes. Slowly, she fished through the mayhem and found her underwear. The ache ran all the way into her stomach, sharp, stabbing. Gingerly, she pulled on the purple pair, a favorite, and went about getting dressed. She searched the house and found 56 sleeping in the guest bedroom. Ostrowski snored on the floor with one of the couch cushions tucked under his head. He wore only boxers and the shirt with the stains still on it. No Jake, no Curtis, no Matt, no Kaylyn. When she woke 56, he blinked as if he didn't recognize her. Without saying anything, he dressed, and she followed him upstairs, past the massive puddle of reeking puke that coated the kitchen linoleum. It wasn't until she saw this that she began quietly weeping.

They drove, and she tried to suck back her tears. It wasn't that she was confused about what had happened. She hurt so badly that there was no question. Yet it all seemed so bizarre, she couldn't quite make sense of it.

"Was it just you?" she asked. A stupid question, and he looked at her like it was stupid.

"You wanted it from everyone in the room, babe. You kept asking for it." Splotchy red patches broke out on his neck—the same hot flush she'd seen in Friendly's on their first date.

She wanted to explain that she didn't remember anything beyond that drink, but she knew that was stupid too.

"I think I need to go to a doctor," she said. "I'm bleeding."

He looked over at her, then back at the road. "Sorry if things got wild. We'll just sometimes do stuff like that. Share stuff like brothers, you know? Don't make more a deal of it than it really is. You kept saying you were into it . . ."

She wanted him to stop stammering his explanation. She could still feel the gluey gunk the tape had left on her face.

When he dropped her off, she went to the bathroom and put a towel between her legs and knelt over the toilet until she threw up. Then she shredded the note she'd written and left it in the trash. For a day and night she pretended she had homework, locked herself in her room, and agonized about whether or not she needed to go to the hospital. But the bleeding stopped, if not the crush of the pain. For the next week, she thought about telling her mom what had happened. Maybe she would know what to do. But the more she thought about it, the worse an idea it seemed. After all, what had happened? Those guys would say she'd wanted to do all that, and she wouldn't have any proof she'd tried to stop them. Then everyone at school, at church, and in the town would think she was a liar, a slut, both. Maybe some people would believe her, but mostly they wouldn't. Mostly they'd think she was trying to get attention for herself. The more she thought about saying something the more awful the consequences manifested in her imagination. As the heat of the pain dulled, the idea of telling did as well.

At school, she'd pass some of the guys who'd been there that night and avoid their gazes, although she could sense them whispering about her. Fifty-six carried on like nothing out of the ordinary had gone on. He came up behind her and patted her butt. He put his arm around her in the hallway. He talked about recruiting letters. That week, Kaylyn stopped beside her locker.

"How was that party?"

Tina honestly couldn't tell what lay in the older girl's smile. Was she making fun of her? She wanted to run away. Instead, she said, "Fine. Had a great time."

Kaylyn gathered her eyebrows in delight. She put her lips next to her ear. "Don't worry, honey, I got it on tape. I'll make sure your initiation stays in the right hands." She winked and walked away.

A week after the incident, 56 drove her out to a secluded spot of woods off Stillwater Road. As he eased closer to her and his breath covered her neck and face, she began to cry. He pulled back and asked her what was wrong, not concerned so much as annoyed.

"I just don't want to black out like that again. And not remember what happened. I didn't want my first time to be like that."

She was about to tell him what Kaylyn had said to her when it got scary. Whereas he'd seemed embarrassed the morning after Ostrowski's, a fury descended over him now, so quickly that she didn't have time to so much as stutter an objection. "You wanted it," he hissed, then began snatching her clothes off. His hands were enormous construction cranes picking apart her outfit. She made the most half-hearted effort to slow him down, but he took her wrists aside with one crushing vise of a hand and pushed her face against the window until she stopped fighting him. Years later, after she'd been with a few other men, she'd understand how truly *large* 56 was. So soon after the previous weekend—and her first time conscious—it felt like she was being split in half. Each time she cried out, it seemed to spur more vicious actions from him, and when she flailed an arm behind her and tried to tell him to stop, he grabbed a fistful of her hair and smacked her face into the door. The rest of it passed with her drifting into a dream, one that felt more real than what was actually happening.

When he was done, he slumped back to the driver's side and pointed to himself, thick, pink, and uncircumcised. This was the first time she'd ever seen a man in this frankly sexual way. He was covered in her blood.

"Jesus Christ," he muttered, trying to wipe it off with the rim of his underwear.

She needed to throw up, and it took everything in her to swallow the urge.

As he finished buckling he glanced at her, and now he looked as sick as she felt. "I'm sorry." His voice retreated, and he had to look away. "I'm just crazy about you." He started the truck. "It'll get easier."

She wanted to be furious at him—or at least she considered that as a reaction. Yet he rubbed the back of her neck on the way back to town. One hand on the steering wheel, the other massaged her shoulder, tickled the down at the nape, and climbed to scratch at her scalp. The clouds had a wonderful blue glow in the early evening sky. The way the sun colored their borders. This wasn't a cruelty in him, she decided. He was just hotheaded, full of power and desire. He didn't understand how harsh he could be. She just had to make him understand he had to be more gentle.

Even if he was the love of her life, this incident terrified her. She never wanted to feel that kind of helplessness again. He was perfectly reasonable, she learned, if she just went to Ostrowski's and went along with everything. He liked watching his friends with her, and her compliance with the team made him gentler, tamed him. Mostly they were like any high school couple: they parked at the Brew or out in the woods off Stillwater or waited for his mom to be out of the house. But once or twice a month, they'd go to

Ostrowski's, that dim basement, and he and his friends would take turns with her. She forgot about Kaylyn's taunt, bordering on a veiled threat—she did what she did because that's what *he* wanted. They told her what to do, and she did it. They had her do things she never would have imagined herself capable of. They put on movies and re-created the scenes with her. They moved her around like a doll. She didn't pretend to understand how he could like watching her this way. Moretti's rat face perched over her, his hand pinching her breast. Ostrowski's fat heaving against her. Levy biting his lip in a snarl. Matt Moore pulling her hair like he hadn't known her since she was six when they played the Bible character game in Youth Group. How could 56 like this? Then they'd whisper gross, cruel things to her at school. Moretti showed her a banana from his lunch, and with Hailey less than five feet away: "Think I could get this all the way in you?"

The one time she managed the courage to tell 56 she didn't want to do this anymore, didn't want to be a toy for the team, he got frighteningly angry with her—what she'd seen that time in his truck. "You think that's about them? Don't be a fucking retard, Tina. That's for me. You think when I get to the NFL there ain't gonna be fifty fucking girls hotter than you lined up to do whatever turns me on? I want that girl to be you but don't think that it's gotta be." These words were barked with such fury, she'd have agreed to anything to calm him. "Those guys are like my brothers," he went on. "We share everything." But this refrain wasn't quite true. A few times other guys from the team came over, and 56 instructed her to suck them off. A freshman named Chase Gobbert had been invited because he'd once recovered a key fumble. She heard Ostrowski say as much to him ("We got a reward for you, rookie"). Gobbert had grabbed her head in such a way that she'd gagged. When she caught her breath they were all laughing, and she'd laughed along. She'd learned to construct all this as normality. Years would pass before she understood it was not. She was in love. And love made you do things you'd never expect, things so far beyond yourself or who you thought you were that you don't even recognize the person who does them. Love was what God gave you to make you both unbearably strong and intolerably weak. Love was the ghost of yourself, a mirror image you saw in a crowd—different life, different ideals, different map of the world—but somehow still you.

She opened the trunk. In the bag was a roll of duct tape. She went around the side of the car, listening to the crickets, and opened the passenger door. Fifty-six sat with his head slumped forward, chin resting on his chest. Carefully, she took his body in her hands and eased him forward until his forehead rested on the dash. A bit of crystal drool escaped his lips and oozed to the floor. She had to work quickly. She'd given him a much lower dose than Cole because she wanted him to come to. She slipped the Buckeyes hat off and dropped it to the center console. Taking his right wrist, she wound the tape around twice, then passed it along his gut and wound it around his other wrist. Then around his back. The tape screeched horribly each time she played out more of it. Fifty-six made a soft sound in the back of his throat, and her heart beat faster. If he woke up now—the tape just looked so flimsy, so ineffectual compared to his size. She wound it around his torso and chest again and again, climbing up his arms until she'd taped all the way to his shoulders.

He stirred and the duct tape crinkled. She tore off the tape, rolled out more, and began winding it around his ankles. She coated his boots with it and then coiled it around his shins all the way to his knees. Satisfied, she stepped back. He looked like a gray mummy.

With 56 secured to the point of immobility, she tore free a strip the length of a pencil, tilted his head back and placed it gently across his lips. She patted it firmly into place.

*   *   *

Roughly a year before this night, Cole had taken her out to one of the access roads near the cornfields where the first wave of wind turbines had gone up. This was when they still seemed positively alien, swooshing in the dark, those distant lights at the towers' tops blinking simultaneously. They'd sat on the hood of his car and watched them wink.

"These things are crazy. Just really nuts," she'd said. She could tell he was nervous, trying to cut through his own anxiety and instead sitting without saying anything.

Maybe she knew what he was about to do. She couldn't remember except that eventually she'd asked, "What's on your mind?"

He launched into it then. A speech he must have rehearsed for weeks, maybe months. "I know you can do better than me probably, Tina. I know you got guys coming at you from all sides, but sometimes I think you let them use you. You know, take what they want from you and don't really respect you or nothing."

"Maybe that's my choice," she snapped. More harshly than she'd intended. You could recognize something was true, see it in a man like Travis of the electronics department, and still do nothing about it.

"No, I know. Alls I'm saying is that I'm not that guy. I'll never be the most impressive guy you could be with. I got a job I'm really good at, though, and I think you're amazing. It's not just that I want to take care of you, but—I don't know—I think you can take care of me too. Sometimes I'm just like—it's a feeling like it's the last day of school before Christmas but you gotta get done with a math test first. That feeling. Like you're going to burst and you can't believe you have to sit there and do it. Only it's like that all the time with me. The only time it's not is when I'm with you."

Then he was holding a ring in front of her. It was thin with a small diamond at the top. "This was my mom's before she died." He didn't look at her but instead considered the ring pinched between his fingers. The turbines caught the cool wind and the blades whipped on, backlit by the stars.

He sat watching her.

Before she discovered she'd say yes, she first thought of 56, and a plan—a daydream, really—that had grown to occupy so many of her idle moments. She thought of what she'd have to do if she ever wanted to close that chapter of her life, which would forever threaten everything Cole promised, which kept her sad and hurt and fearful, which kept her going back to the Travises, which kept her perpetually haunted by a life she never got to have and that, the deepest part of her knew, was nothing more than a drowning fantasy in the first place.

Fifty-six moaned sleepily and his eyes fluttered. He had to breathe through his nose and the change led him to stir. Now came the hard part. From the trunk she retrieved the Terrain Deer Drag Sled ($39.97 at Walmart) and placed it on the ground by the door. She lifted his legs out of the car, which were heavy enough. She had to throw her whole back into grabbing his torso, and even then he felt impossibly dense. A hunk of granite she was trying to heave bodily. Straining, she managed to more or less topple him out of the car and onto the sled. His shoulder landed first, but his head thumped against the plastic and this briefly roused him. His eyes fluttered open and she heard the sticky crinkle of the tape as he explored its confinement. Facing away, she wrapped both arms around his legs, used her hip as added leverage, and heaved the rest of him onto the sled. She took the rope around her chest and began dragging him across the field. Once she'd pulled him away from the car, she had to stop and rest. She looked around. Other than the crickets, the meadow was empty. She went back to the trunk, grabbed a plastic Walmart bag and another item: ammonia inhalants.

She'd found out about them when she googled *smelling salts* on her parents' computer. They were for "arousing consciousness."

She tucked the bag into the back pocket of her jeans and walked back to 56. He lay on the sled, struggling against the tape and the G, his eyes twitching. She stripped one of the salts from the package, knelt down, and held it to his nose. He muttered his head away but didn't come to.

It took her three more salts before his nostrils flared, and he was able to overcome the drug. His head whipped back, his eyes popped open, and he surged against his bonds.

"Shhh," she said, putting a hand on his face. She caressed the stubble on his cheek. "Hold on, babe. Hold on."

He shouted into the tape, muffled barks at her, and she remembered the power of his voice when he called for a last-second shift in the defense. "Just hold on a minute, babe. I just need to . . . I just need to talk to you for a second."

He kept screaming through his gag, eyebrows writhing in fury. He bucked against the tape. She shushed him again and stroked his chest.

"Just listen for a second." Finally, he ceased, but he kept his head off the ground, glaring at her. Breath pulsed furiously from his nostrils. "Just listen."

She kept stroking his chest and the gut he'd grown since high school.

"I want you to know . . ." She stopped and thought about how to restart. All that time in the car. All that planning and she still had no idea how to describe what she felt. "This was the only way to see you. To get you to listen to me. I knew if I just called you or showed up at your door, you'd think I was insane and still in love with you and . . . Okay, I mean I am still in love with you. You know? But

I knew I'd never get you to listen unless I did something drastic, okay? Don't be scared." Her fingers crept under the rim of his jeans where she hadn't constricted him with the tape. She felt the patch of his pubic hair. Felt him stir. The fury in his face twitched in the oddest way. This wasn't at all what she'd thought she'd say. Even after all this time, all the perspective she thought she'd gained, a ghost remained inside of her. "It was just you never let me talk to you after you ended it. You never really explained, and I never believed your reason. But that's not why I'm here. I'm here because I want you to know . . ." She undid his belt buckle, undid the button on his jeans, unzipped the fly. "I loved you, Todd. I loved you so, so much." Despite his situation, he helped her lower his pants by tilting his hips off the ground. His eyes went from pure fury to that pure longing. She'd seen it so many times before. In the cab of his truck. In Ostrowski's basement while his best friends had her two at a time. He was hard instantly. With experience in the years since high school, she knew how enormous, how aberrant he was. She spit into her hand and began working it. The way he'd taught her. "If you had just explained to me what happened, maybe I could have done something to fix it. And then maybe everything would have been different, you know? Maybe you would've had me to care about you, so you wouldn't have gotten into all that stuff you did at OSU and Mount Union. You would've stayed away from drinking and the pills and whatever else. You would've played like you should have played and you would've gotten drafted." Tears came to her eyes, but she'd expected that. "And we could have had everything. Our kids would've grown up without worrying about anything. I could have had kids in the first place. You know I can't? I can't get pregnant anymore. My uterus is damaged. But I don't think it would've been, you know? If you'd just stayed with me. Everything would've worked out differently." His eyes closed and his head tilted back on the ground. He heaved breaths through his nose. She worked her hand up and down faster. She lowered her face and met him with her mouth for a moment or two, just to keep it wet. "I'm getting married now, though. His name is Cole."

Fifty-six did not appear to hear this. She put him back in her mouth, savored him. A moment later, he came, an impossible amount of that salty male fluid erupting over her tongue and spilling onto her hand, arching into the air as she pulled her head away. His spine curved toward the stars, and he made a pleasured sound beneath the tape. That sensation of trying to gulp, choke, and spit all at once reminded her of her first time doing this while the others looked on, hip-hop pulsing in the background. Slowly 56 came to rest on the sled. She wiped her hand on his jeans, crawled on top of him so that she straddled him. His chest was so broad her knees barely touched the ground on either side. She peeled the tape back from his mouth.

"You," he said, breathing heavily. "You are the craziest fucking bitch I've ever met in my life." He rolled his eyes. "Christ . . ."

She stared at him, tears beginning to cloud her eyes. Twelve years waiting for this moment. "You shouldn't have done that to me. You shouldn't have left me like that."

She slapped the tape back on his mouth and pulled the Walmart bag from her back pocket. She slipped it over his head just as his eyes went wide. She wrapped the bag tight around his face, knotting a ball of plastic at the base of his chin to cut off any air. She grabbed his nose with the other hand and pinched.

He thrashed, and all his strength, all his power, was immediate and visceral beneath her. He bucked and twisted, screamed into the tape, the sound baking in his throat. His head whipped back and forth and she lost her grip on his nose, tried to recapture it, but he fought her hand, ducking and dodging his head. She pulled the bag down harder and could see the place where his nostrils sucked the plastic against those two small dark holes then released it. Sucked

it back, released it. He heaved, and she almost fell off. He tried
to scissor his arms and legs while the tape screeched and cracked.
She grabbed his head with both hands to try to keep the bag in
place, and just when she thought he would give up, he jerked his
entire body to the left and sent her sprawling into the grass. The
bag opened around his neck, and he could get air again. His breath
heaving. She'd banged her left wrist against the ground when she
fell off him and could feel the sprain creep up into her arm and
fingers. She couldn't believe it: He had managed to work a good
deal of the tape up his arms. He'd stretched it away from his body,
so his forearms now had room to work, the duct tape having rolled
into sticky threads. Even more unbelievably, he'd managed to get a
foot out of his boot, and now the foot was caught in the bottom of
his jeans but close to being free. Because his jeans and underwear
were down around his thighs, he didn't have far to go before he'd
be able to pull it out and stand. All that strength and something
else—some kind of fury deep inside him, a fury he'd used to knock
that Marysville quarterback's brain against the inside of his skull,
a fury he'd used to pin her face to the window of his truck only a
few miles from here—made her understand how quickly he could
get free.

With his grunts and the squeak of protesting tape behind her,
she sprinted to the car. In the trunk, she slapped aside blue plastic
bags, scrambling, but there was nothing useful. Her panic surged
when she heard his voice behind her.

"Help! Helllllllp!"

He had managed to work the tape off with his tongue. She
thought of the shovel in the woods but it was so far, and she'd have
to leave him alone for so long.

Then she remembered the tire iron.

She pulled it from the compartment beneath the floor of the
trunk. A perfect cross of sturdy metal. She jogged back to 56, who'd

rolled onto his back and nearly had his right leg free. He bucked and thrashed his legs to pull it from the last stretch of pant leg.

"I'm gonna fucking kill you," he screamed. *"I'm going to fucking snap your neck you fucking whore . . ."*

And as he carried on in that manner she hit him on the head with the tire iron. The blow was too light, though, and he just grunted in pain and then screamed louder. She knelt on the ground and hit him again. He moaned, a high-pitched peal like a pig led to slaughter. His struggling slowed. So she hit him again, and the Walmart bag tore and collected a mist of blood on the inside. She'd found the side of his skull, the ear and temple. She hammered at it three more times, huffing with each blow. Finally, she heard a crack and felt the hardness of the bone go soft with a sound like a plate dropped on the kitchen floor. Then 56 was still. Motionless, pants now around his ankles, the semen on his belly glowed in the starlight.

She sat back in the grass, gasping, trying to think about how this changed her plan.

She examined the tire iron. Because he'd still had the bag on his head, there was no blood on it that she could see. She took it to the car and put it back in the trunk. What did she have to worry about? Blood. She had to move him before he bled too much.

She positioned the heavy-duty rope diagonally across her chest like she'd seen her father do when he dragged game. She'd chosen a precise spot where a natural slope allowed gravity to make an otherwise backbreaking task easier. Still, the rope bit into her clavicle as she began hauling him toward the woods. Near the end of the clearing she saw the branch she'd leaned against the tree to mark her way. From there it was only about five minutes to the depths of the woods, though several times she thought she lost the path. She followed the soft sounds of the Cattawa River. All this planning, and it hadn't occurred to her to bring a flashlight.

A gray tarp near a pile of dirt stretched over the earth, weighted down with six large rocks. Two cans of gasoline sat nearby, a twenty-dollar bill and a note *(Just paying you back for the gas and food. Thnx)* poked out from between them. Her plan, when she'd dug the hole four days ago on her day off, was that if anyone wandered by, they'd think her little setup had something to do with camping. That person would take the twenty and she'd know her site had been compromised. As it stood now, no one had stumbled upon the scene, and the hole that took her an hour to dig, until her back and arms throbbed and she'd had to take one of her dad's old Vicodins to dispatch the pain, was still her secret. She dropped 56 by the tarp, tossed the rocks off, and pulled it back. The cavity in the ground, maybe four feet deep, was noticeably darker than the woods around it. She peered in and could see some water had collected at the bottom but just a puddle. It had been a dry summer. She dragged 56 to the edge, and when she went to push him in, she heard his breath. It came in a ragged hiss that whistled against the bag tucked over his face. She peeled back the slippery blue hood to peek. One eye was blacked out, the nose ruined, and the hissing sound was his breath going through a gap where she'd knocked out several teeth.

She lowered her shoulder into him, and shoved him over the edge. He landed with a wet thud and an *oomph*. Another slow moan. Then he began to say her name.

"Tina." It sounded surprisingly coherent despite the G and the work of the tire iron. "Tina, stop this. Go get help."

She could hear the place where his teeth were missing.

She did not feel like climbing down into the hole with the tire iron. The plan had gone mostly right so far. No point in deviating now.

"Please get help . . . Tina."

As he called her name again, she pocketed the twenty and tossed the note on top of him. She unscrewed the first gas can.

When the cold fuel splashed against him and the air filled with that pungent gasoline scent, as distinct as coffee or barbecue only dangerous, he started crying. She hadn't planned on him being alive for this. He was supposed to pass quietly with the bag over his head. "I'm sorry," she told him. "This will only hurt for a second."

He was crying and apologizing and begging and finally, she knew, lying. Pleading, *"I'm gonna be a dad a dad a dad . . ."* over and over. She'd been watching him on her days off for nearly a year. It seemed like his only haunts were bars and his trailer. His only companions Ostrowski and the gray-haired mutt that lived with him.

She spilled half the contents of one can, and he finally managed to kick a leg free. Naked from the waist down, he was trying to get his legs under him. To stand up. So tenacious. She felt for the matches in her jeans pocket, tore one free, and said a prayer. She'd wondered endlessly if when this moment came she would flinch, but she felt no wobble in her heart. She'd already made this right with God, but she would keep making it right for the rest of her days on this earth. He was screaming for help and had finally shimmied to a sitting position when she lit the book and tossed it at him. It landed in his lap and the flames wrapped around him like armor, encased him, a blue-orange knight. He screamed and fell onto his back. The night went bright and the tops of the trees glowed yellow from the power of the blaze. His cries made her understand she'd never actually heard a person scream before. Not like that. Not even close to the scream that had brought her mom running when she cut too deep. Not with madness and pleading and desperate hope that you're about to wake up from a nightmare. His screams grew louder for a moment and then faded to a choking sound as his esophagus or voice box melted. The last thing she saw was his skin blistering, huge boils forming on his arms and thighs, fat bubbling from the tissue like bacon grease sizzling in a pan, the fabric of his shirt and the duct tape melting quickly away. He pulled his skin off in slithering, sizzling strips. The blue Walmart bag fried to his face. She kicked the sled in after him. Then she turned, walked a ways to the edge of the woods where the air was cool and clean. Though she could no longer see him, the glow beamed out of the pit. The river murmured, and the flames threw mischievous, dancing shadows across the surrounding woods. Like a gash in the earth had opened to reveal a bit of hell.

She went back with the gas can and emptied it onto him. He didn't protest. It was strange looking at him now, once a human being she'd known and cared for and now just a log of char. The flames once again went white-hot, the sled burned purple as it melted to him; the heat steamed her face, and sweat beaded across her brow and in her armpits. She couldn't smell him cooking, only the gasoline. She stepped back into the cool of the woods again. She waited until the flames had died down some, and then began emptying the second gas can into the pit, stepping back each time the flames grew too hot. Like she'd hoped, there wasn't much left of 56 by the time she'd emptied both cans. The love of her life was nothing but blackened, smoking shards of bone. She took the heavy rocks she'd used to weigh down the tarp and spent a few minutes hurling them at the skull. Squatting in front of the pit with that acrid scent now more barbecue, she turned the last recognizable feature of his skeleton to smoking scraps. They looked like broken bits of ancient pottery. She saw the chain necklace, filthy and blackened, but there were no longer dog tags looped to the chain. It was a locket, like a grandmother would wear. She fished it out with a stick and pocketed it. Then she covered what remained with the tarp, took the shovel from its perch in the dirt, and began filling in the hole.

"Why're you always reading that gruesome stuff?" Cole had asked her once. She was at lunch in the break room, riveted by a book about JonBenét Ramsey. She'd spent all morning stocking in the grocery section, pulling around cases of apple juice and baby food and frozen dinners on the pallet jack, and she wanted to be left alone for just a minute. She kept her answer short.

"It's interesting."

"Doesn't seem interesting. Seems weird."

"You like horror movies. This stuff's like real-life horror."

Maybe she was thinking about her plan even back then when Cole first began to pursue her, before she'd even had an inkling about what she would do. The example of poor JonBenét served her well, though, when her mind got wandering about how she might do this. Misdirection. Disappearance. Time.

Buried beneath four feet of earth, covered in branches and a young fallen tree toppled prematurely by a storm that she dragged across the disturbed soil, 56 would almost certainly not be discovered. At least not for a good long while. If he were found in a few years, forensic experts—the CSI guys—would have only bone fragments to go on. Dental records would be tough with the skull and jaw in pieces. Wallet and clothes and identifying marks would all be burned up. Perhaps they'd use DNA to identify the victim, but then they'd have to ask what happened to him. Who was he last with? Who did he know? Who'd have reason to hurt him? So few of those questions would have even a remote chance of directing attention to her. His car would be sitting in the parking space across from the Lincoln Lounge with a flat tire. In a few days it would be towed. After three or four days of not showing up for work and not answering his phone, his employer (or maybe Ryan Ostrowski) would call his mother. A missing persons report would be filed. Yet there were plenty of reasons a guy like 56 might want to flee town. Everyone was fleeing everywhere these days. At Walmart, temp associates up and left because a child payment came due or a warrant went out for violating a parole offense or someone had a court date they didn't want to show up to or just plain old debt they could never pay. Without a body, that would be the first assumption. Later, they would first and foremost suspect men. As long as Cole was fast asleep back home, no one would have reason to suspect she'd been anywhere but her own bed on this particular night (and there was no reason he wouldn't be: for four months she'd practiced finding the dosage that would put him under for the night, tapping it into his dinner Mountain Dew). She'd show up for work a bit tired tomorrow but would power through with a Red Bull just fine.

Even if a pair of eyes had spotted 56 climbing into the blue Cobalt, that was okay. She and Cole had already spoken about getting a new used car. She'd suggest they finally pull the trigger this week. There was certainly video footage of her pulling into the gas station on Route 30, but by the time they found him (if anyone found him) this footage and the Cobalt would be ancient history.

She'd shower before Cole woke. She'd get rid of the tire iron, the Buckeyes hat, the gas cans, the little whiskey bottles, the duct tape, and the shovel in the next few weeks. Find them new homes, toss them in dumpsters, or abandon them in places no one would ever look. What was left? Without investigators stumbling upon a huge stroke of luck that tied her to 56 on this night, would she even make the top twenty in a list of suspects? The top fifty?

She suspected not. She also suspected that when 56 turned up missing, New Canaan's police department would assume that he'd either run somewhere or—if he was the victim of a violent crime—it was somehow related to the distribution of methamphetamines, prescription pills, and heroin in the county. He'd said so himself how he was still friends with characters like the Flood brothers. She wasn't worried. She'd have many secrets to keep, but she was an expert at living with secrets. She planned on returning home, living her life with Cole, riding her new bike to work, adopting two children, a boy and a girl, and never hearing about 56 again. She'd sleep happily in her bed, and he in his. Because what she'd finally decided was that Love sometimes called upon people to do drastic things in order to secure it. God would take 56 into His arms and allow him all the happiness that had eluded him, that had made him cruel in life.

And yet, her face grew wet with tears as she remembered him in his backyard cutting burrs out of Symphony's hair.

She turned onto the dirt road that led back to Stillwater. As she approached the pavement that would take her back to Route 30, which would take her home, a lightness bloomed from within. She'd done it. Not perfectly, but as her mother said, *Nothing in life goes perfectly. That's why it's life and not heaven.*

Crawling back up the dirt road, past the fields of summer grass, she kept the headlights off and drove by the light of the moon. She saw movement ahead as a critter, a small blob of dark on dark, jetted across the road on its way to survive somewhere. She imagined the stress of that creature. Constantly in danger of a savage death by beak, talon, or jaw, its enemies were everywhere. Being ripped apart and devoured was nothing but a constant background terror. A possibility every single day of its short existence. Its life would likely end, and it would be nothing more than a carcass to be picked over by lesser predators.

She brought the car to the gate, which she'd closed after going through—just in case anyone drove by at this late hour and wondered why it was open. She knew from experience that if you drove the same country road enough you got to know it intimately: the curves of the asphalt, the seasonal decorations of the houses, the trees with branches that groped too far into your path, the fences, the signposts, all markers of distance from home. All it would take was one late-night driver to recall that this gate, normally closed, had been open.

She flicked on her lights, left the car running, hopped out, and pushed the gate wide.

This was about disappearing. People, she'd come to understand, disappeared all the time. The world simply opened its jaws and swallowed them whole. They vanished, and unless they were rich or famous or particularly beautiful, they did so almost without comment. There was bitterness at murder, grief at accidents, and fury at suicide. But to disappear—well, there was only mystery. And mystery was all three of those things bundled together and made more frightening by the impossibility of it. There were Facebook and iPhones now. People weren't supposed to disappear anymore, and that made it all the more unnerving. At least to those who would wonder about a former football star, who went out for a drink, got a flat tire, and never made it home.

She climbed back into the Cobalt and drove to the other side of the fence. She parked it at the side of the road while she closed the gate. This time, mindless habit led her to shut off the engine, not giving it a second thought. She took the bolt, dangling from its chain, and fixed it back into the hasp. She glanced briefly at the sky, at a flash of very distant lightning. When she slid back into the car, her hand automatically turned the key. In the same moment that the starter did its little choked wheeze, she wondered why on earth she hadn't just left the car idling.

Her stomach turned liquid. Sweat broke out as if once again she faced the heat of her fire pit. She tried it again. She tried it a third time. The engine had started just fine in the clearing. She'd thought of everything except for Cole's failing car. She tried it a fifth time. A tenth. The wheeze was down to a rattle.

She couldn't panic. If she panicked she might do something stupid. She was so close. She got out of the car, though she was not sure why. She popped the hood, but even after all this time with Cole, she knew nothing about cars other than how to drive one.

"Okay," she said. "Okay. Please."

The car probably just needed a jump. But she'd left her phone plugged in on her nightstand in Van Wert. She could walk to a nearby house, claim she was on her way back from a party and the engine had quit. But then there would be a record to follow. Witnesses. Proof she'd been in New Canaan tonight. She'd have to pay with a credit card, and Cole would see the charge.

So instead she just stood there, staring at the shadows of the engine, indecisive, panic swelling. She ripped hair from the spot on the back of her head and felt how wide the bald patch had grown.

She lost track of how long she stood there screaming inside her skull.

When the sound of a car and the glow of headlights both crept into the distance, she wanted to weep. Because this was both what she needed and what scared her the most. The car came from the east, from the direction of town, heading toward the country. The tears came out of her unbidden, but she moved to the road anyway, waited for the headlights to find her, and waved both arms above her head.

The car, an old boxy Jeep, slowed, hesitated, and then pulled to the side, nose to nose with the Cobalt. A figure emerged, a young woman, her face hidden by the glare of the headlights.

"Howdy," said the woman.

She didn't respond. Tina didn't want the first word she spoke to be a sob. Now she was shaking.

"Hey," the woman said, coming around the side. "Holy shit. Tina?"

Of course it was someone who knew her.

"Tina? Hey— What? Are you all right?"

It was the woman in the summer dress she'd seen outside the Lincoln. Tina knew her. The face was eminently familiar in the way a face can be when you can still not summon the person's name. She'd been Tina's best childhood friend. Such was her disbelief, her terror, that this simple, memorable name would not come to her. She ripped at the hairs with two fingers. She had to pee. She had to scream.

She thought of Cole to center her. Finally, she was able to push words out.

"Hey," she said. "Hey. Wow. What are the odds."

Such a stupid way to begin, and she practically wept each word. She wiped her eyes.

"Jesus, are you all right?" She came over and put a hand on Tina's arm. Tina couldn't look her in the eyes.

"Yeah, no, I'm fine. I'm sorry." She waved a hand in the air spastically to clear it. "I just. My car died out here, and my phone's—" *Forgotten, your phone's forgotten.* "I forgot my phone. And I just. This is so far out, I was afraid I'd be out here all night."

The woman stared down at her. The familiar pixie face, cute, eerily similar to both her brothers'. She'd cut her hair into an odd, ugly, spiky mess. Memories of sneaking downstairs to the family snack drawer in search of Fruit Roll-Ups. Her name was right there in every sense but the sounds of the letters.

"It's okay, girl. We'll get this fixed."

"Yeah—no, I'm sorry. I'm really sorry. I was just— Before you came I was panicking. I don't know anything about cars."

"Okay." She nodded. "Can I try it?"

She walked around and got in the driver's seat, tried the key. Same result.

"Totally fine. It just needs a jump. I have cables in my car."

She walked to her trunk, feet crunching over the grit of the road.

"You know how to jump a car?" Tina asked.

"Are you kidding? Do you even remember my dad? He practically made me take classes on jumper cables and changing tires before he'd let me get my license. Also, haven't you ever seen *SVU*? There are pervs out there—you gotta know how to jump a car."

She hefted her jumper cables.

"I've been running into everyone tonight! I thought you and your folks moved away."

"We did." Tina struggled for an explanation. "I was back in town running some errands."

This sounded less than convincing, and it was impossible to tell how the woman took it. She popped the hood and came around, found the release, lifted.

"What are you up to now?" she asked.

"Not much. Nothing exciting. Live in Van Wert by the Indiana line. Work at Walmart."

She wondered if the woman would remember the exact spot she'd helped Tina. If she'd remember it was by this gate and the road leading into the woods. Suddenly, she was sure the light of the fire must have been visible to the woman as she came up the road, but this was ridiculous. That was over an hour ago, and from Stillwater it would have been nothing but a dim ember in the deep. Now the woman was staring at her car, though. Studying it.

"You were just driving and the car died?"

"Yeah, well, I stopped. Just to, you know. Get out and look at the stars. This used to be one of my favorite places to come and think."

Tina watched as she hooked the hungry jaws of the jumper cables up to her battery, then to Tina's. She added another black cable, and attached the open clamp to a piece of metal near the Cobalt's engine.

Only now did Tina smell herself and recall that she reeked of smoke. She'd seen the woman's nose wonder at the stench, and the power of the smell returned to her anew. *I built a fire in the woods. I took a walk and built a fire.* So ridiculous.

The woman walked back to her car and started the engine.

"We gotta let it run for a couple minutes."

Tina tried to imagine the forces that had brought the two of them here, what had bound them for each other on this same lonely stretch of Stillwater. God's plan, always unavailable. But here they were in the cosmic shimmering.

The woman applied the gas, revving the engine so it growled like a suspicious dog.

Tina's skin was clammy. Her shoulders and back throbbed from the pulling and the digging. The sprain in her wrist ached. She could feel the woman watching her through the windshield.

The woman came out. How ridiculous that she could not think of her name but could recall the dances and Vicky's and sleepovers and her face beside the orange lockers and in the stadium bleachers.

"Did you pick up Todd Beaufort earlier? Outside the Lincoln?"

"Todd?" She heard her voice squeal, the tinny sound murder on the bones inside her ears. "No. No, I haven't seen him in a while. A long time."

The woman only nodded.

"Okay, let's give it a try."

She slipped into the driver's seat of the Cobalt. The ignition turned over with a weak sputter on the first try.

"Ha ha! Success. I'm your hero, Ross."

Without warning, a sob escaped her throat. The woman looked up.

"I'm sorry," said Tina. "I'm so stupid—just. Thank you. I'm sorry."

She got out of the Cobalt, and before Tina could stop her, the woman wrapped her arms around her. She was warm and strong.

"It's okay, girl," she said. "You'll be on your way. No worries."

When she let go, Tina wiped her eyes and thanked her again, but her face fluttered with unease. She smelled like a house fire. If she didn't throw up, she'd pass out. The woman didn't stop staring at her.

"I'm fine," she mumbled. "I really need to go now."

The woman said nothing and went to remove the jumper cables.

Tina took the opportunity to amble back to her trunk. She found Cole's windbreaker stuffed into the clutter in the back. She folded it over the tire iron and walked back around to the front of the car.

The woman was saying, "Look, I don't know what's going on, but if you want I can give you a ride back into—" when Tina dropped the windbreaker and swung the tire iron at her face as hard as she could.

The name came to her as she caught her long-ago friend on the skull with a sharp crack. A spackle of blood jettied from her scalp, and she fell onto her butt on the asphalt. With the name came a memory: how this friend used to crack her up by flipping up her eyelids so they stuck, like her face had turned inside out. She was still sitting up, clutching her jumper cables, gazing up at Tina, more bewildered than anything: *Just, wait—why?* when Tina cocked both arms, fire searing through her chest muscles. Tina pictured her head coming apart. She would hit until some unseen bone in her face gave way and her eye popped out. She would hit until the tire iron and the ground and the woman's head of carefully combed blond was wet and black with blood. She would hit until she was sure this woman could never tell her story. She would hit until she could see Cole on the other side of this awful moment. She would hit while she wept, while she prayed, while realms of the watching dead pried her eyes open and made her see the endless answers to what her skull too would look like.

But Tina didn't swing. So instead, the woman got to her feet. She actually took a moment to wipe dirt from her behind. The wound on her head bled down the side of her face; Tina had more raked her across the scalp than anything else. Her arms were exhausted from swinging, from digging, and Stacey was a foot taller, an athlete, a tough girl. She took a step and easily ripped the tire iron from Tina's hand. She shoved her back against the car, pinning her arms.

"What the fuck is wrong with you?" Stacey hissed into her face. "What did you do that for?"

The panic, the sob, and the terror began all at once in her chest, and rose like a mushroom cloud up her throat. The sound she made was a child's wail.

"I'm sorry," she whispered. "I'm so sorry. I'm really so sorry."

"Why did you do that, Tina?" Stacey relaxed her grip. "What is going on with you?"

Tina flapped her hands the way she had when she panicked as a little girl. The reality of what she'd done returned to her, a snaking desolation. Seeing this person from her past, from a separate, untroubled life, broke her away from what she'd seen in the woods. She was Lot's wife peering over her shoulder. She saw the blisters forming on his skin. Another sob escaped.

"Todd was with you, wasn't he?"

Tina began to weep in full.

"I don't know," she gasped. "I don't know what I did what I did why I did."

"Tina, easy. Easy." Stacey took her chin. Blood continued to trickle down her blond. "What do you mean? What happened?" She hesitated. "Was Todd with you?"

"What I did," she repeated. Then wailed. "*Why I did what I did.*" She crumpled to the ground, knees tucked under her. The surface of the road felt gritty and cool.

"What did you do? What happened?"

"I don't know," she sobbed. Snot bubbled in her nose, and she moaned. "*I don't know I didn't know I didn't know.*"

Heaving in the dark, both cars' engines a steady drone, Tina began to scream. She screamed until the screaming turned back to weeping, the weeping to whimpering. She was barely aware of Stacey scrambling in the car for her phone.

She left herself behind then. The first police car came. They put her in handcuffs and had her sit in the back of the patrol car while Stacey explained what had happened and what Tina had said. She thought of Cole back home in their bed, dead to the world, unaware of what his fiancée had done for a least a little while longer. Her head hurt from crying. She couldn't wipe her nose or eyes, so the moisture just hung on her face. A female officer came into the car. She was old and wore her hair in a tight gray bun. She asked her who she'd been with that night, what had happened. Tina wasn't sure she heard these words leave her mouth, but later they would tell her it's what she said: "I left him in the woods."

An ambulance took Stacey away, and more police began to arrive. Ryan Ostrowski was one of the officers who came next. He looked at her first with curiosity, and then with great fear. He wouldn't go near her. She could hear the other officers asking him to go talk to her, but he refused. She could hear him saying it wasn't appropriate, that he knew her ("It's goddamn New Canaan, Strow, we all know someone!"). All the flashing lights were too much. They drove her brain crazy, and she closed her eyes.

When she opened them, Marty Brinklan was standing over her. He took off the handcuffs and sat with her in the back of another ambulance while a paramedic shone a light in her eyes. When the medic finished looking her over, Mr. Brinklan asked her if she was okay.

"My head hurts," she said. He still had a thick white mustache and kind, silent eyes. His face was ancient and weary. Gray tufts of hair protruded from the wide nostrils of his battered nose.

"Tina, you need to tell me what happened here."

She said nothing.

"I'm Marty. I know your folks from growing up. You knew my son."

She sat silently, not knowing what to say. In the distance, she could hear the rumble of thunder. She wanted only to pass into an entombed, dreamless sleep.

He said, "You know they called me out here, Tina, because you said you hurt somebody. We found a little bit of blood in your car. How did it get there?"

She watched the leaves of a nearby sycamore turning over, blown by a furious wind.

"Who was with you? Stacey said she saw you leave a bar with someone."

She said nothing. To even think his name spread inexhaustible dread through the veins of her arms.

"Where is this person? You said you left him in the woods? Is he hurt?"

She said nothing.

"Why were you out here?"

Stacey coming along when she did was her last necessary evidence for the presence of God in all things. He had seen Tina on this road tonight, and He had tested her, she was sure. She had failed the test.

"Tina, there's a storm on the way. If there's someone in the woods, and they're hurt, we need to find them. Right away. Now."

She looked over his shoulder and took in the view. This part of Stillwater rose along the crest of a hill before dropping back down into the woods. From this vantage point the lights of New Canaan glowed, the town nestled into a broad, shallow valley. The way the sky dropped down on the horizon made it feel like they were in one of those planetarium theaters. Not just stars overhead but almost a dome. From the west, the thunderclouds drifted steadily closer. She could see the glowing bursts of lightning in them. How unsettling it was that they all lived out their lives—every triumph and sorrow—confined to this same sliver of God's creation. That they pinballed around one another until someone was dead or born.

"I left him in the woods," she said. "We were in love."

The wind blew harder, a staggering blast of air raking across the fields, shrieking like the sharpening of knives and scattering hair into her face. With it came the smell of fire, the acrid scent of char and carbon that tingles the nose. A thunderstorm swept in. Lightning split the night, and the downpour roared, accompanied by the frequent mortar fire of thunder. Rain like shards of glass streaking out of the sky. They took her away. Not that it mattered. Never again would she sleep through a night and not feel the sunburn heat of the fire. A recurring dream, month after month, year after year, always the same raging fire blasting through the fields and towns and forests, searing the night, swallowing the known world, as she struggled for a cool breath at the edge of the woods. The storm descended over the blue-black nighttime hills, threading through her, savage and beautiful, settling in her heart, her home.

Coda

Lisa Han and the Void at Night's End

ON A BLUSTERY AUTUMN DAY WITH LEAVES SCRAPING ACROSS the parking lot of the Masjid Al-Amin Mosque in Columbus, just north of Ohio State University in the affluent suburb of Upper Arlington, two men sat parked in a 2003 Dodge RAM pickup. In the cab they had an AR-15 semiautomatic assault rifle, a TEC-9 semiautomatic pistol, and a cheap CZ-82 handgun as well as roughly two hundred rounds of ammunition between the three weapons. Their compatriot, who'd arrived in another vehicle and parked at a nearby strip mall, had entered the mosque early Friday morning before worshipers arrived. He carried in a backpack an explosive device built around a block of Semtex-10, which he placed in the women's bathroom. Though security cameras captured his image, this did not keep the device from detonating at ten to noon, just as the Friday prayer service was about to get underway.

The plan was for the explosion to send people running to the front exit where, as they spilled out, they would be caught in a pincer movement line of fire. In the minds of the perpetrators this would serve as a warning to the religious group they saw as most responsible for the troubles of their homeland. Like many young men convinced of their cause but with only vague notions of how the murder of innocent people will advance the interests of their tribe, they had no particular end game in mind, only to rack up as many kills as possible. In their fantasies, they saw it sparking the final crusade, the war for the heart of their nation, in which those with white skin would finally band together and push out all invading faiths and bloodlines.

Instead, when the man in the driver's seat saw the first people pour out, he found he couldn't leave the truck. He saw an old man, blood streaming down his head into a massive Rorschach inkblot on his cream shirt, carrying a young girl with most of her face gone. People and smoke followed behind him, including the girl's father, who was stripping off his shirt to tear into a tourniquet, his shaky hands struggling with tough Brooks Brothers fabric. The driver, Amos Flood, had the assault rifle on his lap, but he never even picked it up. He started blubbering, tears pouring down his fleshy pink face. The little girl just looked too much like a little girl. After a moment, his brother said, "Let's go," and Amos started the car and drove them back home to their farm in New Canaan, Ohio, a little over an hour north.

Three people were seriously injured in the blast and one killed. The injured included the old man, Ali Usman, who lost part of his left hand and received treatment for second-degree burns. He'd run into the fire to pull out the child. The girl, who'd been in the bathroom at the time eating a chocolate bar stolen from her mother's purse, died in the parking lot. Her name was Maisha Rizvi. She was ten years old and a star student in Mrs. Paul-Heen's fifth-grade class at Barrington Road Elementary School in Upper Arlington. Her father was the head of the multimedia department for the Triple-A minor league baseball team the Columbus Clippers. Because they had season tickets, Maisha was a die-hard Clippers fan, knew the names of every player and their stat lines as far into the weeds as on-base percentage. She developed fierce crushes, depending on who was playing well, and if those crushes moved up to the major leagues, she would follow their careers with fervent, desperate hope. A highlight of her short life came when her father arranged a pregame tour of the clubhouse where she met all the players and gathered each of their signatures on a baseball. Dante Orillio, a stout first baseman from the Bronx, carrying a not-unwarranted grudge that the Indians had sent him back down, took the ball from her, and noted the headscarf she'd taken to wearing (as if it could more quickly usher in puberty and therefore adulthood and therefore independence). As he signed his name, he said, "Assalamu alaikum, sister."

She could barely breathe back "Wa alaikum salaam," and after the game, she used an advance on her allowance, begged and pleaded from her father, to buy an Orillio poster, which she kissed on the mouth each night before she went to sleep. Her mother objected to the poster, and they fought bitterly over its appropriateness. This was seven weeks before she saw the chocolate in her mom's purse and—a streak of preteen rebelliousness already blooming—decided she'd rather eat it in the bathroom than sit through the first part of services.

The men who orchestrated the attack were quickly found. The security cameras caught the truck and its license plate, as well as an image of the man who'd left the bomb. It took police only fifteen hours to make an arrest, the FBI joining with local law enforcement to descend on a sad farm in Northeast Ohio to take into custody Amos Andrew Flood, Francis David Flood, and Kirk Radville Strothers. Upon returning home, the three men had had a heated argument about what went wrong, Kirk having successfully planted the bomb while his cousins "pussed out." Then they sat down to drink and smoke marijuana until the authorities arrived. They were so inebriated when they were taken into custody that the police had to put them in the drunk tank and wait to book them. All three would make plea deals to avoid the death penalty. Kirk was sentenced to life in prison, Francis and Amos to twenty years each. There was some outrage at the latter sentences and even more so at the popular narrative that accompanied the attack. The media tended to shy away from the word *terrorism* in this case, which many found indefensible. The incident certainly vanished from the national outlets quickly, buried under the news cycle's accelerated avalanche. Even the hometown paper *The Columbus*

Dispatch found that reporting on the subject had an adverse effect. Daily circulation and website traffic declined noticeably whenever they ran front-page news about the case, and editors learned to keep any updates relegated to the interior of the paper.

After the arrests, Martin Brinklan, chief investigator for the New Canaan Police Department, put in his retirement papers— three years later than he'd planned. He'd always been one to stay busy, to stay working long after everyone else had shut off their lights and returned home to their televisions, but there comes a point when a man can no longer spend all his waking hours look- ing at the stupid cruelty people regularly visit upon one another. In his consultations with the FBI, he'd grown frustrated by their disinterest in following all the tributaries of the case. For instance, how had the three men financed the operation? They had a small marijuana farm on their property, ran a little methamphetamine, and salvaged spare parts from old cars, but this was dumb chump change. He'd known about these boys when his son was in school, and they were always a few fries short of a Happy Meal. Certainly not criminal masterminds of any kind. He was convinced some- one had given them a good chunk of cash for this, but he could never prove it. Additionally, the brothers gave up their connection in Louisiana, an ex-navy guy who'd sold them the explosive, but that man claimed he'd never met Strothers or either of the Floods. He claimed he'd made a deal with a woman and made the ex- change with yet another party: an unidentified twentysomething white male. Prosecutors found the scope of this plot unrealistic. They thought the seller was trying to get himself a deal to reduce his time by implicating imaginary co-conspirators. Marty suspected other players. Individuals who had melted away.

He moved down to the Florida Panhandle to retire, and to be near his living son. His hometown, where he'd lived all sixty-seven years of his life, no longer felt like home. He planned to make yearly trips on Rick's birthday to visit his grave and to talk to him in the quiet of Dryland Creek Cemetery. On headphones, he'd listen to songs written by his son's friend. He would talk about the family, how he missed Rick's mother but not enough to call her, and he felt his son's prayers coming from somewhere—either heaven or the deepest parts of his memory, he was never so sure—while the hot, bright day passed into a sunset that hurt his eyes.

This stupid act of cruelty, as utterly pointless as the bullet that had taken Marty's youngest boy, set off a second, disparate chain of unwinding mystery. The way Ben Harrington once explained it in a crude early song was that love may be planned and violence may be aberrant, but both ripple outward all the same. The mostly failed massacre at Masjid Al-Amin, which garnered national attention for only a handful of days before other gruesome incidents, public political catfights, tech and finance saturnalia, and celebrity gossip swallowed it whole, set in motion a series of events that, four years later, would send a woman to Chicago in search of answers from a long-lost friend.

Like that bizarre night of the confluence, in the spring of 2017 an evening of unstable air and lift brought with it a mighty storm. When the rain began, the first stout drops hit the pavement similar to the way excess dew shakes free of a leaf, droplets too fat to come from the clouds. But then came the wind, tearing off Lake Michigan like the breath of God, scattering loose, abandoned sheets of newspaper down the streets, picking up trash and blasting it down city blocks, driving every pedestrian to seek shelter as the full-fledged midwestern thunderstorm barreled in: a hard, sluicing downpour the city was seeing more frequently in recent years, bursts of meteorological wrath more akin to fetal typhoons. You could only run for cover or face it like a bull rider, as a beast that flexed and bucked. The rain came sideways, from overhead, it even seemed to spring forth from the soaking macadam grid. It filled the river; it turned the surface of the lake into a foaming white-capped stew. The airports shut down, the wildlife hid, the gutters overflowed, and the streets filled with inches of dirty water. The gray-blue tint of dusk gave way to a deep midnight hue. The believers out there could squint and almost imagine this as the much talked about End of Days, the season of Noah's flood rather than the fire next time. Many of them secretly wished for it.

The downpour dragged on, and because it was a Sunday and past business hours, the unfortunate few caught in the deluge had little opportunity for shelter. When the storm exploded in the sky without warning, the woman made a futile gesture of putting her handbag over her head before scavenging an umbrella from a nearby Walgreens. Even with the umbrella, she ended up running, her flats slapping sharply over the roar of the rain. The bar tucked away downtown on the corner of Hubbard and Franklin was one of the few places open. She recognized the point of rendezvous from online images, all glass and warm light, an antique sign overhead advertising Phillies Cigars for five cents. She managed to get in the door before the downpour began in full fury.

The man was not so lucky. Dressed in a suit, making the walk from his hotel, the thunderstorm whipped up, and his umbrella was inside out and flaccid within minutes. He chucked it, ran the remaining two blocks, and was soaked through to his underwear. The light from the bar cut a slice of dark from the pavement, and it was this slice that led him, his shoes beating sprays of rain into his socks. He let out a sharp breath of relief even as his hand skidded off the slick brass door handle. Three heads turned as he tore inside—a couple, twiddling straws at the bar, and a bartender in dark clothes and a bleach-white apron. And then there was Stacey Moore, waiting for him in a booth, fourteen years after Bill Ashcraft had last seen her. She thought he looked remarkably similar, but not in a good way. He'd grown a thick black beard stitched through with premature gray, like someone had shoddily aged him via computer program and wrapped him in a lousy suit and tie. From Bill's perspective, she'd changed drastically from the girl he'd known, the one Ben Harrington had once described as "the hottest church-camp girl in the school." Now she had a messy boy's haircut, tattoos on her arms, on her fingers, and one peeking out from her clavicle, red and black threads that appeared to spool down her chest. She'd gained weight, and her eyes (like cirrus clouds, pale, gossamer blue) were now each surrounded by a haiku of wrinkles. He noticed a faint scar on the side of her skull, above the ear, a thin pink line where the hair no longer grew.

Despite the ugly, uncertain reasons for this reunion, Bill couldn't help but smile when he saw her, and she couldn't help but return it.

"You don't live here then?" she asked him.

"No, just passing through."

Bill wiped the rain from his eyes and checked on the rest of the bar. A couple waited out the storm with a couple of cocktails: a sleepy-eyed black man in a sports coat and a pretty Latina in a vintage red dress. The bar had the shape of an acute triangle, and the couple sat at its shortest side. The bartender brought Bill a clean bar towel from the pile by the maraschino cherries. He thanked him and began scrubbing the rain from his hair.

"Why Chicago?" she asked.

"Had some work here in the city anyway. Seemed convenient with you in St. Louis."

"What kind of work?"

"Politics."

"Like for a candidate? An issue?"

"Something a bit different."

He wouldn't say more, and this worried her. She had not found him via the standard routes, striking out with both Facebook and Google searches. He was a ghost online. She'd called his mother five months earlier, trying to track him down. Unenthused, even vacant, Joni Ashcraft simply said she had no idea where her son was. It didn't sound like she much cared either. Other avenues proved fruitless, and she thought she might give up. Then a month ago, she'd received an e-mail that looked like junk mail. Bizarrely, it requested that she create an anonymous, encrypted e-mail address. Thus began her correspondence with Bill. They finally agreed on a date, a time, and a bar in a specific city. She and Maddy had only recently moved to St. Louis, where Maddy had a job offer after sticking it out in Michigan for the duration of Stacey's doctoral work. She'd lied to Maddy about where she was going and who she was seeing this week.

"This is Fitz. He's two." She showed him her phone. A picture of her son with his bowl haircut, slim eyes, and gaping alligator-sized smile. Bill flipped through a few and handed it back.

"Fitz?"

"For Fitzwilliam. You know, Mr. Darcy?"

"Oof. That's gonna be miserable for him in about seven years."

"Half the reason we did it. If he decides he's gender fluid, he can switch to Darcy."

"Why'd you do it? Have a kid I mean. World's on its way out."

She gave him an unpleasant look and cupped her phone as if this could protect her son.

"My brother Patrick, he calls it 'God,' I call it 'energy'—but just learning to direct your heart somewhere where it can do some honest good, Bill."

He nodded, uninterested in hearing about Patrick: her years of tense phone calls and avoidance on holidays, her mother's tearful attempts to reconcile them, her father's cancer diagnosis, and her angry confrontation with Patrick in the hospital following their dad's surgery. How Patrick was still not all right with Maddy, and likely never would be, even though he'd promised to bury it. How she loved him all the same.

The bartender brought their drinks, a light beer for him and a vodka and soda water for her.

"What did you tell her? Your wife."

She crossed one panted leg over the other and played with her ring finger tattoo as though it were a real wedding band. The Latin: *manibus*. To grasp hands. "I told her I was going to see an old friend."

"So pretty much true."

"In Ohio."

He nodded carefully. "Thank you for agreeing to that."

"Can I ask then? Why we're meeting like spies."

He still had that calm, cold gaze beneath dangerous black eyebrows. There was less playfulness in his face now. The beard made him look like a killer. Finally, he said, "I was surprised by how good it was to hear from you. I haven't spoken to anyone from New Canaan in what feels like millennia." Not for a beat did he take his eyes off her. "Still. Maybe we start with why you're here."

Her eyes went sideways to the couple and the handsome silver-haired bartender. He smirked at something the couple said to him, grabbed a stack of dirty glasses, and disappeared into the back. It was a nice joint: polished oak walls with pictures of the city throughout its history. There were the stockyards at the turn of the century, State Street teeming with horses in the growth years after the Civil War, the first Model Ts rattling along streets still lit by gas lamp, speakeasies crowded with flirting men and women during Al Capone's reign. Lights with the dim authority of candles lined the walls, and the stools at the bar were bolted down with a nice metal bar on which to rest one's tired, soaking feet. She recognized the music playing softly in the background: Miles Davis, *Kind of Blue*.

He watched as she reached into her handbag and withdrew a battered spiral-bound notebook with a large coffee stain melting through the lower right-hand corner of every page. She opened it to a place marked with a paper clip. The edges of the paper curled from too much flipping. She set it on the wood, clasped her hands.

"I came all this way because you're one of the last people who might be able to help me." She took a breath. "A while back—years ago now—I decided to track down Lisa."

And she told him the story of what had happened between her and Lisa Han. They'd fallen in love, she claimed. Bill searched his memory of his high school girlfriend to decide if he'd seen this in her but came up empty. Then again, he had never anticipated she'd leave home the way she did. No one could know anyone that young.

"Bill, when was the last time you saw her?"

"I was in Cambodia actually. This must've been 2010 or so. I got in touch with her so we could meet up. Not for anything hanky-panky-like," he quickly added. "I just wanted to catch up. We couldn't make it work out, though."

"You talked to her while you were there?"

"Yeah."

"You sure?"

"Of course."

"I mean did you hear her voice?"

"No. We traded Facebook messages."

Stacey sat back, her eyes hot and knowing. "When I decided to try to find her again, it was the summer of 2013. We e-mailed back and forth for a few months, and then suddenly she stopped replying. All her social media accounts went idle. She hasn't used them since.

So almost a whole year goes by, and I go see her mother because she's the one who asked me to help find her in the first place. And she shows me the postcards Lisa's sent her over the years. And I'm looking at these postcards, and I don't know—they bothered me."

She pulled a postcard, paper-clipped onto a page, and set it in front of him.

Bill used the opportunity to look past this simple tourist's communication and steal a glance at Stacey's notebook: honey-yellow paper scrawled full with dates and locations ("New Canaan," "Hanoi," "Alliance, Ohio") in messy but cordoned chunks.

"It took forever—and I'll be totally up-front with you: I got a little obsessed. Here I am getting married, working my ass off on my doctorate, and beginning the process of Maddy getting pregnant with Fitz, and I basically have another fucking life I'm living, Bill. I'm lying to everybody because I think there's something wrong about all of it."

"Wrong about what?"

The bartender returned with a crate of clean glasses, which he put in a stack next to the sink, and glanced at them. Bill noticed his gaze. Ever since he realized what it was he'd carried north four years ago, he now noticed everyone who noticed him. The rain's fury surely covered their conversation.

"Bethany told me that when Lisa left home, she wrote a note. Bethany doesn't have it anymore, but she remembered the note saying that I drove her to the airport, that I helped her pack and leave."

"Did you?"

"No."

Bill pressed forward in the booth, staring at the postcard and its looping cursive.

"Did you follow the sentencing for those guys from New Canaan? The ones who killed that little girl."

He continued to stare at the postcard, and Stacey read only five percent of what went through him at that question. It was why he'd risked meeting her at all: to find out what she knew. After all, she too had been home the night of his return.

"A little bit."

"The date when they killed her—it stuck with me because Lisa's e-mails, her accounts, they all went dark at almost exactly the same time."

He had spent years moving the pieces of this emotional puzzle around, trying to find any way to put it together so that he would not feel the puncture wound of guilt and the rot that spread from it. He would never forgive himself for his role in what happened, but ultimately that was beside the point.

"Between that shit and the thing with Tina, it was a hell of a year for New Canaan," he said neutrally.

She watched his eyes for signs and tells.

"You know what else happened after they were arrested?"

Bill waited for it.

"Kaylyn. She disappeared. No one in New Canaan—not her mother, not anyone—knows what happened to her. And look at this . . ."

She set another scrap of paper next to the postcard, a photocopied blurb: *You're a real hot bitch, Stace. Great being your friend and setting up your spikes! Stay in touch. –K.*

"That's what Kaylyn wrote in my yearbook."

The two sets of handwriting were similar, but not exactly the same. Probably half the teenage girls in North America had that bubbled, loopy style.

"You've lost me, Moore." He couldn't keep track of all the dots she expected him to connect, but he was gathering that this was not about what he'd feared. Something far weirder.

She sat back in the booth and raised one tattooed arm, rubbed a cheek so that it looked like she was pulling the flesh from her face.

The wind picked up outside, and it made Bill think of a wolf's howl. Blue lightning streaked the sky, its tributaries like all the random jags of the rivers feeding the Mississippi. It was beautiful, bright, and then it was gone. Followed by the roar of thunder.

"I started trying to track people down—anyone who might know anything about where Lisa might be. I was back in New Canaan almost every month. To see my dad when he got sick but also . . ."

"I might get scotch," Bill interrupted. "I don't know why I ordered this light crap."

Her face spasmed, but the irk quickly passed. "Sure."

When Bill returned with the glass of peat-smelling amber liquid, Stacey squeezed her notebook so that it formed an upside-down U.

"Who did you talk to?" he asked.

"A lot of people. It doesn't matter. What's important, Bill, is it all comes back to one person."

When the name Todd Beaufort came up, Bill couldn't help but let loose a grim chuckle. He would never get away from this guy. At some point they had to cut these ghosts down from the trees. Couldn't just leave them all up there swinging. He listened to this story, drowning in the noise of the storm and looked out the window to the cars cutting through the flooding streets.

"Just listen. I know. I sound nuts. I feel nuts. Just . . . listen." She flipped to another page in her notebook. She went through Beaufort's history of sexual assault, this being the reason he never played a game for the Buckeyes. The young woman never pressed charges, but he had to transfer to Mount Union. His criminal record later included theft and forging prescriptions.

"So what?" Bill tasted his drink and enjoyed the warmth in the back of his throat and the burn in his stomach. "Beaufort was a dirtbag? If that's what you came here to tell me, believe me, I knew that back when we were kids."

"You were in New Canaan that night," she said. "When I found Tina."

The couple, talking in murmurs for so long, broke into laughter as bright as the woman's dress. Bill twirled his scotch glass in clockwise circles.

"What the hell does that have to do with Lisa?"

She pulled a photo from her notebook and handed it to him. It was a picture of a piece of jewelry, blackened and charred, the metal clasp warped. "They found it on Tina when they arrested her that night."

He examined the picture and handed it back.

"I swear to God that locket—it's Lisa's. I remember her wearing it. She used to keep pictures of teeny-bop idols in it. Like as a joke. Jonathan Taylor Thomas and Nick Lachey and all that *Tiger Beat* crap. Do you remember?"

He shook his head.

"So how did Tina have it? Because Todd must have had it. When she did whatever she did to him."

"So you believe she did it?"

Because they'd never found much of Todd Beaufort, new ghost stories erupted in New Canaan. Tina was currently incarcerated and received mental health treatment at the Ohio Reformatory for Women in Marysville, and kids wandered the woods trying to randomly dig up the supposed grave of the ex-football star who'd vanished one warm summer night, whose insane ex-girlfriend chopped him up and buried him there, according to legend. Because a storm had come blasting through in the early-morning hours, similar in size and ferocity to the one blanketing Chicago as they spoke, the police had to call off the search until it passed. Then the Cattawa overflowed its banks, spilling into the nearby woods. In the mud they found fragments of melted plastic, a gas can, DNA that matched Todd Beaufort's, traces of his blood and hair in Tina's car, but never a body. Tina Ross never told where she'd left him and all the search dogs and high-tech equipment proved useless. The flood had carried it all away.

"She did *something* to him," said Stacey. "I've got no clue about the circumstances, but when I found her, Jesus . . ." On that night of the vortex, she'd seen Todd get into that same car, and when she found Tina alone, reeking of smoke, with a frantic misery in her voice, face, and eyes, she knew something terrible had happened. When Tina swung the tire iron at her head, Stacey had almost been ready for it. Like she'd been forewarned in a forgotten dream. "No, she wasn't making fuck-all up."

"So what the hell are you even saying?"

"Christ, Bill . . ." She picked up the postcard and thwapped it against her fingers. "How hard would this be to fake? For someone who knew Lisa? How hard would it be to buy postcards from Vietnam or Thailand online, ship them to one of those countries already written, and pay someone a few bucks to send them back? That same night, the night with Tina, I got a message from Lisa. How hard would it be to get into her e-mail? She only ever had one password, I know that: Romans58. And then, right around 2006, when it got to be a thing, start a few social media accounts for her? I found someone to check the IP addresses on all her e-mails to me. They all originated in Ohio. Mostly in New Canaan, but a few in—"

Bill began to laugh. He was no longer sure if he should be nervous because of what Stacey was saying or if the girl was just batshit.

"Don't fucking laugh at me," she snapped.

He immediately clipped himself, turning a final errant chuckle to a cough.

"Lisa didn't leave. She didn't go on some romantic fantasy jaunt, never to return. Todd killed her. I'm sure of it. And I think

Kaylyn helped him. I don't know what it was about or why or how it went down, but she was clever about it. She catfished Lisa back into existence before anyone had even heard of that word."

How close she was and yet how far. She and Bill were both missing a few pieces, beginning with the videotape, the old camcorder kind, which Lisa found hidden in Kaylyn's drawer of thefts and petty revenge. She was missing how Lisa agonized over what to do with it, who to tell, and just how gut churning it was to watch and then to *own* a secret like that. How it had eaten her up until it was all she could think about day and night. How she couldn't go to the person she really wanted to tell because that girl's brother was among the videotape's demons. How she'd gone to Kaylyn, who she still had love for, and demanded she turn those boys in. How after hearing this, Kaylyn had lured her out to Jericho Lake under a pretense of explanation. How Todd was only supposed to scare her into handing over the tape.

Bill watched the bartender chat with the couple about the midwestern fury beyond the windows. "Like a fist smacking the city," said the bartender, and he poured them another round. They toasted the storm that had brought them together for this fleeting evening.

"Bill." Stacey stared at him until he looked at her. "Do you have any idea where Kaylyn is?"

He set down his scotch, and released a long, careful breath. He'd heard conspiracy theories before. You can't really traffic in left-of-the-left-wing politics and not hear about the thermite charges that brought down the WTC towers or the Bilderberg Group engineering the entire global economy for its benefit. He'd suffered so many disappointments and defeats in his life. He'd lost so many people he cared about. He had no friends, no network, no family he could ever safely return to. He had only his compatriots in this underground experiment and the constant paranoia they shared. He'd battled depression, drug abuse, and so many notions of suicide that he'd forgotten some of the most bizarre ones. (Once, while driving through the Cumberland Mountains he'd noted a guardrail that, if busted through properly, would allow him to die in a kamikaze crash into a piece of dragline machinery currently taking that mountain apart.) He had no patience for fantasy anymore—not his or anyone else's. And yet, when Stacey reached the part about Kaylyn, he returned to his night with her. That night. And he heard her story again and recalled all the holes, odd ends, and blank spaces, which, despite his fog, had seemed eerie and bottomless even then.

As the light outside dimmed and night crept in, the city's skyscrapers looked to him like an infrastructure built from the skeletons of gargantuan monsters and then the marrow set ablaze.

"Kaylyn," said Stacey. "She managed to somehow vanish. I know she was mixed up with Kirk, Frank, and Amos. Kaylyn ran, and when she ran, she had to give up the game. She couldn't risk keeping up the fiction of Lisa."

"And you think I know where she is?" Bill asked.

"Do you?"

"No."

One of the people Stacey spoke to, who provided her with no leads, no clues, no viable information, was Hailey Kowalczyk. She'd cornered Hailey at the retirement home during her trip back to see Bethany Kline (lying to Maddy that she was visiting Patrick and his family so that she'd want no part of the trip). Stacey finagled her old classmate Hailey into inviting her over for a beer. She caught up with Hailey and Eric, got an offer to stay for dinner, and demurred. It wasn't until she asked Hailey to walk her to her car that she managed to ask about Kaylyn. For her part, Hailey thought she acted the role perfectly. Rolled her eyes, crossed her arms, and told Stacey the only story she told anyone: the last time she spoke to Kay was when she drove her back from rehab in 2013. When Stacey pressed her, Hailey explained that she'd wanted nothing more to do with her childhood friend from Rainrock. The girl was either clean or she wasn't. When she gave Kaylyn $1,100 from her savings account and drove her to the bus station in Mansfield, Hailey justified it as she always did: she was her friend's protector, her guardian. Because she was the only person who truly knew Kay, knew every last devil inside her. She had to help Kaylyn because as a girl, she'd been robbed of something, hurt in a way that she could shield from view but never control. It fell to Hailey, time after time, to save her. And she would. Unconditionally.

Hailey volunteered no other information, and Lisa's name never came up.

Stacey had watched Kowalczyk carefully, unable to decide if she believed her. She considered spilling her theory about Lisa, but it still felt outrageous, paranoid, and seeing this version of Hailey, a heavyset wife and mother with bags under her eyes, dressed in nursing garb as she prepared for the late shift, quashed any will to articulate her deepest fear. They embraced before she left, and it amazed Stacey how old they all were. Back home in St. Louis, she and Maddy would fight more than they would fuck, argue more than they would say "I love you," dote over their son, worry about every sharp table corner, wall socket, and fever, and she would remember they were adults. Hugging Hailey, she did not feel like an adult, but perpetually cast back through time. An awkward teenager, jealous and horny and sad and buoyant, forevermore.

Eric, who listened to all this from the kitchen window, knew his wife was lying. Because Hailey had left the house in the middle of the night in October 2013, saying only that Kaylyn had done something stupid and needed her help. Eric, who loathed this junkie woman his wife could never get away from, demanded an explanation. All Hailey had to say about the matter was that it was the final, absolute last time she'd ever help Kay. They'd had a blow-out fight about it. He'd suspected things about Hailey their entire marriage. She was secretive, private. When they'd been in financial jams (so very many times) she'd always have a stash of money to ease them through. He didn't understand why Hailey lied to Stacey Moore, but he also didn't care. After that fall night in 2013, it turned out Kaylyn really was gone. Eric Frye pretended to be putting away dishes when his wife came back inside, and neither of them brought up Stacey's unsettling, probing visit ever again.

Stacey had tried to see Tina Ross at the Ohio Reformatory for Women, but Tina wrote her a polite letter denying the request. In the letter, Tina apologized for trying to hurt her. She was seeing a therapist now and leading a Bible study group. One thing of which Tina was certain, she knew nothing of Kaylyn nor her whereabouts, and it was best for her to stay focused on herself. Dragging up the past was not the way to go about that, she explained. She'd pled guilty to quite a few felony convictions (kidnapping, first-degree manslaughter), but she would be up for parole in just another five years. Cole or her parents visited almost every weekend, and strangely, Tina wondered if prison hadn't changed her for the better. She could focus. She could draw breath. Her therapist told her the only thing she had left to do was to face what scared her. She sometimes thought she could feel God inside of her again, that she had somehow, against all odds, plunged into unfathomable hope.

One of Tina's letters of apology arrived in the mailbox of Allison Beaufort, who tried to read it with hate, but by the time she finished, it had all melted away. She'd liked Tina so much, never understood why Todd dumped her. One thing Allison knew about her son, he was angry. Had been since he was a boy, and rightfully so. Life had done him dirty from the start. She had tried her best. She kept a row of photographs on the mantel in the living room: His senior picture where he wore a blue polo and leaned against a tree. His football picture, on one knee, grinding his upside-down helmet in the grass of the field. His peewee football photo, from maybe fourth or fifth grade, a huge gap in his smile where a front tooth had come out. She took care of the rescue dogs, fed them, gave them a home, and sometimes she sat with one of the oldest and sweetest of the mutts, head on her lap, and together they'd watch the night while she prayed for her son.

Bill stared at the sparkling polish of the table's surface, fixing his eyes on a knot in the wood, a black divot that could have had a map of the world carved into its depths. An uncomfortable silence descended. Stacey felt a hot flash of sweat break out on the small of her back. She'd tripped an unseen wire. She couldn't read Bill's serene face, showing the first ticks of deeper lines, and this infuriated her.

"I haven't heard from Kay. Not since high school."

"But you two had a thing."

"So to speak." He twisted his glass, leaving spirals of moisture on the table, and remembered how he'd once actually believed he'd loved that girl. The storm raging outside reminded him of the first night they'd spent together at her grandmother's house in Dover. "How do you know about that?"

"Doesn't matter."

She'd actually learned this from Dan Eaton, who she met in the visitation room of the Crawford County Correctional Facility in Pennsylvania where he was serving a year for felony assault after beating a man in a grocery store parking lot. Stacey asked him about Kaylyn, but he had no clue. She asked him about Lisa, and he truthfully told her he hadn't spoken to her in over a decade. Stacey pretended her visit was to see how he was doing, and Dan never volunteered the information that might have proved crucial:

what Hailey told him the last night he ever saw her. He'd refused Hailey's visit to Crawford. After his guilty plea, the judge had given him a considerably lenient sentence. One that Dan didn't feel he deserved. What he'd done in the wars? Yeah, that didn't go unnoticed by God. It required payback. *Depression, PTSD, self-blame,* these were buzzwords, he decided, jargon to describe an ancient human hurt written in the bones, sung in the sinews of muscle, ground out in the anamnesis of cells. And yet Danny still had love in him, which is a kind of bravery. He'd spent his year in prison corresponding with Melody Coyle. She'd taken a week off work and left Hanna with Greg's folks to visit him. She so easily saw the decency and courage Greg had spoken of. Dan described the scenario, an encounter in a Neff's grocery store parking lot with a good ole boy hassling a Mexican kid, cussing him out for putting a dent in his Tundra. The guy wore flannel and work boots but had a rich man's haircut; he'd snatched this terrified boy by his T-shirt collar and bounced him off the hood of the kid's decrepit car. Dan saw too many of these bullies in the world now, growing more and more sure of themselves. So Dan grabbed this man's forearm, and brought the heel of his hand down swiftly at a high, brutish angle. How pleasing the sound of that awful crack had been. He hadn't even realized how long he wanted to do something like that. Then he simply kept on going: broke the man's collarbone, five of his ribs, cracked his skull, all in front of the man's wife and two boys. He told all this to Melody in his soft student's voice. Melody Coyle slid a warm hand over his, her eyes as bright as daybreak. How interesting, she thought, that she might very well be about to fall in love with a man who'd held her husband as he died.

"Can I ask you something?" said Bill. "If all this is true—really true—and Todd's the monster you say he is—what's it matter? He's still somewhere out in the woods back home. He got his."

He knew something more, Stacey was sure.

A peal of thunder boomed through the bar, vibrating the glasses, rocking the whole city. A car alarm went off in the distance. The couple and the bartender looked at one another, eyes bugged, and then burst into laughter at how they'd flinched so simultaneously.

"You know what I think?" said Bill. "I think the simplest explanation is usually the right one. Todd Beaufort is rotting in those woods. Kaylyn OD'd in some McDonald's bathroom without an ID on her or tried to coat-hanger her baby out, and Lisa—Lisa just never looked back. Simple as that."

"I still have to know," she said, her nerves too raw, her teeth grinding too painfully, to realize that Bill had just admitted to knowing of Kay's pregnancy. She'd learned this during a forty-second conversation through a screen door with Mrs. Lynn ("Don't know, don't care," she said when asked where her daughter was), but when Bill copped to knowing that Kaylyn had been pregnant, it blew right past her.

Kaylyn, for her part, almost never thought of Stacey, had no idea that it wasn't the pursuit of the authorities that she should fear but her old friend from the volleyball team now working as an adjunct professor of English. She returned from waitressing shifts to her unhappy apartment in a subdivision on the outskirts of Anchorage. She paid Blanca her pittance for watching her son, kissed Scotty in his bed, and collapsed on the couch to breathe black mold she could never quite clean entirely from the ceiling's corners. Then she drank vodka and watched television until she passed out. It was the only way she could sleep. With Hailey's money, she'd chosen the airline ticket that would take her the farthest she could go without a passport, and when she found herself in this land of mountains hurtled together, sheetrock sky crashing against a slate sea, a place where people really could still disappear, she at least knew she'd found something resembling a second chance. The things she had done to con her way to a new identity—she was resourceful, a survivor, and her son would be too. She ignored the passes men made at her at the bar and saved money on laundry detergent by throwing all their clothes in the bathtub with some soap. She and her little guy rolled up their pant legs and danced, and he thought it was a game. The winters were bleak, frigid, lightless, and somehow invigorating. Nothing she could do about the dreams and ghosts, though. As resilient, relentless, and restless as the mold. In the drawer of her nightstand she kept the picture Bill Ashcraft had dropped in her house that night, the one of all of them at homecoming, cut into quarters by the folds. She took it out only when she woke from indissoluble nightmares. Screaming at Todd to stop, wanting to jump on his back and tear him away even as her legs felt rooted in place. *Just please, stop.* It was all she'd been able to say.

The bar could have been a sepulchre, a boneyard for their collected memories. Between them, they had stories they could never tell, and it was these moments intrinsic to their pasts that lingered in this quiet mahogany-and-brass niche of the world, creaking among the connecting joints of the bar stools or the maroon material of the booths, a place where adults would hear settling wood but children would hear spirits. When the dark fell, the pictures of the old city disappeared into shadow. The glasses hanging from a rack above the bar captured light from the street, and that fragrant blend of oil soap wood cleaner and disinfectant wormed its way into their nostrils. For the rest of their time on this earth, that specific scent would forever return them to this place. Even if it was the smell of countless taverns the world over, it would bring them back to consider and dread all these rumors and theories of scattered slag.

"You know, I found your dissertation online." He said it out of the blue, and her wet eyes darted back to him.

"Why?"

"Scared the shit out of me, I gotta say. And now I look around at what's happening, and it's hard not to see it. The world unraveling in this very specific, slow-rolling wave of horror and absurdity. That's why for those of us who want to do something about it . . . To stop it. You know. Those of us who want to stop it." He paused and looked up at her, his mouth hanging open and uncertain for a very long moment. "We now belong underground. We're going to have to do drastic things. Unthinkable things. It's still dawning on people how scary this all is, but it's the only way left."

Stacey chuckled, a tired, exhausted sound. "Bill. My dissertation was eco-crit. It was about literature. What the fuck are you talking about? I came here to ask for your help. In finding Kay. And then finding Lisa."

He gathered himself, simultaneously shook his head and licked his lips. "I need you to trust me. I need you to forget we met. And I need you to understand—I swear to you—that I know nothing about Kaylyn, about Lisa, about any of this."

"And you won't help me."

"I'm not in a position to."

"What are you hiding, you smug fuck?"

He stared at her very hard. "Not what you think I am."

She gritted her teeth, opened her mouth to scream at him, and then closed it.

He reached into his back pocket and removed his wallet. From a photo sleeve, he removed a cocktail napkin folded into quarters. She recognized the handwriting, even after all this time.

There's no such thing as the devil or I would've sold my soul
*   for the fight*
Nothing left now darling but you & me & this last
*   lonesome night*

"Found it the last time I went home. B-list Harrington lyrics from when we ate mushrooms once. I also have one of Rick's medals. His dad gave it to me. I was going to drive it to Washington and pin it to the face of whoever was running the Pentagon at the time, but . . ."

He took the napkin back, folded it tenderly, and returned it to his wallet. Maybe he just couldn't stomach it, the possibility that yet more evil had befallen someone he cared about long ago. But the world had changed, and he had to adapt. There might have been a time in his life when his love for Lisa still endured, when he would have followed Stacey and her bizarre theory to the ends of the earth. That time had passed. He'd lost his picture of all of them at homecoming the night he'd returned to New Canaan. He woke in Rick's old bedroom, his pockets empty except for the cash. Her face—all their faces—were gone.

"My one friend went to Iraq and took a sniper's bullet to the head," he said, already knowing this explanation would be inadequate. "Another died in an apartment fire junked out of his mind. And maybe someone I loved once really was murdered, but . . . I have these dreams—well—they're more than dreams. I wake up from them and it literally takes me a few minutes to understand that they're not real, they just linger that long. In them, I see the world that's coming. The future we're being banished to. I wake up from them and I'm soaked in sweat and shaking, and I never get back to sleep because I feel like I just went walking in another time and place."

In the morning he'd leave his hotel room and trade a backpack with a Saran-wrapped brick of cash for a USB drive packed with the secrets of seemingly invincible institutions. Then he'd vanish down the highway and across the plains. Stacey would return to her new apartment in St. Louis on the Central West End and slide her notebook back into the deep recesses of her desk's junk drawer where Maddy was unlikely to snoop. It would not linger there long.

"We lose people, Stacey," he said carefully. "And it's never fair, and it's never right, and there's always something missing about it. Something unexplained."

Bill stopped speaking so abruptly his jaw clicked shut. Together, in that moment, they remembered Lisa, her raw mouth and giant laugh, and they glanced around because they both felt it. Like she'd been eavesdropping from another booth.

On a cloudless summer night at the edge of a creaking metal dock on Jericho Lake, Lisa Han tried to stare straight up at the glowing fringe of the Milky Way, at the dusting of jeweled stars drawing from one corner of the horizon to the other. She fixed her eyes there so she wouldn't have to watch what Todd Beaufort was doing to her with the knife. She didn't want to give him the satisfaction of screaming, of revealing fear. Kaylyn, pleading from a safe distance, had all but assured they were too far to be heard anyway. Lisa gritted her teeth in agony, in defiance, and tried telling herself how little this would matter—not to those distant worlds, not really.

Todd's sweat dripped into her eye, and she remembered flirting with Bill Ashcraft in her freshman year math class. How his sweet-boy grin bloomed whenever she teased him. How overjoyed she was when he asked if she wanted to go to the movies that first time. This melted into her childhood when her mom moved them to New Canaan, and Lisa spent all her time at the public library scouring the children's books while her mom used the computers to search for a job. It was where she met Kaylyn and Hailey, two impossibly cute, impossibly friendly girls whose class she'd join in the fall. To them Lisa was this crazy, fierce goddess dropped out of the sky who knew exactly how babies were made and could describe it in gory, gut-bustingly funny detail. And a few months later, she would befriend this kid Danny across the street, a cute, dorky ginger who looked like he'd been chosen for a trip to the moon when she let him have her copy of *Where the Red Fern Grows*. "You're like my kid brother," she explained to him once. "I'm older than you!" he objected. "You're like my cute little baby brother who I'm going to stuff in a locker with a bag of dog food and not let you out until you eat the whole thing." And then she sucked the entire length of her index finger and jammed it in his ear until he shrieked.

Todd drove the knife into her until it stopped hurting, until her whole body went numb and cold and indifferent, and then, instead of screaming, she laughed in his face. She was thinking of Stacey's funny little church-chick manner, this air of rosy, Christian, good-golly-Miss-Molly-ain't-that-swell!-ness about her, and what a total gutter whore she was once you got in her pants. Lisa laughed because she was thinking of how hilarious it had been to tease Stacey about this dichotomy, to turn around out of the blue in their senior year English class and whisper, "Stop thinking about these titties, you scag." It was just too easy to crack her ass up. So while she was being stabbed to death, Lisa had to laugh because it was so funny how in love she was. How weird. Who the fuck would've seen that coming? Her defiant chortling carried a mist of spittle and blood straight up into Todd Beaufort's panicked mouth.

Finally, she remembered being eight years old and waking to find her mom curled up in the bathtub. There was no water in it. Fully clothed, she hugged her knees, sobbing. So Lisa went to the kitchen and figured out how to make blueberry pancakes. A half hour and a couple of failed prototype pancakes later, she brought them on a tray to the tub. Bethany wiped her eyes and studied the breakfast like a foreign currency. "How did you make these?" she asked.

"Mom, I can, like, read directions." She unrolled some toilet paper and set knife, fork, and this makeshift napkin on the tray. "Also, you know, most directions are at like a fifth-grade reading level? And I'm already at an eighth-grade level or at least sixth. Does it make you feel better?"

Bethany gasped, sucked back tears, nodded furiously. "Yeah, babe, it makes me feel better. So much better. You're a tough little girl."

"Uh duh, I know." And Lisa sat on the closed toilet to stuff a syrupy, blueberry-packed forkful into her own mouth. "I'm a freaking samurai, Mom."

How much she still had planned. How eager she was to get started. All the people she would have touched, all the hearts she would have broken. She'd wanted to get strange tattoos and pierce the tops of her ears, her tongue, her nipples; wear garish makeup and collect odd gypsy clothes; travel like a wind-borne petal, fight through the muddy crowds of psychedelic bacchanals; write a deranged novel where a woman's periods come to life each month to follow her ghostlike, quipping about dating life and making Marxist critiques of assorted makeup products. She'd wanted to learn to play the guitar like Ben Harrington and take all her wholesome smut poetry and set it to music, to buy a camera and stalk the globe taking pictures of twisted scenes she found beautiful and then render the beautiful vistas with menace, danger, and gore. She wanted to steal unpredictable books from public libraries in Omaha and hostels in Florence and the shelves of her one-night stands, slipping her lovers' most beloved, dog-eared copies into her bag and vanishing without leaving a phone number. She'd wanted to leap over vast chasms and coax others to follow, find herself and her companions all run out of food, matches, maps, water, and opinions so that they'd have to fashion fire from a glasses lens and arguments from half-remembered philosophies. She'd wanted to lead revolutions with barbaric compassion, face down all immutable phenomena, and charge over the shadowlands between the unknown and the unknowable.

On the dock, before Todd Beaufort, sweaty and weeping, finished the deed that would follow him till his death, before he sank her into the depths of that man-made lake, down to the flooded ghost town at the bottom where she drifted into the wreckage of a drugstore on a forgotten Main Street, she understood, vividly, that the most astonishing gift of consciousness was also our tragedy, our cliché, our great curse: Love's absolute refusal to ever surrender.

And then she was on her way.

Whether you face it abruptly or following a long drift into senescence, there's that eternal moment the prophets all gossip about: when you see the whole span of yourself, how astonishing and alive you were. However, as Lisa discovered, this eternity feels like nothing at all compared to the length and depth of the Night that comes after. When you cruise by fallen stars and far-flung quasars, forests of staggering pines and winter snows, granite mountains and impenetrable clouds, cooling lava, black oceans and the rivers that feed them, singing caterpillars and screaming bats, the lonely moan of a whale, endless prairies wrung with wind, purple skies and silver rain, the soil of your strange realm. Even the Night has an end, though, beyond which there is only the void, the abyss. It's the kind of darkness you knew before you feared it. It's the kind of darkness so inky, oily perfect that even as you stretch your pupils to pull light in, it only grows deeper, and all you can feel is the pressure of cold air on your eyeballs. Oblivion is viewing all of time backward and forward, your voice locked forever in all that dust and collapse and depthless sorrow. But what you can never know, what you could never have believed or hoped to believe on the long and staggering journey home, is that this abyss is holy all the same. You understand even the void is impermanent, that nothingness is unstable and bound, practically galloping, toward new creation on foreign shores.

*　　*　　*

Stacey and Bill left the bar and stepped into the night. The rain had stopped. A cool, wet sheen covered the pavements, the cars, the sewer grates, and an internal heat leached steam into the air, white specters rising into the ether. Before they could go their separate ways, Bill took Stacey's arm and pulled her into an embrace.

"You have no idea how much I miss all of them," he said. "How sorry I am for everything."

"I know," she whispered.

She would carry with her what Bill said next.

"Keep searching, Moore." He pulled away so he could look her in the eye. "Fight like hell. It's the only thing I've ever truly believed. Always, always, always fight like hell."

And they were gone, these infinitesimal creatures, walking the surface of time, trying and failing to articulate the dreams of ages, born and wandering across the lonesome heavens.

Acknowledgments

I can't be the first author to believe he's mostly clueless, who understands his real skill in life has been to pull into his orbit a vast array of tireless mentors and fearless fellow travelers who, like an antigravitational force, have kept the walls of his wormhole from caving in time after time. But I have to keep this hulking paragraph narrowed down to those specific to this book, who offered counsel, consolation, and compassion during the four years of its gestation. (Rest assured, I've kept a list of grudges, rivalries, bitter recriminations, and plans for petty revenge in a separate Word doc.) First, there is the vast panoply of tornadic personalities, gutsy genius, and shameless alcoholism that is Iowa. Some very smart writers read and reacted to early portions of this book, including Fatima Mirza, Tim Taranto, Anna Bruno, Willa Richards, Noel Carver, Jennie Lin, Anna Parker, Jed Cohen, Harry Stecopoulos, and Katelyn Williams. Three of my great friends, Jamel Brinkley, Charlotte Crowe, and Patrick Connelly, read early drafts and offered important guidance on the way forward. Ethan Canin is about as generous, headstrong, and brilliant a teacher and writer as you'll find walking the earth. He read this novel in an embryonic stage and his encouragement allowed me to navigate the confusing choices and subtle anarchies that were to come. Sam Chang, Nimo Johnson, Charlie D'Ambrosio, and Karen Russell have my blind allegiance forever. I'd drive all night to bail any of you out of jail. Deb, Connie, and Jan—you three outrageously and transparently collect thank-yous in the acknowledgments pages of contemporary novels, and here's one more. Drew Emerson, Jon Erwin, and Kevin Hanson provided me with deep insight into military life and the incommunicable nature of deployment, of being at war in the twenty-first century, but also with unexpected and enduring friendships, for which I'm far more grateful. Delaney Nolan never read a word of this book, but she inadvertently helped me think through the nature of loss, of wanting something of yourself back that has departed, one night when we broke into a backyard tree house on Maple Street to smoke a joint and hide from an insane thunderstorm. Susan Golomb threw elbows, broke noses, and dislocated shoulders to get this book sold. I owe her forever. They say editors don't edit anymore, but then what the hell was Cary Goldstein doing? This book took a quantum leap when Cary got involved. And even after I thought I'd *Beautiful Minded* this thing to asymptotic perfection, Jonathan Evans supervised Dominick Montalto as he scoured it with a staggering attention to detail (I'll never forgive myself for misremembering the Cavs' 2007 playoff run). Steven Bauer continues to ride herd and remains the most important mentor I met as a wandering youth. As for my weird nuclear cell, Laurie, Bob, Lucinda, and Hannah, thank you for your DNA, your support, and your general tolerance of my irreducible rascality. However, the greatest debt of gratitude I owe is to Karen Parkman, a stunning human, a brave mind, a soulful witch, who read my future, who helped me to cross the finish line, who laughed and cried at all the bizarre stories of my wild home. Finally, I have to acknowledge the friends and peers who, as I worked, were never far from my mind: Nick Savoia, Sarah Pressler, Dustin Whitford, Ben Laymon, Tim Barnes, Brent Jones, Carl Culbertson, Josh McCoy, Nate Smith, and Chris O'Hara. Over the years, in different ways, you all have followed me, haunted me, and made me wonder how things might have been different.

About the Author

STEPHEN MARKLEY is an author, screenwriter, and journalist. A graduate of the Iowa Writer's Workshop, Markley's previous books include the memoir *Publish This Book: The Unbelievable True Story of How I Wrote, Sold, and Published This Very Book*, and the travelogue *Tales of Iceland*. He lives in Los Angeles.

BOOK
CLUB
FAVORITES

READER'S
GUIDE

OHIO

STEPHEN MARKLEY

This reading group guide for Ohio *includes an introduction, discussion questions, ideas for enhancing your book club, and a Q&A with author Stephen Markley. The suggested questions are intended to help your reading group find new and interesting angles and topics for your discussion. We hope that these ideas will enrich your conversation and increase your enjoyment of the book.*

Introduction

Since the turn of the century, a generation has come of age knowing only war, recession, political gridlock, racial hostility, and a simmering fear of environmental calamity. In the country's forgotten pockets, where industry long ago fled, where foreclosures, Walmarts, and opiates riddle the land, death rates for rural whites have skyrocketed, fueled by suicide, addiction, and a rampant sense of marginalization and disillusionment. This is the world the characters in Stephen Markley's brilliant debut novel, *Ohio*, inherit. This is New Canaan.

On one fateful summer night in 2013, four former classmates converge on the Rust Belt town where they grew up, each of them with a mission, all of them haunted by regrets, secrets, lost loves. There's Bill Ashcraft, an alcoholic, drug-abusing activist, whose fruitless ambitions have taken him from Cambodia to Zuccotti Park to New Orleans, and now back to "The Cane" with a mysterious package strapped to the underside of his truck; Stacey Moore, a doctoral candidate reluctantly confronting the mother of her former lover; Dan Eaton, a shy veteran of three tours in Iraq, home for a dinner date with the high school sweetheart he's tried to forget; and the beautiful, fragile Tina Ross, whose rendezvous with the captain of the football team triggers the novel's shocking climax.

At once a murder mystery and a social critique, *Ohio* ingeniously captures the fractured zeitgeist of a nation through the viewfinder of an embattled Midwestern town, and offers a prescient vision for America at the dawn of a turbulent new age.

Questions for Discussion

1. Discuss your first impressions of New Canaan in the prelude. How are these impressions reinforced—or changed—throughout the course of the novel?

2. Consider the structure of the novel—how imperative do you feel it is to the reading experience?

3. "In them, I see the world that's coming. The world we're being banished to" (477). In what ways might the novel's events feel microcosmic to current events and politics?

4. Consider Bill Ashcraft's "T-shirt incident," which unites many of the novel's central characters. How does this incident echo throughout the novel? How does it define Bill? Also, discuss the incident from the other characters' points of view.

5. "In the last decade, everyone had learned to be a truth masseuse" (106). Discuss the novel in the frame of "post-truth." Are the narrators reliable? Consider the different angles and perspectives in which we view the characters and their stories. How do these alternating views affect your overall perception of the characters?

6. *Ohio* is a novel fraught with power dynamics between its characters. How do they differ between the men and the women?

7. "Because people only act—they only change—with a gun to their head" (125) says Bill. Do you think this statement is true in regards to the characters of *Ohio*? Do you think any of the characters grew or changed for the better from who they were in high school? Contrast this bleak statement with the opti-

mistic words of Mr. Clifton later on in the novel: "I see some of you kids I had in class years and years ago, and I can never believe the way you grow into yourselves as adults. . . . It still makes me want to cry tears of joy every time" (232).

8. When driving with Bill through town, Dan observes that "New Canaan was one of the minor places that bore the aftershocks of deindustrialization" (283). How else do we see these aftershocks manifest on both macro and micro levels?

9. Hilde tells Stacey that she often makes "self-denigrating comments" towards her "bumblefuck town,'" and advises her to "break yourself of that habit. You're here. You're curious about the world" (192). How are Stacey and the other characters in the novel who do leave New Canaan—Bill, Dan, Rick, Ben—still bound to their hometown even as they explore the world? In what ways do they remain distinctly "Ohio"? What makes you think they feel this way?

10. "Where does a girl who's lost her religion go to find meaning? What replaces the hole that faith, cast off, leaves behind?" (214). Discuss how religion—specifically, Evangelical Christianity—permeates the lives of characters in *Ohio*, and what replaces "that hole" for each character.

11. "Clichéd inspirational posters making success sound as if it had nothing to do with socioeconomics" (53). How do the characters in *Ohio* define success? How do their circumstances inhibit or encourage their individual definitions? Do you feel any of the characters might have been doomed from the beginning by their circumstances, or do you feel they sabotaged themselves?

12. "If there's a gun hanging on the wall in the first act, in the third act, it must be fired"—a "Chekhov's gun" is a literary principle that advises writers to make sure every element in their stories comes into play at some point. Discuss how author

Stephen Markley makes use of this principle. What would be the "Chekov's guns," so to speak, in *Ohio*?

13. The heartbeat of *Ohio* lies in its vivid characters. Is there one you relate to most, or one that reminds you of someone you know? Discuss with your book club.

14. Dan Eaton pins two quotes to his corkboard before he leaves for basic training: Thomas Paine's "Those who expect to reap the blessings of freedom must, like men, undergo the fatigue of supporting it" and Abraham Lincoln's "I like to see a man proud of the place in which he lives. I like to see a man live so that his place will be proud of him." Discuss these quotes in relation to the events of the novel.

15. "I once read this book about how literature was this vast conversation that mocked all of the borders we normally think of: state boundaries, our own life spans, continents, millennia" (191). Does *Ohio* hold up to this definition? What borders do you think it mocks?

16. Choose an epigraph for the novel—be it a lyric, a line from a poem, a snippet from a news outlet, or anything else, find a quote that you feel captures the spirit, themes, and tone of *Ohio*. Share with your book club.

17. In the novel, Dan and Hailey bond over a love of *Calvin and Hobbes,* a comic strip inspired by and set in the same suburban Midwest where its creator, Bill Waterson, grew up. Read a few Calvin and Hobbes strips—in what ways might Calvin's surroundings feel similar to New Canaan, and the childhoods of the characters of *Ohio*?

18. The cover photograph of *Ohio* is one image from a photo series by Harlan Erskine. Take a look at the rest of series on Erskine's website: http://www.harlanerskine.com/ten-convenient-stores/tencstores-3. How do the rest of the images feel evocative to the mood and motifs of *Ohio*?

A Conversation with Stephen Markley

Congratulations on your first novel. Can you talk about what lit that initial spark that inspired you to write *Ohio*?

I'd been trying to write a version of this book for maybe a decade. I think many young authors typically try to explicate the place they're from in their early work. Everyone has a sense that we need to prove where we come from matters (usually because it does). I finally began to stumble upon the framework that would become the novel after this bad night I had back home bouncing around a few bars, not unlike a few characters in the book. All I'll say is inspiration is fickle and unpredictable.

Did you grow up in Ohio or the Midwest yourself? If so, how did it inform the writing process—and if not, how were you able to channel such a strong sense of familiarity with a community like New Canaan?

Yes, I did grow up in a small town in Ohio. Also, once I got my driver's license in high school and my friends and I could sort of venture out to the surrounding towns and cities I became fascinated by the mythology of places that maybe other people wouldn't find very fascinating: Mansfield, Cleveland, Columbus, Youngstown, Akron, and every tiny burgh and rural highway that connects them. The history, the burdens, the creepy backwoods stories—so much of it was sitting around in my head waiting to be used.

Can you talk about your experiences in the Iowa Writer's Workshop? Did you start working on *Ohio* while still a student?

I went into Iowa extremely skeptical, to say the least, about what I'd get from the experience. Stubbornly, I never thought I'd go the MFA route, but there I found myself, and within two months, I was just chugging the Kool-Aid. I had early pieces of *Ohio* written before I went in, but it went through a Cambrian Explosion–style evolution once I arrived there. It was a completely life-changing experience, not only due to the people heading the classes but also because of my peers, who turned out to be a crop of such funny, fearless, brilliant people. I can't even name names because the list is too long and full of too much dirt that would compromise people's careers in the best kinds of ways.

Besides a fiction writer, you also work as a screenwriter and journalist. How do these other types of writing inform your fiction?

Probably discipline, research, and curiosity. Having always worked with a deadline, I basically can't imagine not finishing a piece of writing when I've set a date to finish it. This means I'm at my desk every day working even when I'd rather not. It may sound like a small thing, but having met all the talented writers who go days, weeks, months without writing a word, I realize what an asset it is. There's also this old Kurt Vonnegut interview banging around somewhere in which he says (I'm paraphrasing), "Great fiction writers tend to have things on their minds other than just fiction." In other words, interviewing a healthcare policy wonk about the ramifications of the Affordable Care Act or a filmmaker working on a documentary about violence interrupters on the South Side of Chicago remains one of my best routes into fiction.

Can you talk about what kind of research you might have done to write *Ohio*?

A better question: "What kind of research did you say, 'Eh, that might be a little much'?" Which is to say, I'm a total psycho. If I'd had any more time with the book, I would have been looking up shift change schedules at Jeld-Wen Windows and Doors plants because a fifth-string character happens to work at one. As a reader can probably tell, I spent a lot of time on the U.S. Army and the combat experience, a lot of time wandering around Walmarts striking up conversations with employees from which I'd later jank ideas. Most insanely, I practically wrote Stacey's dissertation on ecological catastrophe in the context of the global novel only to cut 97% of it from the final draft. But for me it's not so much getting this detail or that detail right, but in fully inhabiting the character, in seeing the world through their eyes entirely. So even if I end up cutting 97% of this thing I spent a year researching, I still have it all in mind's eye. I get how Stacey views her interaction with a waitress spouting off an unexpected line of poetry because I've sunk all that time and effort into being in her brain.

The characters of *Ohio* **are so visceral, each so vividly alive, and strikingly unique. Can you talk about how you crafted their individual voices, created their backstories, and decided how their lives would intersect? Is there one you relate to most?**

That's tough. You steal a little from people you know here and there, a little from your own experience, and then the rest just follows. Pretty soon, they are as alive and real to you in your head as, say, a good friend you grew up with. You can predict what they'll do most of the time, and then at others they surprise you. It helps that I wanted each character to have a central preoccupation (as I think we all do), a wound that's never healed, and a way of viewing the world that is distinct and hard-won. One of the most surprising scenes to write was when Bill, this brazen antiwar activist, is telling Dan, a vet, that Dan fought these wars for nothing, that his experiences in these theaters and the people he lost to these conflicts were a waste. I had it in my head that Dan would come back at him hard, challenge him directly. But then I got to the page and Dan's voice guided the scene elsewhere. He allows Bill keep talking and talking and suddenly the power between the two characters flips entirely. And the result, I think, is much more interesting, much more wrenching. There's this weird thing where you have to let your characters behave as they would behave, even if it goes against what you had planned.

Similarly, even though many of the characters commit acts of cruelty, violence, or selfishness, you also render them with sympathy and humanity. Can you talk about how you prevented any character in *Ohio* from feeling like a clear-cut villain? Did you feel it was important for you to do so? Do you feel like there's any hope left for them?

One of the clearest lines in the book is that notions of "villains" or "evil" are basically childhood fairytales adults tell themselves. I've heard people refer to a certain character in the book as a "monster" and though I'm way too polite to correct them, I think the novel speaks for itself about the danger of these simplistic categorizations. Behind what we think of as evil acts there are wounds, there is damage, there is grief, insecurity, fear, and loss. This is not a relativistic philosophy either. One can acknowledge and combat the horrible philosophies and dogmas and individual behaviors of our fellow human beings without doing ourselves the enormous disservice of simply grafting "evil" onto people we don't like or don't understand. But in imagining villains and heroes, I always keep in my head that villains love and are loved deeply by others while heroes frequently do terrible, unspeakable things for which they can never forgive themselves.

Did you always envision *Ohio* to be organized in overlapping sections (plus a prelude and coda), each focusing on one character? What challenges or rewards did you experience structuring the story this way?

The four characters in four sections was always the base of the novel, and the coda and prelude sort of grew out of suggestions from my agent and editor. *Sula* by Toni Morrison (not a bad Ohio author herself) also played an enormous role. The introduction to that novel just comes at you like a Scud missile, and Morrison talks about how the introduction was the very last part of the book she wrote. I'd had this moment that kept coming up over and over, of the parade following the return of a dead soldier. As soon as I started writing it, I knew that was the way in. Beyond that, I just loved the idea of being lost in each character's world, of viewing all of their lives backward and forward and getting these miniature climaxes on the way to an accelerating ending. The organization, I hope, gives the book a kind of propulsion, it hurtles the reader forward as he or she tries to decipher how it will all come together. So far, I've not heard anyone say, "Markley, c'mon, I saw that coming." You just want those last forty pages to shock the shit out of you and yet feel totally inevitable in retrospect. To leave you scrambling to unearth all the hidden depths of New Canaan.

Were there any particular books, music, films, or anything else that inspired or informed *Ohio*?

I'm very bad at this question, panic, and answer it differently every time. Like I think saying Bruce Springsteen and Toni Morrison is not innacurate, but neither is Quentin Tarantino and Dead Prez or Edward Hopper and the poet Lisa Wells. It's not that one seeks to be influenced but that pieces of art and reportage and the irreducibly bizarre experience of being alive act upon your central vision at all times in ways you can never predict or understand.

Can you talk about what you're working on now? Do you think you'll ever return to the characters of *Ohio* or the town of New Canaan?

I'm still trying to wrap my head around the fact that I'm in this place right now, with a book that, no matter what happens with sales or reviews and all that other glitter, is something I'm deeply proud of, that has this team of incredible people behind it and who believe in it. I don't want to take any of that for granted.

If you had to name a single emotion or feeling that you feel drives *Ohio*, what would it be? What overarching feeling do you want to leave readers with after they finish the book? What do you want them to take away?

The interaction between the writer and the reader is the mystical, ethereal, inexplicable place, right? Like I know what I think is in my book and what it should be evoking and how it should be read, but as with every piece of literature, the reader will bring his or her own hopes, biases, determinations, and dogmas to it. Like I can say that it's a novel about love and loss and war and recession and addiction and ecology and religion and trauma and hope in the dark, but I'm not sure that means much except to taint that inexplicable encounter. Hell, I'm not even sure authors should answer questions about their novels! It breaks the Spell, even if just by a sliver of a degree. Mostly, I want people to close the book and say what all authors want to hear, which is, "Damn. I would throw my grandmother out a window to get an advance copy of whatever this guy writes next."